The G...
The Mar...

By

Arron Hickman

To Tracy

My Silkie Hen

Thank you for your continued support of a miserable old git

From the Large Cock

xxx

Copyright © 2024 Arron Hickman

ISBN: 978-1-917425-99-5

All rights reserved, including the right to reproduce this book, or portions thereof in any form. No part of this text may be reproduced, transmitted, downloaded, decompiled, reverse engineered, or stored, in any form or introduced into any information storage and retrieval system, in any form or by any means, whether electronic or mechanical without the express written permission of the author.

This is a work of fiction. Names, characters, businesses, places, events, locales, and incidents are either the products of the author's imagination or used in a fictitious manner. Any resemblance to actual persons, living or dead, or actual events is purely coincidental.

For my father

May your eternal rest be full of Tottenham Hotspur cup wins

Prologue

The why not the how

1

There it was—the ad I'd been waiting for, buried deep in the back pages of the local independent newspaper. Among the listings for handymen, second-hand children's toys, and old LPs, her offer sat. Simple, unassuming, like someone trying to offload a forgotten trinket:

"For sale: Antique Wood Metronome. Enquire for further details."

I grabbed my phone and dialled my friend immediately.

"Check the back of the *Independent*," I said, my voice edged with urgency. "I've found it."

There was a pause, the sound of rustling paper on the other end, and then a sharp intake of breath.

"Do you think it's the same one?" he asked.

"It has to be," I said. "How many antique metronomes do you see for sale in the back of a newspaper?"

"But why here? Why not sell it online?" he wondered.

It was a fair question—one I'd asked myself plenty of times. In an age of online marketplaces, why this? I'd wasted hours combing through every sales platform, every antiques website, every forum, chasing dead ends.

"Maybe she knew I'd look there first," I said. "Maybe she thought she was being clever, hiding it in the local paper, hoping I'd give up."

"When are you going to get it?" he asked, a note of caution his voice. He probably believed I was getting ahead of myself.

"First, your sister needs to make the call. If they recognise my voice, they might vanish before I even get close."

"Do you want me to come with you?" he offered.

"No," I replied, more confidently than I felt. "I can handle it."

"And if she's there? What will you do?"

"I'll deal with it, if it happens," I said, sidestepping the real answer. Then I hung up, heart racing.

A short time later, his sister made the call, using an untraceable number. The seller turned out to be an old man in Barnet, North London, not far from the train station—someone I suspected I already knew. Everything was falling into place, just as I'd meticulously planned for weeks. His sister posed as a potential buyer, requesting an inspection by an antiques expert before agreeing on a price. Unbeknownst to him, I would be that expert. Desperate to make the sale, the old man agreed without hesitation.

On the day of the meeting, I took the underground to Totteridge and Whetstone, one stop before High Barnet. The walk to his house gave me time to clear my head and slip into character. I was William Hertford, antiques valuer extraordinaire. I wasn't entirely sure how someone like that should dress, so I'd spent the previous day binge-watching *Antiques Roadshow* and cobbled together a look: freshly ironed blue shirt, grey chinos, and brown leather shoes. No tweed blazer or silk tie, but I hoped I exuded the aura of someone who knew the worth of old things.

I arrived at the address ten minutes early. The house stood out—a red-brick terraced property, older than the more modern surroundings. Its white sash windows framed by decorative curtains, and a vibrant blue front door stood out against the dull street. A gleaming brass knocker shaped like a dog's head caught the sunlight. Above the door, a stained-glass transom window cast colourful patterns across the entrance. The front garden was small but meticulously kept, bordered by a low wrought iron fence, with neat hedges and bright flowers adding a splash of colour.

This wasn't her house—too clean, too well-kept. But from what stood before me, I had a clearer picture of who I was about to meet. My heart pounded as I approached. I took a deep breath, steeling myself, and knocked twice, the sound heavy in the still air. I'd spent so much time plotting for this that I hadn't fully considered what I'd do if she was actually here. But as the latch clicked and the door creaked open, I realised the time for planning had run out.

Standing in the doorway was a short, old man with long grey hair, a goatee, and a sharp nose. His face twisted into a grimace as he looked up at me. There he was—the father of the girl who had driven my brother to his grave. There was no surprise in his eyes. Either my disguise had failed, or it had worked too well.

Unfortunately for me, it was the former.

"You're too late," he grumbled, his voice laced with finality. "She left with it this morning."

My brother met her eight years ago. He was twenty-five, and she was twenty-one. They first crossed paths at a local pub where he and I would meet every Friday after work. It was a dingy little dive, the kind of place where the carpets stuck to your shoes, and shadowy corners hid the regulars—most of them unremarkable, unwashed, and too far gone to care. But the pub had one thing we both valued: cheap, reliable alcohol. In the midst of this forgettable crowd, she stood out.

She was a barmaid back then—petite, with dark hair always pulled into a bun. She wore the typical uniform—white t-shirt, black jeans—but her willowy frame and confident posture made it look effortlessly stylish. When the rush died down, she'd retreat to the far end of the bar, elbows on the counter, completely absorbed in a book.

Their relationship started with those books. My brother, a casual reader of horror novels, needed a little nudge to talk to her. She was into counterculture literature, something foreign to him, and she had a fire about her, a need to prove she was a bigger part of a smaller whole. This was during the height of the girl-power movement, and she, a self-proclaimed anarchist, was dead set on challenging the system, one protest and radical idea at a time. Her punkish, rebellious nature was in absolute contrast to my brother's laid-back, easy-going style. With his foppish hair and love for hip-hop and indie music, he never seemed the type to get caught up in politics or social causes. Yet, despite—or maybe because of—these differences, they were pulled toward each other with a force none of us could quite explain.

Books and records became their language. For every Stephen King novel or Wu-Tang Clan album my brother passed her way, she handed him something from Bikini Kill or Sleater-Kinney, alongside a battered copy of a Peter Kropotkin book. I remember him once confessing to me that, although he admired her choices, he didn't really understand them. But he didn't care. They were passionate, mismatched lovers—deeply in love but often at odds with each other's worldview. Where she saw revolution, he saw chaos. Where he sought relaxation, she demanded action.

After a few months, the cracks began to show. One night, during a visit to his flat, my brother confided that they had agreed to an open relationship.

"I love her," he said, nursing a glass of whiskey, "but she told me she needed to figure out who she was. And I agreed to let her."

"And what about you?" I asked, sensing the danger in his words, worried he'd opened a door that could hurt him more than he grasped.

"What else could I do?" he replied, his voice heavy with exhaustion. "All she wants to do is go to secret anarchist meetings or punk rock concerts. No matter how hard I try, that's just not my scene. So, I told her she could go find herself, as long as she came back to me in the end."

He paused, swirling the whiskey in his glass, the ice clinking gently. He looked lost, his thoughts betraying the firm front he tried to put up.

"And did she agree to it?"

"She did... I think. She said she felt confined—not by me, but by her parents' expectations. It was simple: either we stay as we are, always on edge, or we give each other space."

One summer day, I bumped into her at the mall. I hadn't seen her in a while, so I invited her to lunch. We ended up at a retro American-style diner, where 50s and 60s beach rock played overhead. The servers, none of whom were even born until decades later, took our orders in exaggerated American accents. Sitting across from her, I couldn't help but notice how much she had transformed from the quiet, bookish girl I'd first met.

She now wore a military-style jacket adorned with a Che Guevara patch, and anarchist symbols woven into the sleeves. Her once dark hair now had streaks of bright pink running through it, and she'd traded her thick glasses for contact lenses. The shift in her appearance was startling, as though she had completely shed the person my brother had fallen in love with.

Over burgers and fries, we talked about everything but him. She was animated, passionate—telling me about the latest protests she'd attended and the political causes she was fighting for. Every word was filled with fervour, as if she were carrying the world on her shoulders. When I finally asked about my brother, her energy faltered for a split-second

"I haven't seen you with Adam much lately," I said, trying to keep the conversation light.

"Well, you know, I've been busy with the team," she replied, taking a bite of her burger. "The group I'm with has big plans—we're organizing a series of anti-government protests and civil rights workshops. I'm on the design team, so I've been working on pamphlets, coordinating with other groups, and helping plan some direct-action events."

It was clear that this activism meant everything to her, but to me, it sounded rehearsed—like she was playing the role of a young revolutionary, a socialist protester angry at the system but not fully understanding why. I figured it was something she'd eventually grow out of when she was ready to settle down. Yet, in her entire spiel about protests and activism, not once did she mention my brother.

"It sounds like you have a lot going on," I said, "but where does my brother fit into all of this?"

She hesitated for a split second, before forcing a smile. "I know he doesn't always get why I'm so invested in this, but he's supportive. He respects it. I've told him he's always welcome to join us at events." Her voice was steady, but there was a slight strain in it, as if she were trying to convince herself as much as she was convincing me.

As I listened, it hit me how little I really knew about her—and how little my brother seemed to know as well. When I'd asked him to tell me more about her past, he had almost nothing to offer. She'd had a falling out with her middle-class family, but the details were vague. We both assumed it had something to do with her lifestyle choices. She grew up in a household of professors and doctors—not exactly the kind of environment that encouraged becoming an anarchist.

She'd left school at sixteen to study graphic design but dropped out shortly after. She then moved to Scotland to live with her aunt. Why Scotland? Adam didn't know, and she never told him. It was there, though, that she got involved with the anarchist movements she was so passionate about. By eighteen, she was back in London, working at the bar and joining local activist groups. That was it. That was all my brother knew. Her story remained a mystery, and I wished he had pushed for more—if only for his own sake. Maybe he could have foreseen the trouble before it started and avoided the pain it eventually caused him.

As his older brother, I could've pressed harder too. But I was thirty, with little in the way of prospects myself—too caught up in trying to make something of my own life to worry about anyone else's. I was stuck in the repetitiveness of nine-to-five office hours, disillusioned by anything that smelled like the 'greater good.' While I was busy chasing my own dreams, life kept moving on without me. I shut my eyes to what was happening with him, ignoring his relationship problems as I focused on my own ambitions. How many times had I brushed off his issues, too preoccupied with my own desire to escape life's inevitable decline to notice the weight he was carrying?

Eventually, the strain became too much for Adam, and he finally came to me for help. It was a conversation from a cold winter five years ago, one that I would replay over and over, searching for something I could have done differently. Autumn had passed by peacefully, our lives moving forward without much change. The leaves of November had fallen, blanketing the ground in a carpet of brown decay, marking the slow passage into December's bitter embrace.

Adam called me early that day, asking if we could meet at the town park. The weather was bright but freezing, and when we met, our hands were buried deep in our pockets, faces wrapped in scarves. As we walked in silence through the park, I could sense something heavy pressing on him. His brow was furrowed, deep lines etched into his forehead.

"You're brooding," I told him, my breath mingling with the winter chill.

"Am I?" he replied, trying to sound dismissive.

"If you called me here just to get out for some exercise, that's fine," I said, hoping to lighten his mood. "But at least act like you're glad to see me. I haven't heard from you in weeks."

He approached a bench and sat down, pulling out a cigarette. He lit it and stared straight ahead at the frozen pond, his breath mixing with the cigarette smoke in ghostly patterns. I watched him wrestle with whatever he needed to say, as if mapping out a path and unsure of its destination.

"Do you ever have dreams?" he asked, still not looking at me.

Across the pond, some ducks waddled, ignoring the two figures sitting on the bench, as if the cold was nothing to them.

"Of course I dream. Just last night, I dreamed I was in a tag team match with Macho Man Randy Savage," I said, hoping a joke would break the friction.

"Not those kinds of dreams," he snapped.

"Calm down, Adam, it was just a joke," I said, placing a hand on his shoulder. "Just tell me what's going on."

In the distance, a dog barked, sending the ducks scattering into the clouded sky, chased by a black Labrador puppy. We watched them disappear. My brother leaned back on the bench, kicking his heels into the dirt.

"Is it Emily?" I asked. He didn't respond, just kept kicking at the ground, his heels digging grooves into the dirt. "If something's happened between you two, you know you can tell me."

I heard a brief, stifled sob, followed by a deep breath. "She's gone," he finally admitted, his voice heavy with despair.

"Gone? What do you mean, gone?"

"She left yesterday. Took half my stuff with her, including Dad's old metronome."

"What?" I exclaimed, feeling anger flare within me. "Why the hell would she take that?" My fury surged—not just for my brother, but for what he had now lost.

"I don't understand," he continued, his voice trembling. The last time I'd seen him in this much pain was when our father died. "I gave her all the space she needed. Let her do as she wished. If she found someone else, all she had to do was tell me. Not just leave—and take my stuff with her."

I stood up, searching for something reassuring to say. "We'll get it all back," I promised, though I wasn't sure how. "We'll find her and make this right."

He nodded, but the look in his eyes told me he was unconvinced. "It's just… I never thought she'd hurt me like this. I knew we were different, but I gave her all the space she wanted. I trusted her. And now she's gone, and I don't know what I'm meant to do."

"Come on," I said gently. "Let's go back to my place and get out of this cold. You can tell me everything, and we'll figure out where to start searching."

As we walked back through the park, a sense of foreboding settled deep in my chest. This felt like the beginning of a long, difficult journey—one that had already upended our lives in just a few short hours. I couldn't shake my worry, the fear that I might not be able to keep up with what lay ahead. I had a sinking feeling this wasn't just about a breakup or stolen things. There was something else that neither of us could fully grasp yet.

Now, as I stood on that doorstep, staring into the weathered face of her father—a man who had shielded his daughter with secrets and lies—the memory of that painful conversation with Adam surged back. The ache of his betrayal, of Emily's cold abandonment, hit me like a wave I hadn't braced for. Every ounce of anger, every unspoken word, begging to be released.

I wanted to bellow, to rage at him for letting her slip away without facing the consequences—for raising a daughter who could do so much damage and walk away unscathed. But instead, I swallowed the fire burning in my throat, forcing myself to remain calm, steady. The rage simmered, but I wouldn't let it rule me. Not here, not now.

"When you see her again," I said, my voice cold, "tell her my brother killed himself a few weeks ago."

Part 1

Five years later

2

I waited for the soft click of the apartment door closing before I opened my eyes to the darkness. Still hazy from an evening of alcohol and sex, I swung my legs out from under the sheets and sat up. My bladder urged me to head to the bathroom, and I wasn't in the mood to argue. Navigating through the shadows of the early morning, a strange thought crossed my mind: I could probably find my way around this place if I ever went blind. Why was I thinking that? I blamed the bottle of vodka she and I had emptied last night.

After relieving myself, I wandered back to the bedroom. The watch on my nightstand read 3:17 a.m., but sleep had already slipped away, leaving me adrift. The stale scent of sex lingered in the air, mixing with her faint perfume. I found my cigarettes in the bedside drawer and lit one. Standing naked by the open window, I observed the stillness of Langley Crescent from my third-floor apartment.

The town lay quiet, bathed in the soft glow of streetlights. The occasional hum of a distant car was the only reminder that even a sleeping town never truly rests. Across the street, rows of houses stood dark and lifeless, save for a few flickers of light from other insomniacs or early risers. It was late May, and the cool air carried the faint scent of rain. Everything felt suspended, as if time itself had paused in the fragile space between night and day.

I finished the cigarette, flicked the stub into the ashtray, and closed the window. The room felt aimless in its silence, and though I wasn't tired, I couldn't shake the feeling that it was too early for anything other than sleep. Then my stomach growled, interrupting the quiet—a not-so-subtle hint that being awake at this hour should involve food.

Wrapping myself in my dressing gown, I wandered into the kitchen. The fridge offered slim pickings: two eggs, a couple of wilted tomatoes, and a small jar of pickles. I checked the date on the eggs—they were still good. I set them to boil, threw a couple of slices of bread in the toaster, and sat down at the dining table, listening to the gentle bubbling of the water.

The rhythmic sound of boiling eggs became a soothing background to the early morning calm. Dim light from the approaching dawn filtered through the blinds, and the smoke from my earlier cigarette lingered in the air, giving the moment a timeless, noir quality. I suddenly felt like a character in a 1950s detective film—a weary cop finding serenity in the quiet of the night, haunted by a case he can't solve, sitting alone in the kitchen as the world continued to turn outside.

"Serenity"—that word always brings back a memory I can't shake. Her, sitting right here at this table, head bowed low. What stands out the most are her blue high-heeled shoes, placed neatly beside her bare feet. Her long, dyed-blonde hair hung over her face, hiding her eyes as they avoided mine. She wore the sleeveless, black, low-cut dress I'd bought her as a gift.

"Well then," I said, breaking the heavy silence. "What happens now?"

She didn't respond. If it weren't for the faint sound of her breathing in the thick, tense air, she could have been a statue. I sat down beside her, removing my watch and slipping off my jewellery, hoping that she would speak to me at some point.

"Do you want coffee, or something stronger?" Still nothing. "Fine, two cups of strong coffee it is. Ground or instant?" Her silence begged me to fill the void. "Instant it is."

I got up, leaving her to whatever thoughts had her trapped. It was 1:30 in the morning, and I was too tired to keep this going, but there was no choice. Outside, a cat cried into the night, its unanswered calls echoing through the streets. I knew exactly how it felt. I placed a mug in front of her and sat back down.

"Shall I put the radio on?" I asked, trying to break the suffocating quiet. "This drink will keep us awake for a while and I'm bored of listening to my heartbeat."

She slowly lifted her head and looked at me. Mascara-streaked tears had left dark, delicate rivers down her cheeks.

"Why are you always so patient with me?" she asked, her voice trembling.

I handed her a tissue from the counter. She dabbed at her eyes, giving a small, bitter giggle.

"I must look a state."

"Only if you're looking for it," I replied, my attempt at humour falling flat.

"I planned to be long gone by now," she said, brushing her hair from her face. "But I couldn't leave without saying goodbye."

"Why not?"

"I was worried about you. I didn't know how you'd react, and look at you now—still calm, still composed."

"Where are you going?" I asked, ignoring her analysis of me. Truthfully, I felt like a blank canvas, waiting for someone to paint the emotions I should be feeling.

"I have a friend in Leeds who said I could stay with her."

"And is *he* going with you?"

Her eyes glistened again as she sighed, steadying herself. "No, that's over. I never felt anything for him; it was never more than sex. I only did it to hurt you."

"Well, that's something, I guess. I think I'd feel a hundred times worse if you'd told me you loved him."

I lit a cigarette, took a deep drag, and handed it to her. Leaning my head back against the wall, I exhaled, watching the smoke curl upward, forming lazy patterns above us. I tried to find images in the smoke—my own personal ink-blot test.

"No anger?" she asked. "No rage? It's like I've done nothing wrong."

"Would it help?" I replied, my voice edged with frustration. "Do you *want* me to argue with you?"

"I want you to talk to me!" she shouted, her words erupting from the silence.

I stubbed out the cigarette and looked at her. "Fine," I retorted sharply, "let's talk. Ask me something. Go on."

"Oh don't be childish!" she snapped back.

"No, I mean it. I'll answer anything you want to know."

"How did your brother die?" she asked tenderly.

"What—out of everything you could ask, you want to know that?" I said, my voice quieter now.

"It matters because you've mentioned it, but you've never opened up about it. You hardly open up about anything at all."

"I'm sorry about that; I truly am," I said, and I meant it. I'd always kept things close, ever since I was a kid, and it had become second nature. The coffee had grown cold and tasted faintly of ash. "I'm going to have a cool drink. Do you want one?"

She shook her head, her expression distant. The air between us felt thick with unspoken words and regret—a chasm we couldn't bridge, no matter how hard we tried.

"If you must know, my brother died by a self-inflicted wound," I admitted after a long pause.

"I'm so sorry. How?"

"That's between me and him, and that's how it's going to stay."

She let out a bitter laugh, her eyes narrowing. "See, this is exactly what I mean. You're the kind of person I thought you were all along."

"What kind is that?" I asked.

"You're the kind of person who could witness a car crash, watch it unfold right in front of you, and brush it off like it didn't affect you. You'd never tell anyone how you *really* felt about it. Sometimes, you're like a cold, unmoving statue—something people admire from afar, but you never show anything but silence. Stoic, indifferent."

"That's quite a description. I should write it down."

"You're either being sarcastic or deadly serious. I can never tell with you."

I took a deep breath, drumming my fingers on the table. "So, what do we do?"

She pushed her chair back and stood up, and despite knowing exactly where this was heading, I still felt attracted to her, a pull I couldn't shake.

"*We* aren't going to do anything," she said, her voice steady but with a finality that left no room for argument. "I'm going to pack my things and sleep on the sofa. Later this morning, I'll be gone."

"What about the rest of your stuff?" I asked, trying to keep my tone neutral.

"Keep it. I don't want anything more than I need."

"I can forward it to you, if you want."

She paused, looking back at me with a mix of sadness and resolve. "No, it's better for both of us if you don't know where I am. Keep whatever you want and give the rest away." She started to walk away but then stopped, turning back. Leaning down, she cupped my face in her hands and kissed me on the lips. "For what it's worth, I'll always hope for the best for you."

With that, she left, her footsteps fading softly on the floor. I watched her go, feeling her absence settle into the room like the hollow stillness of an empty chapel. The silence that followed was suffocating. The strain had lifted, but it left me with something worse: an emotional vacuum, the kind that makes everything feel weightless and heavy all at once.

I sat alone for a while, staring at the space she'd just occupied, trying to comprehend the truth that I was a single man again. My life had taken another sharp turn, and yet, I felt no immediate grief—just numbness. Then, as if on autopilot, I headed to bed, too drained to think about anything else.

She kept her word. When I woke a few hours later, she was gone. The apartment felt eerily still, as though it had already adjusted to her absence. I took a long shower, letting the water run until it turned cold, then went about clearing away the remnants of the night—the mugs, the ashtrays, the half-smoked cigarettes. Wiping down the counter where we had sat felt surreal, like I was cleaning away the last traces of her.

Though I had cooked for one many times before, this morning felt profoundly different. This time, there was no one else coming to join me later. The permanence of her left a noticeable void in the space she had once existed—her mind, body, and spirit no longer filling the apartment. I caught myself glancing back at the chair where she had sat, her final image burned into my mind: head in hands, tear-streaked cheeks, and those last, quiet goodbyes.

I had no idea what to do next. I felt like a lost child trapped in the body of a weary wanderer, untethered. There was no roadmap for this—no clear instructions on how to dismantle a shared life. The apartment felt like a time capsule, holding pieces of her that I didn't know how to handle. Her makeup and toiletries could go to charity, but the keepsakes—the gifts I'd bought her, the photos of us together—what about those? Should I keep them for myself, as reminders of what we once had? Or was it better to let them go and try to forget?

I thought of that movie where a man asks scientists to erase the memories of someone he once loved, though I couldn't recall its name. In some way, it felt like that—like the temptation to remove every trace of her would make it easier to move on. But I knew better; memories don't disappear that easily.

In the end, it seemed easier to just pack everything into bags and move on. I sorted through her drawers and cupboards, dividing her belongings into two piles. After three years together—our lives woven in ways I would never get back—this was the final act of our relationship: charity or trash. Should her things be preserved as relics of love, or erased along with the memories?

I chose the latter. It felt brutal but necessary. Like ripping off the plaster off a wound that had already healed.

The sting of a burning cigarette nearing my fingers pulled me out of my thoughts. The pot of water was boiling over. I turned off the stove, drained the hot water, and filled the pan with cold to cool the eggs. Despite the lingering ache of her memory, a small sense of relief crept in, gradually overshadowing the sadness. Our life together had run its course, and she had chosen to walk away. There was nothing I could have done to change that.

The best thing now was to lock the memories away, make some food, light another cigarette, and maybe, eventually, crawl back into bed.

3

When I was twelve, my uncle Cliff invited me to spend a day at the beach with him and his new girlfriend. I was always excited to see him, and I eagerly agreed, though I knew that spending time with him often came with its own set of challenges—mainly because of who he was. My uncle wasn't exactly my mother's favourite person, and my father always regarded him with suspicion due to his wild lifestyle. A roadie by trade, Cliff spent much of his adult life touring with rock and metal bands, soaking up their chaotic world. My mother often said he had picked up far too many bad habits to be trusted with a twelve-year-old. But to me, he was a rockstar.

With his long brown hair, a goatee that almost reached the top of his ribcage, and silver rings on every finger, he was the coolest person I knew. He lived life entirely on his own terms—always flying by the seat of his pants, rolling with the punches, and flipping a defiant middle finger to anyone who tried to rein him in.

On that sunny summer morning, my mother finally gave in to my pleading and reluctantly handed Cliff a list of strict rules. It was full of things I found laughably obvious: *Christopher mustn't drink alcohol, mustn't do any drugs, mustn't break any laws, mustn't spend time with people of questionable morals.* But the last one was the kicker: *Christopher mustn't be left alone with any woman Cliff introduces him to.* I couldn't help myself—I muttered something sarcastic about her still treating me like a child. My mom shot back without missing a beat, "It's not you I'm worried about."

Cliff, of course, just grinned through the entire lecture, nodding along as if he actually cared about my mother's concerns. He even gave me a sly wink when she wasn't looking. Like I said—rockstar.

We set off on our beach adventure in his old trailer—the same one he proudly called home. It was a one-bed campervan that had carried him across the length and breadth of England, plastered with posters of bands like Motörhead, Iron Maiden, and Venom. Every available inch of wall space was covered, giving it the feel of a rock 'n' roll shrine on wheels. Inside, it had everything he needed—a bed, a tiny kitchen, and an even tinier toilet. Cliff always claimed this van was special, despite my dad's constant reminders that he needed to mature, settle down and get a real place. But for Cliff, that camper was his castle, and nothing would change that.

We were heading to a secluded beach where we could park the trailer right on the sand, fling open the doors, and soak in the carefree spirit of the ocean. It was a perfect day—the kind of day that made you feel like you were in California rather than some coastal spot in England. We didn't have surfboards, or anything fancy like that, but it didn't matter. All we needed was the sun, sand, and sea.

Before we could fully dive into our beach day, though, we had to pick up Cliff's new girlfriend, Vanity. Her name alone intrigued me, and I asked him what she was like. He just grinned and said she was 26, had a good job, and for some reason, preferred his company over the "dull, regular blokes" she could have dated. Typical Uncle Cliff—never one to shy away from a bit of self-praise.

When we pulled up to her place, I quickly understood why he was so taken with her. Vanity was striking. Beneath layers of cheap makeup, there was a natural beauty that stood out. She was petite—no more than 5'2"—though her chunky platform boots added a few extra inches. Her hair was a mass of heavily lacquered curls, the kind that looked stiff even in the wind, but there was something captivating about her. She greeted me politely but kept her distance for most of the drive, only chiming in when I spoke directly to her.

For the trip, she was quiet while my uncle couldn't keep his hands off her, constantly touching her face or running his fingers through her hair, telling her how gorgeous she looked. I had to admit, even at my age, I could see why he was so infatuated.

When we arrived at the beach and drove onto the sand, I stuck my head out of the van window, letting the salty breeze tickle nostrils. The coastline stretched out like a postcard—endless golden sand meeting deep blue waves. It felt like we'd stumbled onto a Californian beach rather than a stretch of English coast. As soon as we stepped out of the van, I could tell it was going to be a perfect day. The shore was almost deserted, with only a few people scattered about. The soothing sounds of the ocean mingled with the occasional call of seagulls, and the sun shimmered off the water, casting a golden glow across the horizon. It was a scene that promised adventure—at least for a young boy like me, eager to seize the afternoon.

The day unfolded like a dream. We ran barefoot through the warm sand, swam in the cool, welcoming sea, and capped it off with a beach barbecue. My uncle and I played football while Vanity stretched out on a towel, soaking up the sun in her bikini. As the afternoon wore on and the sun began its slow descent toward the horizon, my uncle cranked up the radio in the van, blasting classic rock from his worn-out CD collection.

With Vanity by the waist, they danced like carefree teenagers, spinning and laughing until they collapsed into the sand. Their joy was infectious, and I couldn't resist joining them. In that place, surrounded by the vastness of the ocean and the endless sky, I felt an exhilarating sense of freedom. It was the kind of freedom my uncle always talked about—the kind where nothing mattered except the present. I couldn't help but remember one of his favourite sayings: *"When life tries to bring you down, stick a finger in the air and say, 'You can't beat this bastard!'"*

But as memorable as the day at the beach was, it was the drive home that stayed with me. Exhausted but content, we all sat in comfortable silence, the kind that only comes after a day spent under the sun. Vanity, who had been reserved at first, had loosened up by now, cracking jokes and teasing my uncle playfully. In return, he half-jokingly told me to avoid girls like her, hinting that my mother had been right—they'd only lead me astray.

When we dropped Vanity off at her apartment, my uncle walked her to the door. I watched from the van, wondering if I'd ever have a love like theirs. As they shared a kiss goodbye, I saw him slip her a small envelope before he flashed her a final grin. Climbing back into the van, he turned to me with a wink. "Let's get you home before your mum sends the police after me," he joked.

4

"Did you ever find out what was in the envelope?" she asked, her voice curious as she nestled closer, her arm draped lazily across me.

"The same thing the rich hand over to you when their time is up," I replied, brushing her hair gently away from her forehead.

"Money? She was an escort?" she asked.

"Yep, a one-hundred-percent, dyed-in-the-wool call girl," I chuckled. "But my uncle never cared. That's just how he was. I guess I get that from him."

"That was a good story," she murmured, pressing her forehead against my chin. At twenty-six, her skin was still as soft as ever, her slender, tanned body warm against mine. By day, she was just another humanities and arts student. But nights like these, she was only a phone call away from being someone's perfect paying companion. I never asked if she enjoyed the work; she never complained. She would meet up with me whenever she was free, unless she had other bookings.

She was a natural—fiercely intelligent and undeniably beautiful. Her elfin features and soft, middle-class London accent complemented her sharp understanding of people, especially men. Standing around 5'9" with long legs, I always told her she could easily model lingerie while charming intellectuals on the side. She'd laugh it off, dismissing my comments with a smile. She claimed she did this side of her life for fun, and to pay her way through university.

"Why don't you get a normal job?" I asked her once.

"Like what?" she replied, flashing a playful smirk.

"Something where your talents are appreciated without any strings attached," I suggested. "Where you don't have to deal with guys like me."

"Maybe someday," she shrugged. "But for now, this works for me. Besides, how do you know I don't enjoy hanging around with guys like you?"

She worked for a company called *Sunsets and Starlight*. I never knew where their headquarters were, but the woman who took the bookings had a thick, no-nonsense northern accent. Whenever I wanted to see Dominique, I'd ask for her by name, though I knew that wasn't her real one. I never pushed for more. If she wasn't available, I'd leave a message with the agency.

Dominique once told me that the woman who ran the agency had found her by chance, stopping her on the street to compliment her looks. She asked if Dominique would be interested in being a "gentleman's companion" for good money. Dominique was juggling her studies and a part-time job that barely covered rent. The agency owner had sensed her vulnerability, seen her as the perfect recruit. She'd assured that most of her clients were lonely, wealthy old men looking for pleasant company. Curious and in need of extra cash, Dominique agreed to give it a try. What did she have to lose?

That was three years ago, and since then, hundreds of bookings had come and gone. Most of her clients were celebrities, foreign businessmen, sports figures, or politicians passing through London, hoping their double lives—away from work and wives—remained hidden. Dominique never revealed their secrets, not even to me; she was fiercely professional, taking her work seriously. Despite the attention she got from powerful men who could offer her far more than I ever could, I often found myself wondering what she saw in someone like me—someone with average looks and an average life.

Then, one day, as if reading my thoughts, she said, "I like you; you're genuine."

I looked at her, surprised, and she continued, her eyes reflecting a rare sincerity. "You don't put on airs. You don't pretend to be someone you're not. With you, there's no pretence, no façade. You treat me like a person, not just an object or a means to an end. And in this world, that kind of honesty is a luxury."

I first became acquainted with her after an overnight stay in a Central London hotel. It was early summer, and my company had sent me to interview a high-profile businessman for our publication. The electronics firm I worked for was undergoing a major expansion, and the director I was set to meet was in town to review its progress. We needed his insights to energise the company's productivity and meet year-end growth targets—or, at least, that's how my boss spun it.

The interview itself had been a slog, a dismal experience that left a foul taste in my mouth. The director was full of self-importance, convinced that every word out of his mouth was gospel. I played along, nodding in all the right places while my phone filled up with recordings of his banal slogans and lifeless corporate jargon. As someone who had never really embraced the "company man" mindset, the thought of transcribing his drivel filled me with dread. Needing a reset, I decided to expunge my discontent with a few strong drinks—courtesy of the company tab.

I had settled into the hotel bar, already two drinks deep, when I saw her. Or rather, I couldn't not see her—the young woman in the red dress. She entered the room with such grace and presence that every eye, including mine, followed her. The dress clung perfectly to her form, its vivid colour striking against the dim, ambient gold lighting. Her dark hair cascaded over her shoulders, and she moved with a confidence that was equal parts alluring and intimidating.

She approached the bar, her voice soft but distinct, blending effortlessly with the low hum of the piano in the background. She greeted the barman with a kiss on the cheek—a casual, intimate gesture that made me wonder about their relationship. I couldn't help but hope they weren't together, though I had no real reason to think so. With practiced ease, the barman slipped a small, folded note into her hand. She glanced at it, gave a slight nod, and murmured her thanks before her eyes swept the room.

Her gaze caught mine for just a second, and she smiled—a smile full of curiosity and something more, something hidden. It was the kind of smile that lingered in your mind long after it was gone. She held my attention just long enough for me to feel the weight of her presence, then, as gracefully as she had arrived, she left the bar.

I gestured the barman over. "Excuse me," I said, glancing at his nametag, "Esteban. The woman who just left—who is she?" I tried to sound casual, though the curiosity in my voice was hard to hide.

"Just a woman," he replied with a knowing smile.

"Obviously," I said, a little sharper than I intended. "But what's her name? Does she work here or something?"

"No sir, she's merely visiting someone," Esteban replied casually, sizing me up. "If I may say so, sir, not wishing to offend, but if there's a reason you wish to know her, she's probably a bit out of your league. She has a very particular clientele, if you catch my drift."

His smile told me everything. I wasn't the first to ask, and I wouldn't be the last. His expression suggested I should drop the matter, but something about her wouldn't let me.

"Ah," I said slowly, the realisation dawning. She wasn't just beyond my reach financially, but in every other way too. Yet, even knowing this, curiosity still nibbled at me.

I shifted uncomfortably. "Maybe I could just have her name?" I asked, my voice faltering. "You know, for the future."

Esteban smirked, clearly amused by my persistence. "Tell you what," he said, leaning in slightly, "I'll do you a favour. Call this number and ask for Dominique. If she thinks you're right for her, she'll let you know. Good luck, sir. You might just need it."

He handed me a sleek card with a discreet phone number and the company name *Sunsets and Starlight* elegantly scripted in cursive.

"Thanks," I muttered, a mix of excitement and apprehension stirring inside me.

That night, back in my hotel room, I stared at the card for what felt like hours before finally dialling the number. A stern female voice answered, and I nervously left a message for Dominique to contact me.

I lay on the bed, waiting, anticipation prickling under my skin. Eventually, exhaustion overtook me, and I drifted off with her image still vivid in my mind.

In the early hours of the morning, my phone rang. Jolted awake, I fumbled to answer, my heart pounding. Her voice came through the line—cool, professional, and to the point.

"How did you come to know about me?" she asked, her tone calm but direct, leaving no room for misunderstanding.

"Esteban," I said, hoping it was the right answer.

The silence that followed was excruciating. Had I cocked up? Did I sound too eager, too naive? Had I come across as though I was wasting her time?

Finally, after what felt like an eternity, she responded, her voice composed but decisive.

"8 p.m., Tuesday, Sanderson Hotel Bar. Wear a blue shirt."

And just like that, the call ended, leaving me wide awake and breathless.

Tuesday came, and I arrived at the hotel bar early, choosing a seat at the back where I could observe the room without being too conspicuous. As per her instructions, I wore a blue dinner shirt with black evening trousers. Worried that I might not stand out in a sea of similarly dressed diners, I paired the outfit with an outlandish, blue-striped tie—a long-forgotten gift from a friend that had languished, still wrapped, at the bottom of my drawer for years.

Sitting alone at a large table, I nervously checked my watch every few minutes. The seconds dragged on painfully, and by 8 p.m., insecurity started to sneak in. Had she changed her mind? Or worse, had I been stood up? I ordered a Long Island iced tea to steady my nerves, but by 8:15, with the waiter's polite but persistent suggestions to order food, I began contemplating leaving. Maybe she'd been called away by a high-paying regular—someone who could offer her more than a mere dinner with me.

Just as I was about to ask for the bill, the door swung open. There she was—not the stunning, sultry figure I had imagined from our brief encounter at the bar. She was dressed down, almost unremarkably, in black trousers and a red shirt, topped off with a beret. Her appearance took me by surprise. Gone was the high-glamour femme fatale; instead, she looked like someone who might be making jam or hosting a local craft fair. It wasn't what I expected, and I wasn't sure how to feel. On one hand, it removed the fear that I would look like a client paying for her time; on the other, I'd hoped she might make a little more effort for me.

"I thought it might be you," she said coolly as she sat down, removing her beret with a flick of her wrist. "I called Esteban to confirm you were legitimate."

"Oh, everything's above board," I replied hastily, suddenly unsure of how to act. Desperately, I reached for bad comedy. "I was in Esteban's company for a while... uh, he makes a mean glass of wine."

As soon as the words left my mouth, I regretted them. My inner voice screamed at me for sounding so dumb.

She ignored my awkward attempt at humour, casually picking up the menu. "Shall we order?" she asked, her tone nonchalant, as if this were just another evening for her.

"Yes, of course," I stammered, trying to regain my composure. I was flustered, thrown off by how effortlessly she navigated the situation while I fumbled to find the right words. She hadn't even greeted me; was this just a job for her? Was she here to get it over with as quickly as possible?

Sensing my discomfort, she took pity on me, her expression softening. "Buying me dinner is usually how these things start," she said with a gentle smile, as though guiding me through the unspoken rules of an arrangement I clearly didn't understand.

I quickly flagged down the waiter and we ordered. The restaurant, surprisingly quiet for a Tuesday evening, had a warm, intimate ambiance. The scent of roasted meats and fresh herbs filled the air, mingling with the comforting aroma of freshly baked bread. Despite the cozy atmosphere, I could barely concentrate on anything other than her—this enigmatic woman seated across from me. I had come seeking an encounter, but what I found was an unexpected hostility between curiosity and my own insecurities.

I picked up the menu and discreetly glanced at the prices. This night was going to cost me about two weeks' wages. Without looking up, I asked, "This is a nice place. Do you come here often?"

"Only on business," she replied.

Business. I couldn't forget that. This wasn't a date for her; it was a transaction, a business meeting between a client and a provider. I felt like a window shopper wandering around a pricey boutique—polite enough to browse its wares but destined to leave empty-handed. I wanted to say, "It's okay, I'm just looking," but the words stuck in my throat.

I studied the wine list, trying to hide my nerves. I chose an elegant-sounding, medium-priced Merlot called *Keepsake* for us to share. She didn't disagree. When the waiter brought the bottle, he opened it with a pleasant pop, and the deep red liquid flowed into our glasses like a guarantee of something more.

"Thank you, George," she said to the waiter, smiling.

"No problem, Angelique," George replied in a playful, exaggerated French accent

Angelique? I thought her name was Dominique. Was that her real name, or just another alias? And who was George to her—a co-conspirator, a confidant, or just another player in this intricate dance? The thought of how many layers of mystery surrounded her made me uneasy. What was her real currency—money, or something more personal?

"Would you like to order food?" George asked, snapping me out of my thoughts.

"For starters, I'll have the dolmades, and for the main, my usual," she said, not missing a beat.

George's demeanour shifted from formal to familiar. "Fillet of swordfish, very well. And for you, sir?"

"I'll have the same," I said, trying to keep my voice steady while praying my credit card wouldn't give up on me tonight.

George gave a theatrical click of his heels and left, leaving us in an awkward silence that seemed to grow thicker by the second.

I fumbled for something—anything—to say. "So, the reason I called—"

"It's fine. You can skip the pretence," she cut in, her voice casual as she sipped her wine. "Whatever excuse you were about to come up with, spare me. I've heard them all before." She gave a sly smile, her confidence equal parts intimidating and disarming.

"Thank God for that," I said. "I'm just... not used to this sort of thing."

She raised an eyebrow, watching me closely. "And what sort of 'thing' do you think this is?"

Her question caught me off guard, and I fumbled for an answer. Was she truly curious, or testing me? What *was* this? I knew it wasn't a date, not romance or some whimsical fantasy. It was business—a transaction. Yet, there was something in me that wanted it to be more, to step outside the boundaries of whatever this arrangement was supposed to be.

"That's just it: I don't know. I'm not even sure I should be here. To be brutally honest, I don't usually eat in places this fancy."

"What do you usually eat when you're out?" she asked, picking up on the emotional rollercoaster I was trying to get off of.

"When I get the chance? Bar food, mostly."

"What kind?" She leaned in slightly, her curiosity evident.

"The usual—cheap and cheerful. Fish and chips, burgers, chicken wings."

"A proper bar diet, then," she said, flashing a small smile.

"Yep, that's it," I admitted, a strange pang of embarrassment hitting me, though I couldn't quite explain why.

"How often do you indulge in this gourmet fare?" she asked, her voice playful, but with a teasing edge.

"Once a week, maybe twice if I'm lucky."

She raised an eyebrow, clearly amused. "So, your weekly indulgence is... greasy bar food?"

I couldn't help but laugh, feeling my nerves loosen just a little. "Pretty much, yeah."

"Hmm," was all she said, the sound more thoughtful than judgmental.

Our starters arrived, and I ogled the dish in front of me. The dolmades—stuffed vine leaves glistening with olive oil—looked foreign and intimidating. I'd never had them before and wasn't sure I wanted to start now.

Noticing my apprehension, she smiled. "Don't worry, they're just filled with rice. They're delicious."

I laughed falsely, still trying to shake off the nerves. "Like I said, bar food is more my speed."

She took a bite of her dolmades, her lips closing around the vine leaf with a slow, deliberate motion that was almost mesmerizing. Was it all part of the act? A performance designed to keep me captivated, compliant? Whatever it was, it was working.

The waiter, George, returned to check on us. "Is everything to your liking?" he asked, his tone professional.

"Very much so," she replied smoothly, before turning to me. "Don't you think?"

I nodded, not trusting myself to say anything coherent. George smiled, as if he was in on some shared joke, clicked his heels again, and left us to our conversation.

"So," she said, her smile widening just a little, "shall we talk business?"

My stomach dropped. I had been dreading this—the inevitable discussion of payment. "Oh, right, yes," I stammered, fumbling for words.

"You've never done this before have you?" She giggled, amused by my anxiety. "Relax, I don't bite."

"I'm sorry," I confessed, putting down my fork, "I have no idea how any of this works. I thought I'd come in and tell you I was a photographer, see what happened. But truth is, I'm just a first-timer caught in the headlights."

"Like a terrified rabbit?" she asked, raising an eyebrow.

"Exactly," I replied with a laugh.

"First off, relax. This is a first for me as well." She took another bite of her food, her eyes still locked on mine. "Normally,

I'd be discussing the terms of my service, what's included and what's not, and of course, my price. If you couldn't afford me—which, I'm fairly certain you can't—I'd thank you for dinner, and we'd part ways. But," she paused, "you seem different, so I'm going to give you the benefit of the doubt. Tell me a little about yourself, and we'll see how this night unfolds."

Her calm confidence was oddly encouraging. The power dynamic between us felt unfamiliar, but I found myself willing to play along. "What would you like to know?" I asked cautiously.

"What do you do for a living?" she asked.

"It's not very interesting," I hedged, "and I'd hate to bore you before dessert."

She smirked. "Can I guess? I'm very good at reading people."

"Is that so? What's your success rate?"

"Around ninety-five percent," she said, her eyes gleaming with playful conviction.

"That's good enough for me," I said, intrigued, giving her full permission to read me.

She leaned forward slightly, her eyes narrowing as if peeling back layers to see right through me. "I have a picture in my head—of you behind a screen, typing away into the early hours of the morning."

The waiter arrived to clear our plates, letting us know the main course was on its way.

"Go on," I encouraged, grateful that the conversation had moved away from the uncomfortable topic of money.

"You're not a manual labourer—you don't have the hands for it. There's something creative about you, but not the pretentiousness of an artist. And with the slight panic you showed when you glanced at the menu prices," she smiled knowingly, "it's clear you earn money—just not the kind that affords you dinners like this on the regular."

I cringed inwardly. Was I really that transparent?

She smiled wider, almost as though she could read my thoughts. "You seem like the kind of man who's stuck in a job with no passion, but it pays the bills, so you stay."

Her observations hit disturbingly close to home. "Your process is impressively accurate," I admitted, pouring us both another glass of wine, noticing the bottle was already half-empty. "You're building quite the profile."

"You write, don't you?" Her voice took on a tone of certainty.

I nodded, surprised by how easily she could pin me down.

"But you're not an author... more like a journalist." She tapped her fingers on the table. "You write for a... magazine."

I sighed, raising my hands in defeat. "I'm glad I didn't bet any money on this. You've nailed it. How do you do that?"

She touched her nose, grinning. "That's a professional secret."

The waiter returned, presenting us with our main course: a perfectly cooked swordfish fillet, draped in rich hollandaise sauce and served with crisp, steamed vegetables. The aroma teased my senses, a gentle invitation to let the evening's worries dissolve into the indulgence before us.

"So, tell me your story," she said, her voice smooth, inviting.

"It's pretty ordinary," I replied, taking my first bite of the meal, savouring the luxurious flavours.

"I like ordinary," she said, slowly enjoying her own food with a deliberate, almost provocative grace.

"My name's Chris Charles. I was born in 1989 and grew up in North London. My mother was a bank clerk, and my dad was a concert pianist. I had a younger brother, five years behind me. We lived in a neat, well-kept townhouse where nothing ever seemed to go wrong. Then, when I turned thirteen, mum decided she didn't want a family anymore and left us for another man. My dad raised us on his own after that."

I paused, taking another bite. "Am I boring you yet?"

She swirled her wine, studying me with interest. "No, it's fascinating. Go on."

"School was a blur. I didn't have much direction, so I went with journalism at university—it seemed like a safe choice. Meanwhile, my brother followed in my dad's footsteps and became a musician. He was doing well for himself. After graduation, I drifted through jobs until I landed where I am now, writing for a business publication. I live in a flat I'd rather leave, hike when I can, and enjoy Italian and Mexican food. I listen to rock music, don't believe in ghosts, like cats but don't have one, and today's youth baffle me. That's about the whole picture."

"Utterly absorbing," she said, a hint of a smile playing on her lips.

"You're mocking me," I replied, feeling a twinge of embarrassment. "It's a boring life, and it'll probably only get more boring from here."

"No, it isn't," she countered, her eyes locked on mine. "Consider tonight—will this be a boring part of any future stories you tell?"

I took another bite of the swordfish, the flavours unexpectedly perfect with the red wine. "You're right about that. Do you always ask men to tell their life stories?"

"It depends on why I'm meeting them," she said with a slight shrug. "In my line of work, I like to get a man to open up, as much as he's willing. It usually makes the evening go better for both of us. Most men who see me just want to feel listened to. The physical part is secondary."

I felt a twinge of guilt. "I think you've already figured out I can't afford much more than this dinner."

"You misunderstand," she said, her tone soft but intent. "Throughout my life and work, I've encountered countless lives—each unique in its own way—but most have left me feeling indifferent, as if I was only there to witness them perform. Hearing your story, though, makes this evening feel like something more... something almost like providence. With others, I was there because I was asked to be, but with you, it feels like I'm here because I *want* to be. It feels like your life holds more for you than you realise."

"Does it?" I asked, the question slipping out more earnestly than I'd intended. "Because to me, it feels like I'm just drifting—waiting for excitement to finally arrive or for death to step in first."

"That's a bleak outlook," she remarked, placing her fork down with a soft clink. She leaned forward, setting her plate aside, and reached across the table. "Give me your hand."

I offered it without hesitation. Her touch was soft, her fingers warm and slender. "You don't realise it yet, but tonight is just a part of your story. A chapter you'll come back to, again and again. You'll remember this dinner, this conversation, and you'll smile—whether it's a happy smile or a sad one, you *will* smile."

She released my hand, and with it, the warmth of her touch faded. Around us, the restaurant thrummed with life—the clink of glasses, the low hum of conversations, and the rich scents of the kitchen drifting through the air. Late diners trickled in, their laughter mingling with the quiet rhythm of the evening.

She was an enigma—her words cloaked in secrets, her true name still unknown. And yet, I found myself drawn in, willingly following her lead, unsure where it would take me.

As the waiter returned to clear our plates, she reached up, her fingers deftly unpinning the intricate bun that had held her hair in place. A cascade of long, black locks spilled over her shoulders, shimmering like liquid ink. It felt otherworldly, like she'd stepped out of a dream.

"Something wrong?" she asked, her eyes twinkling in the soft glow of the restaurant's lights.

I couldn't find the words. I was completely captivated, as if everything else had faded into the background. Never in my life had I seen such beauty, a beauty that felt almost unreal. I had the strange sensation that, if I glanced around, I'd see the other diners equally spellbound, their lives briefly interrupted by her presence.

Before I knew what I was saying, the words spilled out. "I want you." The confession echoing in my mind like a voice bouncing through an empty room. It wasn't just lust—though that played its part—it was something innate, as though my entire existence had shifted out of the mundane.

She reached across the table, her movements slow and deliberate. Her fingers grazed the back of my hand before intertwining with mine. A simple touch, yet it sent a shudder down my spine, making the moment feel dreamlike, as though I had known her far longer than I had.

"And I want you," she whispered, her voice barely audible. "No charge."

5

After that night at the restaurant, we began meeting once or twice a week, whenever her schedule allowed. Some evenings were filled with passionate sex; on others, we simply sat across from each other on my worn sofa, eating, drinking, and trading stories. I'd recount tales from my past—of which there were plenty—while she shared anecdotes from the people in her present. When it came to her own past, though, any questions I asked were met with polite deflection. I never pushed, fearing that pushing too hard might cause her to disappear entirely. Instead, I learned to be content with the knowledge she offered, especially the insights from her education, which she patiently explained in ways I could comprehend.

Despite the joy I found in her company, a persistent confusion aggravated me—why was a woman like her interested in someone like me? Almost weekly, I'd ask her why she was with me, but her answers remained vague, frustratingly so at times. I didn't feel any more special than the clients she saw professionally. I wasn't a rich politician or a charismatic rock star. My life felt small in comparison to the vibrant world she seemed to navigate effortlessly. Compared to the colourful characters in her orbit, I was just a bland shade of magnolia.

"You're you," she said one day, her voice contemplative. "What we have here is a normal story with normal people. We're having an out-of-body experience, watching ourselves on a stage, acting out a simple, slice-of-life scene. Until my character exits, stage right."

"That sounds a bit too philosophical for our situation," I replied, trying to grasp the meaning behind her words.

She laughed, that light, melodic sound that always eased my tension. "You're right. I just love seeing that confused look on your face. But if you really want to know, I like that you sought me out."

"I only did what any other man would do, surely?" I said, still perplexed by her interest.

"No," she said, her tone softening. "You sought me out—not just for sex, but because you *wanted* to see me. There's a difference. And despite what you think, you're far more interesting than you give yourself credit for."

And so, our relationship continued. We saw each other whenever we could, and on the days her work called her away, I was at peace with it. Surprisingly, I felt no jealousy, no anxiety over the fact that she was with other people. To outsiders, it might have looked like I was suffering from a severe lack of self-respect, allowing her to carry on with her clients without objection. But to me, it was never like that.

What she did when she wasn't with me was her *professional* life. I was the sole member of her personal life. The two worlds never collided. She never brought her work home, never spoke of her clients, and never compared me—sexually or otherwise—to anyone else. It was as if, when we were together, I was the only one who mattered. And in that strange stability was the magic of what we had.

That late August, we decided to escape for a long weekend, taking a break from our busy lives. Her new term at university was just around the corner, and with her studies and work consuming most of her time, being together would soon become rare—a pause before the inevitable rush of reality pulled us apart.

We chose a secluded hotel by the beach. Most of the day was spent in a blissful haze, the distant rhythm of the sea blending with our sighs of passion. Afterward, as the sweat cooled on our skin under the gentle breeze of the ceiling fan, a memory surfaced—the day I spent with my uncle and his mysterious companion.

When I finished telling the story of my uncle and his girl, she slipped out of bed and walked naked to the bathroom. Seconds later, the sound of running water echoed through the room, steam seeping out under the door.

"So, what happened to your uncle when you got back?" she called out from the shower.

"Nothing much," I replied. "He dropped me off, and that was that. The funny thing is, I told my parents about his girlfriend, Vanity, and you should've seen their faces—they looked like they'd been slapped. That was the first time I ever heard the word 'escort.'" I smiled, remembering the awkward conversation my dad had with me afterward.

"Did you ever see her again?"

I could hear the water running, and I was planning to join her soon. But first, I lit a cigarette.

"No, my mother wouldn't let me go anywhere near my uncle if Vanity was around. She said a woman like that wasn't appropriate for teenage boys." I took a drag, the smoke curling up toward the ceiling. "I was angry back then because I liked her, but I kind of get it now."

"Didn't your uncle say anything? I would've been upset if my partner meant I couldn't see my nephew."

"No, he was too scared of my mum," I said with a small laugh, though a pang of regret followed. I wished I hadn't listened to my mother, especially since she left us not long after. "Anyway, they didn't last. He moved to Wales, and I only saw him on special occasions."

I sat in silence, recalling how upset I'd been about rarely seeing my uncle. The last time I saw him was at my father's funeral, and he was a pale shadow of his former self. Drugs had turned him from a vibrant man into a living skeleton, slurring his words and barely able to string a sentence together. I hadn't heard from him since.

"So, are you going to sit there with the look of a sad puppy, or are you coming in here?"

How did she know? Even from behind the bathroom door, steam swirling around her, she could sense when I drifted into the past. She definitely had a gift for reading people. "I'm coming," I called, stubbing out the cigarette.

As I approached the bathroom, the promise of sharing a shower with the most beautiful woman I'd ever been with sent a surge of desire through me. I was about to step in when my phone rang, its shrill tone cutting through the mood.

She stopped the shower and peeked her head from behind the glass screen. "Don't answer that," she said, her voice tense.

"Why?" I asked, confused.

"I don't know, just... don't." She stepped out, water dripping from her wet hair, dripping down her naked body. Her skin gleamed under the dim light, and my desire flared again.

I reached into my coat pocket and glanced at the screen. Seeing the name, I smiled. "It's just Duncan," I said, trying to calm her. "What are you so worked up about?"

"I have a bad feeling. If you take that call, we won't know where it leads." Her voice was tight, her earlier sensuality replaced by sudden uncertainty. The shift caught me off guard.

"It's probably just a quick chat," I said, trying to brush it off, though her anxiety was starting to seep into me.

"Don't," she pleaded, stepping closer, her eyes locking onto mine, filled with urgency. "Please don't."

But curiosity got the better of me. Ignoring her, I lifted the phone to my ear. "Hello?"

Part 2

The tale begins

6

I had known my friend Duncan since early childhood. We'd grown up together, gone to school together, and navigated the pitfalls of adulthood side by side. We used to joke that we'd take a bullet for each other, but even the best of friends can sometimes be a puzzle. Duncan was that kind of friend—loyal and steadfast one minute, unpredictable and volatile the next. Alcohol had a strong hand in shaping the man he'd become, but it was his growing disdain for society that truly defined him in recent years.

It hadn't always been that way. Once, Duncan was the life of every party—the king of every gathering. His easy-going nature, his shaggy-dog charm, and his reckless humour drew people in. His world back then revolved around two things: girls and burning the candle at both ends. But like all flames that burn too brightly, Duncan's couldn't last. His carefree life was cut short in a way no one could have anticipated, leaving him a shadow of the man he used to be.

The accident came out of nowhere. It was a dark, wet winter evening, the road slick with an icy sheen. Duncan had been on his way to a Christmas party when a car, driven by a kid high on weed, came careening around a blind corner and hit him head-on. The impact sent Duncan flying several feet. He wasn't killed, but he might as well have been. His foot was pointing in the wrong direction when the paramedics got to him.

What followed were months of painful recuperation. Duncan's ankle had been shattered in the accident, and it took extensive surgery to rebuild it—rods and pins holding together the fragments of bone. The doctors warned that he'd walk with a limp for the rest of his life, and on bad days, he might need a cane to get around. But the accident had cost him more than just his physical mobility; it had broken his spirit. The light that had once made him the heart of every party was dimmed, snuffed out by a bitterness that seemed to spread with every bottle he reached for—not just to dull the physical pain, but to drown the anger and frustration of being sidelined by something entirely beyond his control.

Despite it all, I held onto the hope that Duncan would somehow find his way back to the man he used to be. I wanted to be there when he did, to help him remember the vibrant, magnetic guy who could light up a room with nothing more than a laugh and a half-baked observation about life. Duncan had always had a gift for seeing the absurdity in things, turning the mundane into something profound or hilarious, and people flocked to him for it. His stories—whether rooted in fact or not—were captivating, his laughter infectious.

I tried to support him through those dark times, clinging to the fragments of the old Duncan whenever they surfaced. During his better days, I'd visit, and we'd chat like we used to—about anything and everything, from the ridiculous to the profound. It felt, for a moment, like the friend I'd known for years was still in there, just waiting to re-emerge. But those occasions became rarer, and the darker days grew more frequent.

I kept hoping that with age, Duncan might find some peace, that the passage of time would dull the sharp edges of his bitterness. There were occasions when it seemed possible. Every now and then, he'd show signs of trying to straighten himself out. He'd talk about getting his life back on track, about finding a way to move forward. For a while, it would seem like he was brushing off the weight of his frustrations, trying to reclaim some sense of normalcy.

But it never lasted. Something—a memory, a disappointment, a bad day—would set him off, like a trigger being pulled on the gun he kept pointed at his own happiness. He'd spiral back into that dark place, and each time, it seemed harder for him to climb out. The anger, the self-loathing, the resentment—it all came rushing back, dragging him deeper. I worried that one day, he wouldn't be able to pull himself out at all.

Still, I couldn't walk away. No matter how hard it got, I stayed by his side. Because that's what you do for someone who's been with you through it all, even if they no longer resemble the person they once were. Not when they've been part of your life for as long as Duncan had been part of mine.

I stood on the far side of Duncan's office, watching as he limped back behind his desk. The heat was suffocating, with the summer sun pouring in through the windows. Despite owning an air conditioner, he kept it off most days—the cold aggravated the metal pins still lodged in his bones. Outside, I could hear his secretary arranging a delivery, her voice muffled behind the door.

Duncan gestured toward the worn plastic chair across from him. "You don't usually need an invitation," he said, easing himself into his old leather recliner, which groaned under his weight.

I sat down, taking in the cramped space. His office, no bigger than a standard living room, felt even smaller with the clutter. An old metal filing cabinet took up one corner, while a fan lazily spun in the other, barely cutting through the heavy air. Dust motes floated in the sunbeams slicing through the room. For a guy running a wedding videography and photography agency, his setup was anything but glamorous.

I couldn't help but notice Duncan looked different. For a weekday, it was unusual not to catch a whiff of alcohol on him by this hour—proof he must've come straight from a meeting or reviewing footage. Duncan was a high-functioning semi-alcoholic, never letting his habits interfere with work, at least not visibly.

"So," he said, tapping his fingers on the desk.

"So," I echoed, smiling despite myself. No matter how much of a mess Duncan could be, I was always glad to see him.

"I haven't heard from you in weeks," he said, narrowing his eyes.

"Sorry, I've been a bit busy."

"Too busy for your best bud? Got something going on that you're not telling me?"

"No, nothing like that. Just… other things."

"Other things like… maybe seeing someone?" he asked, raising an eyebrow.

I laughed, caught off guard. "Is it that obvious?"

"Come on, man. That goofy smile of yours says it all."

"What smile?"

Duncan reached into his desk drawer and, to my surprise, pulled out a can of iced tea instead of his usual vodka. I figured he had another meeting lined up after this one.

"You get this weird look on your face when you're getting some, like you've been sucking helium from a balloon," he said, cracking open the can and taking a sip.

I had no idea what he meant by that. How does someone even look after inhaling helium? I felt fine, and when I looked in the mirror this morning, everything seemed normal. Before I could respond, we heard the office door click shut as Linda, his secretary, left to give us some privacy.

Duncan grinned mischievously, leaned under his desk, and pulled out a vodka bottle, pouring a shot into his iced tea. So much for a sober conversation. The mood shifted instantly, and I knew I wouldn't be staying long.

"I promised Linda I wouldn't drink during business hours," Duncan said, swirling the vodka in his glass with a smirk. "But what she doesn't know won't hurt her, right?" He offered me the glass, but I waved it off politely. He shrugged, taking a generous gulp.

"So, what's going on with you? What's her name?" he asked, settling back into his chair with a curious glint in his eyes.

"Dominique," I said, almost sheepishly.

"Ooh, la-de-da, French, is she?" he teased, raising his eyebrows with exaggerated flair. He took another sip, and a drop of the vodka-laced tea fell onto his tie. I noticed but didn't bother pointing it out.

"No, she's English," I corrected.

"With a name like that? Huh." He sniggered, the corners of his mouth twitching as if he were piecing together some half-baked joke.

Duncan sat there in his typical business attire—a grey shirt he swore was perfect for hiding stains and a black tie so dark it seemed to absorb all the light around it. His recent short-back-

and-sides haircut gave him a polished, professional look to anyone who didn't know him as well as I did. Meanwhile, I sat across from him in jeans and an old Aerosmith T-shirt, my laid-back '70s rock vibe.

"So, when do I get to meet this, Dominique?" he leaned in with a grin that told me he was already plotting ways to embarrass me. "I've got a bunch of stories lined up to make sure she knows the *real* you."

"Soon," I replied, dodging the prospect as best as I could. "She's busy with school and work, but we'll figure something out."

Duncan raised an eyebrow. "What does she do for a living?"

I hesitated. How much could I tell him? Would he even believe me if I said she was a high-class escort? And more importantly, would he understand? I decided to keep things vague.

"She works for an agency that collaborates with government departments and private sectors," I said, hoping that would be enough to steer the conversation elsewhere.

His curiosity only deepened. "And how exactly did you meet a girl like that?"

Before I could muster up an answer, Duncan cut in, his tone shifting. "Oh, did I tell you I bumped into Alice a couple of months ago?"

I shook my head. "I thought she was living in Leeds now. How is she?"

"She was down visiting her parents. Seemed fine—she's seeing someone new." He said it casually, but I could sense a subtle undertone in his voice.

"That's good," I said, feeling a flicker of nostalgia.

"She asked about you," Duncan added. "I didn't know what you'd want me to say, so I just told her you were keeping busy, staying out of trouble. She asked me to say hello."

The room was getting stuffy, so I stood and walked over to the window. Outside, the city moved as it always did—people hurrying from one place to the next, faces taut with dissatisfaction or blank with fatigue. A large van below was being unloaded, workmen stacking boxes without a care that someone might be watching. I lit a cigarette and offered one to Duncan.

"No thanks, trying to quit," he said, shaking his head before taking another sip of his drink. The irony wasn't lost on me—quitting cigarettes but still holding tight to the bottle.

"They were happy times, weren't they?" he asked, nudging me lightly with his knee.

I stubbed out the cigarette halfway, breathing in the humid summer air. "If you're about to launch into another speech about how I left the business, save it."

Duncan raised his hands in mock surrender. "Hey, calm down. I'm just saying... when we worked together, things were good."

"And now you're going to follow that up with how everything went downhill the moment I left to 'pursue my own goals,' right?" I said, sitting back down, though part of me wanted to walk right out.

"We were doing well. We weren't raking in millions, but we had enough to get by and then some. We were a great team—you had Alice, and I had..."

He trailed off, his mind clearly drifting to the accident and all that had come after.

"You had us," I finished for him. "And I told you from the start, my role in this was always going to be temporary. I helped get the business off the ground, but I never planned to stay forever. It wasn't my path."

"And writing for a monthly business publication is?" he shot back.

The silence between us grew charged with all the unsaid things hanging between old friends. Duncan knew exactly what he was doing—digging up the past, trying to get a reaction from me. I thought about leaving, letting him sit in his insecurities and drown his frustrations in the bottle, only to call me tomorrow with an apology, as he always did.

"I'm sorry," he said after a long pause. "Seeing Alice brought back all the memories. We used to have fun—wild nights, crazy adventures—and now it's just paperwork, taxes, and dealing with agency workers who barely show up on time. The grind of it all just... gets to me sometimes."

"That's called growing up," I replied, my tone blunter than I intended. "Happens to ninety-nine percent of people."

"Well, I guess I'm stuck in that one percent," he muttered, a hint of bitterness in his voice.

It was then that my eyes caught the framed photo above Duncan's head—a picture I hadn't noticed before. A canvas shot of Alice, Duncan, and me, taken at a cabaret show years ago. Alice stood between us, radiant, her smile lighting up the whole frame. I was on the left, my long hair almost hiding my eyes, while Duncan grinned widely, that infectious, carefree grin that used to make him the life of the party. The photo was a snapshot of pure joy—one that felt like a lifetime ago. Had that always been there, or had I just become too blind to see it?

I took a deep breath. "Whatever's knocked your confidence, you can get past it," I said, choosing my words carefully. "You just need to start believing in yourself again."

Duncan gave me a crooked smile, the kind that said he didn't quite buy what I was selling. "Says the guy whose version of self-belief is wrapped in weary cynicism about everything."

I couldn't argue with that.

He reached for his drink, but before he could take a sip, I placed my hand over the glass. "Maybe what you really need is a few months off the booze. Give yourself a chance to see the world through sober eyes."

"So, you think I'm an alcoholic?" he asked, his voice teetering between defensiveness and weariness.

"I'm saying, put the glass down. Stop dwelling on the past, especially when it wasn't as great as you remember. And instead, tell me more about that visitor you mentioned when you called yesterday."

Duncan hesitated, his fingers twitching as they lingered near the glass. Then, in a move I hadn't expected, he slowly pushed it across the desk toward me. It was a small gesture, but it carried a lot of weight—his silent way of asking for help. And despite everything, I was glad to offer it.

"You're right," he said, taking a deep breath, "where do I start?"

"From the beginning," I replied, grimacing as I finished the last of the sickly-sweet tea.

7

"It was early yesterday morning when they came in," Duncan began, leaning forward, his tone serious. "I was just *relaxing* after a 'high-powered business meeting' with a supermarket owner about sponsorship."

I gave him a look. "What were you really doing?"

He sighed, conceding with a grin. "Fine. I was trolling commenters on news forums."

"As you do," I said with a smirk, shaking my head.

A small man in a perfectly tailored charcoal grey suit strode in, flanked by two massive figures whose suits were darker and less refined. They moved with an air of authority, as if the space already belonged to them. They stopped in front of Linda's desk, their eyes cold and unblinking. She was mid-conversation with a friend, but the second she saw them, her instincts flared. Something was off.

Muttering a hasty goodbye, finished the conversation.

The small man smiled at her—a rigid, chilling smile that never reached his eyes. "I would like to speak to the owner of this establishment," he said, his voice smooth but dripping with a quiet menace.

Linda tried to compose herself, but it was clear she was rattled. "Do you have an appointment?" she asked, her voice barely steady.

"No," the man replied, his tone flat as he inspected the room with a sense of ownership. "But since we're here, and you don't seem too busy, perhaps you could schedule me in for a meeting—say, right now?" He tapped his gloved fingers on her desk, the sound sharp and deliberate, like a warning.

"I'll need to check his availability," she said, the words shaky. "We don't usually take walk-ins."

"Oh, I'm sure he'll be more than happy to see us," the man said, his voice laced with something dark, leaving no room for refusal.

Linda, clearly unnerved, hurried into my office. When she came back, she was pale as a sheet. "Yes, he'll see you now," she said nervously.

I followed his stare to the door, my curiosity spiking. "Who were they?"

Duncan hesitated, his expression serious. "If I had to guess—in one word: gangsters."

The small man looked no older than fifty, but his presence was commanding—like a little fascist general. His Italian suit was tailored to perfection, giving him an illusion of size, and a crisp white shirt peeked from beneath the jacket. The open collar revealed a thick gold chain gleaming against his skin. His movements were precise, deliberate, and his polished shoes reflected the dim overhead light. His slicked-back hair, streaked with grey, framed cold, unblinking eyes that seemed to take in everything—and miss nothing.

Behind him, the two hulking figures loomed like silent sentinels, each at least a foot taller. Their muscular frames strained against the fabric of their black shirts, making the small man appear even more imposing. The first had a shaved head, a detailed dragon tattoo coiling around his right ear. The second, with jet-black hair framing a face crisscrossed by scars, wore an expression that told silent, violent stories. Both men sported heavy black leather gloves—the kind that vowed brutality if required.

The small man extended a gloved hand. "Thank you for seeing me on such short notice." His voice was smooth, controlled, but it carried an undertone of something darker. The gesture wasn't a request—it was a command. Without hesitation, my friend took it.

"Though small, his grip was like iron," Duncan said uneasily.

"From the smallest acorns grow the greatest oaks," I muttered, though I wasn't sure why the phrase came to mind.

Linda, who had followed the men into the room, seemed bewildered by the sudden chill that filled the air. As she shut the door, she mouthed a single word of apology to Duncan: "Sorry."

"Please, take a seat, Mister...?" Duncan began, trying to regain control of the situation.

"You can call me Smith," the man said, seating himself with the precision of someone who owned the room. His voice sliced through the air like a chisel through soft wood. Despite his efforts to sound refined, Duncan caught the unmistakable South London accent woven through his words.

"We only have one seat, I'm afraid," Duncan said, gesturing to the spartan room.

"Do not worry. I won't be here long, and my associates are quite happy to stand." The two men nodded in unison, standing like stone golems, awaiting orders from their smaller master.

"So, what can I do for you, Mr. Smith? Would you like to discuss a booking?" Duncan asked, attempting to steer the conversation toward familiar ground.

"Nothing of the sort," Smith replied, his voice touched with a subtle, mocking scoff. "I'm here on behalf of someone I work for. We have a small request of you."

"Anything I can do to help, Mr. Smith," Duncan said, barely managing to keep his composure.

Smith's smile was as polished as his suit, as artificial as a billboard model's. "Good," he said, rapping his gloved hand lightly on the table. "You handle various ceremonies for business, don't you?"

"Photography, videography—it's my bread and butter. Though I'm no David Bailey or Michael Winterbottom," Duncan said, injecting a touch of humour, hoping to lighten the mood.

"It would be better for both of us if you didn't make light of this situation," Smith replied, his smile vanishing into thin, taut lines of pink flesh against expertly shaved skin. His polished accent slipped, revealing a harsh cockney drawl. "Now, may I continue, or do you wish to mock me further with your childish jokes?"

"I... I apologise," Duncan stammered, his bravado crumbling. "I meant no offense."

Smith didn't respond. His hawk-like gaze remained fixed on Duncan as he raised a gloved hand, beckoning the bald lackey over. The man reached inside his coat and pulled out an iPad Mini, handing it to Smith, who turned it on and slid it across the desk toward Duncan.

The screen lit up, revealing a single image—a man Duncan recognised instantly.

"The man in this photo," Smith growled, his voice low and menacing, "Do you know him?"

Duncan swallowed hard. "Uh, yes, I do. It's—"

"Adam?" I said, stunned.

Duncan nodded. "It was the picture I took of him at that summer festival."

"What do they want with my brother?"

"I'll get to that," Duncan muttered, his eyes wide with disbelief. "It gets stranger."

Smith tapped the image on the screen, the sharp sound of his gloved finger like a gavel striking down. "Were you with him before and after this picture was taken?" he asked, his tone colder now.

"Yes," Duncan admitted, barely audible. "I was."

Smith tapped the image on the screen with a gloved finger. "Were you with him before and after this picture was taken?"

"Yes, I was," Duncan admitted, his voice barely audible.

"That is good," Smith said, his smile returning, though colder this time. "Our conversation is off to a good start, wouldn't you say?"

Smith's thin smile reappeared, colder than before. "Good," he said, his voice as smooth as glass but just as hard. "Our conversation is off to a promising start, wouldn't you say?"

Duncan nodded, but he was in fight-or-flight mode. His eyes flicked to the window, perhaps calculating the odds of escape, considering how far a third-floor jump might take him. The door was out of the question; the two enormous figures behind Smith stood like unmovable walls. Yet, as unrealistic as it was, throwing himself out of the window seemed like a plausible option.

"If you say so, yes" he muttered.

Smith leaned forward slightly, his voice dropping to a razor-sharp edge. "Did you know Adam Charles well?"

Duncan shifted uncomfortably in his chair. "Very well. He was the brother of my best friend. I always took the photos when he played live. But... if you're looking for Adam, you'll have a problem. He died five years ago."

Smith's cold smile vanished, replaced with an expression void of emotion. "We're aware of that," he said flatly. "What I want to know is if you're familiar with any of his acquaintances—those he may have been in contact within the weeks before his death."

Duncan's hands were slick with sweat. He was barely holding it together, the urge for a drink biting at him. He swallowed hard, shaking his head. "Adam kept to himself toward the end. I only knew his close family. Anyone else... they were just passing faces, people I wouldn't remember."

Smith's eyes narrowed, his stare drilling into Duncan's with a mix of calculation and threat. "My friend," he said, his tone softening, almost coaxing, "you don't need to be nervous. All we want is a simple piece of information—someone Adam may have known. Think of this as a consultation between two professionals. And if it goes well, you could find yourself very generously rewarded. Now, once more—was there any friend, any face, which stood out?"

Duncan hesitated, his mind scrambling for answers. But the looming presence of Smith's men and the fear left him paralyzed, terrified of giving the wrong answer and sending this tense exchange spiralling into something far worse.

"I'd like to help, I really would, but you'd need to speak to his brother. He knew more of Adam's friends than I did," Duncan whimpered, barely holding his composure.

I shot him a glare. "So, you dropped me in it?"

"What was I supposed to do? It's the truth!" Duncan stammered guiltily. "But that's not all…"

The small man, Smith, leaned further forward, his eyes narrowing as they drilled into Duncan's soul. Duncan thought he might crack, and cry for forgiveness. But then, just as quickly, Smith leaned back and smiled—a thin, chilling smile that made Duncan's blood run cold.

"I believe you," Smith said, his voice unnervingly calm.

Duncan barely suppressed a sigh. "Thank God," he muttered under his breath, thinking the worst had passed.

But Smith wasn't finished. His smile twisted, his tone sharpening like the edge of a knife. "However," he continued, "I now need further assistance from you."

Duncan's momentary relief vanished, and he could feel the sweat trickling down his spine. "Anything you need," he forced out, his voice trembling.

Smith raised his gloved hand, and one of the henchmen stepped forward, pulling a small notepad and pen from his pocket. He handed them to Duncan, along with a small note card. "Memorise the number and address written here," Smith instructed, his tone clipped and commanding. "Then write them down and give them to Adam's brother."

Duncan's hands shook violently as he scribbled the details onto the notepad. The fear made his handwriting barely legible, but the second he finished, the card was snatched away.

Smith's eyes never left Duncan as his voice dropped to a menacing whisper. "Now, two things must happen. First, your friend must go to that address and call the number. Once that's done, he is to destroy the details—tear them up, burn them, eat them for all I care. But they must disappear. And make no mistake—we'll know if he doesn't."

"Eat them..." Duncan repeated, his voice cracking as he struggled to keep his hand steady. The absurdity of the instruction might have been laughable under different circumstances, but fear crushed any sense of humour.

Smith's expression darkened as he straightened up. "Second," he continued, "if either of you so much as whispers a word about this meeting," he gestured casually toward the figures standing like behind him, "Cliff and Trevor here will ensure that, after razing this little operation of yours to the ground, you and your friend will never feel safe in this town again. Do you understand?"

Duncan nodded frantically, sweat trickling down his temple.

"I said," Smith growled, leaning closer, "do you *understand*?"

"I understand," Duncan croaked, barely able to find his voice.

Smith clapped his hands together, the sharp sound making Duncan flinch. "Good, very good." He turned to his henchmen. "You see, boys? This is what happens when two hardworking men conduct themselves in a civil, business-like manner."

"Yes, Mr. Smith," Clifford replied, his dragon tattoo shifting with the nod of his head.

"Yes, Mr. Smith," echoed Trevor, his scarred face remaining disturbingly blank.

"Excellent," Smith said, a smile curling back onto his lips. Reaching into his jacket, he produced a thick envelope, and with a flick of his wrist, slid it across the desk toward Duncan. "This should cover any business losses you might have incurred during our little chat."

As the three men turned to leave, Duncan gingerly opened the envelope. Inside, a stack of fifty-pound notes. Too thick to count with them still in the room, watching him. His hands trembled as he mumbled, "Thank you, Mr. Smith. That's... very generous."

Smith gave a polite nod, though his smile never reached his eyes. "Remember, no telling anyone. If you do, we'll find out."

Duncan swallowed hard. "No, Mr. Smith, I won't say a word."

Smith's eyes darkened. "Good boy."

With that, the three men walked out, the door clicking shut behind them. But the oppressive unease they'd brought with them remained, lingering in the air like a choking vapour. Duncan sat frozen at his desk, heart pounding, eyes fixed on the envelope as if it might explode at any second.

8

The cigarette burned between my fingers as I looked at the note, the address scrawled in Duncan's shaky handwriting. "I can't figure this out," I muttered. "What do they want with my brother?"

"Beats me," Duncan replied, rubbing the back of his neck. "But is there anything about that guy that stands out to you?"

"Other than the fact that he sounds like the walking stereotype of a gangster? Not really," I said,

"What do you think they want?"

"What makes you think I'd know?" I snapped, frustrated.

"Hey, I'm just asking," he shot back. "Don't shoot the messenger."

I scowled but kept quiet.

"Seriously though," Duncan continued, "did Adam ever mention anything shady? Something off?"

"Not once." I shook my head. "You knew him—he was straight as a damn ruler. Criminal stuff? Not his scene." The idea of some mobster being involved with my brother felt wrong.

"They seemed to know him, though," Duncan said, glancing down at the note again.

"Doesn't mean he was in any trouble," I countered, a bit sharper than I'd intended.

Duncan then asked the question I'd been trying not to think about. "You don't think… they had anything to do with his death, do you?"

I bit my lip, staring at the ashtray on the desk as I tried to work everything out. Could they have? I didn't want to believe it, but I couldn't disprove it out of hand.

"I don't know," I admitted.

"So, what now?" Duncan asked, watching me as I paced up and down his small office.

I exhaled heavily. "What else can I do? I either follow their instructions and see what they want, or I don't—and they rip our lives apart."

"You could go to the police," Duncan suggested, though he didn't sound convinced.

"Yeah, and what would I say?" I said, stopping to face him. "The guy walked in here like he owned the place, made his threats, and left with nothing but a whisper of evidence. Besides, if they're bold enough to show up like that, then they're not scared of the law."

Duncan sighed, sinking into his chair. "Yeah, you're probably right. They've likely got connections anyway; it would be our word against theirs."

"The only real option is to go to the address, call the number, and find out what the hell they want. Maybe I can get some answers—figure out how Adam got mixed up with these people. Best-case scenario, I help them enough to make them leave us alone."

Duncan looked at me, his brow furrowed in concern. "Do you want me to come with you?"

I shook my head. "No. It's me they want. You've done what they asked—don't get yourself deeper into this. I'll be fine."

There was a sadness in Duncan's eyes as he nodded. Sober, he was a good friend—reliable, thoughtful. But I knew that once I left, he'd crawl back into a bottle, his worries vanishing with each drink.

"What're you going to do until then?" he asked.

"I'm heading home. I'll watch the footage from that gig—the charity ball. Maybe there's something there that makes sense." I flicked the cigarette into the ashtray and grabbed my coat.

Duncan leaned forward, his voice earnest. "Look, if you need anything—anything—you call me. Smith and his crew? They're bad news. I've been in some rough situations, but this… this feels worse. Just be careful, okay?"

I nodded, truly appreciating his consideration of my well-being. As I stepped outside into the heavy, late-summer air, my girlfriend's words from the night before echoed in my mind: *We won't know where this leads.*

9

We're simple creatures, moving aimlessly from Place A to Place B without a second thought, oblivious to the journey we're actually on. Life becomes a blur—days, weeks, even years passing in a haze while the world continues spinning, indifferent to our pace. But when we stop, really stop, and reflect on the path between those points, we realise the grand design we once trusted starts to fall apart. It unravels slowly, like a loose thread pulled from the hem of a cotton blouse—fragile, barely held together.

Take, for example, a man sitting on his sofa, a glass of lager in one hand, a half-smoked cigarette in the other. Just this morning, he learned that dangerous people—serious, sinister people—wanted to meet him. They had questions, demands, all about someone his brother might have known. And yet, what could he possibly offer them? He hadn't spoken to his brother in those final, tragic weeks. He was as lost to that part of his brother's life as anyone. But now, despite knowing nothing, he had no choice but to help, or risk becoming their next target.

Place A was where the bombshell dropped, where everything began to unravel. Place B was supposed to be his refuge, his home, his so-called "safe space." But the journey between those two points? A blur—a void in his memory. He couldn't even recall how he got there. His brain registered nothing but the thick exhaust fumes from passing cars, the acrid scent of diesel clinging to his skin. The rush of traffic, the honking horns, and the hum of engines drowned out his thoughts. The people he passed were nothing more than shadows, ephemeral ghosts in the periphery.

Yet, once he arrived home, clarity returned, harsh and unforgiving, and the memories began carving themselves into his psyche, reshaping what he thought he knew. The world as he understood it had shifted—violently, irreversibly. What once seemed familiar now felt foreign, as if the very ground beneath his feet had reorientated. From this point on, his life was destined to veer off its course—whether it was for better or for worse, only time would tell. But one thing was certain: the man who had walked into his home was not the same man who had left it that morning.

    From the sofa, I stared listlessly at the screen before me. The room was still, save for the rhythmic whir of the fan oscillating in the corner. The world beyond the walls seemed irrelevant, as though it no longer existed. My focus was consumed by the paused image of my brother, frozen on the screen—a life now lost but preserved in these digital moments.

    The fan's steady hum was the only thing grounding me, its cool breeze brushing against my face as I sat, eyes fixed on the image of Adam mid-performance. The cigarette between my fingers had burned down to the filter, long forgotten, its embers now cold. My mind, however, was still trapped in that space—still lost in the concert footage, the spring day when Adam's music filled the air, and none of us had any inkling of what was to come.

    I'd watched this video more times than I could count, desperately hoping to find something—some clue, some hidden detail—that might explain why those men, and Smith, were so interested in him. This footage was all I had left of my brother's last performance—a simple charity concert, held in a field near his home. It had been a joyous occasion, and Adam had been in his element. On that stage, with his acoustic guitar and his voice echoing across the field, he was alive, happy, completely immersed in his music.

    The camera panned across the audience, faces blurred by distance and motion. I scanned them for what felt like the hundredth time, searching for something out of place, but nothing jumped out. The crowd was just that—a crowd, filled with smiling faces, clapping hands, and swaying bodies, none of them distinct, none offering any answers.

Eight times I'd watched it, and eight times I'd come up empty. What did Smith's men expect me to find? Why had they targeted Adam?

Frustration mounted as I crushed the cigarette into the ashtray, rubbing my tired eyes. I was grasping at shadows, searching for answers I unsure even existed. There was no point in continuing, no revelation waiting for me in these frames.

I closed the concert footage, ready to shut off my laptop when my eyes landed on another file—one I hadn't touched in years. "Adam's Celebration of Life." It had sat on my desktop, untouched for three years, a relic of grief I had carefully locked away and allowed to gather virtual dust. I had avoided watching it, not because I feared the memories, but because I had worked so hard to leave them behind.

Now, though, with Smith's sudden appearance and the resurfacing questions about Adam, that file felt like a door to the past—a ghost reaching out, urging me to open it, to relive the emotions I had buried.

After a second's hesitation, I clicked play.

The screen flickered to life, pulling me back to that bittersweet day—Adam's celebration of life. The hall was packed with family and friends, their faces filled with a mix of sorrow and reverence as they gathered to honour my brother. I watched the ceremony unfold, feeling strangely detached, like I were observing a drama in a parallel universe.

People stood one by one to pay tribute, reading poetry Adam would've dismissed as "too sentimental." Some chose to perform the songs he had loved, each note laced with nostalgia. Then came the bit that stood out—Courtney, Adam's best friend, plugging in his electric guitar. He stepped up to the mic and belted out a raw, passionate rendition of "Time Is On My Side" by The Rolling Stones—Adam's favourite song. The irony wasn't lost on anyone. The choice felt almost cruel, mocking the harsh truth that time hadn't been on Adam's side after all.

With emotions simmering beneath the surface, I paused the video. I needed a break, so I headed to the kitchen and cracked open another beer. As I took several gulps, the cold liquid settled into my stomach but did little to ease my sadness. A noise outside drew my attention, and I watched as two pigeons landed on the windowsill. They bobbed their heads excitedly, oblivious to the world they shared with me. "I wonder if they know what they're doing," I murmured. "Because I certainly don't."

Leaving the pigeons to their business, I went back to the sofa, lying down, eyes fixed on the ceiling. My thoughts wandered back to that day—Adam's memorial. The weather had been unseasonably perfect, with a soft October sun bathing the gathering in warmth. Hundreds of people had shown up, their grief palpable, their laughter strained. They weren't just mourning Adam's death; they were mourning the void he left behind.

I tried to recall who had been there, but the faces blurred in my memory. Instead, I could only remember the emotions—the sobs, the smiles, the way people clung to shared stories of Adam as if keeping him alive for just a little while longer. I strained to pull names from the fog, but my thoughts played tricks on me, offering up characters from films and novels, not the reality I was trying to grasp.

Frustrated, I turned onto my side and picked up my phone. I wanted to call Dominique, to hear her voice, but she was at work, and I didn't want to disturb her. I imagined her saying something wise or calming, some pearl of comfort, even if she couldn't fix anything. Sleep would come eventually, I told myself. Tomorrow was waiting, and it would bring with it more questions, more uncertainties. Yet I was strangely eager to face it.

10

The next morning, I caught a cab and made my way to the address I'd been given, arriving a few minutes early. As I stepped out of the car, I was met by a desolate, rundown industrial area of South London. Whatever this place had once been—a factory, a warehouse, a hub of some forgotten dismantled enterprise—it was nothing now. The air smelled stale, a mix of decay and dust that clung to the back of my throat. I stood there, hesitating, taking it all in.

The cab driver lingered, leaning out of his window. "You sure you want to be here, mate?" he asked, his tone dripping with worry.

Every instinct I had told me to say no, to jump back in the car and tell him to drive as far away from this place as possible. But I forced myself to swallow the rising dread, nodded, and paid the fare. The driver gave me one last doubtful look before speeding off, the sound of his tires crunching on loose gravel kicking up a cloud of dust that lingered in the air.

I stood alone, facing a decrepit warehouse. The rusted metal doors were covered in grime and layers of graffiti. Amidst the chaotic scrawl of colours and half-faded gang names, one bold word loomed large in chipped blue paint: **"Nevermore."** I nearly laughed at the irony of it. Poe would be rolling in his grave if he knew his words were being used to decorate a place that seemed a perfect candidate for despair. Most of the windows were shattered, jagged shards still clinging to the frames like broken teeth, while green moss and creeping yellow weeds twisted their way up through crumbling brickwork. If this building wasn't condemned already, it should have been.

I pulled the note from my pocket, double-checking the address. It was correct—this was where I was supposed to be. With minutes to spare before the appointed time, I dialled the number scrawled on the paper. It rang twice before a baritone voice, heavy with authority, answered.

"Are you there?"

"I am," I replied. "What now?"

"We'll be there shortly. Now, destroy the note."

The line clicked dead before I could respond.

I pulled a lighter from my jacket pocket and set the corner ablaze. The flame devoured it hungrily, curling the edges into blackened tendrils before the whole thing crumbled to ash. I flicked the charred remains into the gutter, watching as they scattered and dissolved into the grime.

No sooner had the last bits of ash vanished than a sleek, black SUV turned onto the street, its tires crunching over the littered ground. It rolled to a stop in front of me, engine rumbling softly. The driver's door swung open, and out stepped a bear of a man. His shoulders were broad enough to fill the entire frame of the door. A thick brown beard, flecked with grey, climbed up his cheeks, and his long hair was pulled back into a taut ponytail. His expression was carved in stone—hard, unyielding—his deep-set eyes boring into me like drill bits.

"Hi," I said, forcing a smile that felt brittle. "I assume you're here for me?"

He didn't respond, just kept scowling as he moved to the passenger door and pulled it open. "Get in," he growled, his voice soft yet carrying menace—the sort of tone you'd expect from someone who made their living enforcing the South End of London

I felt his eyes burn into my back as I slid into the seat. The interior of the SUV was almost jarringly luxurious compared to the derelict surroundings outside. Rich, cream-colored leather seats gave off a faint, spicy scent—cinnamon, maybe—and the polished wood and brushed aluminium details on the dashboard gleamed in the muted morning light. A massive touchscreen display dominated the console, its exterior pristine and reflective, flashing digital indicators that seemed to pulse with life. Everything inside looked new, immaculate—each stitch, each button, an obscene display of wealth

In the back, the seats cradled me like a wolfskin rug. Between them, a sleek console housed built-in controls for heating, air-conditioning, and even massaging backs and behinds - luxuries I'd only ever seen in glossy magazines. A smaller panel controlled the entertainment system, with a discreet screen tucked away, waiting to spring to life at a touch. Even the cup holders, nestled in a pull-down tray behind the driver's seat, were lined with felt to prevent the slightest rattle from disturbing the silence. Every detail whispered to the passenger: "You'll never be able to afford anything like this." It wasn't just a car; it was a palace on wheels.

The man climbed in beside me, the seat creaking slightly under his weight. He shut the door with a soft *thunk* that felt final, as if sealing me in for good. Before I even felt the engine rumble into life, we were moving, gliding like a giant black swan across water. Just the suspension of this silent beast was probably worth more than I'd make in a decade.

Not knowing how far we'd be driving and unwilling to sit in tense silence, I decided to break the ice. "So, where are we off to?" I asked, doing my best to sound casual, even cheerful.

"You'll see," came the curt response.

"How long is the drive?"

"About fifty minutes, give or take," he said, scratching his neck. That's when I noticed a snake tattoo coiled around his fingers, the movement of his knuckles making it look like it was slowly devouring prey.

"My name's Charles," I offered, grasping at anything that might lighten the mood.

"Keith," he replied bluntly, nodding slightly.

"What kind of car is this?" I asked.

"The sort that costs money," he grunted, clearly uninterested in chatting.

"Expensive tastes," I murmured, glancing around at the luxurious interior. "Do they normally send you to do the driving?"

"Do you normally ask so many questions?" His voice carried a warning edge.

"Only when I'm nervous," I admitted, catching his look in the rearview mirror. "Is this your car?"

Keith's eyes flicked away from mine, settling back on the road. "Do I look like the sort of person who can afford a car like this? It belongs to people who matter. That's all you need to know."

I leaned back into the plush seat, letting his words sink in. *People who matter.* The phrase suspended in air like a stubborn fog, reminding me that I was in a world where people like Keith—and his unseen superiors—made the rules. Rules I didn't dare break. All I could do was sit tight and hope I didn't say or do anything that would lead to a fatal misunderstanding. Yet a part of me, rebellious and agitated by the absurdity of the situation, felt an almost reckless urge to keep probing.

"It's a beautiful car, but I bet maintaining it costs a fortune. What do you tell the boss if you ever scratch it?" I ventured, half-joking.

Keith's expression stayed stern, but there was the faintest twitch at the corner of his mouth—almost as if he were suppressing a smirk. "Depends which boss I tell."

"More than one, huh?" I joked, leaning in just a bit. "I know that feeling. Passing information up the chain of command can be a nightmare. Is it the same in your line of work?"

"Only when things go wrong."

I noted the subtle shift in his demeanour. He seemed to be softening, just a fraction, and I wasn't about to let go of the opportunity. I needed every scrap of goodwill I could get before we arrived at… wherever the hell we were going.

"So," I began, keeping my tone light, "Seagull managers, eh?"

"What's that?" he asked, his scowl softening, replaced by a flicker of curiosity.

"It's an idiom for managers who swoop in, make a lot of noise, crap all over everything, and then fly off, leaving you to clean up the shit."

He laughed—a low, gravelly sound that caught me off-guard. My gentle prodding was working. The big man seemed almost… human.

But just as I thought I was making progress, he shut down again, like a steel door slamming shut. "I know what you're trying to do, and it isn't going to work," he said, his voice dropping back into that stone-cold tone. "I don't know anything about anything."

Damn, I'd pushed too far, too fast. I needed to backpedal before I lost whatever small ground I'd gained.

"You just do what the boss says, no questions asked," I stated, careful to keep my voice neutral.

"And that is all I do," he replied, his tone brokering no argument. The brief glimmer of warmth had vanished, replaced by the same blank, unreadable expression I'd seen when he first picked me up. "So, the best thing for both of us is for you to sit back there and not ask any questions that'll get you in more trouble than necessary."

I clenched my teeth, frustrated but recognizing the invisible wall I'd hit. The banter was over, and I was back to being a passenger, barrelling toward a destination I didn't want to reach, heading deeper into a world I didn't understand. All I could do now was hope that whatever awaited me wasn't as ominous as it felt.

Not knowing how far we'd be driving and unwilling to sit in tense silence, I decided to break the ice. "So, where are we off to?" I asked, doing my best to sound casual, even cheerful.

"You'll see," came the curt response.

"How long is the drive?"

"About fifty minutes, give or take," he said, scratching his neck. That's when I noticed a snake tattoo coiled around his fingers, the movement of his knuckles making it look like it was slowly devouring prey.

"Can we at least listen to some music?" I asked, the request coming out more timidly than I'd intended.

Keith considered this, then reached forward and pressed a button on the touchscreen. A soft harp melody floated through the speakers, gentle and strangely serene.

"Harp music?" I asked, surprised.

"Helps me concentrate," he grunted.

I leaned back, letting the soft hum of the engine and the gentle curve of the country roads lull me into a state of half-sleep. The car glided smoothly through the empty lanes, and the tranquil melody playing from the speakers wrapped around me like a warm blanket. I felt the pressure in my shoulders ease, my thoughts drifting somewhere between the present and the surreal. Somewhere in the haze, I heard the partition glass between the front and back seats slide up with a soft, mechanical hum, cutting me off completely from Keith. It was a firm, unspoken end to our brief conversation.

With no distractions and nothing to anchor me in the now, I slipped into a dream. I saw Dominique and me on a secluded Mediterranean beach, our bodies entwined under the sun's gentle glow. The sea shimmered like liquid sapphire, and the air was thick with the scent of salt and sun-warmed sand.

"This is the sort of place I could stay forever with you," I murmured, my fingers tracing the curve of her back. My other hand moved lazily in the air, sketching invisible patterns against the deep blue sky.

"Forever isn't a concept that works for me," she replied, her voice like the breeze whispering over the waves. She tilted her head, studying me as if weighing each word. "Whatever happens now, remember—nothing can be forever. And whatever you think forever means, it is so much more."

"I think I understand," I said slowly, the words tasting unfamiliar on my tongue. Suddenly, a quill appeared in my hand, its feather brushing against my fingers. "But you need to write it down—your beliefs about space and time—so I can make sense of it."

She took the quill from me, its soft plume brushing her lips as she considered. "Space and time are just things we've created to make sense of what we can't truly grasp," she said, her eyes shifting to the horizon. Standing up, she took the canvas I offered and began walking toward the sea, her bare feet kicking up little puffs of golden sand. "This place—this moment—exists outside all that. So, what I tell you now, you'll remember forever."

"And what's that?" I called after her, watching as she slowly waded into the water, her silhouette dissolving in the shimmering tide.

"It's—"

"Hey!" Keith's voice cut through, and a sharp prod jarred me awake "We're here," he announced curtly.

Groggy and disoriented, I blinked and looked around. "Where's here?" I mumbled, climbing out of the car and stretching, the midday sun hitting me like a wall of heat. I took in my surroundings—an empty, desolate stretch of road with no sign of civilization in sight. The only thing that stood before us was a massive cast-iron gate set into ancient, dark brick walls, the surface nearly black with age. The wrought-iron bars on top were shaped like clubs from a deck of cards, their pointed tips more menacing than decorative.

Keith stepped forward and pressed the intercom button embedded in the stone pillar. A crackle of static erupted, followed by a low, distorted voice. "Morning Keith."

A pause, then the gates slowly creaked open, the iron bars groaning as if reluctant to welcome me in. Keith gestured for me to follow. "Through the gate and down the road. That's where you're going," he instructed, his expression unreadable.

With a nod, I stepped past the threshold, feeling the gravel crunch beneath my feet as I moved forward. But my thoughts were elsewhere, still lingering in that dream. As we walked, I couldn't shake the image of Dominique wading into the sea, her words echoing in my mind: *"What I tell you now, you'll remember forever."* What had she meant? What truth was she about to tell me.

11

I followed Keith quietly, our footsteps muffled by the soft earth underfoot, as we moved through a dense tunnel of trees that arched overhead, their branches intertwined like fingers clasped in prayer. The only sounds were the natural ones: birds singing hidden deep within the green canopy, and in the distance, the rapid staccato tapping of a woodpecker drilling into bark. Other than that, there was silence—no cars, no voices—just us and the ceaseless murmurs of nature.

Though I knew where we were headed, I found myself in no hurry to get there. The stillness of the place was hypnotic, urging me to take it slow, to savour the calm before I stepped into whatever awaited beyond the gates of this old estate. I wondered if Dominique's cryptic warning had been playing in my subconscious all along, guiding me to this strange quiet before the inevitable storm.

After a few more minutes, the narrow trail widened into a grand drive, revealing the destination in all its grandeur: an imposing old country house. It stood like a sentinel of another era, its stately presence rising above the treetops. Pea green ivy clung to its stone walls, and tall, narrow windows caught the sunlight, glinting like watchful eyes. The slate roof, weathered by time and moss, crowned the structure, while a massive double wide oak door marked the entrance—inviting yet formidable. The house was framed by perfectly manicured lawns, the verdant surroundings exuding elegance.

This wasn't the kind of hideout I'd envisioned for men like Smith. If anything, I'd expected something darker—an office above a grimy club in Hackney or a smoky den of sin tucked away in a seedy alley. Not… this. Perhaps that was the point, I mused. Perhaps the refined exterior masked the darkness inside—a room for torture, another for stripper orgies, and maybe one for planning armed robberies, maps pinned to the walls.

"This *isn't* your place, I take it?" I asked, letting sarcasm bleed into my voice as I glanced at Keith.

He snorted, his lips twitching in a reluctant smile. "Are you taking the piss?"

"You don't live here, then?"

"What do you think?"

"Doesn't it have any staff quarters?" I quipped, glancing around as if expecting to spot a butler in the shrubbery.

"Wise arse," he muttered, but his tone was lighter, the antagonism between us softening. For a second, I believed that under different circumstances, we might have shared a laugh—maybe even a pint at some pub.

As we continued, I noticed a meticulously manicured lawn at the centre of the circular drive, dotted with sculpted stone nymphs, each one carved in hauntingly lifelike detail. The statues, arranged with care among wildflowers blooming in careful disarray, seemed to float above the grass. One statue, larger than the others, stood at the head of the lawn: a marble angel with its wings spread wide, as if welcoming each visitor who dared approach the house.

"I wouldn't want to be the gardener here," I said with a grin. "I have a feeling one wrong clip of a flower, and it won't just be the roses that get pruned."

Keith shook his head, but I caught the faintest flicker of amusement in his eyes. "Just keep walking," he muttered, giving me a gentle nudge forward. "The boss likes punctuality."

To the right of the door was a cast-iron alarm pull—a Victorian relic of craftsmanship with a round handle attached to a pulley mounted on the aged brickwork. Keith gave it a strong tug, and from behind the thick wooden door, we heard the deep clang of a bell reverberating through the house's interior. The sound carried with it a sense of conclusiveness, as though marking the end of any chance I had to walk away from this encounter.

As I stood there, I found myself slipping into unwanted thoughts about Dominique. The people who lived in homes like this, with their statues of Greek gods and sprawling estates, were the very same ones who could afford her services. Had she been to places like this before? Had she wandered through corridors lined with priceless artwork, dined at mahogany tables under the soft glow of crystal chandeliers, her laughter mingling with the clink of wine glasses? Had she ever lain in antique four-poster beds draped in rich, ruby satin sheets, her presence an indulgence they savoured, even if only for a night?

"No, I mustn't think of that now," I muttered, not realising I'd spoken aloud until Keith shot me a curious look—one that made it clear he was eager to be done with his part in this arrangement.

I was about to stammer an apology for my odd remark when we heard footsteps approaching from the other side. My imagination ran wild, conjuring images of horror movie butlers—tall, gaunt figures shrouded in shadow, leading unwitting visitors to their doom. But when the door finally creaked open, I was met with a rather unexpected sight.

Standing there was a small, round man in a perfectly tailored blue suit. His soft features and the almost cartoonish part in his greying hair made him seem more suited to a Dickens novel than a scene like this. The hair was parted so precisely on both sides that it left a shining bald patch exposed at the top, which seemed destined to expand with each passing year. He looked more like a genteel solicitor than an emissary for a gangster.

"Welcome," he said, his voice almost a whisper. He glanced at Keith and offered a courteous nod.

"Morning, Arthur," Keith greeted him, his tone unusually respectful. "I've brought him, as requested."

The man smiled, though it didn't reach his eyes. "He will be most pleased," he replied, his polished accent dripping with the kind of upper-class English that marked him as someone accustomed to servitude in such a grand household.

Keith shifted, glancing back at me briefly. "Does he need me for anything else?"

"No, that will be all for now," the man—Arthur, apparently—replied, holding the door open for me to step through. "Thank you, Keith."

Keith turned to me, and for the first time since this entire ordeal began, I thought I saw something almost like care in his features. "Good luck," he murmured under his breath, then turned and strode back down the path, his shoulders slightly hunched as if relieved to be free of his task.

"Sir, if you would," Arthur said. His small hand gestured for me to step inside; his manner polite but with an edge that brooked no delay. I swallowed hard and stepped through the doorway, my body tensing as I crossed the threshold.

The cool air inside hit me like a slap. It smelled of aged wood and faint polish, mixed with a subtle fragrance of flowers—lilies, I thought. The entrance hall was vast, its high ceilings adorned with intricate plasterwork that curled and spiralled in elegant patterns. An opulent chandelier hung overhead, casting a gentle glow that made the polished marble floors gleam. Thick carpets muffled my steps as John led me deeper into the house.

The walls were adorned with framed paintings of idyllic countryside scenes: rolling hills, serene lakes, and golden fields under vibrant blue skies. Beneath them stood solid oak sideboards, polished to a gleaming shine, arranged with ornate vases and delicate porcelain figurines, creating an atmosphere that felt both stately and carefully curated.

The butler moved with a deliberate precision, each step slow and measured. I noticed a slight limp, subtle but present, as he guided me down the long hallway. He didn't speak, and his gloved hand occasionally brushed the sideboards, steadying himself as he walked. The faint, uneven rhythm of his steps echoed in the expansive silence, stretching out the journey.

We stopped at a heavy, dark-stained door to our right. The butler, his expression carefully neutral, raised a hand and gave a gentle knock—three soft, deliberate raps that seemed to reverberate through the wood. There was a brief pause, and then a deep voice called out from within:

"Come in."

The butler glanced at me, a look that betrayed nothing of what awaited inside. Then, with a slight bow, he pushed the door open, and we stepped inside.

Part 3

Omnipotence and my brother

12

Letter from my brother – Dated 01st March 2019

Hey bro,
I don't know why I'm writing this instead of just calling you. I usually prefer talking to sending letters, texts, or emails, but some things are better written down. I won't say much, because there is too much I want to say, but I want you to know that I do realise that running out on you that morning and leaving just a note was a pretty shitty thing to do. But if I had stayed, I know you would have talked me out of leaving, and I couldn't let that happen.

You're probably pissed at me, and I get it. I'm sorry for how I handled it, but I'm not sorry for why I did it. I needed to go, even if it hurt the people I care about most. I know that doesn't make it any easier, but I didn't just disappear on you—I didn't tell any of my friends either. I'm sure you've been swamped with calls asking where I am, and I hope it hasn't stressed you out too much.

As for where I am and where I've been… Well, I've been all over. I've been crashing on sofas, staying in random hostels, and occasionally renting a room for a night or two. I've met strangers, gotten myself into some odd situations—stuff I could tell you about, but I'm not sure I want to. People say secrets eat away at you, but I think some are better kept. Don't worry, I haven't betrayed who I am by breaking any laws, though you'd probably like me to. :-)

I've been drifting from place to place. I was in Sussex recently, staying with a drummer I know. We drank, talked about life, and bonded over feeling like outsiders—too bad to be overachievers, too good to be underachievers. He took me to a local bar to hear some blues musicians. It was nice, but I felt out of place among the depressed music teachers and beat poets. I met a dancer there, and we had some meaningless sex—nice but empty.

After Sussex, I rented a room in another town, spent lazy hours writing songs, and drifting in and out of dreams. I even toyed with the idea of quitting music altogether and living a life where I create new identities—changing my name and job with every new place. Imagine people believing I'm a radiotherapist from America or a former tennis player cut down in his prime by some incurable disorder. It could be fun, don't you think?

One thing I know for sure—right now, I'm a nomad. I keep moving when what I probably need is to settle down and focus, but I just can't. With so many paths to choose from, I'm afraid of ending up in the wrong place. So, I avoid making decisions and keep drifting. Who knows what comes next? Each place I land is different, and that in itself teaches me more about who I am.

I can imagine what you'd do in my shoes. You'd choose something relatable, settle down, and make something of yourself, all while observing the flaws in your choice. I've always thought you'd make a great satirist or standup comedian. I know you'll scoff at the idea, but I think you should give it a shot.

The other day, I was thinking about the games we played as kids. Remember when our annoying cousin Sam stayed with us for the weekend? We pretended we were on a sinking ship, and Sam had to choose which of us to save. You said you only had a chicken and a hot meal waiting for you. I had a whole family I would leave behind if she let me drown. And yet, she chose you. I never understood why, but maybe she saw something in you worth saving. I don't know why I thought about that—it's funny where the mind wanders when you're trying to write music.

Anyway, I'm going to wrap this up for now. I'm packing my things and hitting the road tomorrow. I haven't decided where I'm heading yet, but that's part of the fun. I'll probably flip a coin or throw some dice and let fate decide.

Take it easy, bro.

Adam

13

Second letter from my brother – dated 17th April 2019

Hey bro,
It's me again, floating through life like a piece of flotsam on the horizon. My last letter might have sounded a bit bleak, but that wasn't my intention. I was just in one of those reflective moods—the kind where the best thinking happens. Thoughts turn into ideas, ideas recede into memories, and those memories become creations. Right after I signed my name, I started jotting down ideas for a song, so something good came out of all that introspection.

I've come close to abandoning this little tour of mine and heading back home, but the thought of returning still scares me. So, I push those thoughts aside and keep dragging myself to the next place. I've even toyed with the idea of learning meditation, maybe even embracing a Buddhist life—giving up all my worldly possessions, detaching from everything, and focusing on personal wisdom. It sounds appealing, but would I have to give up my music? If so, bugger that!

On a different note, I think I've finally found a place where I want to settle for a little while. The village is peaceful and quiet, letting me be alone with my thoughts. I found a room in a lovely couple's cottage. It's cheap and cheerful, but it has what I need. I've spent the past two weeks reading and writing music. When the weather's nice, I sit in their quaint little garden with my headphones on, listening to Dr. Dre or N.W.A. A strange mix of rap music and village life, don't you think? It helps me focus on my work and keeps my emotional baggage at bay. I'm in a much better place, both physically and mentally.

The nearest town is about ninety minutes away, and sometimes I hike along the river path that runs from here. I rarely encounter anyone, and those I do meet feel like kindred spirits—

just like me in many ways. I met a lovely woman in her sixties recently. We sat on a bench by the path for an hour, talking about the surroundings. She was a farmer's wife with many tales about the village. It was… nice. When she left, I felt a bit sad that it was over. Those feelings of connection have been hitting me more lately.

Being in a place this isolated, I expected to lose interest in people. Instead, I've found the opposite. It's like everything about me is part of a vast machine, and society is the oil that keeps it running smoothly. The people I encounter seem like technicians with instruction manuals on how my machine works. I'm sure that if I broke down, they'd fix me easily.

That's not to say I've suddenly become a social butterfly; far from it. I haven't met a woman in weeks that I've felt the urge to sleep with, and I don't find that unsettling. I still crave the excitement of attraction, but I'm less interested in the actual sex. Maybe my sexual mojo has faded, and honestly, I'm not sure I care. Perhaps my new path lies in celibacy. If I were Catholic, I'd be a prime candidate for priesthood.

I have a request for you. I'm not sure if it's simple or even possible, but here goes. Do you remember that girl you dated for a few months… Lucy, wasn't it? She was a folk musician from Crawley. We went to her place once for a party—her birthday, I think—and she had this big picture on the wall of a melting cello. That picture always made me feel sad, and I never knew why. It still pops up in my mind now and then. Do you know whatever happened to Lucy? Are you still in touch? If by any chance you are, could you see if she still has that picture? Maybe she'd be willing to sell it. I can cover whatever she asks for it. If she agrees, I'll let you know where to send it.

Recently, I walked up into the hills, found a secluded spot, and played my guitar among the trees. Do you think they listened? They didn't react, or if they did, they couldn't show it.

Take care of yourself,

Adam

14

Based on Duncan's description, the man seated behind the desk was unmistakably the same one who had paid him a menacing visit just days earlier. Dressed in a sharp black suit, he wore a single black glove, a detail that seemed almost theatrical. Without a word, he gestured for me to enter. The office itself was a testament to understated luxury—dark wood panelling lined the walls, and heavy velvet drapes framed tall windows, allowing only thin slivers of daylight to seep through. An imposing antique desk sat atop a richly patterned Persian rug that swallowed the sound of my footsteps.

"Your visitor, sir," the butler announced before leaving us alone in the study.

The man remained seated, his cold eyes fixed on me in silence. His face was a mask of calm, with an enigmatic smile that offered nothing. It was as if he held all the cards and enjoyed watching me squirm. If I could have read his thoughts, I suspected I would've liked what I found.

He extracted a cigarette from a silver case, lighting it with deliberate care. "Please, have a seat," he said, gesturing with the unlit cigarette toward a leather armchair opposite him. He then extended the cigarette case toward me. I declined, wary of accepting anything from him. With the same meticulous precision, he placed the case back on his pristine desk. Everything on it—the silver cigarette case, a red fountain pen with a gold-tipped lid, and a slim case file folder—was perfectly aligned, as if arranged by someone with an obsessive eye for detail.

It dawned on me that I was still standing. Quickly, I moved to the chair and sat down, trying to appear more composed than I felt.

"Thank you for coming," he said, his voice adopting a polished, almost mockingly refined accent that hinted at a cultivated façade.

"It wasn't exactly a request I felt I could refuse," I replied, working hard to keep my tone steady.

He stood and crossed to a well-stocked bar nestled against the wall. "May I offer you a drink?" he asked, pouring whiskey from a crystal decanter with a deliberate, almost flamboyant flourish.

Though I'd refused the cigarette, I felt a stiff drink might help me survive this meeting. "Yes, please. One cube of ice," I said cautiously.

His smile widened, as if he could see through me. "A man after my own heart," he murmured, placing the drink gently on the desk before retreating to his seat. He settled back down, crossing his legs and absently flicking away an invisible speck of lint from his trousers.

The room was engulfed in a heavy silence—the kind that makes the air feel thick with unspoken threats. Though spacious, the office felt oppressive, as if the walls were pressing in, shrinking the space around us. I glanced at the tall windows, longing to crack one open just to prove to myself that there was still a world outside this suffocating quiet.

"I wish to extend my condolences for the loss of your brother," he said softly, his gaze momentarily lowering. "I've lost close family myself. It's a pain we carry, like a weight pressing down beneath the ocean."

His sincerity caught me off guard. There was no trace of sarcasm or pretence in his tone. "Thank you," I replied, genuinely touched by the unexpected display of empathy. Unsure of how to navigate the sudden shift, I glanced around the opulent room, searching for safer ground. "This is an impressive house," I offered, gesturing to the richly decorated surroundings. "I commend you on your choice."

"Oh, it isn't mine," he murmured, his eyes drifting lazily around the room as if he were counting each piece of furniture. "I merely run it on behalf of its owner."

"Clearly, you run it very well."

"Thank you," he said, inclining his head slightly. And just like that, the softness vanished. His face sharpened, and the mean, clipped tone returned. "With the pleasantries out of the way, let's get down to business." He straightened in his chair, his posture like that of a cobra preparing to strike. "Your friend was very forthcoming with your name." His smile returned—a thin, slicing smile, as cold as a scalpel. "He seems like a decent bloke."

The subtle cockney accent that had lurked behind his words now surfaced fully, stripping away the polished veneer he had maintained so far. It was unsettling, like a crack appearing in a flawless mask. I didn't know how to respond. How does one talk to a man who can switch between genteel host and streetwise thug in the blink of an eye?

Sensing my hesitation, he continued, his voice now devoid of the earlier warmth. "If you and I conduct this meeting in an honest and straightforward manner, it'll be over quickly, and you can walk out of here without any complications." He gestured casually toward the door. "But know this—I'm exceptionally good at detecting when someone is feeding me bullshit. Should that happen, it will put me in a very… difficult position." He leaned forward, the smile gone. "Do you understand?"

"I do," I replied.

"Good." He leaned back again, relaxing as if we were old friends. "I hate bad situations. They take time and energy to clean up, and my time is far too valuable to waste on other people's mistakes."

I nodded, gripping my glass a little more firmly. "I understand."

"Excellent," he replied, his eyes never leaving mine.

He waited as I took a sip of my drink, watching as the ice melted, tiny droplets running down the inside of the glass like tears. "May I ask a question?" I ventured, the words slipping out before I could stop myself.

"Of course," he said, spreading his hands in an almost generous gesture. "Ask away."

"What does this have to do with my brother?"

"Nothing," he said, the answer quick and dismissive.

"Nothing?"

"Then why am I here?" I asked.

"Because we asked you to come," he replied, his grin stretching wider, dark amusement gleaming in his eyes.

Was he being deliberately vague to rattle me, or was this some twisted game meant to keep me off balance? "I don't understand," I said, my irritation bubbling away.

"Your brother is of no consequence to us," he replied calmly. "You're here because my employer—the man who owns this estate—wants information on someone your brother knows."

"Knew," I corrected.

"My apologies," he said, placing his gloved hand on his chest in a mock display of sincerity. "*Knew*. We believe you might be able to help us locate this person. All we ask is a name and, if possible, a location—nothing more, nothing less."

"And why would you think I could help?" I asked. "It's been five years since my brother died. I wasn't even in contact with him at the end."

"That is true," he conceded. "But as his brother, you might know something even he wasn't aware he'd left behind. A thread—small but significant—that connects him to this person."

"Why are you after them? If they're in some kind of trouble, I don't want to be involved."

"It's nothing of the sort," he said with a sly grin. "Quite the opposite. This person is... *important* to my employer."

He reached into the slim case file on his desk and extracted a single photograph, sliding it toward me. "Take a look and tell me what you see," he said, tapping the image with his finger.

He opened the case file and pulled out a large photo, sliding it across the desk to me.

"Please, study this photo and tell me what you see," he said, tapping it with his gloved finger.

He reached into the slim case file on his desk and extracted a single photograph, sliding it toward me. "Take a look and tell me what you see," he said, tapping the image with his finger.

The 7x10 black-and-white photo showed my brother sitting on a grassy hill. Behind him, the crumbling ruins of an old castle loomed against a cloudy sky. I'd never seen this shot before, and something about it left me sullen.

"It's Adam," I said. "Looks like some sort of promo shoot."

"Do you know where it was taken?"

I shook my head. "No idea."

"Are you sure?" he pressed, leaning in slightly.

"He was a musician. There are plenty of photos of him out there, some I've never even seen. This is one of them," I said defensively.

"Take another look," he urged. "Does anything stand out to you?"

I scrutinised the image, forcing myself to slow down and really see. There, further back on the hill, almost swallowed by the backdrop, was a solitary figure—a girl standing soundlessly among the ruins, her eyes fixed on something beyond the frame.

"The only thing I see is... the girl further up the hill," I said slowly, unsure.

"Correct," he murmured, rubbing his hands together in a gesture that made my skin crawl. "That's the person we're looking for. Do you know who she is?"

He pointed at the photo with his ungloved hand. Beneath his fingertip was the woman with light hair, the features of her face blurred by distance and shadow. Even in black and white, her hair shimmered in the photo like strands of moonlight caught in the wind.

I leaned in closer, squinting. "I can't tell... she's too far away. Just a blur."

"I thought as much," he said, setting the tablet aside. He flipped open the file folder again, revealing that it was brimming with photographs. "We had the image enhanced."

He handed me an A4-sized printout, a larger, slightly clearer shot of the girl. I held it up, feeling his eyes boring into me as I tried to piece together something familiar from the grainy details. Her face, though larger now, was still indistinct—a smudge of pale skin framed by a halo of fair hair.

Does this help?" he asked, the words dripping with expectation.

"Not really," I answered.

If he was disappointed, he didn't show it. "Look harder, do you notice anything... unusual about her?"

I squinted again, willing the image to give up its secrets. But the girl remained as she was, standing silently. Her golden hair shone like a beacon even in the monochrome stillness, and her skin was so pale it seemed almost translucent. I still didn't know who she was, but I suddenly felt like I needed to.

Smith could see I was struggling. "Look at her left cheek, around her eye," he said, his voice almost coaxing.

I leaned in closer, frowning. He was right. There was something there—a shadow, a smudge, like an ink blot that shouldn't be on her face. "That's probably just a flaw in the image," I said, desperate to dismiss it. "A glitch in the camera."

He shook his head slowly. "We've had the photo analysed. There's no flaw. That mark..." He tapped the image lightly. "We believe it's a birthmark."

"A birthmark?" I repeated, staring harder. The smudge became clearer the longer I looked—a dark, irregular stain that wrapped around her eye like a mask of ink. "You might be right," I said, taking another drink, "but it still doesn't help. I don't know who she is."

"But she must have known your brother," he insisted, his voice sharpening. "Think harder. Did he ever mention anyone like her? Even in passing?"

"There were a lot of people in his life I didn't know," I said, "musicians, colleagues, friends... There are so many people who might've passed through his life without me ever meeting them. I'm sorry, but I really don't think I can help you. Believe me, I wish I could."

Silence stretched between us, thick and oppressive. It was the kind of silence that demanded to be filled, chewing at my nerves until I wanted to scream, to laugh, to say *something* just to make it go away.

Finally, Smith leaned back. "You're telling the truth." He stated directly, almost to himself. "Or at least, you believe you are." He steepled his fingers, his expression unreadable. "But that's the problem, isn't it? Truth is a slippery thing. So often, the things we *think* we know turn out to be lies we tell ourselves."

"If you believe me," I said, letting out a sigh, "does that mean I can go?"

He bit his bottom lip thoughtfully and then said, almost playfully, "Not just yet." With a deliberate slowness, he reached into his jacket pocket and pulled out a small earpiece. He held it up, letting me see it, as if its presence alone would explain everything. "Just give me a moment," he told me, slipping it into his ear. "I'm going to contact the man in charge."

Every muscle in my body screamed at me to get up, to bolt from this room and not look back, but I forced myself to stay seated. I took a sip of my watered-down whiskey, feeling the fiery liquid scorch a path down my throat. The burn was sharp, invigorating, and I clung to that sensation like a lifeline. I needed to stay grounded, clear-headed. This would be my one and only drink, I decided. After this, I'm out of here—no matter what he says.

"Hello, boss," he said into the earpiece, his tone cheerful, almost chummy. "Did you get all of that?"

What did he mean, "Did you get all of that"? Was his boss listening in? My eyes darted around the room, scanning the shelves crammed with leather-bound books, searching for a hidden microphone or the telltale trace of a camera lens. Spy movies had taught me to expect these things, and now I was kicking myself for thinking they were all just Hollywood exaggerations.

"Yeah... no... uh huh..." Smith murmured into the earpiece. His eyes narrowed, sharp as blades. "No, I don't think he's lying..."

He winked, sending me a message I didn't want to decipher. Was he warning me? Mocking me?

"Do you give me authorisation to proceed?" He paused, listening intently. "Good, good. Yes... will do... speak soon."

"Proceed with what?" I blurted out, the whiskey loosening my tongue just enough to speak against my better judgment.

"In a rush, are we?" he teased, his tone dripping with mockery. "Patience, Mr. Charles, all will be made clear."

He leaned forward, folding his hands neatly on the desk as if we were about to discuss business over tea and biscuits. "Though it's unfortunate that you couldn't provide us with any concrete information about the girl in the photo, we believe you may be able to help us in other ways. Our organisation has methods to locate this person, but they are... time-consuming, expensive, and complicated." His expression hardened, the friendly mask slipping ever so slightly. "And if there's one thing we cannot afford, it's complications. That's where you come in."

"Yes, you," he said firmly. "We want *you* to find her."

"Me?" I snorted, pointing an incredulous finger at myself. "You can't be serious. How am I supposed to find a girl I don't even know?" I waved the grainy photo in the air. "If your organization is as capable as you claim, surely you can track her down faster than I ever could."

He gave me a thin smile, as if humouring a stubborn child. "You were close to your brother, were you not?"

I hesitated, then nodded slowly. "As close as I could be, considering... everything."

"Precisely," he replied. "By the simple process of elimination, which puts *you* in the best position to find her."

"Position?" I scoffed. "What position? I don't even know where to start. Surely you have more than just this picture of my brother to go on."

"The only clues we have are in that picture... and these." He reached into his desk drawer and slid a thin, leather-bound folder across the table. "Open it. Perhaps seeing what's inside will broaden your understanding of why we want her found."

I eyed him warily, then slowly flipped open the folder, bracing myself for what it might contain. Inside was another photograph—this one much older, the edges yellowed and frayed. It was a black-and-white image of a young boy sitting on a bench at what looked like a fairground, surrounded by four other boys, all holding ice cream cones. They were nearly identical—dark cropped hair, pudgy faces—but one stood out because of a jagged scar running down his cheek.

"Who is this?" I asked, looking up.

"We'll get to that," Smith replied smoothly. "Look at the next one."

Beneath the first photo was an even older image, which appeared at first glance to have been taken some point before World War II. It showed a family of three standing proudly beside a polished town car—an English naval officer in full uniform, his wife dressed in elegant Sunday best, and in her arms, a young baby swaddled in a blanket.

"These are interesting, but I don't see how they're relevant," I said, my patience wearing thin.

Smith leaned forward, eyes gleaming. He reached into a side drawer and pulled out a small magnifying glass. "Look closer. It is a photo taken in the 50's. The boy with the scar—that's the man I work for. Now, focus on the background, far left corner, near the candy floss stand."

I squinted through the magnifying glass, moving it carefully across the photograph until I found the spot he indicated. My stomach twisted as I saw it—a small, indistinct figure standing half in shadow. Long shining hair cascaded down her back, and even in the grainy black and white, I could just make out the faint outline of a birthmark around her left eye.

"I think I can see what you're getting at, but it must be a mistake."

"There's no mistake," Smith murmured, his voice a low rumble of certainty. "Now look at the second photo. Taking in the 1920's, it is of a Lord and his family. He died shortly after this was taken. Look to the right, near the garden fence."

With a sense of dread, I shifted the magnifying glass to the edge of the image, where a tiny figure stood near the hedgerow. The clarity was even worse than the first photo, but it was unmistakable: the same long hair, the same ethereal outline, and... the same dark smudge around the left eye.

My pulse pounded in my ears as I looked up at him. "You're saying... it's the same girl in all of these photos? But that's impossible. They're separated by nearly one hundred years."

"Impossible?" Smith echoed, tilting his head. "That's a very limiting word, don't you think?"

"Who the hell is she?" I breathed, more to myself than to him. The room felt smaller, closing in on me. "No," I said, shaking my head as if I could shake off this insanity. "This is a joke, a setup. Why are you doing this?" I laughed—a hollow, bitter sound, more of a plea than anything else.

"We are not joking," he replied, his tone cold and measured. "Nor is this a prank. We believe the girl in the photo with your brother is the same one seen with the boss and the Lord."

"You're wrong," I snapped, my voice laced with a mix of anger and disbelief. "What you're suggesting is—it's absurd! This kind of thing doesn't happen in real life."

"Be careful, Mr. Charles." His voice dropped to an icy whisper, every syllable a warning. "Whether you believe it or not doesn't change the fact that you've been tasked to find her. Right now, we're asking politely. But if you continue to resist, that civility could turn into something more... demanding." He twirled his gloved fingers in the air, his grin darkening. "I think you understand."

I swallowed hard; the implications obvious. "The threats are all well and good," I managed, struggling to remain steady, "but even if I *did* believe you, how do you expect me to find someone like her?"

"How you find her is up to you," he said, leaning forward until his face was only inches from mine. His eyes were like pits of black ice. "But find her, you *must*."

"I can't just drop everything!" I burst out. "I have a life—a job!"

"You no longer need to worry about such things." He pulled out another cigarette, lighting it with an almost casual indifference, then offered me one. I took it, my hands trembling as I accepted. My nerves were hanging by a thread. "We know everything about you, Mr. Charles. We've acted accordingly. As of yesterday, you no longer work for Harrogate Systems. An email was sent resigning on your behalf, and it was accepted."

I shot to my feet, fury surging through me like fire. "You did *what?!*"

"It must surprise you how easily your employer let you go," Smith continued calmly, exhaling a cloud of smoke. "But no one is indispensable these days."

The shock hit me like a freight train. I had to grip the back of the chair to keep from stumbling. "You had no right," I spat, the words venomous. "You had no right to interfere in my life like that."

"Rights are subjective, Mr. Charles." He shrugged, his expression devoid of remorse. "In our world, control and influence outweigh any perceived rights you think you have. We needed your full attention—" He spread his hands, as if presenting some grand revelation. "—and now we have it."

I glared at him, chest heaving, the urge to punch that smug look off his face almost overwhelming. But I knew better. Violence wouldn't get me out of this; it would only dig the hole deeper.

"You know what? Fuck you, and fuck all of this. Do what you want; I'm not doing anything for you."

I stood straight-backed, letting my anger fuel every step as I marched toward the door. Whatever fear I'd felt before was swallowed by the inferno of hate burning within me.

"We know of Dominique, Mr. Charles," Smith shouted after me.

I froze. My entire world shrank down to that single, weighted name. I knew the power of it—knew the threat veiled behind that soft-spoken syllable. Slowly, I turned back, shoulders sagging, and slumped into the chair. The fight drained out of me, replaced by a nauseating sense of defeat.

"Good," Smith said smoothly, folding his hands as if my compliance had been a matter of etiquette. "Screaming and shouting is not a dignified way of handling business. To me, threats are so passé and shouldn't be needed if the conversation isn't ended before all the cards have been placed on the table."

"Just get this over with," I muttered, the words tasting like ash in my mouth.

"Though you no longer have an employer, all is not lost," he continued, ignoring my tone. "My employer has authorised me to extend a contract of terms. We will give you one month to find the girl, and for those four weeks, you will be paid *handsomely*. Should you locate her within that timeframe, you will receive a bonus that will last you for a very, very long time. It is a generous offer for such a small window of effort."

"And if I don't find her?"

"Failure is not an option." His eyes unflinching. "Should you not find her, your life—and those of your friends—will become... *unpleasantly* complicated. I like you, Mr. Charles. I would not like to see anything happen to you."

There was no way out of this. I was stuck. "Fine," I said, each syllable a bitter surrender.

Smith clapped his hands together, the sound sharp in the oppressive silence. "Great. I am so glad that you have agreed."

Smith clapped his hands together, the sharp sound reverberating in the suffocating silence. "Excellent! I am so glad we have reached an agreement."

"It's not like you gave me any choice," I growled.

"We all have a choice, Mr. Charles." He leaned back in his chair, adopting a pose of exaggerated contemplation. "It is just that some choices only have one outcome—one we surreptitiously make without even knowing why." His lips twisted into a smirk. He reached into a drawer, producing a sleek phone, and began tapping the screen. "I have sent this month's compensation—including a generous allowance for expenses—to your bank account. From tomorrow and for the next several weeks, you shall be working exclusively for us. Should you have any requests, my driver, Keith, will provide you with a phone number. Each time you use it, you will destroy it, and we will issue you a new one. This will continue until the month is up, or you find the girl."

I pulled out my own phone and opened my banking app. Sure enough, the balance had shot up significantly—far more than I'd expected. Part of me wanted to question how they knew my bank details, but I knew better than to ask. These people clearly had resources far beyond what I could fathom. What was a bank account to men who could erase an identity with a few strokes of a keyboard?

The throb of a migraine began to pulse behind my eyes, the pressure building with every beat of my heart. Their threats, their demands, the sudden termination of my job—it was too much. I was trapped. Caged. And they were dangling both the carrot and the stick in front of me, forcing me to choose.

"I just have one question," I said, swallowing the last of the whiskey in a single gulp. "If you want me to do this, you owe me an answer."

Smith smiled, a cold, calculated expression that sent a chill down my spine. Not for the first time today, I wanted to smack it off his face.

"For that I need to tell you a story," he said.

15

"The one thing the boss values more than anything in this world is knowledge. Power, money, sex—it's all part of a bigger game. But knowledge... knowledge is the key to having all of those and more," Smith explained, his voice steady, almost reverent. "The boss knows many things, and he will die knowing many more. He sometimes wields that knowledge like a weapon, other times as a shield. But mostly, it serves a purpose only he understands."

"He sounds like a great man," I replied, fighting to keep the sarcasm out of my voice but unsure if I succeeded.

Smith didn't flinch. "May I ask you a question, Mr. Charles?"

"Nothing's stopped you so far," I shot back, irritated.

"Do you find your life boring and uneventful?" he asked, leaning forward slightly.

"I lead a life like most normal men," I answered curtly, feeling my annoyance flare. "I have a job, friends, people I care about."

"I'm not belittling you," Smith continued calmly, "when I say that I believe you live a most unextraordinary life."

"Not anymore, it isn't," I scoffed, gesturing around us.

"Compared to the man in charge, yours is a mundane existence," he carried on, still void of malice. "Think of this: at this very minute, there is a man—an exceptional man—sitting on a private beach in Barbados. With a single word, he can bring down a multinational institution or elevate someone to the highest echelons of power. Can you imagine that? No, I don't think you can."

He moved over to the bar and poured us both another drink, placing the glass in front of me. "Right now, that man is thinking of two people." He motioned toward me and then pointed to the scattered photos. "You and her. Nothing else occupies his mind. Can you feel the weight of his expectations, the heaviness of it?" Smith shuddered as if the thought alone made him tremble.

Exasperation simmered within me. Would this man ever get to the point? He was spinning words, like some demented storyteller. But as Smith continued, I realised with a sinking feeling that my anger wasn't just about their manipulation. It was about the helplessness I felt.

"I'm going to tell you the tale of this man," he murmured, lowering his voice as if sharing a secret. "And I want you to listen to every word. Because once you understand, you'll want to do as this man says. For one reason, and one reason alone: to please him."

"This man was born in the autumn of 1953, in a small village in eastern Russia," Smith began, his voice low and measured, as if relishing every word. "He was the oldest of three brothers, raised in a family of five. His formative years were spent working alongside his father, tending fields of wheat. Life was harsh and unrelenting. Money was scarce, and there was barely enough food to go around. So, at fifteen, he made a decision that would alter his life forever. He left. He hoped that by taking his meagre appetite off the family's table, his younger siblings might stand a better chance."

Smith paused, his fingers tracing the rim of his glass. He seemed almost lost in the tale, as if every word pulled him deeper into the memory of someone else's life.

"With a sack slung over his shoulder—containing all his worldly possessions—and wearing shoes bound by string to keep the soles from falling apart, he set out. He walked for days, finally reaching the city. Alone, destitute, he begged for work wherever he could find it: factories, construction sites—any menial job that would pay a few Rubles. Survival was all that mattered."

"His education was minimal, barely enough to read and write," Smith continued, "but he was clever—sharper than most. Maybe it was the desperation of hunger that made him shrewd, or the endless labour that honed his mind as much as his body. In the city, he quickly come to appreciate that the true currency wasn't money, but people—connections. He needed to know the right ones, to befriend them, to exploit them. Smith's eyes locked onto mine; his admiration for this boss was almost reverential.

Smith's eyes met mine, a flicker of something like admiration lighting his eyes.

"By twenty, he had moved up from being just another cog in the factory to the assistant of a textile warehouse manager. That's when his true calling emerged."

"And what was that?" I asked, unable to hide my curiosity.

Smith leaned forward, the reverence in his voice palpable. "The power of knowledge."

The way he said it—like it was a holy mantra—sent a chill down my spine. This wasn't just a story to him; it was a creed.

"He would spend his evenings drinking with the warehouse manager, plying him with vodka, asking him about the ins and outs of the business, the secrets no one was supposed to know. Because drunk lips are loose lips. And it wasn't long before he discovered that the manager was having an affair with the wife of a local political party member."

Smith smiled thinly, the corners of his lips tugging upward like a predator scenting blood. "Now, tell me, Mr. Charles, what would you do with such knowledge?"

"Blackmail him for money?" I offered.

Smith's smile vanished. "Such small-minded thinking. Were you even listening? Money was never the goal. Power was."

His eyes blazed, as if offended on behalf of the man he was speaking of. "He didn't blackmail the manager. No, he went after the mistress. He used her secret to secure an introduction to her husband. If she didn't comply, the truth would be revealed, and she would be ruined. And so, she did. That one favour landed him a position in her husband's department, a stepping stone that put him in the path of people who mattered."

Smith's voice dropped, dark and intense. "From there, he used his knowledge like a blade, cutting down those who opposed him and elevating those who served his interests. Every favour he granted was paid back with a secret. And every secret was a tool. By twenty-five, he was manipulating governments."

"All of this is fascinating," I interrupted, "but if he was that powerful, why did he leave Russia? Why is he here, worrying about me?"

"Because he was smart enough to know that in Russia, even the most powerful men have their limits," Smith replied, his tone chillingly calm. "He saw what happens to those who overreach—how quickly the winds of politics can change. In 1982, he walked into a British embassy with a dossier full of Soviet secrets so explosive, they couldn't move fast enough to grant him political asylum. By the time he left, he had not only asylum but a new identity, citizenship, and a passport."

"His old friends must have loved that," I muttered, barely able to keep the sarcasm out of my voice.

"Oh, they were furious," Smith agreed. "But they couldn't touch him. He had kept back just enough secrets—names, locations, operations—to ensure that they would leave him alone. He became a ghost, flitting between governments, corporations, and criminal organizations, trading secrets like stocks. His empire grew—wealth, influence, control."

Smith spread his hands wide, gesturing to the opulence around us. "But he never settled. He never stopped. Because, in the end, the chase for knowledge never ends. That's why he's here now. Yet you sit here believing us to be nothing more than petty criminals."

"What else am I supposed to think?" I snapped. "I'm not dealing with some high-level politician. You're the man in charge of...well, a gang."

"You may see us as thugs," Smith said, "but we are simply another arm of a man who commands power on a scale you can't comprehend."

"Where does the girl fit into all of this?" I demanded, growing impatient with his cryptic storytelling.

"That is a story within a story," Smith murmured, his voice dropping to a low, almost reverent tone. "When the boss first arrived here, he brought with him a circle of trusted men—advisors who had escaped the Soviet Union with their own dark secrets. But unlike him, they were not as untouchable. One of them was found dead not long after their arrival—a warning. His throat was slit, and the word 'traitor' carved into his belly."

I stifled a yawn, struggling to keep my focus as he continued, but something in his tone shifted.

"That man was one of the boss's closest friends," Smith said. "When they laid him to rest, the boss himself carried the coffin into the church. He sat at the front, holding court over the mourning. Nothing more will be said on that—what matters is what happened next. Among the mourners, the boss noticed a girl. A girl with a distinct birthmark on her face—the same one in your brother's photo. He recognised her instantly."

"Recognised her?" I scoffed. "From where?"

Smith leaned forward, his eyes locking onto mine. "From a day decades earlier, in a small village fair back in his hometown. She looked exactly the same—hadn't aged a single day. Imagine that Mr. Charles. All those years... and she appeared just as she had back then."

"Wait," I said, incredulous. "You're telling me this girl hasn't aged in decades? That's impossible. She'd be what... fifty now? And in the photo with my brother, she doesn't look a day over twenty-five."

Smith nodded slowly. "I know. It defies logic, doesn't it? But here we are. Whether you believe she's the same girl or not doesn't change a thing. The boss has spent years—decades—trying to find her again, but she's always slipped away just as he was about to grasp her. Now, finally, we have another chance, and he expects us to bring her to him."

"What did she say to him? What has him so obsessed?"

"I don't know. No one does. All I have is the information he's deemed fit for me to share. But again, it doesn't matter. I am merely the vessel through which his will is carried out. That will now include you, Mr. Charles. You will find the girl and deliver her to him—or at the very least, tell us where she is."

"And what happens when he finds her?" I asked.

Smith's expression darkened, his eyes narrowing into slits. "I do not care," he replied, each word biting and final. "And neither should you. This is far beyond the comprehension of minds like ours. My purpose is to carry out his commands, and I will do so until my dying breath. If that means bringing him the girl by fair means or foul, then it will be done. It would be wise for you to adopt the same attitude."

His words were heavy and suffocating, as though the entire house had been enveloped by the invisible authority of his boss. Every wall, every object, seemed bound to the will of a man I hadn't even met. The silence that followed was oppressive, and I found myself staring down at the photo of my brother, wondering how I had ended up here.

"You must not discuss a word of this to anyone outside of our agreement," Smith warned, his voice slicing through my thoughts. "We will know if you do."

His eyes bored into me, unblinking, making me feel small—like a fly trapped beneath a glass, waiting for someone to decide whether to let it live or squash it. I had more questions, so many more, but something in me had gone quiet. There was nothing left to say.

"Now, if you have no further questions, our business is concluded. I have other pressing matters to attend to, so it's time for you to go." He gestured dismissively toward the door. "Keith will drive you home."

I stood up slowly, biting back the urge to argue. There was no winning here, no room for negotiation. I headed for the door, clutching the folder—the one holding what might be the last photo ever taken of my brother. I felt relieved knowing that this confrontation was over—for now. The situation had shifted from menacing to surreal. I was knee-deep in something twisted, something far beyond my control. I had no choice but to play along.

Just as my hand gripped the door handle, a sudden thought struck me. I turned back to face Smith. "One last thing," I said, my voice firmer than I felt. "How did you know about my brother? He couldn't have been involved with you or your operation."

It felt like an eternity before he finally spoke, his voice low and deliberate. "Are you sure of that?"

The implication of his answer froze the retort on my lips. I opened my mouth, ready to demand answers, but before I could, he cut me off.

"Leave now, Mr. Charles," he said, his tone final and unyielding.

And just like that, the conversation was over. No more questions. No more answers. I turned and walked out, leaving Smith behind with his secrets and his twisted loyalties.

16

"Where do you want me to take you?" Keith asked, glancing at me in the rearview mirror.

I slumped in the backseat, my blood still simmering from the tense meeting. My head throbbed; my thoughts jumbled. The first thing I wanted to do was tell him to take me home, but then I realised Smith and his people probably already knew where I lived. Somehow, home didn't feel like a refuge right now. If this was my last chance at a normal night, I wanted to hold on to it for just a little longer, to pretend I still had control over something.

"Do you know The Transit Bar in Epping?" I asked.

"No," he replied, already typing it into the GPS. "But I'll find it."

The drive wasn't straightforward. A jack-knifed lorry had blocked the motorway, forcing us onto the backroads. The journey stretched on, the winding lanes of the countryside swallowing us in shadows. Time became elastic, warping and twisting as it often does when you're stuck in the monotony of a moving vehicle. Whenever I tried to keep track of it, it seemed to slow to a crawl, like a snail inching through thick mud.

I couldn't take it anymore. "What do you do when you're waiting for instructions?" I asked, breaking the silence just to fill the void.

"I either sleep or read," Keith replied, his tone flat, eyes steady on the road ahead. "Unless the boss asks me to do something else."

"What kind of 'something else'?"

"Best not to ask," he warned.

We passed a field of cows. Their vacant eyes followed us, chewing methodically, drool hanging from their slack mouths. I studied at them, wondering if they ever sensed when they were being led to slaughter, if they felt a glimmer of fear in those final seconds. I shuddered and turned away.

"What are you currently reading?" I asked, desperate to keep the conversation going.

"Dostoyevsky's *The House of the Dead*," he said.

"Really?" I couldn't hide my surprise. Keith didn't strike me as the type to enjoy classic literature. I had expected him to say something like a tabloid or a crime novel. Something less... cerebral.

"Just because I drive a car and clean up trouble doesn't mean I'm illiterate," he said, sensing my reaction. "We're not all mindless thugs."

A flush of embarrassment crept over me. "I'm sorry," I stammered. "I didn't mean to... well, I'm usually the first to say not to judge a book by its cover, and here I am, doing exactly that."

He paused, considering the question. "It used to," he admitted. "But after a while, you get used to it. People see what they want to see. They hear 'chauffeur' or 'security' and assume you're just muscle with no brains. But that's their problem, not mine. If I let little things like that irritate me, I'd be useless to the boss."

"He sounds like someone who inspires the people under him," I said.

"He does," Keith replied staunchly. "He found me at a low point in my life, and I owe him for that. Despite what Smith might have you believe; he's always been good to me."

"Does he have a name?" I asked.

"I assume so," Keith said with a hint of a smirk.

"You don't know?" I pressed.

"There's never been a reason to ask."

"If you don't know his name, then what do you and your... colleagues call him?"

"It's either 'the boss,' 'the man,' or simply 'the Russian.'"

The Russian. My mind reeled, trying to piece together an image of this unseen figure—a puppet master with ties everywhere, a man who seemed more like a political force than a criminal overlord. Less of a Jim Jones or Charles Manson, more of a James Bond villain.

"The Russian, huh? I wonder if I'll ever meet him?" I mused.

"He'll meet you when he chooses to," Keith said flatly. "*If* he chooses to."

We were nearing the outskirts of Epping now, where fields and forests met the edges of the village. The bar I'd chosen sat in the heart of town, nestled between old brick townhouses and narrow cobbled streets. As we passed a grand three-story home with iron gates and tall white columns, Keith nodded toward it.

"One day, I'll have something like that," he said thoughtfully.

"Does this work pay that well?" I asked, surprised. He didn't seem high enough up the ladder to dream of estates like that.

"Not enough for a place like that, not yet. But I'll get there."

"Why not quit and find something that pays better?" I suggested.

Keith shook his head, a shadow of something unreadable passing across his face. "I don't do this just for the money," he said. "There's something... noble about the work."

"Noble?" I couldn't keep the scepticism out of my voice. Were they really so deluded as to believe they were serving some righteous cause? Followers of a criminal mastermind, treating him like a messianic figure?

"Not like that," Keith replied, almost as if he could read my thoughts. "We work for someone who doesn't demand more than we're willing to give, and yet we all push ourselves beyond our limits for him. Is there anything more noble than offering your life to someone who commands respect and whom you serve freely, without hesitation?"

"When you put it that way... I guess not," I muttered, though the disbelief must have been clear in my voice.

"Don't you have anything in your life that drives you to go beyond what you think you're capable of?" he asked, swerving to avoid a deep pothole. The car jolted, and I slid across the backseat, cursing myself for not wearing a seatbelt.

"Not really," I admitted. "I do what I'm good at, and if that seems unambitious, so be it. I'm content. Or at least I was until today, when I got handed a job I didn't ask for and a bank account full of money I never earned."

"You don't believe in anything? No higher purpose, no god pulling you toward something greater?"

"No offence, but there's no god guiding or judging me," I replied flatly. "I live how I think a normal person should live."

Keith didn't seem phased by my bluntness. "Maybe when this is over, you can ask the boss for guidance."

"Maybe," I whispered, though I knew there was no chance I'd want anything to do with this man—if I even survived long enough to meet him.

With that, the conversation died. The rest of the drive passed in tense silence, the only sound the muted hum of the engine and the occasional thump of a pothole. I stared out the window, watching the countryside melt into shadow, wondering how I had stumbled into a den of zealots, following a Russian oligarch with a cult-like hold over his followers.

17

By the time we reached the bar, it was early evening. People were heading home from work, their faces lit up with the promise of the weekend. The sun dipped behind the buildings, painting the sky in soft shades of pink and orange. I took a deep breath, savouring the fresh evening air. For the briefest moment, it felt like I was back in my old life—a place where the craziest thing I had to deal with was rush hour traffic. Despite Smith's best attempts to drag me into his world of shadows and threats, a small part of me clung to a sense of normalcy. I needed that right now.

Inside, *The Transit Bar* was already buzzing with the energy of Friday night regulars, their laughter bouncing off the wood-panelled walls. The faint scent of fried food mixed with the smell of spilled beer and cheap aftershave. It wasn't glamorous, but it felt real—grounded in a way that soothed me. I ordered a lager and a chicken club sandwich at the bar, then found a quiet corner table, away from the noise, and slumped into the worn leather seat.

When the sandwich arrived, I wolfed it down in a few bites, then ordered another beer and a whiskey chaser. I tried to piece together everything that had happened before my meeting with Smith, but it was all a blur. The day had dropped an avalanche of information on me: Russian gangsters, a girl who hadn't aged in decades, and—worst of all—Adam, my brother. Thinking about him left me more than just depressed—it left me desperate for someone to talk to, someone who could support me.

On a whim, I pulled it out and dialled Dominique's number. It went straight to voicemail. She was probably busy with a client—someone who needed her attention more than I did right now. But jealousy stabbed through me all the same. While I was sitting here, drowning in confusion and fear, she was off with some stranger. It wasn't fair, I thought bitterly. I needed her right now. I needed someone. But that was her life, her choices—choices I'd accepted when we first got together.

My second round of drinks arrived, and I considered calling Duncan, the one person who might understand just how crazy all of this sounded. But Duncan would only get caught up in the drama, diving headfirst into it like it was some dark adventure movie. He'd be thrilled by it, eager to play detective, forcing me to make choices I wasn't happy with. And by the end of the night, he'd be six drinks deep, ranting about his own disordered life while mine went unaddressed.

No, I didn't need that tonight. Tonight was mine, and I needed to keep it that way.

I sighed, resigning myself to drinking alone. If I got drunk enough, maybe I'd stumble home, sleep it off, and wake up with a clear head. But what else could I do? I had no job to worry about, no one waiting for me, a bank account full of unearned money and the guarantee of finding myself knee-deep in whatever shit Smiths boss had planned for me.

A burst of laughter erupted from the table next to me. A group of girls, faces flushed from alcohol, leaned into each other, sharing a joke. One caught my eye and smiled—a flirty, playful look that made me consider, for just a second, joining them. What would it matter if I ended up in bed with one of them? Dominique was busy with someone else, wasn't she? Why shouldn't I be? But even as the thought crossed my mind, I pushed it away. That wasn't what I needed. It was the alcohol talking, whispering possibilities of reassurance that would only make everything worse in the long run.

Instead, I leaned back and watched as a small jazz band began setting up at the far end of the bar. The soft, mournful music floated through the room, and everyone stopped what they were doing to listen. A waitress with bubble-gum-pink hair came by to clear my table, asking if I needed anything else. I ordered another whiskey and a bag of chili peanuts, then settled into the chair.

"Can I join you?" a familiar voice asked.

I opened my eyes to find Keith already seated across from me. "Looks like you already have," I said with a wry smile.

The waitress arrived with my order, and Keith asked for a Diet Coke.

"Not drinking?" I asked. "Still on the clock?"

"I don't drink," he replied flatly. "Gave it up years ago. Let's just say alcohol and I didn't get along."

I raised my beer bottle. "You have my sympathy. So, are always working?"

"Twenty-four hours a day," he replied. "My phone's never off."

"That must wreak havoc on your personal life."

"What social life?" he shot back with a grin.

I glanced around the bar, then looked out the window at the fading light. A thought hit me. "Wait a minute... if this isn't a social thing, are you here to keep an eye on me?"

"The boss has invested money in you. He just wants to make sure nothing happens that might... hinder his investment," Keith said, tapping the neck of my beer bottle. "He expects results."

I rolled my eyes. "I get it. I don't like it, but I get it."

Keith leaned in slightly, his voice dropping to a low murmur. "Look, I don't know why, but I like you. So let me give you some advice—don't overthink this. Don't question it. Just do the job. I've seen people self-destruct, because they couldn't keep their heads straight. You're in this now. Consider me the guy who helps keep you on track."

I raised an eyebrow. "So, you're like *big brother*? Always watching, always listening? And what happens if I step off track, hmm? What will you do?"

"Whatever it takes to get you back on it," he said firmly. There was no hint of menace—just an unwavering sense of duty.

"You sound like you're trying to seal the cork back in my bottle," I said, lifting my beer in a mock toast. "In more ways than one."

"Call it whatever you want, but you *are* going to make this your last drink, go home, have something to eat, sleep, and wake up tomorrow with nothing but focus. You'll thank me later."

I thought about ignoring him, staying exactly where I was, and ordering round after round just to spite him. But he was right.

Sitting here, drowning my frustrations, was just burning hours I didn't have. The last thing I needed was to wake up tomorrow with a hangover and Keith's eyes boring into me, waiting for me to slip up. I already felt the crosshairs aimed at my head; I didn't want to give anyone a reason to pull the trigger.

I sighed, drained the last of my whiskey, and stood up. Keith watched me carefully, nodding in approval as I gathered my things and made my way toward the door.

Tonight's fleeting taste of freedom was over.

18

When I got home, I peeled off my clothes and tossed them into the laundry basket, feeling like I needed to shed more than just fabric. I jumped into the shower, hoping the hot water would wash away the grime of stress clinging to my skin. As the steam filled the small bathroom, the day's tension seemed to lift, evaporating with the rising mist. After drying off, I checked the time: 9:43 PM. Still early enough to crack open another beer, but my body craved something lighter—iced water sounded better.

I lit a cigarette and settled into the shadows of my living room. From my coat pocket, I pulled out the photo of Adam that Smith had given me. I held it, the edges slightly crumpled from handling, feeling its weight not just in my fingers, but somewhere deeper. I considered taking a closer look—maybe I'd missed something. But Keith's words from earlier rang in my mind: *Don't overthink it.*

With a sigh, I tossed the photo onto the table, stubbed out the cigarette, and stretched out on the sofa. Before long, sleep pulled me under.

The next morning, I awoke to the intoxicating smell of bacon sizzling. Blinking against the early light, I sat up, momentarily disoriented. It took a second to realise I was still in the living room. My girlfriend was already in the kitchen, wearing my old Black Sabbath T-shirt, her bare legs peeking out as she stood over the grill, carefully tending to several rashers of bacon.

The aroma was heavenly. I wandered over and wrapped my arms around her from behind, pressing my face into the curve of her neck.

"Mmm, I don't know what smells better—the bacon or you," I murmured, the words muffled against her skin.

"Probably the bacon, but I taste better," she teased, glancing over her shoulder with a mischievous grin.

I patted her playfully on the backside and slumped into a chair at the kitchen table. The wall clock read 6:14 AM. "When did you get in last night?"

"About three hours ago," she replied casually, not missing a beat as she flipped the bacon.

"Three hours?" I stared at her in disbelief. She looked flawless—her skin fresh, hair neatly brushed, smelling faintly of rose water and vanilla. She radiated energy, as if she'd just come from a spa instead of from three hours of sleep.

"How do you look this good on no sleep?" I asked, shaking my head.

"Good genes," she said with a wink. "But why'd you crash on the couch? Got lazy, or was it something else?"

I sighed and launched into a rundown of the last forty-eight hours—the surprise visit to Duncan's office, the unsettling meeting with Smith, the tense car rides with Keith, the stories that sounded like they belonged in a thriller novel, the veiled threats, and the shocking revelation about my brother. Throughout it all, she listened silently, her expression inscrutable. It was almost eerie how she took it in stride, as if discussions of Russian mobsters and strange, ageless women were as mundane as chatting about the weather.

"So, you don't know who the girl is?" she asked calmly, sliding a plate of bacon and toast across the table.

"Nope," I replied, biting into a crispy strip, savouring the salty goodness.

"And Adam never mentioned her?"

"Not once." I shook my head.

"So, he might not have known her at all," she mused, stirring her tea thoughtfully.

"If he did, he kept quiet about it," I said with a shrug.

"So, what's your next move?"

I got up and poured two glasses of orange juice. As I handed her one, I glanced out the window, half-expecting to see Keith's car parked down the street, lurking in the shadows. But if he was there, he was successfully blending into the surroundings—just another piece of suburban scenery. I wondered if I'd ever truly know when I was being watched, or if I'd have to spend the rest of my life looking over my shoulder.

I sat back down and took a long sip of juice. "Find the girl, I guess."

"It's a big world out there. Hunting down one girl is going to be nearly impossible. What if you don't find her in four weeks?"

"Then I'll probably be fitted for concrete shoes somewhere," I said dryly.

"Don't joke, this is serious." She lightly punched my arm, her eyes flashing with agitation. "If she *is* someone your brother knew, how many people could that realistically be? And what if she was just a fan? His Facebook group alone has over three thousand followers. It'll be like finding a needle in a haystack—if the haystack was the size of a small town."

"Wait, he had a Facebook group?" I asked, honestly surprised.

"You didn't know?"

"I'm not on social media, never have been. I know he did some online stuff, but I didn't pay attention to it."

She flicked open her phone and, within a couple of taps, pulled up Adam's Facebook page. His profile photo showed him mid-gig, guitar held high, his face sanguine, lost in his art. Stage lights cast a halo around his head; it looked like he was glowing—alive and vibrant, just like I remembered him.

She was right. Under the image was the number: **3,013 followers**.

"If you want, I could upload a picture of her to his page," she suggested. "Even if she's not on there, someone might recognise her."

"No can do." I shook my head firmly. "Smith warned me not to tell *anyone* about this. I'm not even sure I should be telling you." I paused, rubbing the back of my neck. "Besides, I have a plan... well, part of one... sort of."

She lit a cigarette and started tapping away on her phone, her bright orange fingernails clicking gently against the screen. "I may not know everything," she said without looking at me, "but I know when someone's grasping in the dark."

"Who says I'm grasping?" I shot back, the comment stinging more than I wanted to admit. "I'm going to ask around the few friends I know of his. Maybe he reached out to them when he didn't want to talk to me."

She didn't respond, just took another drag from her cigarette. I couldn't blame her. It was a long shot, and I knew it. But it was the only one I'd come up with in the short, chaotic hours since I'd been dragged into this. Sighing, I cleared the plates from the table and dumped them in the dishwasher. I glanced at the clock. Was there a specific time I was supposed to start the search? Was this a 9-to-5 role, or was I expected to be on call 24/7 like Keith?

"Little Ashton," Dominique said suddenly, breaking my thoughts.

"What?"

"That's where your brother was when the photo was taken—Little Ashton," she repeated, a small smile playing on her lips.

I stared at her, confused. "How do you know that?"

She held up her phone, the screen displaying a picture of old castle ruins, identical to the ones in the photograph of Adam and the girl. "It's a distinctive building. I just ran it through a reverse image search. Came up immediately."

My jaw dropped. "You did that in... what, ten seconds? How?"

"Come on," she teased, her grin widening, "you're only thirty-five. Surely technology like this isn't beyond you?"

"No, I mean—how did you even know to look for that building?" I stammered.

Her smile faltered, and she shifted awkwardly. "I have to admit something," she said. "While you were asleep, I... I looked at the photo you left on the table."

"You what?" I felt a flicker of irritation, but more than that, I was surprised.

"I know I shouldn't have," she continued hurriedly, "but you looked so strained, even in your sleep. I thought maybe I could help somehow, so... I took a picture of it with my phone, just in case."

"I—well…" I tried to form a coherent response, but all I could manage was a half-laugh, half-sigh. "Give me a break. I've lost my job, I'm being threatened by strangers, and now my girlfriend's sneaking around taking pictures of my stuff."

"I'm sorry," she said apologetically. "But look—at least I found something, right? In less time than it takes to smoke a cigarette."

"That you did," I murmured, shaking my head in disbelief. "That you did." I couldn't argue with her there.

"And you're going to have to buck your ideas up if we're going to find this girl."

"We?" I blinked, taken aback as I settled back into my chair.

She moved closer and slid onto my lap, brushing a stray lock of hair away from my eyes. "You don't think I'd let you handle something this dumb on your own, do you?" She leaned in, kissing the side of my neck.

Outside, a car horn blared twice—short and sharp. I stiffened. Was that Keith's way of telling me time was wasting?

"No," I said firmly. "I don't want you involved in this. If everything goes wrong, and Smith and his cronies come after me, I'm the one who should take the hit, not you."

"You're so cute when you try to be chivalrous," she murmured, her lips brushing against my ear. "That's why I'm so into you. But you're wrong. I've been in this since you took that call from your friend. It's my choice to go with you." She kissed me softly, then pulled back. "You need brains for something like this. And let's face it—you're not exactly a master strategist."

I sighed, torn between wanting to protect her and knowing she was right. Smith already knew who she was; keeping her out of it would be nearly impossible. And the truth was, if I left her behind, I'd spend every second I was away worrying about what Smith might do. At least if she was with me, I'd have some control.

"Fine," I said, exhaling deeply. "But we'd better get started."

I tried to rise, but she stiffened her legs around me, holding me in place, a playful smile tugging at her lips.

"First things first," she whispered, her fingers teasing at the hem of her shirt. Slowly, she slipped it over her head, her eyes locked on mine. "I need to apologise for sneaking around behind your back."

We had sex right there at the kitchen table, her apology gratefully accepted. Keith - and everything else – could wait.

19

Sexually satisfied with our earlier escapades, I sat naked in the kitchen while Dominique showered and got dressed. Feeling adrift, I switched on the radio, letting the soft hum of easy-listening music fill the space. It was Sunday, my so-called 'day of rest,' a day I typically reserved for lounging, eating a lazy breakfast, and mentally gearing up for the week ahead. But now, with no job to worry about, that ritual was dead.

The clatter of the letterbox broke the silence, followed by a soft thump as something hit the doormat. I picked up the delivery—mostly junk mail and local editorials. One envelope caught my eye, though: an info pack I'd requested from a tech firm a while back, outlining software designed to detect and dismantle criminal networks. Ironic, considering my new employer. There was also a pamphlet from a small startup offering bespoke software solutions. Out of curiosity, I glanced at my phone and looked up the company—it was based in Danswich, just seven miles from Little Ashton.

I studied the flyer, and on impulse, I reached for the note Smith had given me and dialled the number. Four rings later, Keith picked up, his voice terse.

"What do you need?" he asked.

"And a good morning to you too," I replied, feigning cheerfulness.

"Yeah, morning," he grumbled, clearly not in the mood for pleasantries. "What is it you want?"

"Nothing urgent," I said lightly. "Just curious—do you believe in coincidences?"

There was a pause, and I could almost hear him rolling his eyes on the other end. "When you were given this number, it wasn't meant for casual chats."

"I know, but it's just something that popped into my head. And since you're the only one I can actually call to talk about the job, I figured I'd ask."

Keith let out a sigh, like he was debating whether to hang up or humour me. "No, I don't believe in coincidences," he finally said, his tone flat.

"Really? So, when weird connections show up, you just chalk it up to random chance? Never had any strange luck—good or bad—catch you off guard?"

"I make my own luck," he replied curtly. "What I *do* believe in is people getting on with their job instead of wasting pointless calls."

I glanced out the window, half-expecting to see his car parked somewhere down the street. "Ah, so you *are* watching me," I said. "Where are you hiding?"

"I'm exactly where I need to be," Keith replied, his voice taking on a sharper edge. "And I wouldn't have to be if you'd just get on with things like you're supposed to."

"See, I have a problem with constant surveillance," I said, leaning against the windowsill. "If I'm going to do this, I need space. I can't work with you breathing down my neck. Tell Smith that I'm going to look for the girl, but I'll be doing it my way. No threats, no shadowing, no micromanaging. If you want results, I need the freedom to get them."

"Listen, mate, you're not exactly in a position to make demands."

"Oh, but I am." My tone strengthened by annoyance. "Your 'organisation' has already cost me my job, turned my future upside down, and put me in a situation where failure means I'm as good as dead. What else do I have left to lose?"

"More than you think," Keith replied coldly. "The boss doesn't like complications. He'll burn someone's entire life to the ground if it serves his needs, and I've seen him do it. Believe me, you don't want to be on the wrong end of that. I'll pass your request on to Smith, but that's the best I can do."

"Fine. Point taken."

"Now, destroy this number," he ordered, voice flat. "I'll send you a new one soon."

Before I could respond, he went. Frustrated, I ripped the note to shreds and tossed it out the window. Sure, I was littering, but if Keith was watching, I wanted to make sure he saw the damn thing go.

The thought of Keith out there somewhere, lurking in the shadows, watching my every move, made my skin crawl. I could almost feel him surveying me, reporting my every breath back to Smith. I needed to shake off this paranoia—to clear my head and burn off the irritation twisting in my gut.

I headed to the bedroom and threw on a pair of faded grey jogging shorts, an old workout vest, and my running shoes. I caught a glimpse of myself in the mirror—looking like a cliché of the thirty-something trying to "get back into shape." In truth, I hadn't run in weeks, and my muscles ached for the release. I called out to Dominique, telling her I was heading to the local shop and asking if she needed anything. Without waiting for a reply, I grabbed my keys and stepped out.

Setting off at a steady jog, I let my legs find their rhythm. Each thud of my sneakers on the pavement was a small victory, driving out the noise in my head. The streets were quiet, almost serene for a Sunday morning. I wound through the neighbourhood, taking unfamiliar routes, testing how far I could push myself without veering into my usual patterns. Something about straying off course felt safer—more unpredictable.

When I finally reached the shop, I quickly ran through a mental list: travel kit, snacks, toiletries, cigarettes. Dominique would be fine—she was always ten steps ahead, like she'd been preparing for this long before I'd even considered it. If I was going to face whatever lay ahead in Little Ashton, I needed to start thinking like her.

When I finished my shopping, I wandered into a small coffee shop next door. The place was cozy, its walls lined with eclectic art, and the air was filled with the aroma of fresh pastries. I ordered a blueberry-banana smoothie and two lemon drizzle muffins—one for myself, and one to share with Dominique later. As I sat there, sipping my smoothie, I found myself smiling at the thought of her. Despite all the chaos swirling around us, I felt an odd sense of gratitude that she'd chosen to come along. At least I wouldn't be facing it alone.

The other patrons shot me curious glances, probably wondering what I was grinning about, but I didn't care. I pulled out my phone and began searching for tickets to Little Ashton. With the cash Smith had given me, I went ahead and booked two first-class seats. If we were heading into unknown territory, we might as well do it comfortably. Spending money so freely felt strange. Normally, I'd be stressing over whether I could cover my bills, planning out each expense. But now, with my bank account brimming and no job to go back to, I felt oddly unmoored, like I'd lost the very worries that kept me tethered.

On my way home, I took the long route through the park, the peaceful surroundings settling me. My mind drifted back to Alice and when we last spoke. She'd told me she wanted the best for me, but I'd never quite understood what that meant. What would she think if she could see me now? Would she be as steadfast as Dominique, ready to charge ahead with me? Or would she have done what she did before—turned away and left me to fend for myself?

I shook my head, pushing thoughts of Alice aside. She was part of the past, like the fallen leaves the wind was now sweeping into the bushes. A ghost, lost in the breeze and long forgotten.

When I finally got home, I found Dominique stretched out on the sofa, lazily flipping through *The Collected Horror Stories of Charles Dickens*. She looked effortlessly casual in her green yoga pants and a loose t-shirt emblazoned with a teddy bear clutching a bloodied knife.

"Did you get what you needed?" she asked, setting the book aside and smiling up at me.

I dropped the shopping bags beside the sofa and sank down next to her. She swung her legs over mine, and as she started running her fingers through my hair, I handed her the muffin I'd picked up earlier. "Yep. Just need to pack, and I'm good to go."

She took a bite, crumbs spilling onto her chest, and grinned. "I'll have everything ready by tonight."

Leaning closer, I breathed in the familiar scent of her shampoo—apple blossom with a hint of citrus. "This is your last chance to back out."

Dominique shook her head. "I'm not backing out of anything. I'm with you all the way to Little Ashton and beyond."

"You do realise that if this goes sideways, 'beyond' might mean hiding for the rest of our lives?"

She shrugged, utterly unfazed. "Doesn't matter. At least I'd be hiding with you."

Her words struck harder than I'd expected. A part of me wanted to argue, to tell her that I was making the decision for both of us and that she was not to come, but I knew she wouldn't listen. Once Dominique made up her mind, there was no turning back. "Thank you," I murmured, pulling her closer and kissing her. Her lips tasted faintly of lemon.

We sat in silence after that, the calm of her presence filling the room. She finished the muffin, and I peered out the window, watching birds flit across the hazy sky. The peacefulness felt fragile, as if I needed to capture it and hold it forever in a glass bubble—just her, me, and the quiet sky.

"What are you thinking?" she asked gently, breaking the spell.

"Everything and nothing," I replied.

"That sounds like a lot," she murmured.

I traced my fingers lightly along her neck. "If you'd asked ten-year-old me where he'd be twenty-five years down the line, he'd have painted a completely different picture."

"What did he want?" she asked, curiosity softening her tone.

"He wanted to be an American wrestler," I said, a wry smile tugging at my lips. "With a flashy car, a massive house, and a swimming pool so big, you could swim right off the edge of the world."

"What about fifteen-year-old him?" she asked.

"Oh, that was different," I sniggered. "For him, it was all about girls and sex."

"And now?"

"Now? I'd settle for a quiet life, no stresses, no worries… and sex, of course."

She slid off the sofa and knelt in front of me, her eyes playful. Taking my hands, she cupped them to her pert breasts. "Well, I can help with that last part."

We made love for the second occasion that day, our bodies entwined on the soft blue rug in my living room, giving every inch of ourselves as if it might be our last chance at happiness. When it was over, we lay there, breathless and bare, staring up at the cream-coloured ceiling. Lost in our thoughts, we simply held on to the moment.

"This must be hard for you," she muttered, turning her face to mine.

"The sex? No, that's the easy part," I quipped, letting out a soft laugh.

"No, silly, I mean everything else—what's happening with you. You act like you're handling it, but I can see it in your eyes," she said gently.

I sighed, the humour slipping away. "I just want to know what any of this has to do with my brother."

"Then let's find out," she suggested, beginning to sit up.

"Soon," I said, pulling her back into my arms. "But let's stay here a little longer, just like this."

For the next twenty minutes, we lay there, wrapped in each other's warmth, feeling the world turn around us.

20

When I awoke from a nap, still sprawled naked on the living room floor, I saw Dominique standing by the mirror, carefully applying her makeup. She was dressed in a tight black evening dress that hugged her figure, paired with elegant four-inch heels. Her hair was swept up into a sleek bun, a few loose tendrils falling artfully around her face. The sight of her like that—a vision of sophistication and poise—made me feel like a wild animal in comparison.

"Look who's awake," she teased, pouting her lips as she perfected a deep red shade of lipstick.

"What time is it?" I asked groggily.

"1 PM," she replied, giving me a playful smirk. "You certainly know how to sleep when you're satisfied."

I stood up and stretched, feeling the stiffness in my back. My elbows were raw with carpet burns, and lint clung to my bare skin. "Heading out?" I asked, brushing stray fibres from my thighs, only now realising just how intense our earlier romp had been.

She glanced at me through the mirror, adjusting her dress. "I've got a booking—afternoon slot. I'll be back by 10 PM, bag packed, and ready for our trip. I hate that I have to go, but this was booked weeks ago."

I wandered into the bathroom, switched on the shower, then leaned against the doorframe. "And while we're away?"

She snapped her makeup bag shut and slipped it into her purse. She looked incredible, and it ached knowing she'd be leaving, looking like that, for someone else. "Don't worry about it. After tonight, I'm telling the agency I quit."

I blinked. "You're quitting?"

"Yep. From tomorrow, I'm all yours," she said, stepping towards me and brushing her hand across my cheek. With a confident smile, she picked up her bag and disappeared out the door.

I stood under the hot spray of the shower, letting it clean away the morning's intensity. I felt like things were falling into place. Dominique was all in with me, and that gave me a peace I hadn't had in a long while. Whatever the next month would bring didn't matter anymore. It felt like I'd hit the jackpot.

Afterwards, I made a simple tuna salad, paired it with a cold beer, and settled on the couch. I flipped through some of the editorials I'd picked up earlier, but none of the articles could hold my attention. Bored, I switched on the TV—only to be met with the usual Sunday afternoon lineup: antique auctions, religious sermons, lawn bowling. All of it was mindless, background noise.

A ping alerted me to a message on my phone. It was from Keith, sent from a new number: *"Once this number is used, delete it from your phone. K."*

Without hesitation, I dialled.

"You're doing this just to wind me up, aren't you?" Keith answered, his voice rough and impatient.

"No, not now. I need a couple of things."

"What things?"

"First, did you talk to Smith? Is he going to give me some space?"

"He agreed—partially. You need to keep me updated regularly if you find anything. If you can commit to that, he'll give you the room you need to work."

"Fine," I muttered, idly picking some lint from under my fingernail. How had it survived a hot shower?

"What's the next thing?"

"My girlfriend's coming with me."

"There's going to be two of you?" His voice sharpened with surprise.

"Yeah. I know Smith warned me not to tell anyone, but how could I disappear for a month without explaining something to her? She wants to come, and frankly, I think she'll be a great help. Two sets of eyes are better than one."

"I don't know how he'll react to that," Keith said, and I could hear the scratch of a pen. "But I'll let him know. Is that everything?"

"No, one more thing."

He sighed. "If this is about coincidence, fate, or any of that bullshit again, just hang up now."

"It's not. I wanted to ask if you knew my brother, Adam."

Silence. I thought the call had dropped. "Why do you ask?" Keith finally said, his tone wary.

"Smith hinted that my brother might have been involved with your organisation in some way, but that doesn't make sense. Sure, he could be impulsive, but getting mixed up in criminal activity? No way, he would've told me."

"You're sure about that?" Keith asked.

I hesitated. The truth was, I wasn't sure. The last few months of my brother's life had been distant, with him disappearing off to parts unknown. If he had gotten involved in something dangerous, I would not have known, because he couldn't be bothered to pick up the phone and tell me.

Keith must've sensed my uncertainty. "Look, Smith hasn't told me anything about your brother. All I know is what you know: he encountered the girl we're after. That's it."

"Thank you," I said, the pressure easing just a little. "I mean it."

"Good, now wait for the new number and don't call again unless you're dying. I'll meet you downstairs at 9:30 tomorrow," Keith said, ending the call.

I stared at my phone, the silence in the flat amplifying my unease. It was nearing dusk, and the last traces of daylight filtered through the blinds, casting slanted shadows across the room. With a deep breath, I knew it was time to pack.

The forecast told us that there were clear days ahead, with the occasional shower, so I kept it simple: a few t-shirts, joggers, underwear, and the toiletries I'd picked up earlier. I threw in smart shirts and grey chino shorts for good measure. For footwear, I opted for my hiking sandals and a decent pair of shoes. Anything else, I'd figure out along the way.

All that remained was to wait for Dominique to get back. Time seemed to crawl, so to keep from spiralling, I called my friend to give him a brief update.

"Thank God you called!" he blurted out the second he answered. "I've been worried sick."

"Sorry I didn't ring sooner," I replied, guiltily. "Everything's been... chaotic. I wanted to wait until I had something concrete to share."

"So, what the hell's going on?" he asked.

Just like I had with Dominique, I summarised the essentials, careful to avoid the more dangerous details. He'd already done enough by connecting Smith to me, and I didn't want to drag him deeper. I didn't want him to feel guilty, I couldn't add that to my conscience.

"Sheesh, man... Is there anything I can do to help?" The worry in his voice was palpable.

"No," I said firmly. "I just need you to keep this between us. Not a word to anyone. If it gets out, we're both in deep shit."

"Yeah, no problem. Linda's been asking what this is all about, but I just told her it's some future project they want documented. She knows I'm lying, though."

"I don't know how long I'll be gone—days, maybe weeks. If things go south, I might not be coming back at all."

"Don't say that mate," he pleaded. "You'll get through it. You always do."

"I'm trying to stay positive," I sighed, rubbing my temples, "but it's hard when you're dealing with people like them."

"Just keep your head down, do the job, and get out. That's all it takes."

"I wish it were that simple," I muttered. "But it's more than that now. As soon as I saw that picture of Adam, it stopped being about a job. I must know what role he played in this, what he got caught up in. And that girl... What's her connection to him? If it's nothing more than a random photo, that's fine. But if it's something deeper..."

"He was going through a lot," my friend said softly. "I've been there myself, still trying to piece my own life together. That girl he was seeing really messed him up, and he wasn't built like you. You've always managed to get through life without it leaving to strong a mark on you. Remember the day you found that note from him saying he needed to leave for a while? You didn't question it because you knew he had to go. He was your brother—you knew him. And if you believe he wasn't involved with these people, then he wasn't."

"I hope you're right," I murmured, doubt still nagging at me. I took a long swig of beer, letting his words linger. How well did I really know Adam in those final days?

"Hello? You still there?" he asked after a pause.

"Yeah, sorry. Just thinking," I replied, distracted.

"It'll be fine," he reassured. "You'll go to that village, find the girl, figure out what really happened with your brother, and then come back home. We'll grab a beer or three, laugh about this whole thing, and remember the good times with Adam. I don't want to be doing that alone."

I glanced at the TV, where an American pastor was fervently preaching to an audience caught up in rapture. The subtitles displayed his sermon: *"Those that are lost are never truly gone and can be found when we give ourselves over to Christ."* Had that been what my brother was chasing when he disappeared? Some kind of spiritual rebirth? Whatever it was, it hadn't saved him in the end.

"Duncan, can you do something for me?" I asked suddenly.

"Anything, mate."

"I probably won't call again until this is over. In the meantime, can you promise me one thing? Don't touch a drop of alcohol."

There was a long silence. It was a request I'd wanted to make for years but never had the courage to.

"Umm…"

"I mean it. Just this one small thing. Make it through the next few days without drinking, and you'll see it's possible for the long haul."

"I don't know if I have that kind of self-control, but... I'll try. I promise."

"Thank you. And one more thing—ask Linda out for dinner. She cares about you. Someone like her could be good for you."

He laughed, a hearty sound I hadn't heard in a long while. "Alright, bud. For you, I'll do it."

"I really value your friendship. Our time together has been good, really good. I'll see you, one way or another, on the other side of this."

"You take care, yeah?"

I ended the call and stared at the blank screen, feeling a strange mix of consolation and sadness. I'd carried the burden of worrying about his drinking for so long, always feeling like I had to keep an eye on him. If he stuck to his commitment to me, that was one less responsibility waiting for me when I returned.

As I sank back into the couch, I wondered—would I ever get back to this life? To these mundane conversations and ordinary problems? Would I make it back to the person I used to be? The odds didn't look good, but I pushed the thought aside. For now, I just needed to focus on finding that girl.

Part 3

Little Ashton

21

Letter from Adam – dated 30th April 2019

Hey bro,
The village here has this regular hiking group that meets up once a week, and treks into the hills. It's usually four to eight people, early morning, heading to the top for a picnic before trekking back down. They say it's for exercise, but I think it's more of an excuse to get together and have a good gossip. I spotted the ad for it on the village's Facebook page and thought, why not? I can already picture you scratching your head, wondering, *"Since when has Adam ever been the outdoorsy type?"* But there's something about this place—it's hard to explain. It's like it's calling me to get involved, to slot myself into its rhythm.

There were six of us: me, an older couple named Jan and Clive who run a little bric-a-brac shop, a local restaurant owner named Claude, and a young mother called Marie, who runs the village camping store. We met outside Claude's restaurant around 7:30 a.m., and as the new guy, I had to give a little introduction. I only gave the briefest of rundowns of myself, but it reminded me of being the new kid in school—awkwardly standing in front of a room full of people who already know each other. After the pleasantries were done, we set off. The weather was perfect: not too hot, not too cold, just that rare kind of day that begs you to be outside.

The hike up took about an hour, and I ended up walking beside Claude. We talked about our lives—his as a busy restaurateur in a quiet village, and mine as a musician struggling to reclaim a lost sense of purpose. You know, you never realise how little you understand yourself until someone asks you to explain it. I kept saying the same old lines: *"I'm a musician, trying to find my inspiration again,"* but when Claude asked me what that really meant, I found myself stumbling, trying to make sense of my own story.

At the top, we reached a white stone structure. Clive explained it was a Trig Point—a triangulation marker used for mapping. Leaning against it, I took in the view. The valley below stretched out like a giant patchwork quilt of greens and browns, dotted with hedgerows and winding dirt paths. I thought about snapping a photo for you, but it wouldn't have done the place justice. There's something rarefied up there—a sense of acceptance that no matter what, a man can survive anything.

You know, bruv, despite all the trips and tours I've been on—from sitting in a sweat lodge in Iceland to climbing Machu Picchu—this felt different. This wasn't about chasing an epic view or having some profound spiritual experience. It was just a group of people walking up a hill, sharing a bit of food, and enjoying the peace. And yet, it resonated more deeply than anything else has these past months. I felt... solid, like I was part of something real again.

Lunch was simple—sandwiches, sausage rolls, and tea—courtesy of Jan and Clive. We sat together, chatting about the village, its history, and the people living here. They were straightforward, no airs or graces. Life here isn't fancy, but there's a strength to it. When problems arise, they just handle them, face-on. No pretentiousness, no fuss. It made me realise how different it is from the chaos of the city, where people pretend their problems don't exist until they explode. Up here, you deal with things, or you get left behind.

On the way back down, I walked beside Marie. She's only a couple of years older than me, but she's been through hell. Her boyfriend, a corporal in the army, was killed by an IED, leaving her to raise their two little girls alone, along with managing the store and looking after her ill mother. I told her how much I admired her strength. She just smiled and said, "No one's struggle is worse or better than anyone else's." Funny, isn't it? I remember you saying that to me once, too. Life has a way of bringing old lessons back around.

When we got back to the village, they started planning the next walk. I said I'd join, but honestly, I'm not sure I want to. There's a part of me that wants to keep that short time on the hill to myself, like it was something precious that I don't want to tarnish.

It's strange, after leaving you, I thought wandering around, playing gigs, drinking, and meeting people would inspire me to write again. But none of it worked. And yet, here in this quiet little northern village, I think I finally found it—the spark I've been chasing.

I'll leave it there for now. Maybe I'll finally manage to get some of that music out of my head and onto paper.

Take care,
Adam

22

Letter from Adam – dated 17th May 2019

Hey bruv,
Yesterday, I met up with Marie for a drink. It wasn't anything serious—she's just one of the few people around here my age, so it was nice of her to reach out. And before you start getting ideas, don't. Despite our easy conversation, there was this mutual, unspoken understanding that it was purely platonic. I have no feelings for her beyond respect. If anything, I admire her strength after everything she's been through.

Marie was born and raised in this village, and unlike most of the younger crowd, she never felt the pull to leave. She wanted her kids to grow up here, in the same place where she and their father were born. They met during college, and after a few years together, she got pregnant with their first. Feeling the pressure to provide, he enlisted in the army. Three tours and another child later, he was killed. I kept apologising, saying how sorry I was, but she just brushed it off. Said her kids are her reason to keep going. Now, she works at her father's store, looks after her mother, and is even planning to study for a degree. The way she manages all of that… I can't even begin to fathom it.

I felt small in comparison. There I was, wrapped up in my own trivial problems, not wanting her to ask me about them. But she never made me feel lesser. It was humbling, really. Eventually, she did ask, and I gave her a watered-down version of my life. Skipped over the ugly parts and instead focused on the music—something I'm always more comfortable talking about.

Turns out, I was the first semi-professional musician she'd ever met. She laughed and said it was exciting, and I joked that it was probably for the best, since most of us are complicated souls—craving attention and hating it when it comes. But as we kept talking, I found myself opening up a bit more about my musical struggles. She suggested I look around the countryside for the answer. Mentioned a place where her father used to go to paint—a secluded part of the woods called *Potter's Glade*.

She didn't know where the name came from, but when she was young, it was where all the local kids used to hang out. As they grew up and moved away, it became one of those forgotten corners of the forest. To get there, she had to draw me a map from memory—a series of landmarks and half-remembered trails. I agreed to check it out the next day, more out of curiosity than hope.

So, this morning, I packed my guitar and headed out to find *Potter's Glade*. I followed Marie's directions, winding through the woods, searching for the signs she'd described—a tree twisted like a corkscrew, a moss-covered boulder, a hidden path between two birches. It was harder than I thought. Nature has a way of shifting over the years, making the familiar seem foreign. I came across an old stone circle—crumbled and overtaken by weeds. I tried to remember if Marie told me they were supposed to mean something, but the story eluded me.

The deeper I went, the more the path seemed to disappear. It felt like the forest itself was stopping me, branches snagging at my clothes as if trying to hold me back. It almost felt wrong to push them aside, but I kept going. If this place was as special as Marie told me it was, I had to see it for myself.

When I finally found it… bruv, it was something else.

The forest opened into a small, circular clearing—no bigger than a schoolyard. Immediately I knew this was the glade. The trees formed a dense canopy overhead, creating a natural dome that felt both sheltering and overpowering. The air was still, like the world itself was holding its breath, waiting for me to disturb it. In the centre was an old, weathered log, surrounded by tiny white flowers—so delicate they looked like they'd shatter at a touch.

I sat on that log, guitar in hand, just staring. The silence was almost sacred. I didn't want to break it with something loud or brash. If I was going to play, it had to be something gentle, something that felt like it belonged. And then I remembered a day long ago—do you remember? You and I sitting on the floor, watching Dad at his piano. You must've been, what, sixteen? It was about a year before he died. He was playing some of his favourite Elvis songs, and I just picked up my guitar and strummed along.

Right there, in that clearing, I started playing those same songs. It felt right, somehow, like it was what the place had been waiting for. Despite being outside, the sound was perfect, each note resonating through the woods. The boundaries between me and the forest blurred. I can't explain it better than that. I played for hours, lost in the music and the memory, and when I finally stopped, the ache in my fingers felt like a blessing.

And you know what else? I realised something as I played. The order of those songs Dad used to play—they weren't random. They were his way of speaking to us, even if we didn't understand it at the time. Look at the titles:

"A Boy Like Me, A Girl Like You"
"We'll Be Together"
"As Long As I Have You"
"Just Pretend"
"It's Only Love"
"Don't Leave Me Now"
"I'm Counting on You"
"Don't Cry Daddy"

They're all about Mum, aren't they? I wasn't old enough to notice what was happening between them, but you witnessed it all, but like Dad, never let your anger show. You always told me she didn't matter, that Dad was enough. But I think he missed her more than he let on. All those times we'd sit there, thinking it was just another session of Dad messing around with his music... he was trying to tell us how he felt. How he never got over her leaving us all.

I wish we'd seen it sooner. Maybe we could've talked to him about it. Maybe we could've helped.

Anyway, I'll leave it there for now. Just needed to get that out. Hindsight's a real bastard, isn't it?

Adam

23

"Keith?" Dominique said, her voice trembling.

"Clara, is that you?" he replied, his eyes widening in recognition.

"Who is Clara?" I mumbled to her, confused.

"Get over here, little lady," he shouted excitedly, leaning down and opening his arms wide.

She rushed over to him, throwing herself into his embrace, leaving me standing on the steps of my building with both our travel bags in hand. It was like she'd forgotten I existed. She looked so small in his massive arms, her head barely reaching his chin. I stood there, mouth agape, feeling like a man who'd just been sentenced to the guillotine. Who the hell was Clara, and how did she know Smith's driver?

Keith had arrived at exactly 9:30 a.m. in a long silver Mercedes-Benz, so spotless it seemed to shimmer. The sky had clouded over since yesterday, and the air was thick with humidity. Sweat was already pooling under my T-shirt. There was a charge in the atmosphere, a faint scent of electricity, as if a storm was brewing. Watching them hug, like long-lost lovers, I found myself silently wishing for that storm to break—if only to muddy his pristine car and ruin their little reunion.

Dominique—or Clara, as she now appeared to be—had returned around 2 a.m. last night. She woke me up, and we spent the next hour getting everything in order: covering the mortgage for the next two months, cancelling deliveries, and shutting off the mains. All the little mundane details that no longer seemed relevant. Now, as I glanced up at my apartment window, I realised I'd spent the better part of the last decade boxed into those four walls, and today might be the last time I ever looked back at them. But there was no sadness, no pang of regret. Maybe I'd mentally checked out months ago. Maybe that place had become nothing more than a mausoleum I kept coming back to out of habit—a casket masquerading as a home.

Dominique broke away from Keith and came back over, grabbing her bag from my hand. "You didn't tell me it was Keith driving us?"

"He wasn't someone I expected you to know," I replied, perhaps a bit too sharply.

Dominique casually wrapped her arm around Keith's waist and smiled up at him, her eyes closed. If she was trying to stir something in me, it was working. "I've known him for a while, but I haven't seen him in…" She looked at Keith for the answer.

"Shit, it must be two years," he said, squeezing her face affectionately in his massive hand.

"Too long," she grinned.

"Yes… too long," I echoed, forcing a smile as I thrust my bag into his arms. "I assume you want these in the boot?" Without waiting for a response, I yanked the door open and nudged Dominique inside.

As I walked around to get in beside her, I caught Keith muttering under his breath. The whole reunion scene was grating on me. I barely registered the plush interior of his gleaming Mercedes. A petty urge flared up inside me—to scuff the leather with my shoes or drop crumbs on the immaculate carpet. My jealousy, that ugly bear that usually slumbered in its cave, was now wide awake and stretching its claws, ready to lash out.

"What's up?" Dominique asked, poking me in the side.

"Nothing, *Clara*," I lied, though I knew my face was probably betraying me.

"You're lying. You look like something's bugging you." She grinned, clearly enjoying my distress. "Wait… are you jealous?"

"Jealous? Me? No!" I scoffed, though my tone was a bit too defensive. She pointed out the window to Keith, who was just passing by on his way to the driver's seat.

"Him?" I shook my head, my inner bear growling. "What would I have to be jealous of?"

Keith entered the car, dressed more casually today: no jacket, no tie, just a crisp white shirt unbuttoned at the neck and black trousers. He looked relaxed, like a man meeting old friends rather than transporting two people into potential danger.

"Before we leave," Dominique said, turning to Keith, "can you please reassure my *lover* here that there's no need for him to be jealous?"

Keith laughed. "He's jealous?"

"I'm *not* jealous," I snapped, feeling my irritation flare.

Keith raised his hand, showing off a gleaming platinum wedding ring. "No need for jealousy, mate," he said, clearly enjoying this. "I'm married."

My bear sharpened its claws. "Wearing a ring doesn't mean much these days. Plenty of people have affairs," I muttered, letting my irritation take a swipe at him.

Keith's laughter was rich and unbothered. "Yeah, but I'm married to a *bloke*."

"Oh," I mumbled awkwardly, my inner bear retracting its claws and slinking back into the cave.

"I know Keith because he used to work for one of my old clients, you big dumb fool," Dominique explained, playfully pinching my arm. "He used to drive me to and from meetings."

"How was I supposed to know?" I grumbled, trying to save face. "One minute you're Dominique, then Angelique, now Clara. When some random chauffeur—no offense, Keith—hugs you like a long-lost lover, it's confusing. What was I supposed to think? You were secret siblings?"

"I'd be lucky to have Clara as a sister. She's a little darling."

Dominique shook her head, smiling indulgently at my idiocy, then turned to Keith. "How's Harold?"

Keith's face fell slightly as he shifted the car into gear. "He passed a couple of years ago. Cancer finally caught up with him."

Dominique's smile faded, her lips curving into a soft pout. "That's a shame. I always liked him more than the others."

My bear stuck its head out of the cave again. There's nothing like a little envy to wake it from hibernation.

"A regular client, was he?" I asked, the bear already baring its teeth.

"Yes, but it wasn't what you're thinking," she said quietly. "He'd lost his daughter, Clara, when she was only eighteen. It shattered him. So, he hired me—not for sex, but to role-play as his daughter. I'd cook for him, chat about my imaginary day at college, ask how *his* day had been. We'd talk, laugh. Then, when our time was up, he'd thank me as Clara, kiss my cheek, and say how sorry he was that our meeting was always so short. It was… heartbreaking."

"That's…" I hesitated, feeling a pang of shame for my earlier jealousy. "That's tragic."

At that, my inner bear, embarrassed by its own growling, slunk back into its cave, dragging a "Do Not Disturb" sign behind it.

"So how long have you two been together?" Keith asked, breaking the heavy silence.

"Long enough for *Mr. Charles* here to jump to conclusions," Dominique quipped, giving me a teasing side-eye.

I could have retorted, could have defended myself, but I'd already made myself look ridiculous. No point stoking the fire further.

Keith's eyes flicked to me in the rearview mirror. "Coincidences," he muttered, throwing out the word in a way that felt like a challenge.

"Sorry?" I asked, caught off guard by the sudden shift.

"When you called me yesterday, you asked if I believed in coincidences, and I said no. And yet, here we are. What are the odds of me running into *Clara* with you today?"

"Is it really a coincidence, though?" I countered, considering his point. "I'd call it probability. You work for wealthy men, the type who might hire high-end escorts. So, the odds of you two crossing paths again weren't exactly slim."

Keith shook his head. "Maybe. But what's the probability of a bloke like *you* managing to land a girl that *rich men* fall over themselves for?"

"Are you saying I couldn't get a girl like her?" I snapped, my pride flaring.

"She's a *real beauty*," Keith said, as if it were an undeniable fact. "And you, well… you're not exactly Casanova, are you? I doubt you could afford even five minutes with her."

"Hey, you two!" Dominique interrupted, cutting off my rebuttal, her voice sharp. "I'm sitting right here in the car, you know."

Talking about her past like this—especially with Keith—felt wrong, like it cheapened her, reduced her to just another woman. I hated it. But Keith seemed determined to needle me, to put me in my place, and I wasn't about to let him get the better of me.

"You might have a point," I said slowly, keeping my voice steady. "But consider this: the probability of you seeing Dominique—*Clara*—again would've been just as high, whether I was in the picture or not. My presence here doesn't change the odds, in fact, it probably lessens them. So, your argument? Still doesn't hold."

Keith glanced at me, grinning in the rearview mirror. "I'm not so sure about that."

"Neither am I," I muttered, more to myself than to him.

Dominique shifted, resting her head gently on my shoulder and slipping her hand into mine. "Well, whatever it is—coincidence or probability—I'm just happy it's brought us all together," she murmured with a soft smile.

Traffic for a Monday morning was surprisingly light. As we rolled through the streets, we passed clusters of cyclists in brightly coloured spandex, their bibs adorned with charity logos. Keith slowed down, letting the lead rider cautiously glance at the car, his helmet cam swivelling to record our every move. Keith cracked open the window, letting in a cool breeze—a welcome reprieve from the simmering conversation.

"So, where are you two heading?" Keith asked casually.

"Little Ashton," Dominique answered before I could stop her. I winced inwardly; I hadn't wanted Keith to know too much about our plans until I felt more secure about where I was going.

"Never heard of it. Where's that?" he asked, voice neutral.

"Up north," she replied lightly, and I winced again. *Stop giving him information*, I thought.

"Is that you asking, or your boss?" I interjected, trying to re-establish some boundaries.

"Calm down, chief," Keith chortled. "I'm just making conversation. Haven't seen this girl in ages, and I'm not passing on anything we say in here. Just trying to fill the silence, that's all."

"We could always talk about the weather," I said drily, letting mockery coat my words.

"Oh, will you two stop it?" Dominique cut in, her tone halfway between exasperation and amusement. For a second, she sounded just like a teacher chastising two unruly kids.

"Yes, boss," Keith replied, grinning.

I offered a stiff nod, and for a few seconds, the car lapsed into silence. Then, I heard Keith trying—and failing—to stifle a laugh. His attempts sounded like a rusty hinge struggling against the wind, and against my will, I found myself chuckling too. Before long, the three of us were all laughing together, the edginess evaporating like morning mist in sunlight.

Once the laughter ebbed, Keith's voice turned more serious. "Listen, Chris," he said, his eyes briefly meeting mine in the mirror, "keep this girl safe for me, would you? I've missed her, and now that I've seen her again, I'd like to stay in touch."

I glanced at Dominique, the sincerity in his words catching me off guard. "If I can't do anything else, keeping her safe will be my number one goal," I said, meaning every word.

We pulled into the station, and Keith stepped out to retrieve our bags from the boot. Dominique hugged him firmly, looking almost fragile in the embrace of the towering man—like a porcelain figure wrapped in burlap.

Keith turned to me and extended his hand. "Stay safe," he said gruffly, his tone serious but tinged with a warmth I hadn't expected.

"I'll try," I replied, gripping his hand firmly.

My town's train station was modest—a small brick building with a few gates and a lone kiosk. Mid-morning, the place was mostly empty, with just a handful of commuters and travellers drifting by. I stepped aside, letting Dominique take the lead. She was dressed casually in blue cut-off dungarees, a grey t-shirt, and one of my old Metallica baseball caps. Her slender legs ended in sturdy hiking boots, while I'd opted for a simpler look—trainers, light green shorts, and a matching vest. To any passerby, we probably looked like a couple of carefree tourists, gearing up for some hill-walking and muddy trails. If only they knew the truth.

"So, why did you and Keith fall out of contact?" I asked as we stood on the platform, waiting for the train.

"That's a long story," she replied, not bothering to look up from the lifestyle magazine she'd brought along for the ride.

"We've still got fifteen minutes before the train gets here. You could give me the short version," I pressed lightly, hoping to coax something out of her.

She flipped a page. "What I was before today is irrelevant. It's buried. I put that part of me to rest when I woke up this morning. I'm done mourning it, and from here on, my focus is on us. On this life."

Her response caught me off guard. Had she known of, or had any dealings with the Russian before now? Was she running from something? Hiding something? I couldn't tell if she was trying to reassure me or sweep the past under the rug. Either way, I needed to know more.

"Okay," I said cautiously, "but I need you to answer just one thing for me—honestly. Once you do, I will not ask about your past anymore."

Dominique finally looked up from her magazine, her eyes steady and serious. "Go on."

"Do you know any of Keith's current employers—Smith, his boss, anyone?"

"No," she replied instantly. "I cut ties with Keith when I found out who he worked for. I wanted no part of it. You don't have to worry about me being involved with them."

"Good," I murmured, feeling a pressure life. I didn't want to picture her entwined up in their world. Even though some questions still lingered about what, or how much she knew of them, I'd given my word not to pry further.

The train rolled in ten minutes late. We boarded and made our way to the dining carriage. I grabbed a bland-looking chicken salad, and she picked up a ham and cheese sandwich. We found a seat by a window and settled in, watching the countryside blur by as the train picked up speed.

After a while, Dominique broke the silence. "Have you ever heard of the social contract?" she asked, absently picking apart her sandwich.

"I've heard of it," I replied, between mouthfuls of dull lettuce. "But I'm not going to pretend I'm an expert."

"It's the idea that we give up some of our freedoms in exchange for protection and safety. We submit to authority for a kind of mutual benefit."

"Okay..." I said, frowning slightly. I wasn't sure where she was going with this.

"That's how I feel with you," she said, glancing up at me. "Like I've traded in my old freedoms for something better."

I sat there, chewing thoughtfully on my dry, tasteless meal, trying to digest both her words and her meaning.

"Don't frown, I don't mean literally," she continued. "By getting on this train with you and embarking on this crazy adventure, I've left my old self behind and signed a new contract for our future."

"Does that make me an authoritarian who can demand you follow my orders for your safety?" I growled in my best imitation of an evil fantasy villain.

"Well," she growled back playfully, winking, "it depends on what you're demanding of me."

We laughed and settled into the steady rhythm of the carriage. As the train slowed, we passed a large reservoir. Swans glided on the shimmering water, a small murder of crows pecked at the banks, and fishermen sat behind windbreakers, patiently waiting for a bite. The landscape seemed to mirror our situation: tranquil on the surface, yet full of unseen currents below.

"We need to choose where we're staying," I said, taking out my phone.

"Didn't you book already?"

"No, I wanted us to do it together," I replied, flicking through hotel booking sites. "So, what do you prefer—hotel, Airbnb, bed and breakfast, or hostel? Don't worry about the expense. Our friends in the shady organisation are covering it."

"How about something small and quaint rather than big and elaborate? Run through the B&Bs available."

I listed the dozen options that popped up. It was short notice, but being early autumn, most of the tourist crowd had moved on. When I reached the second-to-last B&B on the list, she stopped me.

"That one," she said decisively.

"Hotel Jessica?"

"Yes, that one."

"Why that particular one?"

"Because that's my name," she said, her grin softening, lit by the sunlight pouring through the window.

"Another work name to remember, nice."

"No, you fool, that's my real name—Jessica. Jessica Chastwick."

I put my phone down on the table, staring at her, feeling a sudden rush of connection as if an invisible tether had just been created between us. A name. A real name. It was more intimate, more revealing than all the things we'd done together up until now. "Nice to meet you, Jessica," I said, my heart swelling.

"Nice to meet you, Chris," she whispered, reaching across the table to squeeze my hand.

The sunlight spilled over her like a halo, casting a glow that highlighted the significance of her revelation. I felt like I was seeing the real her—beyond the masks, beyond the personas she'd adopted. If there was to be any good that came from this task, let it be this clarity, this fragile sense of hope that made every struggle, every risk, worth enduring.

24

Three hours later, we finally arrived at our destination. The train only took us as far as a town station about thirty minutes outside of Little Ashton. As we stepped onto the platform, I paused to take in the crisp northern air—cooler, fresher than the city's—and shrugged into a long-sleeved shirt. Jessica, braver as always, stayed in her casual gear. A few cabs waited outside, drivers standing by their vehicles, hoping for the rare weekday fare. After a quick glance, we hopped into one, and it carried us the rest of the way to the village.

"So, what now?" Jessica asked as we climbed out of the cab, both of us stretching after the long ride.

"We've got an hour until we can check in. Let's find a place to grab something hot to drink," I suggested, gesturing to the main street ahead.

We didn't have to look long before we found a small, family-run café. The scent of fresh brewing coffee greeted us along with the studied glares of the few customers there. We ordered our drinks and chose a seat by the window, watching locals shuffle past. I pulled out the file Smith had given me, laying it on the table for her to see.

"So," I began, flipping through the photos, "after we check in, we need to decide where to start. I'm not sure whether we should split up or stick together."

"Divide it," Jessica suggested, sifting through the photos with a practised eye. "I'll hit up the hotels, pubs, anywhere people might remember your brother. I'm good with people."

I nodded thoughtfully. "You're right. While you're doing that, I'll focus on tracking down the exact location of this photo. It's distinctive. Someone around here must recognise it—maybe even know who took it."

"Do we start today?"

I glanced at my watch. "No, not today. I think a shower and a good night's sleep would do us both good. We'll hit the ground running tomorrow."

After finishing our drinks, we decided to walk to the hotel, taking our time to get a feel for the place. Little Ashton might have been officially classified as a village, but it felt like it straddled the line between that and a small town. The high street was lined with charming independent shops—a few antique stores, a bakery, and a florist—interspersed with two pubs and a couple of inviting restaurants. But it wasn't all quaintness. There were the usual signs of creeping modernity: a kebab/pizza place, an Indian takeaway, and even a Chinese restaurant tucked between an express supermarket and a run-down betting shop.

It was the kind of place caught between eras—stubbornly resisting the pull of modernity, yet unable to escape it entirely. The pace of life seemed slower here, a lingering echo of a simpler age, especially when compared to the bustling satellite towns just a few miles away. But that was part of its charm, like it was holding on to its roots with quiet determination, preserving its identity amidst the inevitable march of change.

Jessica squeezed my hand gently as we strolled past an old stone church with a small graveyard nestled beside it. The headstones, some barely legible, stood like silent guards, watching over centuries of people long forgotten.

"Now that we're here, maybe you can tell me what happened with your brother," she said softly, breaking the quiet.

I stopped mid-stride, turning to meet her expectant face. "I've never told you, have I?"

She shook her head slowly, her eyes searching mine. "No. You only ever said he died. I didn't want to push, figured you'd talk about it when you were ready. But if I'm going to help, I need to know more about him."

I led her into the quiet grounds and found a weathered wooden bench nestled among the gravestones in the churchyard, its brass plaque inscribed: *Gregory Summersworth 1904-1989*. I set my bag down beside me and sank onto the seat with a heavy sigh.

"If you're not ready, it's okay," Jessica said delicately, sliding onto the bench and threading her arm through mine.

"It's not that I've been avoiding it," I murmured, staring blankly at the names on the headstones around us. "I just don't ever really think on it. But now that we're here, it's time you knew what happened."

I took a deep breath, feeling the familiar pang of grief as I began to tell her about Adam, my brother—the musician who had been taken from me far too soon.

"My brother was a complicated man," I began, my voice thick with memory. "He saw and felt things more intensely than most people. He was a musical artist through and through. Everything he experienced seemed to resonate inside him, like he had no filter between himself and the world. A breeze wasn't just a breeze; it was a reminder of every farewell he'd ever endured. A song wasn't just a melody; it was a conversation between his past and his future, his hopes and regrets."

I sighed, remembering how easily he'd get swept up by the smallest things. "When Adam loved, it wasn't halfway. It was full force, like he was trying to give away pieces of himself. And when Emily came along, he poured every bit of that intensity into her. But when it fell apart... she didn't just leave. She took something from him, our fathers' metronome."

Jessica tilted her head. "A metronome?"

"To anyone else, it was just an old, ticking gadget our dad used when he played piano. But to Adam, it was like a piece of Dad's soul; he idolised him and was crushed when he died. It was the beat of the metronome that kept him steady when everything else was falling apart. Losing Emily hurt him, but losing that metronome? It was like losing Dad all over again."

An elderly man shuffled past us, wearing a faded raincoat and brown trousers, his small Jack Russell trotting faithfully beside him. He tipped his flat cap in a polite gesture, wishing us a good afternoon in a thick Lancashire accent. We returned the greeting, and the brief interruption gave me a moment to gather myself, the coolness of the air biting at the edges of the memory.

"When Emily left, he was crushed," I continued once the man had moved on. "Lost and aimless. If she'd just ended it, he would've been hurt, sure, but he could have found a way to move on. But when she took his things—especially what our dad left him—it was like she'd ripped the heart out of him. He couldn't understand how someone he loved could be so cruel."

"That's so sad," Jessica murmured, resting her head on my shoulder.

"He stayed with me for a few months after that, desperate to track her down, to reclaim what she'd stolen. I tried to help him, but by then, it was like we were living in completely different worlds. He was slipping away, and no matter what I said, I couldn't bring him back. Then, one morning, he just vanished. Left me a note on the mantelpiece—said not to look for him, that he'd contact me when he was ready."

"You had no idea where he went?" she asked, her voice tinged with disbelief.

I shook my head, feeling the old guilt rise up. "No. He had so many connections through his music, so many places he could've gone. I didn't know where to start. And honestly, I thought... maybe giving him space was what he needed. I was sure he'd come back when he was ready."

Jessica lifted her head slightly to look at me, her eyes warm and patient. "But he didn't, did he?"

I swallowed; the memory of that day as vivid as if it had happened yesterday. "No," I whispered. "A couple of months later, I got a call from the police. They'd found him in his car, parked in a field in the Midlands. The windows were rolled up. He'd run a hose from the exhaust into the car."

Jessica stiffened, her eyes wide. "Oh, God..."

I nodded, the words spilling out, raw and painful. "There was a half-empty bottle of vodka beside him. And his guitar... his guitar was in the passenger seat. The police said he'd been there for hours before someone noticed. I... I never even got to say goodbye."

"Didn't he leave a note?" Jessica asked, squeezing my hand.

"No," I said, squeezing her hand gently. "I didn't know where he'd been, what he'd gone through. I could only guess. For years now, Adam's story was something I recounted so many times that it lost its weight—a rehearsed tale I could tell without flinching, like it happened to someone else. But now, searching for answers I didn't even know I needed, it's dragging up emotions I thought I'd buried. And all these questions… ones I never thought I'd be asking. Isn't that strange?"

"It's not strange," she murmured. "You're just good at compartmentalising. You put things in boxes, stack them neatly in your mind, and only open them when you're ready. What happened after you found out?"

"The only thing I could do—I went looking for Emily. She had Adam's metronome, and I wanted to get it back. For him. For both of us."

"Did you find her?"

"No. When I finally tracked her down, she'd moved on, leaving me to deal with her father. He said he'd pass along my message, but a few months later, I just got a package in the mail—with a short note of apology. Can you believe that?" I shook my head, still feeling the bitterness. "She didn't even have the decency to face me or pick up the phone. Just sent it back like it was nothing. I hated her for so long after that."

Jessica looked at me, her expression gentle. "What did you do with the metronome?"

"If I'd had it, I would have cremated it with Adam. But it came too late, so I just... kept it. It's in the wardrobe with a box of his other keepsakes. I guess I've been holding on to it for both of us."

Without a word, Jessica leaned forward and kissed me gently on the lips. "Thank you for telling me." she whispered, her voice laced with sincerity.

"Alright, enough of the heavy stuff. How about we find the hotel and start fresh?" I stood, stretching out the stiffness in my back, and offered her my hand with a small smile.

"Sounds like a plan," she replied, slipping her fingers into mine. "Let's go make some new memories."

"Good ones?" I asked, pulling her gently into a hug.

"The best ones," she murmured, leaning into me.

The bed-and-breakfast, 'Hotel Jessica,' was a quaint two-level cottage nestled on the outskirts of town. It looked more like a rustic barn than a house, with ivy and yellowing leaves climbing up the weathered stone walls to meet the sagging thatched roof. An old oak wagon wheel, whether an authentic antique or just a decorative piece, was mounted beside the door, lending it a storybook charm. The whole place felt as if it had been lifted from a tale about a countryside retreat where life moved at a more relaxed pace.

Waiting at the worn oak door was a woman in her fifties, her brown-grey hair tied back loosely, peeking out from beneath a woollen green cardigan that seemed to have seen as many seasons as the house itself. She wasn't the "Jessica" we'd half-expected, but she introduced herself as Maureen Langdon, or "Moe" for short, and welcomed us warmly. When we inquired about the name, hoping for some meaningful link, Moe explained that she'd bought the property as it was and didn't have the heart to change it. Jessica looked momentarily disappointed but quickly masked it. I could tell she'd been hoping for a deeper, personal connection—something more symbolic.

The second we stepped inside, a sense of tranquillity hit me, as if I'd stepped through a doorway into a different era, one where the world was slower, quieter. The entrance hall had dark grey slate tiles underfoot, with thick, varnished wooden beams overhead, which hung low enough for me to brush my fingertips against them. Potted plants dotted the room, trailing along the walls, their fragrance blending with the scent of aged wood and fresh linen. At the far end of the hall, a grandfather clock's pendulum swung lazily, its steady tick amplifying the stillness of the place.

Moe took us on a short tour, starting with the parlour. The space had the same inviting, rustic charm as the entrance, with a large stone fireplace dominating one wall, flanked by heavy leather armchairs and a floral-patterned sofa that looked like it had belonged to someone's beloved grandmother. The bookshelf along the back wall overflowed with well-worn books, their spines bent and cracked from years of eager hands. It was the kind of room where you could curl up and lose yourself in a good story, so enveloped in the atmosphere that you'd forget you were a mere guest passing through, rather than someone who belonged here.

Next, Moe led us into the dining room, which seemed to be the heart of the house. Polished oak tables, each set with delicate china and vases of freshly picked wildflowers, filled the room. The walls were adorned with a collection of pastoral paintings and old black-and-white photographs of the property and its people. Faces of coal miners, farmhands, and local villagers stared out from the frames, their expressions stoic yet proud—etched in an era when life was hard, but the community held together. It was easy to imagine the hum of matronly cooks in the kitchen, baking bread and simmering stews over a wood-fired stove.

Finally, she showed us to our room. It was modest but elegant, with a tall four-poster bed draped in patchwork quilts and crisp white sheets. A vintage oak dresser stood against one wall, topped with a simple glass vase of fresh yellow flowers. The window framed a breathtaking view of the surrounding hills and forests, rolling into the distance like a verdant sea. I leaned against the sill, taking in the sweeping landscape that seemed to stretch forever.

"Not bad, eh?" Jessica whispered, slipping her arm around my waist.

"Not bad at all," I murmured, smiling as I glanced around.

Moe cleared her throat softly, and we turned back to the reception desk where she placed the register and an old-fashioned pen in front of us. "If you'd just sign in, we can get everything settled."

I scrawled my name in the book, feeling oddly formal, like I was entering some kind of private club.

"What do you think of the place?" she asked.

"How much would you accept from us to buy this place from you?" Jessica asked, a playful grin spreading across her face.

Moe laughed heartily, shaking her head. "I don't think I could ever part with it," she replied, clearly amused. "But that's the first time someone's tried to buy it before even staying a night!"

As I handed over my credit card, Moe's smile faded into a more scrutinising look, her eyes narrowing slightly as if she were assessing more than just our ability to pay. Maybe she'd seen too many visitors with secrets over the years; maybe she sensed we were more than just tourists. This wasn't the sort of place that entertained the likes of dirty weekends or brief love affairs. It felt rooted in an era of dignity and restraint, one that insisted on knowing the true nature of those who passed through its doors.

"We're here for a mix of business and pleasure," I said. "We've booked for a week, but it might be necessary for us to stay longer. Would extending our booking be possible?"

Moe gave me a wary look, eyebrows drawing together as she ran the numbers in her head. "How much longer are we talking?"

"A month," I said, keeping my tone casual.

"A month?" she echoed, blinking in surprise. "We don't usually allow stays that long."

"I'm happy to pay double the rate," I offered, adding a small, knowing smile. "I'd just like to make sure we're settled."

She chewed her lip thoughtfully calculating the unexpected financial boon, her eyes flicking to Jessica before returning to me. "We're heading into the quiet season," she said slowly, tapping at her keyboard. "I could do it, but you'll have to pay upfront—and there's no refund if you cancel last minute."

"Fair enough," I agreed. "The money's yours, no matter what."

She nodded, still watching me carefully, and then scribbled down the new booking details in the ledger. "Consider it done."

I thanked her and took Jessica's hand, leading her up the narrow staircase to our room. As soon as we stepped inside, I kicked off my shoes and flopped back onto the bed, the soft quilt enveloping me in a vanilla-scented embrace. It was the kind of bed that made you want to stay put forever, sinking deeper into its warmth.

"If it weren't for the fact that we're here on a mission," I murmured, staring up at the wooden beams overhead, "this would feel like a honeymoon."

Jessica paused, one eyebrow raised, as she peeled off her top and headed for the bathroom.

"Honeymoon, huh?" She turned on the taps of the claw-footed bathtub, the sound of rushing water filling the quiet room. "Regretting not choosing a five-star hotel instead?"

"Not in the slightest," I said, watching her reflection in the bathroom mirror. "This place suits you. It's got character, just like you."

She laughed and disappeared into the bathroom, leaving the door slightly ajar. I heard the faint rustle of fabric as she shed the rest of her clothes, then the gentle splash as she eased herself into the steaming water. A long, contented sigh followed, and I considered joining her. But instead, I stayed where I was, staring at the ceiling, lost in thought.

Honeymoon. Where had that come from? I'd never even entertained the idea of marrying Jessica, yet the word had slipped out so naturally. Was it this place? The charm of the countryside, the sense of retreat, of solitude? Or was it something else? Something deeper?

Once this was all over, what then? Would I really ask her to marry me? Could I see us building a life here, in this sleepy, out-of-the-way village? She'd be leaving her friends, her entire world, behind for someone like me. And what would we do? What would I do? Once Smith's money ran out, would I end up working at the local supermarket, stocking shelves for a living?

I heard the splash and a contented sigh as she settled into the bath. I half-considered joining her but instead crossed my legs and closed my eyes. I thought about this town and how its residents probably took it for granted. To us outsiders from the south, these kinds of places felt almost magical, but to them, it was just a backdrop to their daily lives. They went about their routines, accepting visitors' money with grace, while we marvelled at the charm they barely noticed.

The sound of Jessica shifting in the bath drew me back. "Well, are you joining me?" she called, her voice soft and inviting.

"Maybe in a bit," I replied, sitting up and glancing out the window. The view was stunning—rolling green hills dotted with patches of woodlands, sloping away into the distance under a pale blue sky. It was the kind of place city-dwellers like me only saw in postcards or on TV, never truly believing such tranquillity existed. The locals probably took it for granted, going about their routines without a second thought, while people like me stood here marvelling at it, wishing we could just step into their lives.

"Suit yourself," she teased, and I could almost see her smirk. "But don't wait too long, or I'll turn into a prune."

I returned to bed and rolled over, listening to Jessica gently hum a tune. What tune it was, I couldn't place, but the sound of her soft voice was soothing, pulling me closer to sleep. Images swirled in my mind, and slowly, I began to drift.

My thoughts turned to the girl in the photograph—the one with the dark birthmark circling her eye, stark against her pale skin. Had she known my brother? Had she offered him consolation in his final days, a presence that could still the chaos within him? I pictured her as a calming figure, a siren of sorts, her delicate, mournful voice easing the despair that had consumed Adam. But the fundamental question remained: how could she be the same girl who had met Smith's boss thirty years earlier? It seemed impossible—a trick of memory, perhaps, blurred by the passage of time. And yet, a small part of me—something primal—felt that I was facing something unnatural. Something I couldn't yet grasp.

I was roused from my sleep by the warmth of Jessica's body slipping under the sheets beside me. The room had grown darker, the light of dusk giving way to the soft, eerie glow of the moon. Without a word, I discarded the last of my clothes and made my way to the bath, needing the heat to chase away the chill the dream had left behind.

When I returned, I found her waiting, her silhouette illuminated by the pale, silvery light seeping through the window. We came together, no words spoken, just the shared urgency of need. The night deepened, life outside shrinking away as we moved in tandem. The full moon hovered in the sky, casting its ethereal light across the room, bathing us in a glow that felt almost otherworldly.

25

We awoke early the next morning and headed down to the dining room for breakfast. The delicious aroma of sizzling sausages and freshly scented tea set my belly rumbling. An older couple sat at a corner table, chatting animatedly with Moe as they worked through hearty plates of beans, eggs, and sausages. The topic of the day was local hiking trails, and Moe, ever the gracious host, seemed delighted to share her recommendations.

Jessica shot me a mischievous look before I replied with forced nonchalance, "Yeah, great sleep. Out like a light." If Moe knew the truth about how much "rest" we'd really gotten, I'm pretty sure the rest of her hair would've turned grey on the spot.

Moe's eyes twinkled deliberately. "Ah, young love—I was there once," she mused, and I opened my mouth to quip back, but Jessica pre-emptively gave me a sharp pinch on my thigh under the table, a clear signal to zip it.

"Come, take a seat. I'll be right over to get your orders," Moe said, guiding us to a small, sunlit table by the window.

I settled into the comfortable chair and scanned the menu, glancing up at Jessica. "So, what's the plan today?" I asked, my voice low. "The weather's looking good, so I thought I'd head up to the castle ruins and see what I can find out."

"I'll poke around the local inns and guesthouses," she replied. "If anyone's hesitant to share details, I'll say I'm Adam's sister-in-law. So, if you get a call from a suspicious innkeeper checking up on me, you'll know why."

"Good thinking," I murmured as Moe returned to take our orders. I opted for a full English with extra bacon and a glass of fresh orange juice. Jessica ordered two warm croissants with a steaming mug of black earl grey tea.

When Moe bustled away, I leaned in. "Once I'm done at the castle, I'll try tracking down local photographers. Adam must've hired someone from the area, and they might recognise the girl too. If I don't have any luck with that, I'll come back and make a plan of action for the next few days."

Jessica reached across the table and squeezed my hand gently. "You're overthinking it. We'll find her," she said with a reassuring smile.

Just as our breakfast arrived, Moe reappeared with my orange juice, lingering a bit longer than necessary. "So," she said, her tone casual, "I overheard your conversation, are you looking for someone?"

I hesitated before pulling out the photo of Adam and the girl. "Yeah, actually. Have you seen either of these people around? My brother passed through here about five years ago, and I wondered if the girl was local."

Moe adjusted her glasses and squinted at the image, her brow furrowing in concentration. After a few moments, she shook her head slowly. "No, I'm sorry. They don't look familiar."

"Not at all?" I spoke. "He was here around then, and she's got such a distinctive face. I thought maybe they would've stood out."

She gave a small, regretful smile. "I wish I could help, but unless they stayed here, I wouldn't know. And I think I'd remember a young woman like her."

Jessica leaned forward. "What about your husband? Would he have recognised them?"

Moe giggled. "I doubt it. He's been dead for twelve years."

Oh, I'm so sorry!" Jessica stammered, her cheeks flushing pink.

Moe waved it off with a gentle smile. "Don't worry, love, it wasn't your fault. Now, enjoy your breakfast. If I remember anything, I'll be sure to let you know." She laughed and started to head back toward the kitchen but paused mid-step, her finger tapping thoughtfully against her lips. "Actually, you could try the camping shop. Marie sees loads of visitors coming through for gear and hiking guides. They might've made a stop there," she suggested before disappearing behind the kitchen door.

"I'll add the camping shop to the list," I said, turning to Jessica. "But this isn't going to be easy. Five years is a long time for anyone to remember a face—especially visitors passing through. I can barely recall the people I met last month. But this girl... she stands out. Still, the real problem is if she's moved on without leaving any trace behind. I've got no idea what I'll tell Smith if that's the case."

"We'll deal with it when we have to," Jessica replied, her tone calm and steady. "For now, let's just focus on what we can control. We'll meet back here at six?"

I nodded, appreciating her practicality. There was no point worrying about bridges we hadn't even crossed yet. We finished our breakfast with light conversation about the village and its peculiar charm, shared a quick good-luck kiss, and set off in our separate directions.

Though the locals referred to the hill as 'Castle Hill,' the guidebook I'd picked up from Moe clarified that the structure was actually a folly built in the mid-eighteenth century by Lord Ashby. Apparently, the old lord wanted to project an image of longstanding nobility, crafting this faux fortress to create an illusion of grandeur. Locals speculated about his motives—some said it was to impress a woman, others claimed it was to hide a scandal—but the real reason had faded into myth.

From a distance, the folly looked every bit the part: a ruined castle perched dramatically on a rise, its solitary tower standing lookout against the sky. But as I got closer, the illusion unravelled. The 'ruins' seemed too strategically broken, the jagged edges too perfectly placed to be authentic. The single tower, though weathered, was suspiciously symmetrical, and the crumbling battlements seemed almost choreographed in their disarray. The grand archway at its base, wide enough for a carriage, stood intact, serving as a gateway to the hills beyond. The building was impressive, but it lacked the sense of history and life that comes with true castles. No one had ever lived or died within these walls. This place wasn't a relic—it was a monument to vanity.

Still, if it hadn't been for the shadow hanging over my visit, it would have made for a pleasant hike. The folly crowned a steep hill, providing sweeping views of the countryside. The trail, roughly two miles from the edge of the village, wound through quiet farmland, the fields dotted with grazing sheep and lined with dry stone walls that snaked across the land like veins. Here and there, I passed the remnants of old homesteads—stone foundations swallowed by moss and ivy, chimneys standing stubbornly against the encroaching woods. There was a road that led up to the top, narrow and winding, but I opted to walk. It felt more respectful, somehow, like earning the view at the summit.

When I finally reached the folly, I was winded and regretting my decision not to invest in proper hiking boots. The rough terrain had worn through the thin soles of my trainers, and I made a mental note to stop by Marie's shop later for some. For now, though, I stood in the presence of the false castle, catching my breath as I surveyed the area. The folly's roofless shell stretched out in front of me like a ruined cathedral, its empty windows framing patches of the sky. Birds flitted in and out, their calls echoing off the stone.

Whatever its original purpose, the folly had been repurposed into a small visitor centre, complete with a museum that local volunteers curated. A large wooden structure had been attached to one side of the faux castle, blending in just enough to avoid disrupting the visual charm. Inside, the museum featured a few exhibits on the local history, with one of its main attractions being an old crossbow, passed down through Lord Ashby's ancestors and regarded as a 'good luck charm' for the family.

I laughed when I read that. How anyone could consider a weapon to be a source of good luck was beyond me. Then again, the rich and powerful had their own peculiar ways of bending the world to fit their desires.

I wandered through the exhibits, taking in snippets of the village's past. Faded black-and-white photographs lined the walls, showing local gatherings, fairs, and notable figures from decades ago. There was a small diorama of the original village, complete with hand-painted wooden figures and model carts. It was quaint, almost endearing. But I wasn't here for history or village pride. I was here for answers.

With that failure out of the way, my next stop was to search the castle grounds. Wandering around the hillside, I found what I believed to be the approximate spot where my brother had taken the photograph. I sat on the grass, watching some magpies hop about, scavenging for food. I held up the photo, staring at it, trying to wring out any extra bit of information from that still picture of life.

Eventually, I approached the staff, a trio of elderly volunteers who looked thrilled to see a visitor. I showed them the photo and asked if they recognised the faces. One by one, they squinted at the picture, peering at it from various angles as if a different perspective might jog their memories.

"Sorry, love," one of the women said. She handed the photo back with a polite smile. "I don't think I've ever seen either of them."

Another of the volunteers, a frail-looking man in a knitted jumper, leaned closer and adjusted his glasses. "Distinctive girl," he murmured thoughtfully. "But no, I'd remember a face like that."

"Maybe they were just passing through," the third volunteer offered, shrugging. "We get all sorts coming up here for a look around. Could've been anyone, really."

It was disappointing, but not surprising. It was a long time ago for people who barely knew each other to begin with, and even longer for those who came and went. I thanked them anyway and left, heading back out into the grounds with the sinking feeling that I was chasing ghosts.

The hill sloped sharply around the folly, giving way to patches of uneven ground tangled with gnarled trees and clumps of wild bramble. I pulled out the photograph of Adam and the girl, squinting between it and the ruins, searching for any clue that might place them here. If the picture had been taken at this location, it had to be from a very particular angle. I began to circle the perimeter, scrutinising every dip and hollow, hoping for something—anything—to trigger a spark of recognition.

But the grounds felt eerily deserted. There were no signs of people being here, no picnic tables or benches, not even a patch of trampled grass where people might have regularly gathered. It felt like a place suspended, untouched and forgotten. Like stepping onto a stage long after the play had ended—the actors gone, the set abandoned, and only the silence of an empty theatre lingering in the air.

I sat down, cross-legged, and looked at the photo again. My brother stood there, smiling faintly, the girl beside him looking directly at him, her face marked by that strange, dark birthmark. Adam appeared almost happy. Almost. I turned the photo over, as if some hidden clue might appear on the blank back.

A soft rustle nearby caught my attention. I looked up to see a pair of magpies hopping through the grass, pecking at the ground. One of them edged closer, its beady eye watching me warily.

"Hey there, mate," I murmured, digging into my pocket for the packet of peanuts I'd brought along as a snack. I tossed a few in its direction. The bird cocked its head, considering, then cautiously picked up a peanut and began pecking at it.

"I don't suppose you've seen this couple, have you?" I asked dryly, holding up the photo for the magpie's benefit. "The girl especially?"

The bird gave me a baleful look, then snatched up another peanut and fluttered away, its glossy feathers flashing in the sunlight.

"Yeah, thought so," I muttered, stuffing the photo back into my pocket.

For the rest of the morning, I wandered the hill, approaching anyone who looked like they might be familiar with the area. I held up the photograph, repeating the same question over and over: "Do you recognise these people?" Most gave polite but unhelpful responses, offering variations of, "No, sorry," or "She looks unique, but I've never seen her." After what felt like hours of hopeful starts and disappointing finishes, all I had to show for my efforts was the same lack of dead-end I'd started with.

By midday, drained and frustrated, I decided to take a break and made my way back into town. Before leaving I'd stopped by back the tourist centre and picked up a few more guidebooks, grasping at straws in the hope that some overlooked detail might spark a lead. There had to be *something* here—some hidden corner of knowledge I hadn't uncovered.

By midday, I decided to take a break and wandered back into town. I'd picked up some more guidebooks from the tourist centre, hoping something – anything - might give me a lead. I found a cafe, ordered a cappuccino and slumped into a corner table, dropping the stack of guidebooks beside me. Taking a slow sip, I opened the first book and began to leaf through its pages.

The guides were the usual fare—glossy images of scenic walks, maps detailing the local geography, historical titbits, and lists of quaint businesses aimed at tourists with money to spend. One particular book caught my attention: the author, a local historian with a slightly smug-looking grin and wire-framed glasses perched halfway down his nose, seemed to believe he knew the village better than anyone else. His introduction boasted: *"Little Ashton and the surrounding land is built on the ever-changing history of its tales and legends. It's a malleable thing, growing and shrinking with each breath of its residents."*

"Great," I muttered at his photo, rolling my eyes. "You're telling me that Adam might have visited a place that has altered beyond recognition but can't be bothered to tell me how. What good are you?"

By mid-afternoon, I gave up and trudged back to the hotel for a nap, hoping Jessica had fared better in her search.

She hadn't.

We sat on the bed later that evening, both stripped down to our underwear, takeaway pizza boxes strewn between us alongside maps, guidebooks, and scattered notes. A whole day's worth of questioning and wandering wouldn't have filled the back of an envelope.

Jessica sighed, taking a large bite of pepperoni pizza. "The two pubs in this village," she said, jabbing a finger at a spot on one of the maps, "have changed hands at least three times over the last five years. And some of the locals mentioned an influx of hikers and other 'annoyances' passing through town. But once I started asking specifics, they clammed up."

I nodded, biting into my slice and washing it down with a sip of beer. "People have been weirdly cagey, haven't they? I tried getting details from a few folks around the castle earlier, but all I got were vague shrugs and polite smiles."

"Yeah," Jessica agreed, leaning back against the pillows, "almost like they're all in on something we're not. Anyway, I tried heading over to the camping store to talk to Mary. But when I got there, a sign on the door said they're closed for holidays this week."

"I had zero luck at the castle. Before you got back, I even tried tracking down local photographers, but most are based miles away. We've moved exactly two inches from where we started."

Jessica tossed a pillow at me. "Stop being such a downer. We only got here yesterday."

"Yesterday, today, tomorrow—it's all the same. It's been five years since Adam had his picture taken on top of that hill. Every lead we thought we has been a dead end, and I'm running out of ideas." I let out a long breath and took another swig of beer. "Nope, my love, we are stuck in the middle of a very long and very deep creek with two broken paddles and a hole in the boat. I'll do my best to keep you safe before I drown."

She took the bottle from me, took a large swig, and handed it back. "Though it's often cute, your cynical observations can be trying. We've still got several weeks of searching ahead of us—don't base them all on one day of failures."

"Does nothing ever get you down?" I asked.

"Of course things get me down," she replied, her voice softening. "But remember who I am and what I've given up. I'm an ex-escort who has slept with so many different professional men and women that I've picked up loads of tips and tricks on how to handle difficult situations. You think your situation is tough? I was once hired by a man whose wife was about to find out, via the press, about an affair with his much younger advisor. He wasn't sure what the next day would bring, but he was determined to have one last moment of blissful sleep. We didn't even have sex; he just wanted comfort."

"So, what you're trying to say is that my drop from the gallows is still short enough for me to survive?"

"That's your strange way of describing it, but yes. Tomorrow is just another day of us looking, so don't give up hope yet."

After pizza and several more beers, we climbed into bed and made love. Tired legs and minds are no match for testosterone, beer, and the warmth of a beautiful woman beside you.

The next few days became a blur of repetitive, disheartening searches. I'd head off in one direction, Jessica in another, and we'd regroup in the evenings, weary and frustrated. I'd vent my dissatisfaction, and she'd listen patiently before we'd inevitably fall into bed together. Despite the fantastic sex, the task of finding the girl was wearing me down. I didn't want to pile too much of my frustration onto Jessica, but I think she could tell I was running out of options.

We soon decided to expand our search beyond Little Ashton, moving through neighbouring villages and knocking on doors, chasing even the thinnest of leads. I found a shop and bought myself a decent pair of hiking boots and wandered for miles along winding country roads and footpaths, stopping at isolated farms and small hamlets. I'd produce the photo of Adam and the girl, hoping someone might recognise her. But every response was the same: a polite shake of the head, a sympathetic smile, a murmured apology.

As the days dragged on, the skies turned slate grey, casting the landscape in a sombre light. What had once felt vibrant and lush now seemed muted, stripped of life. Even the people we passed on the village streets were beginning to look hollowed out, their faces lined with the weariness of routine. Each failed conversation sucked a little more energy out of me, leaving me feeling like I was stumbling through a ghost town, haunted by my own inadequacies.

"Why don't you pop a note through the door of the camping shop?" Jessica suggested at the end of our seventh fruitless day. We were back at the hotel, sitting on the bed amidst crumpled maps and hastily scribbled notes. "They're due to reopen soon, right? Whoever runs the place might have been around back then. They can call you as soon as they see it. That way, we can take a couple of days off to clear our heads."

I rubbed my temples, feeling the dull throb of a budding headache. "Good idea," I muttered. "Feels like we're running out of options, so it won't hurt."

The following morning, I drafted a simple note, scrawling it in neat, bold letters. I sealed it in an envelope, marking it **URGENT** across the front, and slipped it through the letterbox of the shuttered shop:

'Hello, my name is Chris Charles. I need to speak with you urgently. Please call my number as soon as you read this, or visit me at Hotel Jessica, room 4.'

It felt like a long shot, but it was the best we could do. With nothing left but the waiting game, Jessica and I spent the next couple of days in a state of limbo, hunkering down in our room. Aside from the occasional stroll for a meal, we rarely left. Instead, we used the break to recharge, letting our bodies rest and our minds think about other, more pleasant things.

By the third day, when the phone finally rang, I nearly leapt out of my skin.

"Hello," a woman's voice spoke. "Is this Chris Charles?"

"That's me," I replied, my heart thudding with a mix of anticipation and hope.

"You posted a letter through the shop, asking me to call?"

"Yes, that's right. Is this Marie?"

"It is. Is this about an order or purchase you've made? Because we have official returns data on our website."

"Oh, no, it's nothing like that," I interjected quickly. "I'm in town because I'm looking for some information on someone who visited here a few years back, and I'm hoping to find out if they ever stopped by your shop."

"That explains the strange note," she said slowly, the wariness evident in her voice.

"I'm sorry, I just... I'm running out of options," I admitted, trying to keep my tone steady. "It was the only way I could think to contact you."

"Who are you, then?" she asked, suspicion lacing her words. "You're not the police, so what—are you some sort of investigator?"

"No, I'm just a guy looking for his brother and a girl he was seen with."

"Haven't you called the authorities?" she asked, her tone guarded. It was the same wary suspicion I'd encountered with other locals, as if the village instinctively recoiled from outsiders with probing questions.

"I can't."

"Why not?" Her voice sharpened, sceptical now.

"It's... complicated," I hesitated, choosing my words carefully. "It's hard to explain over the phone. I just need to talk to you, face-to-face. Show you a couple of photos."

"I'm not sure I want to get involved in something like this," she said.

"Please, Marie, you might be the last person I can approach for assistance," I implored, trying to steady my voice. "I've spent the past week searching, talking to everyone I can, and I've got nowhere. What have you got to lose? If you can't help, I'll thank you and walk away. No pressure."

There was a long silence on her end, and I could almost hear her evaluating the risks. Meanwhile, Jessica poked me in the ribs, her eyes wide with curiosity, silently demanding I let her know what was happening.

Finally, Marie sighed. "Alright, fine. Come by the shop tomorrow morning before I open. But just for a few minutes."

Before I could thank her, she finished the call.

"Well?" Jessica asked eagerly.

I relayed the brief conversation, and a triumphant grin spread across her face. "Great! I'd better come with you; your desperation might scare her off."

"Am I really that bad?"

"No," she teased, her eyes softening as she leaned in, "but I think you're adorable, so my opinion's a bit biased."

26

The next morning, we skipped breakfast and headed straight to the camping store. I felt a strange sense that today might bring a breakthrough. Though the shop wasn't due to open until 9 a.m., we arrived early, just after 8:15. The green metal shutters were still down over the wide glass windows, but the entrance itself was clear. I rang the bell.

Movement flickered inside—someone shifting around behind the shelves. A woman appeared, stepping out from behind a row of rucksacks. Her eyes met mine through the glass.

"Chris?" she mouthed.

I nodded. She hesitated, then unlocked the door and motioned for us to enter. The shop seemed much larger on the inside, with its high ceilings and long, cluttered aisles packed with gear for every kind of adventure. Rows of shiny new tents stood beside racks of rugged hiking boots, waterproof jackets, and shelves crammed with hiking essentials. The air was tinged with the scent of canvas and gum, and our footsteps echoed faintly as we ventured deeper inside.

"Follow me to the back," Marie requested.

She was a striking woman, not much shorter than me, with shoulder-length hair dyed blonde, though brown roots peeked through at the parting. Dressed in black cargo trousers and a thick green polo shirt embroidered with her name and the store logo, she had an air of quiet authority that belied her hesitant manner over the phone.

We moved past the cashier's counter and through a set of double doors into a dim storage area. If the shop floor was an organised haven for outdoor enthusiasts, the backroom was chaos. Boxes and bags lay scattered across the floor, shelves crammed haphazardly with gear of every kind. Lanterns, stoves, and cookware were jumbled together beside piles of boots, shoes, and rain jackets. The smell shifted here, more rubber, cardboard, and dust.

In one corner of the cluttered backroom sat a small desk, its top littered with papers and an old PC that hummed under a flickering lamp. An oversized accounting book, worn and dusty, lay neglected, as if it hadn't been touched in years. Three mismatched plastic chairs were arranged around the desk like spectators at a makeshift inquisition.

"Take a seat," Marie said, gesturing to the chairs as she settled behind the desk. "Sorry about the clutter. I was away last week, and we're behind on stock. My assistant isn't in yet to help with the backlog."

Jessica glanced around, taking in the disorganised shelves and stacks of unpacked boxes. "The owner of the guesthouse told me this place is a local family business."

"It is," Marie replied, a hint of something delicate in her voice. "Or it *was*. My dad opened the store back in the eighties. I've been running it ever since he passed." Her expression shifted, cautious once more. "But I'm guessing you're not here to talk about camping gear. What is it you really want to ask me?"

"Firstly, thank you for agreeing to talk to me," I said, leaning forward and resting my forearms on my knees. "I lost someone, too. My brother passed through this town several years ago, and I'm trying to piece together his last days—find out if he met anyone here."

Her look hardened slightly. "Who was he?" she asked bluntly, her tone suggesting she expected this to lead nowhere.

Instead of showing her the same photo I'd flashed around the village, I decided to change tactics. I pulled out my phone and opened a video of my brother performing at an open mic night, strumming his guitar as he sang his song, *Birth of Delight*. The recording was grainy, but Adam's voice—smooth, full of emotion—echoed in the small room. I hoped the music would stir something in her, trigger a real memory instead of a vague recollection.

Marie leaned forward, her brow furrowing as she watched. At first, her face was unreadable, but then her eyes widened with recognition. "That's Adam," she murmured, her voice softer now. She looked up at me, a faint, sad smile forming. "I remember him. God... it must've been... what, five years ago?"

"About that, yeah," I replied, barely able to contain the rush of hope. "Did you know him well?"

"We met up several times," she said slowly, still watching the video as if she could see Adam right in front of her. A soft smile tugged at her lips; the kind reserved for fond memories. "Hiking trips, the odd coffee here and there. He was a lovely guy, always had a smile and was so easy to talk to. When he said he was leaving, he said he would keep in touch, but... I never heard from him again."

I took a deep breath, steadying myself for what I had to say next. "He took his own life not long after that," I said gently, the words heavier than they should have been. "I'm retracing his steps, trying to understand what led him to it."

The smile vanished from her face, replaced by a look of shock and sadness. "Oh, God... I'm so sorry," she whispered. "He seemed so... *together*, you know? There was a light in him, a kind of energy that drew people in. A few of us here really took to him." She blinked rapidly, as if struggling to process what I'd just told her. "He even played a couple of small gigs at a restaurant in town."

"We've been trying to talk to people, we might be imagining it, but no one seems willing to help," Jessica said.

Marie sighed, rubbing her forehead. "You're not imagining it. People around here have been wary of outsiders lately. There's been some trouble with visitors, and now most folks prefer to keep their distance. It's a small-town mentality, I guess—one bad experience, and they close ranks."

She hesitated, looking thoughtful, and handed my phone back to me. "A lot of people have moved on. Chances are, the ones Adam knew are long gone.

"What about you?" Jessica pressed lightly. "You stayed. Why?"

Marie sighed heavily, the weight of unspoken thoughts dragging down her shoulders. "I want to leave," she admitted.

"But with two kids and a shop to run, it's not that simple. My father poured his heart into this place. Selling it off would feel like… like betraying his memory."

I nodded, sensing an opening, and reached into my jacket. Pulling out the photograph, I placed it gently on the desk between us. My nerves felt like exposed wires, crackling, ready to electrocute those stupid enough to touch them. *Please, recognise her. Just give me something.* But I kept my face neutral, willing myself to be steady.

"This picture was taken up on Castle Hill," I said, gesturing to the woman standing behind Adam. "Do you recognise the girl?"

For a minute, the room seemed to still. Marie's eyes flickered with something—recognition, hesitation, fear? I couldn't be sure, but there was something. She stared at the photograph longer than necessary, her fingers trembling ever so slightly as she held it. My heart pounded. We were so close—on the very edge of a breakthrough.

"I remember this photograph," she murmured. "Adam asked me to take it because he needed some promotional shots for the gigs at the restaurant. But the girl…" She trailed off, staring at the image as if willing it to transform into something else. Then, almost reluctantly, she shook her head and handed the photo back, her expression closing off like a door slamming shut. "No. I'm sorry. I don't know who she is."

I leaned forward, strain coiling inside me. *She's lying. She knows more.* "Are you sure? Because for a second there, it looked like—"

"No," she interrupted sharply, cutting through my words. The force of her reply was startling, her voice laced with a defensive edge. "I told you—I've never seen her."

Something was off. Her reaction was too quick, too vehement. There was more here, buried beneath the veil. But would pressing harder get me what I needed, or just push her further away?

"Marie," I said, choosing my words with care. "I just need the truth. Whatever you know, even if it's just a guess—"

"I *said no*, didn't I?" she snapped, almost throwing the picture back at me. Her face was flushed now, eyes narrowed. "Look, I'm sorry about your brother, I really am, but I don't know what else you expect me to say. He showed up, we became friends, we hiked a bit, then he left. Whoever else he was with, whatever he was dealing with—that wasn't my business."

Her words were sharp, final, and tinged with something that felt darker than guilt. Anger, maybe. Or fear. Either way, it was clear I'd hit a nerve, and I wasn't sure pushing her harder would get me what I wanted.

Jessica placed a gentle hand on my arm, squeezing slightly. A silent reminder: back off, or we'll lose her for good.

Calm as ever, Jessica stepped in, her presence like a balm to soothe the pressure thickening the room. She reached out, her voice soft but full of quiet strength. "Marie," she began gently, "I didn't know Adam, but from the way you talk about him, I wish I had. He seems like he was kind, easy to be around."

Marie's gaze flickered again, her expression caught between hesitation and something else I couldn't put my finger on. But she stayed silent.

"We're here because Chris needs to know the truth," Jessica continued. "Whether this girl has something to do with Adam's death, or whether she doesn't, we must find out. For Chris's sake - for the chance to finally understand what happened."

Marie seemed at a loss for words, her face a confused blend of confusion and distress. "I can't," she whispered, her hands falling to her face as if trying to shield herself from what we were asking of her. "This is too much."

"If you know who she is but don't want to tell us, please understand," I interjected softly, trying to keep my voice reassuring, "we're not here to cause trouble. She's not in any danger. I just need to talk to her."

The room fell into an uneasy quiet, broken only by the hum of the extractor fan in the corner. Jessica and I traded worried glances. Had we pushed her too hard? Was she about to shut down completely? Jessica grasped my knee gently, urging me to hold back.

Marie exhaled slowly, a sigh full of exasperation and something that felt almost like surrender. "It's not that," she murmured, shaking her head. "I'm telling you the truth—I don't know her. I've never seen her, never spoken to her. I really don't have a clue who she is. But..."

She faltered, her eyes darting between us. "But what?" Jessica urged delicately.

Marie's shoulders slumped as if the weight of what she was about to say was crushing her. "But... I do know someone who might."

Marie's fingers began drumming anxiously on the desk, a rapid, staccato beat betraying her inner turmoil. "I'd rather you just leave now," she admitted, a trace of fear slipping into her voice. "But I see that's not going to happen, is it? Talking to this person... it won't be easy."

"Please," I said, calmly. "Whatever it takes, just point us in the right direction."

Marie hesitated, then finally relented. Reaching into her desk drawer, she pulled out a stack of papers—receipts, invoices, delivery notices—all seemingly mundane. My heart sank as I tried to discern her intentions, but then she pushed the papers aside and retrieved a small, heavy-looking key.

"I live above the store," she said, holding up the key. "What I have for you is up there. Come with me."

"Alright," I agreed cautiously, standing up. Jessica followed suit, watching Marie intently.

Marie led us out of the storage room and through a heavy wooden door at the back of the shop. We climbed a narrow flight of stairs, each creaking step echoing in the stillness of the flat above. At the top, we found ourselves on a small landing with three doors, each slightly different—one with peeling paint, another polished to a shine, and the last adorned with a faded welcome mat.

Marie paused in front of the middle door, glancing back at us with a conflicted look. It was like she was contemplating whether to turn the key at all. After what felt like an age, she took a deep breath, squared her shoulders, and unlocked the door with a firm turn of the key.

The flat felt lived-in but strangely hollow, as if it were holding its breath. A black leather sofa sat against one wall, its once-springy cushions sagging slightly from years of use. An armchair was positioned beside it, facing a flat-screen TV. Scattered toys dominated the floor—plastic soldiers mounted on tanks, fighter jets locked in eternal combat, and tiny racing cars abandoned mid-race across a cluttered central table. The remnants of childhood chaos against the quiet stillness of the room created an odd, bittersweet atmosphere.

"I haven't had a chance to clear up after the boys," Marie murmured, a hint of self-consciousness

"It's fine," Jessica replied, offering her a reassuring smile.

Marie led us past the chaos and into a smaller, more confined space. It was a home office, compact and meticulously organised—a stark contrast to the disarray of the living room. A sleek, tempered-glass desk held a high-end computer, and a black leather office chair sat neatly tucked in. But it was the large, dull-grey safe nestled in the corner that caught our attention. Its surface was scratched and worn; the metal dulled by use.

Marie pulled out a key from her pocket, the tiny click of the lock breaking the silence. She twisted the dial methodically, a series of faint, rhythmic clicks echoing in the small room. The safe door swung open, revealing a small collection of personal items. Marie reached inside and withdrew a brown, leather-bound sketchbook, its cover scuffed and weathered.

With a slow, deliberate motion, she handed it to me.

"I don't know why I've kept it all these years," she admitted, her voice barely above a whisper. "But I think it's what you're looking for."

"What's this?" I asked, glancing at Jessica, who looked equally puzzled.

"Open it," Marie urged, her stare fixed on the sketchbook. Her expression was guarded, yet there was a fragility in her eyes—a flicker of unease.

I opened the book and began flipping through the pages, each sketch revealing a different facet of Marie's father's talent. Some pages held nothing more than rough doodles—crude sketches of animals and abstract shapes—while others displayed stunning scenes of the countryside, with intricate depictions of birds and flowers.

I turned the cover and began flipping through the pages. The drawings varied in style and subject, revealing glimpses of the artist's skill and sensitivity. There were quick, rough sketches—hastily drawn foxes, deer leaping through meadows, and brambles weaving together to form pretty patterns. But then, the pages transformed into scenes of breathtaking beauty: sweeping landscapes, delicate birds perched on slender branches, and intricate studies of wildflowers.

"In his spare time, Dad loved to sketch out in the woods," Marie explained, a wistful smile tugging at her lips. "He would spend hours capturing the little things most people overlooked. I always thought he could have been a great artist if he'd had the confidence. But instead, he gave everything to this shop."

I lingered on a detailed drawing of a robin, its tiny claws curled around a fragile twig. Each feather was meticulously rendered, and the bird's eye seemed almost alive—bright, watchful, as if caught mid-song.

"These are marvellous," I said, genuinely moved by the talent and patience evident in every stroke. "But I'm not sure how these help us."

"Keep going," Marie urged, "it's at the end of the book. One of the last things he ever drew."

With renewed urgency, I turned page after page, my pulse quickening as anticipation built. Each flip brought me closer to what felt like a revelation. And then I found it—the last drawing in the sketchbook.

Everything stilled.

There she was—the girl I'd been chasing through rumours and fading memories. Her face glared back at me, captured in striking detail. The delicate contours of her features were almost painfully familiar, but it was the birthmark encircling her left eye that held me transfixed. It was as if the artist had poured every ounce of his focus, his obsession, into rendering that mark. The lines were etched with such precision that it seemed to pulse with a life of its own, vivid even in the grayscale of graphite.

Her eyes—dark, intense—seemed to bore into me through the page. There was something in them that defied the flatness of the medium, a haunted quality that made my skin prickle. I half-expected her to blink, to turn her head and acknowledge me, like some ghost caught in the paper.

Heart pounding, I reached into my pocket and retrieved the photograph. Holding it up beside the sketch, I felt my stomach lurch. It was her. There was no mistaking it—the same delicate bone structure, the same sweep of hair, and that birthmark, a stark, almost defiant streak against pale skin. The girl in the photograph and the girl in this sketch—they were the same.

"This can't be," I muttered, my mind spinning. "When did your dad draw this?"

"2012," Marie replied, her voice quiet but certain.

"Who *is* she?" she asked, her voice trembling with urgency.

Marie let out a long, weary sigh, like someone burdened with a secret too heavy to carry alone. "She's someone my father became obsessed with shortly before he died."

I shook my head, disbelief pressing down on me. "It *can't* be the same girl," I said, trying to convince myself more than anyone else. I turned to Marie, locking eyes with her, hoping for some logical explanation that would unravel this impossibility. "Did your dad know who she was? Did he ever mention her by name?" My voice faltered, the distress worming in as I fought to stay composed.

Marie hesitated, her expression a mixture of guilt and confusion. "Dad never mentioned her to me, at least not directly," she began slowly, choosing her words carefully. "But I found out about his obsession shortly before he died. The first time I saw her for myself was when I found this sketchbook."

She glanced down at the drawing, her fingers brushing over the worn leather cover as if it held answers she wished she didn't know. "I was clearing out the loft after he passed and came across this sketchbook in an old suitcase. Among all these peaceful nature drawings, she stood out—like she didn't belong there. I asked Mum about her, but she always dismissed it, said it was just some girl Dad drew from his imagination. But I don't think that's true."

Marie paused, her eyes growing distant, as if caught in a memory she wasn't sure she wanted to relive. "There was something... off about the way Mum brushed it aside. I always had this feeling that she was hiding something, that there was more to the story than she let on."

Amidst the shock of Marie's revelation, a flicker of hope ignited within me.

"Your mother might know more?" I asked, my voice urgent. "Is she still around? Can I talk to her?"

Marie shook her head, a pained expression darkening her features. "No, she's not well. I don't know what would happen if you confronted her."

"Maybe if she understood the urgency, she'd help?" I pressed, desperation edging my tone.

"I'm not sure you'll get anything more from her than I did," Marie murmured. "In the end, I had to stop asking."

"We'd still like to try," Jessica said gently. "If you'll allow us. Please."

Marie sighed deeply, her eyes dropping to the floor as if balancing some invisible burden. "It's not that she won't talk to you... it's that she can't," she said, her words heavy with sadness. "She's bedridden with early-onset Alzheimer's. Some days, she doesn't even know who *I* am."

Jessica reached out and clasped Marie's hand tenderly. "Please, if this weren't so important, we wouldn't ask. If there's a chance, any chance at all, it could help us both find peace."

Marie looked at her, caught between loyalty and empathy. I could see the wariness in her eyes. I couldn't blame her. How would *I* feel if two strangers showed up, asking to speak to my ailing mother about long-buried secrets? But this was our last hope.

With a long, slow sigh, Marie nodded. "Come with me."

She led us down a narrow hallway to a blue door at the end, which opened onto a small landing with three rooms. "These are the bedrooms," Marie explained. From the outside, the flat seemed small and cramped, but the inside was surprisingly spacious, a concealed labyrinth of lives lived in hushed tones.

Marie paused, placing her hand gently on the door handle. "Before we go in," she said, her voice firm, "if she becomes upset at any point, it stops, and you leave. No ifs, ands, or buts—understood?"

I nodded quickly, and Jessica murmured, "Absolutely. We'll follow your lead."

Marie's eyes lingered on us, as if searching for any sign of uncertainty. Then, with a resigned nod, she turned the handle and pushed the door open.

The bedroom felt like a time capsule—a sanctuary where memories clung stubbornly, frozen in place. Faded wallpaper, once vibrant with delicate floral patterns, whispered of an age that had been full of colour. An antique dresser stood against one wall, its mirror reflecting fragments of a life slipping slowly away. Framed photographs, their silver tarnished with age, captured smiling faces long past, the expressions within them slowly fading, mirroring the fragile state of the woman who once filled this space with energy.

Cocooned under a dark blue quilt, the old lady stirred in her sleep, her thin, silver hair fanning across the pillow like scattered rivers of diamonds. Her face, etched deeply by laughter and tears, was a map of a life slowly being erased by the cruel illness afflicting her. Beams of soft sunlight slanted through the half-closed blinds, casting a latticework of light across the bed, a delicate prison that seemed to trap her frail figure within.

"She sleeps most of the day now," Marie whispered, her voice laced with a sadness that felt centuries old. "A carer comes by to check on her, to wash, feed, and give her medication. But the rest of the time… it's just me and the kids. You wouldn't believe it, seeing her now, but a few years ago, this fragile little thing was a strong, no-nonsense northern lass."

Jessica laid a comforting hand on Marie's shoulder, rubbing gently. "It must be so hard for you, juggling everything. The shop, the kids, your mum…"

Marie's shoulders sagged. "I was told to put her in a care home. They said it would be better for everyone. But I just couldn't… not after everything we've been through." Her voice trembled, caught between the memory of the strong, vibrant woman who raised her and the sad reality of the hollow figure lying in the bed before us.

With great care, Marie approached the bed and lowered herself onto its edge, taking her mother's hand with a tenderness born of unconditional love and loss. "Her name is Brenda," she whispered. "Most days, she thinks I'm her older sister, Janet, who she hasn't seen in thirty years. If she thinks you're someone she knows, just go along with it. It's easier that way."

Jessica and I moved closer, each step heavy with the solemnity of the moment. I'd never been in a situation like this—never been this close to such a raw portrayal of decline. My stomach tightened at the thought that I might be intruding, that my presence might disturb a delicate balance Marie was working so hard to preserve.

"Mum," Marie murmured, her voice soft, almost hesitant, "Mum, wake up. We've got some guests. They've come a long way to see you."

At first, Brenda responded with nothing more than a faint, tired groan, the kind that comes when someone is unwillingly pulled from sleep. Had she been dreaming? If so, what kind of memories lived behind those heavy eyelids? Who was I to force her to wake and face the confusion of a world she no longer recognised?

But slowly, with more gentle coaxing from Marie, Brenda's eyes fluttered open. She blinked, her eyes roaming the room with a dazed, unfocused look as if searching for some thread of familiarity to secure herself. Her thin fingers, clasped in Marie's, twitched slightly. "Janet, is that you?" Brenda asked, her voice filled with tentative hope as she squinted at us.

Marie's shoulders slumped slightly as she leaned in closer. "Yes, Brenda, it's me, Janet," she whispered, using the familiar deception. "I've brought some friends to see you."

Brenda's eyes, clouded with confusion, flitted from one face to the next, struggling to connect the fragments of memory. When she finally settled on me, a faint smile crept across her lips, though it was touched with uncertainty—like a glimpse of a long-forgotten dream that couldn't quite take shape.

"Georgie, is that you? Did you come back?" she asked, her voice trembling with a fragile hope. The vulnerability in her tone made my heart ache.

Marie leaned closer, her words barely more than a breath. "George was my dad's name. Go along with it. Remember what I said."

I hesitated, but then Brenda's hand stretched out towards me, trembling slightly, reaching for a ghost she thought had finally returned. Taking a deep breath, I moved closer and knelt beside her, gently taking her hand in mine.

"Yes, it's me... George," I murmured, forcing calm into my voice despite the knot in my throat. "I'm here."

Brenda's eyes lit up with a glimmer of something almost childlike—joy, disbelief, yearning—all blending together in a kaleidoscope of emotions. "You came back," she whispered, a tear sliding down her cheek. "You've been gone so long... I thought... I thought I'd never see you again."

Her words cut through me, raw and heartbreaking. I glanced quickly at Marie, who gave a subtle nod, silently urging me to continue the charade.

"Yes," I managed, my voice cracking. "I'm back now. I've missed you so much."

Brenda lifted her free hand and brushed it against my cheek, her touch light and uncertain. Her skin was cool and clammy, fragile as tissue paper. "Where did you go?" she asked, her eyes wide with the innocence of a child seeking reassurance.

How could I answer that? I had no idea what life she and George had shared, what vows had been broken, what hopes and desires had been left behind. I felt the weight of this woman's anguish pushing back at me, and the stakes of my lie suddenly felt enormous.

"I was away, love," I whispered gently. "But I always planned to come back."

"You left me alone with Marie for so long," she muttered, a hint of accusation in her tone, as if blaming me for abandoning her in a sea of loneliness.

Guilt that wasn't mine churned inside me, and I squeezed her hand tenderly. "I'm sorry," I whispered, feeling the words break apart as they left my mouth. "I didn't mean to be gone for so long, but I never stopped thinking about you. I just got lost, that's all. But I'm home now. I found my way back to you."

"No!" she cried suddenly, her voice sharp and trembling. Tears welled up in her eyes, her frail body shaking with the effort of holding on to whatever pain she felt. "You're lying. You never wanted to come back! You never loved me."

Her outburst sent a shock through the room. I saw Marie flinch, her face crumpling with the force of her mother's anguish. Panic clawed at me. How could I convince this woman—this stranger who had mistaken me for a ghost from her past—that I hadn't abandoned her?

"Shush," I murmured, reaching up to gently stroke her hair. It was thin and brittle, slipping through my fingers. "That's not true. I always wanted to come back. I always thought about you and Marie. Always."

The impetuosity in my voice was real—born not just from the need to soothe her, but from the fear that I was doing more harm than good. I glanced at Marie, searching her face for any sign of what to do next. She was frozen, her eyes shimmering with unshed tears.

"Please believe me," I whispered, leaning in closer, brushing my cheek against hers, a subtle act of compassion from the man she was yearning for. "I love you, Brenda. I never stopped loving you. I came back because I couldn't stay away from you."

Brenda's sobs quieted, and she smiled. Her eyes, though clouded with confusion, glimmered with something that resembled release. "I'm so happy you're back," she whispered.

"So am I," I murmured, squeezing her hand gently. "But... I need your help. Someone is looking for me, and I can't find them. Maybe you could help?"

Brenda's brow furrowed, her gaze drifting away as if searching through the fragmented corridors of her memory. The mention of needing help seemed to drag her further from the present, into a place where time was unreliable, and faces blurred into nothingness. For a second, I thought I'd lost her, that my only chance to get what I came for had disappeared for good.

Desperate, I reached into my pocket and pulled out the sketch Marie's father had drawn—the image of the girl with the unmistakable birthmark. "Do you remember this picture I drew?" I asked softly, leaning in so she could see it clearly.

Brenda's fragile smile crumbled away, her face becoming twisted with an emotion that seemed too strong for her frail frame to contain. "I remember her," she spat, her voice suddenly laced with bitterness. "She took you away from me."

My pulse quickened. "That's good," I blurted out before realising how wrong it sounded. "No, I mean—no one could keep me away from you. No one could ever take me from my Brenda."

A single tear slipped from Brenda's eye, trailing down the lines of her face and landing delicately on the pillow. "You should never have gone there," she grumbled, her voice breaking. "You should have stayed home. With me."

The pain in her voice was like a knife to the heart, each word cutting deeper. Every fibre of my being screamed at me to stop, to let her retreat into the comfort of her memories. But I couldn't. This was the closest we'd come to uncovering a truth.

Where did I go, my love?" I whispered, leaning in, desperate to pull her back to the present—to keep her anchored in the here and now, just a little longer.

Marie shifted beside me, her agitation evident. "Maybe we should stop," she whispered, her voice strained with worry. But Brenda's eyes flared with sudden intensity, her frail body trembling.

"The girl," Brenda whispered, her voice uncertain. "She took you away from me and our daughter. Marie doesn't understand; she keeps asking me about her, but I'll never tell. I'll never tell."

I glanced at Marie, whose face had gone pale, her hand pressed against her mouth as if holding back a cry. This was new. She was hearing things she hadn't known hadn't been told/

"I need to go back, my love," I murmured, trying to keep Brenda focused. "The girl has something of mine..." I scrambled for something plausible, something to keep her talking. "My wedding ring. I left it behind, and I don't want to lose it. But I can't remember where I left it, and I don't want the girl to find it."

"No, I won't say."

"Please, my love," I pleaded, keeping my tone soft, coaxing. "It's the ring you gave me on the happiest day of my life. I don't want it to be lost forever."

"You'll leave us again," she whimpered.

"No, I swear," I said fervently, holding her hand tight. "With all my heart, I'll come back to my family."

Brenda stared at me, her expression lost, torn between fear and longing. Then, slowly, she began to speak, her voice a thin, fragile whisper. "Gunnersby Woods... That's where you went that day. You asked me to go with you, but I said no. You came back and told me about the girl who let you draw her... but you were never the same after that. You should have stayed... you should have stayed."

Gunnersby Woods. My heart pounded. This was it; we were getting somewhere. "Who is she, my darling? Who is the girl I drew?"

But the question shattered something inside her. Brenda let out a loud wail, her body convulsing as sobs tore through her. "Why did you go?" she cried, her voice rising to a piercing shriek. "Why did you leave me? Why?"

"Brenda, please," I urged, imprudence overriding my compassion. "Who is she? What is her name?"

"Oh, my Marie," Brenda wept, her voice breaking, "I didn't want to tell you. I didn't want to hurt you..."

"Who is she Brenda?" I urged. "Who is the girl?"

But Brenda only began to hammer weakly at her own temple, her knuckles trembling, her face contorted in agony. "Why did you go to the woods?" she wailed, her sobs mingling with frantic, broken cries. "Why?"

"That's enough!" Marie's voice cut through the chaos as she stepped between me and her mother, her face full of anger. "You're hurting her. Stop."

"But I need to know her name!" I insisted, leaning around Marie, my voice rising. "Brenda, tell me—what was her name?"

But Brenda was lost, trapped in the storm of her grief. Her fingers continued to claw weakly at her head, her cries escalating into heart-wrenching howls that reverberated through the room, each one a stab of guilt and sorrow that cut into me.

"Just wait outside, both of you," Marie ordered, her tone brooking no argument.

"Come on, Chris," Jessica murmured, her hand wrapping around my arm, gently tugging me back.

I resisted, staring at Brenda's frail form, feeling helpless, torn. Then, slowly, I let Jessica pull me out of the room, my legs feeling like lead as we moved into the narrow hallway. Behind us, Brenda's grief-stricken cries filled the air, echoing around us—a haunting, keening sound that seemed to seep into my bones.

27

Marie joined us in the living room, her face pale and exhausted. She collapsed into an armchair and sighed heavily. "She's gone back to sleep," she murmured, shaking her head slowly. "I've never seen her like that before."

"I'm sorry," I said apologetically. "I shouldn't have pushed her."

"It's fine," Marie replied, but the stiffness in her voice and the way she rubbed her temples told a different story. She looked drained—like she'd aged years since we'd been here.

Jessica and I had been sitting on the sofa before Marie entered, whispering to each other as we tried to piece together Brenda's fragmented words. But without the full story, we were stumbling in the dark. Now that Marie was with us again, it was clear she held the key to filling in the gaps.

"That must've been hard for you to see," Jessica said gently, reaching out to place a hand on Marie's arm.

"I've had that sketchbook for years, and only now… only now do I hear that girl was the reason Dad... the reason he left us." Her voice cracked slightly on the last few words, and she blinked rapidly, as if trying to dispel the memories.

"You recognised what your mother meant when she mentioned Gunnersby Wood?" I asked cautiously.

She swallowed, composing herself. "I know it well," she said, her tone tinged with bittersweet nostalgia. "Dad took me there a lot. It was... his sanctuary. Out of all the places around here, it was his favourite spot to sit and sketch. He called it his *natural muse*. When your brother came through the village, looking for inspiration for his music, I pointed him there. And from what he told me, it was perfect. But that girl…" She shook her head, troubled, as if confronting a recollection she'd tried to bury. "I understand now what Mum meant when she said Dad had changed."

"What happened with your father?" I asked.

"That's a long story," Marie replied, "and not a happy one."

"Maybe if you tell us more about him, we can help make sense of it," Jessica suggested.

Marie let out a long, tired breath and nodded. "Dad moved to Little Ashton in the late '70s. He'd worked on the gas rigs for a while but wanted to settle down, get his feet back on solid ground. There was no work where he grew up, and though he could've joined his father's running the family fish business, he couldn't stand the idea of coming home every night smelling like cod. He wanted something that was his own, away from his family. He was always a bit of a dreamer... a rebel."

She paused, lost in the memory, a faint smile touching her lips.

A sudden knock at the door interrupted her. A young man with cropped hair poked his head in, glancing around uncertainly. "Is it okay to open up, Marie?" he asked, his voice soft, careful not to intrude.

"Go ahead, Luke," she said, waving him off absent-mindedly. "If you need anything, just call."

As he left, Marie shifted in her seat, collecting herself. "Sorry, where was I?" she asked, looking slightly disoriented.

"Your father moved here to find work," Jessica prompted gently.

Marie's eyes softened, and the faint smile returned. "That's right. He had no plan, no clue what he was going to do. He just left it up to chance. Closed his eyes, stuck a pin in a map of England, and that's how he ended up here. Never even looked at where the pin landed until he'd already packed his bags and said goodbye to his family. And then he left, without knowing a thing about this place. His family wasn't exactly thrilled—especially Grandad, who wanted him to stay and run the fish shop. But Dad had bigger dreams."

"Did he find work when he got here?" Jessica asked.

Marie shifted in her chair, a small, bittersweet smile flickering across her lips as she delved into the reminiscences. "He managed, but it wasn't easy at first. This place back then—it was like stepping back in time. Rose-covered cottages, garden parties, fairs on the village green. Quaint but quiet, especially for someone searching for work. But Dad had something others didn't—a big personality. People were wary of this cheerful Scotsman who'd just appeared out of nowhere, asking for jobs, but he quickly became known around town. He made money doing whatever he could—farm work, local handyman jobs, tending bars—anywhere that needed an extra set of hands."

"Did he ever think of leaving, finding something more permanent in a bigger city?" I asked.

"Not once," Marie said, shaking her head firmly. "He loved this place, and he loved the people. His family kept calling, asking him to come back and reconsider, but his answer was always the same—he was happy here. Eventually, they accepted it. If he ever found himself short, they'd send a bit of money down, but he never asked. He was determined to make it on his own terms."

Marie's eyes drifted to the window, as if she could still see the village of her childhood in the reflection. By the 1980s, she explained, the town had started to expand, drawing in visitors and new residents who saw it as an entryway to the countryside. One of those new faces was her mother.

"She was from Danwich—the larger town nearby—and had come here for a weekend away with some friends," Marie continued, her voice softening. "They met in a pub. According to Dad, it was love at first sight. He always said that the moment he saw her, the whole room seemed to shine. They talked all night, and he even walked her back to her guesthouse in the rain, holding his coat over her head to keep her dry. When she left, they talked on the phone nearly every night and saw each other as often as they could. Two months later, she moved in with him. Shortly after, they were married."

"That's so sweet," Jessica murmured, though I could feel my own impatience rising. This wasn't the information I was after, but I bit my tongue. Marie needed to tell her story, and I had to let her.

"Once the town started growing, Dad noticed a rising demand for camping gear. That's when he came up with the idea to open this shop. It became an obsession—his one shot at building something real, instead of scraping by with odd jobs. He saved every penny he earned, working double shifts at the bar, taking on extra gigs wherever he could. Mum was a nurse, working at a hospital a few towns over. She picked up every bit of overtime she could manage. They were so close… until I came along."

Her voice stretched as if each word was pulling her deeper into a realm of thought she hadn't revisited in years.

"All that money they'd put aside for the store. It vanished in a heartbeat—spent on baby clothes, bottles, a pram… everything a new family needs. Mum told me once that dad was devastated, but he never showed it. Can you imagine that? After all those years of planning and hard work, he lost his dream overnight. But he never let me feel like I was a burden. Not once."

She glanced around the room, as if looking for her father's ghost in every corner.

"If your dad spent all his savings," I asked gently, "how did he manage to open the shop?"

"Your guess is as good as mine. One day, out of the blue, he told Mum he had a plan and needed to go to London for a few days. She wasn't happy about it, not with money so scarce and him gone for days without income, but… Dad had a way of making you believe everything would be fine."

"Most dads do," I murmured, thinking of my own.

Marie nodded, her voice dropping to a whisper. "When he came back three days later, he had the cash for the down payment and enough to stock the shelves. Mum was furious—demanded to know where he got that much money. She grilled him for days. But he swore it wasn't a loan, and that no one could ever come asking for it back. A few weeks later, the shop was open."

A heavy silence settled over the three of us. That kind of money didn't just appear, and whatever strings he'd pulled to get it must have left a mark on him.

"You might wonder why I'm telling you all this," Marie said, her eyes locking onto mine. "But I need you to understand what kind of man my dad was. He'd do anything for his family. So when he started acting strange, it was… it was so jarring. So out of character.".".

She took a deep breath, gathering herself. "The shop was a success. Tourists flooded in every summer, looking for hiking and camping gear. Dad hired help, and for the first time, he was able to do what he truly loved. He'd spend whole days in the woods, sketching and wandering. Sometimes he'd take me along, hoisting me up onto his shoulders, whistling old tunes as we hiked. I remember the way he'd wink at me, like we shared some secret with the trees. Those were the happiest days of my life."

Marie paused, her eyes growing distant. "As I got older, the forest lost its magic for me. I was a teenager, wrapped up in my own world, and Dad started going out alone more often. He'd disappear with his sketchbook for hours, but he always came back the same—smiling, eyes sparkling like he'd found something extraordinary out there."

She took a shaky breath. "Then, one day, everything changed."

"What happened?" I prompted.

"He went out like usual, but he was gone far longer than expected. Mum was frantic. She thought he'd gotten lost or hurt. I begged her to let me and my friends go look for him, we knew the woods like the back of our hands, and could search in places people didn't know about, but she refused, scared that we might share whatever fate dad she believed dad had suffered. Hours passed, and just when she was about to call the police, the front door swung open. He walked in at eight o'clock, as if nothing had happened."

Marie's fingers clenched around the arm of the chair, her knuckles turning white. "Mum was livid. She laid into him, demanding to know where he'd been. And all he said was, 'Time got away from me.' Claimed he'd been sketching. But Mum didn't believe it for a second."

"And after that?" Jessica asked.

Marie nodded slowly. "The next day, things seemed normal... at least to us. But he was different. It started small—mood swings, irritability. He'd wake up either sad or seething with anger, and it was like he wasn't fully present anymore. He'd sleep in late, leaving Mum to run the shop alone. And when he did get up, the only thing he wanted to do was head back into the woods. Sketching was the only thing that seemed to bring him peace."

"But it didn't help, did it?" I murmured.

She shook her head, her voice trembling. "No. Things kept getting worse. Some days, he wouldn't get out of bed at all—just lay there, staring blankly at the ceiling. And when he did try to work, it was like... like he wasn't really there. He'd forget the simplest things—orders, deliveries, people's names. And then came the outbursts."

Marie's grip on the chair tensed, a flash of anger burned in her eyes. "He'd lash out over the smallest things—shouting at us, berating the staff. He'd accuse us of betraying him, of breaking promises none of us had made. Said we were all against him."

"It got so bad, it was like *he* had Alzheimer's—drifting in and out of reality, forgetting things that mattered. But the worst... the worst was when he forgot about my husband's funeral—his own son-in-law's funeral. Can you imagine?"

Everything seemed to shrink around us, Marie's grief closing us in, thick and suffocating, until a soft cough echoed from her mother's room. We all tensed, glancing towards the door, half-expecting Brenda to burst in, ready to silence us for digging up these painful ghosts.

"Did he ever see a doctor?" I whispered.

"No," she replied. "He refused—sometimes *violently*. And then... everything changed again." She paused, gathering the strength to go on. "I was in the back, packing items for delivery, when I heard them fighting upstairs. My parents never argued like that—ever. But that day, Mum was screaming, demanding to know who *this girl* was. Why he was so obsessed with finding her in the woods. And he... he just kept crying, saying that if he didn't find her, something inside him would... eat him alive."

Tears welled in Marie's eyes, and Jessica quickly handed her a tissue. She dabbed at her face, struggling to keep herself together.

"What did you do?" Jessica asked, her voice full of sympathy.

Marie let out a bitter laugh. "I ran up there to stop it. The shop was open, customers were coming in, and the poor shop assistant was left to deal with everything. Poor kid," she added with a sad smile. "But when I got upstairs, it was already over. Mum came out, apologised, and told me to leave him be—to let him calm down. I asked her about the woman they were arguing over, but she brushed it off as a misunderstanding, told me to go back downstairs and look after the store. And I... I listened. I didn't check on him. I'll never forgive myself for that. Because by that afternoon... it was too late."

The guilt etched on Marie's face was raw and familiar, the kind that lingers years later.

"Later that day, in the middle of selling a tent to a customer, Dad got a phone call. When it ended, he just placed his personal items on the counter, grabbed his sketch pad, and walked out. The customer told us later that dad had been happily chatting, talking about the best camping gear for a two-day hike. Then, suddenly, his face went pale. He excused himself and walked out, leaving the assistant to finish the sale."

Her voice hesitated, breaking under the burden of the next sentence.

"A few hours later, some local kids found him... floating face down in the river outside of town."

"I'm so sorry," Jessica whispered.

"The police found no signs of foul play," Marie said. "They said he must've slipped off the bank and fallen into the water. But I couldn't believe it. Dad was a strong swimmer—there's no way he could have drowned in just a few feet of water. But Mum... she just wanted to accept it, to move on. She seemed almost... unsurprised. For her sake, I let it go. Those last few weeks had drained her so much. I didn't want to make it harder."

Her hands stiffened around the crumpled tissue. "But do you want to know the strangest part?" Her stare flicked between us, haunted. "When the police found his body, they also found his sketchbook. It was lying on the riverbank, perfectly dry, with the page open... to the face of *that* girl."

Jessica and I exchanged a glance, the weight of Marie's words sinking in like a stone plunging into deep water. We didn't need to say anything—the truth, or some dark shape of it, hovered between us.

"Mum wanted me to burn it," she continued. "But I couldn't. Watching him sketch brought him so much joy... I wanted to hold on to that, to keep that part of him alive. Mum saw how much it meant to me, so she shoved it up in the attic, hoping I'd forget. And for a while... I did. Until last year, when I found it again and asked her about the girl. But by then..." She trailed off. "By then, the Alzheimer's had already started to take her."

"But you think that girl was responsible?" I asked.

"For years, I convinced myself that Dad was having an affair. I thought all those long walks into the woods were to see *her*—that he was unhappy, looking for an escape." Her look toughened, a simmering anger raging. "But Dad loved us too much for that. And now, today, you show me a picture of *that* girl—the same bloody girl—with your brother."

"And he died too," I said, contemplating the thought hanging in the air. I wasn't sure what else to say. What was I supposed to do with this information? File it away under 'faerie stories for the deceased'?

"Whoever she is, she's dangerous," Marie murmured, leaning forward, her elbows resting on her knees. "If what my mother said is true, if Gunnersby Woods—and that girl—had something to do with Dad's decline, then I need to know why. And if I somehow... *somehow*... pointed your brother down the same path "

"No, stop," I snapped, my voice sharper than I'd intended. "Adam was his own man. He chose to end his life because he couldn't bear it any longer. Don't you *dare* put this on yourself. We don't even know if that girl had anything to do with what happened to either your father or my brother."

Marie's eyes narrowed, dark with suppressed rage. "Then give me a better explanation," she challenged, her face unyielding.

I stood up, a surge of anxiety in my chest "Maybe you're right. Maybe your dad *was* having an affair," I said, pacing the small room. "People change. Maybe he wanted out, no matter how much we want to believe he didn't."

Jessica and Marie watched me patiently, their eyes following every restless step.

"Or maybe the truth is simpler—your father was overwhelmed," I continued. "There was stress of running a shop and providing for a family... it sounds to me like he was slipping into depression. Anyway, if what your mum told me is true—that the girl had some power over your father, or if there *is* something strange at play—then tell me this: What does this girl gain from your father's death? From Adam's?"

Neither of them spoke. No one had an answer.

"And if she met *both* of them here, in this tiny, middle-of-nowhere village, why doesn't anyone know who she is?" My frustration bubbled over, my voice rising as I felt the fragments of our fragile theory start to slip away. "Why doesn't anyone *recognise* her?"

Jessica placed a calming hand shoulder. "Chris, quiet—Brenda," she whispered, nodding towards the closed door where Marie's mother rested.

"Sorry," I muttered, forcing myself to take a deep breath, shifting back to Marie as she brushed away a stray tear. "Listen," I said, lowering my voice. "I'm sorry. I'm not angry at you. But this... this whole thing is impossible to make sense of. We're talking about a girl who seems to appear, ruin lives, and disappear again without a trace. You think she's dangerous—I believe you. But why? Why would she do this? What's the *point*?"

"I'm just as lost as you are," she murmured, a hint of frustration mingled with sympathy. She stood abruptly and disappeared into her office. I heard the metallic click of a filing cabinet being unlocked, followed by the soft shuffle of papers. When she reappeared, she was carrying a large, rolled-up map. She unfurled it across the table, revealing a detailed layout of Little Ashton and the surrounding woods.

Her finger traced a path to a small, green patch deep within the dense forest.

"But if there's one place that ties my dad and your brother together," she said, "it's this." She tapped her finger against a tiny clearing. "They both ended up here, alone."

Jessica and I leaned closer, our eyes fixated on the map, staring at the sprawling green area nestled in the heart of the woods.

"You think she lives out there?" I asked, doing my best to temper my scepticism.

Marie shook her head. "Of course not. There's nothing out there but trees, the glade, and the river that winds through here." She drew her finger along a thin blue line snaking its way through the forest. "It starts near the town and flows right to this spot." Her finger stopped at a small symbol near the clearing. "There's an old, abandoned cabin just off the glade. It belonged to the local groundskeeper."

"Lord Ashby," she added, glancing up as if gauging our reactions. "He owned these woods centuries ago, but after his family line died out, the land reverted to the townsfolk. The cabin's been deserted ever since. No one goes near it except the odd hiker. So no, I don't think she's hiding out there. But what else do we have to go on?"

"We need to check it out," Jessica insisted, nudging me lightly. "Together."

I scoffed, the sound devoid of humour. "You want us to go searching through the woods—for what, exactly? Some ghost story?"

Jessica's eyes softened. "I don't know what's out there. But Adam and George both ended up in the same place, drawn by something. Isn't that enough to at least *try*?"

"Yeah, you're right." Turning to Marie, I asked, "How hard is it to get there?"

Marie leaned back in her chair, her brow furrowed in thought. "It's not difficult if you know where to look. I gave your brother directions, but I was shocked when he found the glade on his first attempt. It's easy to miss if you're not careful."

"Could you draw us a more detailed map?" I asked, feeling the first flicker of determination break through the fog of confusion.

Marie's lips curved into a small, determined smile. "I can do better than that." She paused, looking between us. "Normally, it's a 90-minute hike following the riverbank to reach the edge of that part of the forest, but I can drive you closer. There's a gravel trail that goes deeper in. I can drop you off halfway, near an old logging road. From there, it's only about a half-hour trek on foot to reach the glade."

"That would be great. When can we go?" I asked.

"There's just one problem," Marie said, hesitating as she glanced out the window. "I don't know if you've checked the weather, but we're expecting heavy rain for the next forty-eight hours. You really don't want to be hiking through the forest in that. The river floods easily, and it can cut off parts of the trail. We'd be risking it if we tried to go now."

I tensed. Another delay. My frustration must've shown, because Marie quickly continued.

"Thank you," I said. "That's more than I could ask for."

Marie gave a small, half-hearted smile. "If I thought I could talk you out of this, I would," she admitted. "But part of me needs to know the truth, too. Just… be careful, okay?"

"We will," Jessica assured her, her voice steady. No one could guarantee safety, not when we had no idea what we were stepping into.

We exchanged a few more words of gratitude before Marie lead us out of the flat through the back. The moment we stepped outside, the first cold drops of rain splattered against my skin. The storm wasn't waiting; it was already rolling in.

Jessica pulled her jacket around herself, glancing up at the darkening sky. "Looks like we're in for it."

"Yeah," I muttered, glancing back at the shop. Marie stood by the doorway, watching us leave. She looked small and fragile, framed by the warm light of the store. I lifted a hand in farewell, and she offered a strained smile in return before shutting the door.

We made our way to the car, the rain picking up as we walked. When we reached it, we were already damp. I slid into the driver's seat; the windscreen immediately spattered with heavy droplets. Jessica settled in beside me, rubbing her hands together for warmth.

"Well, we've got two days to kill," she said with a wry smile. "How do you plan to pass the time?"

I started the engine, staring out at the curtain of rain already blurring the road ahead. "No idea. Waiting isn't exactly my strong suit."

"No kidding." She let out a soft laugh.

Part 4

Tales and Legends

28

Letter from Adam – dated 26th May 2019

Hey brother,
Though I told you that I wasn't sure whether I would do so again, I finally gave in and joined my new village friends on another of their hikes. And yes, they are exactly as I describe them—friends. It's strange, after all the networking and showmanship in London, to be around people who honestly have no interest in influencing me, either personally or creatively. They don't care what I write or how I perform; they're just interested in me—what I'm doing, how my day's been, if I've seen the weather reports. Sure, they've all got their quirks and flaws—don't we all?—but they seem like good people. Especially Marie, who's become someone I can have deeper conversations with. And even then, my music isn't the focus; it's about two people discussing whatever life is holding up to them to view. I assume she's checked out my stuff online, but whether she likes it or not, she's too polite to say, and I don't feel the need to ask. It's refreshing.

Sorry, I'm rambling. Let me get back to the point.

During the walk, Claude asked if I'd be interested in doing a small set for a special event at his restaurant. Apparently, some folks booked out the place for a 50th birthday party, but the musician he'd hired bailed at the last minute. I was hesitant at first—didn't think anything could get me back on stage just yet—but Claude's been good to me, and I wanted to help him out. I warned him that I haven't played covers in a while, but he just smiled and said not to worry—it was only for a couple of hours, mostly as background music. He even insisted on paying me what he had promised the other guy, plus a bit extra for stepping in last-minute. After a bit of back-and-forth, I agreed. I'm still living off savings, so some pocket money wouldn't hurt.

We set up a time for me to check out the venue, and I was surprised to find it much larger than I'd anticipated. His restaurant is called 'The Scallop'. As the name suggests, it's a fish restaurant, yet it felt more like a modern style gourmet place, with minimalist décor, and polished concrete floors, and a small, temporary, raised stage area set up in the corner for me and my acoustic guitar—no need for soundchecks or anything complicated; I just had to turn up and play. Easy enough for a night's work.

He asked for a photo to put in the window, and online, to let his guests know who'd be performing. That's when I hesitated. It felt wrong to use any of my old promo shots. It's like the person I was before I came here doesn't match who I'm becoming. The man in those photos—polished, posed, styled—isn't me anymore. I didn't want that version to overshadow who I am now. So, I told Claude, I'd send him something new.

The only person I could think to ask for help was Marie. She'd mentioned during one of our meetups that she handles all the promotional shots for her shop. I gave her a call, and although she wasn't sure, worried she wouldn't do it justice, I told her it didn't need to be anything fancy. It's not like Claude's restaurant is the Royal Albert Hall. As long as I was in the picture, that's all that mattered.

So, during her lunch break, we headed up to Castle Hill for a quick photo session—me with my guitar, Marie with her camera. The sun was out, and the recently cut grass was perfect for capturing some moody yet upbeat shots. It felt good—different—doing it in such a relaxed setting, without a professional photographer barking orders: "look this way," "tilt your head," "no, not like that!" Do you remember that shoot for The Hanged Man EP? What was that photographer's name again? Something O'Reilly? I remember he wanted to pose me with flamingos—flamingos, of all things—because he thought they symbolised balance and serenity or some nonsense. We ended up getting drunk, and he tried explaining the whole concept to me in a blur of absinthe-fuelled artspeak. In the end, I ditched the idea and went with a straightforward Hanged Man tarot card cover.

This was nothing like that. It was just the two of us chatting and laughing, Marie snapping shots while I played random chords, experimenting with different angles until we both agreed we'd found something decent. I sent the best photo to Claude. It's a simple shot—me sitting on a low on the grass with the castle ruins in the background, the sun dipping behind me, casting everything in a soft light. It felt… right, in a non-artsy way. I'm curious to see if it's already up when I head over to play.

Sorry, I'm digressing again. Back to the shoot.

We were finishing when Marie received a call from one of her suppliers and stepped away to take it. As I watched her walk a little way down the hill, chatting with her back to me, things took a turn for the weird.

"Hello," a soft voice whispered from behind me.

Startled, I spun around to see a young woman standing a few paces away. She couldn't have been older than her early twenties, with long blonde hair that fell in loose waves around her shoulders. She wore a simple white summer dress that swayed gently in the breeze, and white sandals, making her look almost out of place against the rugged backdrop of Castle Hill. But it wasn't her hair, or the dress, or even the way she seemed to have appeared out of thin air that caught my attention. It was the birthmark.

The blood-red mark covered the area around her left eye, almost like an upturned handprint against her pale skin, vivid and stark against her otherwise flawless complexion. And those eyes—green, impossibly green, like deep moss under sunlight. I found myself staring before I could stop.

"Hello," I mumbled, trying hard to pull my eyes away from that crimson stain.

"Who are you?" she asked, her voice soft yet carrying a strange resonance, like a child's whisper echoing in a cavern.

"My name's Adam," I replied, awkwardly extending my hand. "And you are?"

She looked at my hand but made no move to take it.

"Is that your woman?" she asked, tilting her head slightly, nodding towards Marie, who still stood a distance away, unaware of our conversation.

"Marie? No, no—she's just a good friend," I answered quickly, feeling oddly self-conscious under her scrutiny.

For some reason, she giggled—a light, almost musical sound that made the hairs on the back of my neck stand up.

"You were laughing together, what were you doing?" she asked, stepping closer and starting to walk slowly around me in a circle.

"Marie's just taking some photos of me," I explained, turning to keep her in view. "I'm a musician and—"

"You play music?" she interrupted, her curiosity seemingly piqued.

"Yeah." I lifted my guitar slightly, trying to seem casual. "This isn't just a prop," I sniggered nervously.

"What kind do you play?" She asked, squinting one eye against the suns glare.

"Oh, that's a loaded question for a musician. I dabble in a bit of everything," I said with a half-smile.

"Can you play something for me now?" She tilted her head, blocking the sun with her hand.

"Right now? Here?" I hesitated, glancing around. "I don't know… but I'm playing a small gig in the village in a couple of days, at a place called The Scallop. If you're interested, I—"

"I don't go into the village," she interrupted, shaking her head emphatically. She spun on her toes, almost dancing with a lightness to her step. "But I do like it up here."

"It is beautiful," I agreed, watching her twirl. "I come up here a lot—sometimes I hike through the woods nearby."

"I know," she said, giggling softly. "I've seen you there… with the others."

Her words caught me off guard. "You've seen me? If you'd like, we meet up once a week. You're welcome to join us," I offered, still puzzled by what she found so amusing.

She shook her head slowly, an impish grin on her lips. "I don't really get on with many people."

"That's a shame," I replied, genuinely meaning it.

"But I'd like to go with you," she murmured, stepping closer and poking me lightly with her finger, a playful, intense gesture.

"Oh, um… that would be—" I started, but before I could finish, Marie's voice called out sharply from behind.

"Adam!"

"See you around, Adam," the girl called faintly, her voice carrying on the breeze as she walked away, heading back toward the castle ruins.

I turned just as Marie approached, her phone now tucked back into her pocket. "Okay, the call's done. If we're finished here, I need to get back to the store—lunch hour's over for me, I'm afraid."

"Yes, of course. Let's head back," I replied, still dazed.

Marie must have noticed the look on my face because she frowned slightly. "Are you okay?"

"Yeah, yeah, I'm fine. I was just talking to…" I hesitated, glancing back up the hill. "Well, she didn't give me her name, but she was standing right there—" I turned to point, but the girl was gone. There wasn't a trace of her white dress against the landscape. Just the empty slope and the quiet stone walls of the castle beyond.

"Who were you talking to?" Marie asked with a playful chuckle.

"She was right here… and now she's gone," I murmured, more to myself than to Marie.

"Ooh, a mystery girl," she teased lightly.

We made our way back down the hill, her words hanging in the air. A mystery girl. It sounded ridiculous, like something out of a clichéd novel. But it didn't feel that way. It felt… significant.

I tried describing her to Marie—her height, her white dress, the vivid birthmark that looked almost painted on—but she just shook her head. No one like that lived in the village. She seemed baffled, and I soon gave up talking about it. Trying to explain it made her feel less real, almost as if I'd imagined it, and I didn't want that. For some inexplicable reason, it felt wrong to share the encounter, yet the whole thing lingered like a vivid dream that refused to fade with the dawn.

That was a few days ago, and even now, I find it hard not to think about her, but far harder to speak about it. Even just writing this letter feels strange, like my hand is willing me to write about everything *but* her. I want to see her again. I don't know why, but I do.

The weather's been awful—grey skies, constant drizzle—so I haven't made it back up the hill since that day. But I'll go back soon, that's for sure. Hopefully, she'll be there. Maybe she'll even spot me first, save me the effort of searching.

Anyway, I need to stop rambling. I've got to prep a few songs for the gig tonight, and the rain's let up just enough for me to make it to Claude's without getting drenched. Wish me luck, bruv.

Speak soon,
Adam

29

Letter from Adam – dated 11th June 2019

Hey Chris,
It finally happened. After countless failed attempts to track her down, just when I'd all but given up hope—she found me.

I'd just finished my gig at Claude's restaurant. It went better than I ever could've imagined. The nerves were brutal at first—understandable, considering it was my first live performance in over six months. For the first twenty minutes, I felt like I was in a vice, but then something shifted. I started playing the old covers Dad and I used to jam to, and everything just clicked. The crowd joined in, singing along to the songs they knew. It's funny how a few Elvis and Rolling Stones tunes can light up a room full of well-fed strangers. Marie was there for support, and after the show, Claude treated us to a free meal to celebrate.

The next morning, I was still riding the high. The sky was overcast, but the warmth lingered—perfect for summer clothes. So, I threw on a pair of shorts and headed to my favourite spot in the woods, hoping to "play the music out of me." I hadn't felt that kind of rush since… well, since long before Emily left, and I didn't want it to disappear too soon. Do you remember that day, after one of my gigs, when I was so wired, I couldn't stop playing? I kept going until the early hours while you slept on the sofa. It was like that—mania, the professionals call it.

So there I was, guitar slung over my shoulder, humming those 70s hits from the night before, following the river that snakes up to the forest's edge. It's a nearly two-hour trek for me, mostly along the stream, but I didn't care how long it took. I felt like I'd been plugged into some kind of positivity machine, surging with so much joy I could've run a marathon.

And then, I saw her.

There's a point where the river curves into a farmer's field. An old stone bridge arches over the water, connecting the path to a foot trail that winds through the wheat. That's where I found her—sitting on the riverbank in the same white dress, holding a blue, long-stemmed flower to her nose. When she turned to me, her long blonde hair falling over her shoulders, it was like the world shifted.

"Hello, Adam," she said, waving casually, as if we'd known each other for years.

"Hi," I managed, my voice coming out awkward and boyish.

"I've been waiting to bump into you again," she purred. "Come, sit with me."

Four simple words, yet they felt like a command. I couldn't have resisted even if I'd tried. I set my guitar down and joined her on the riverbank. Had she been sitting here alone, waiting just for me? There was no one else around. Only the quiet murmur of the river and the occasional call of a moorhen broke the silence.

"Where are you going?" she asked, lightly tapping my knee with the flower.

"There's a spot in the forest where I like to play," I said, lifting my guitar as proof.

"Is it the place with the log surrounded by white flowers?" she asked, tilting her head.

I nodded, my pulse quickening. "How do you know?"

"I know it well," she murmured, glancing toward the distant treeline. "I go there myself sometimes, but I'm not sure you'll make it before the rain comes."

I looked up, searching the sky for a sign. But there was nothing. No hint of dark clouds gathering, just a heavy, humid stillness and a soft breeze drifting through the wheat.

"Those of us who've lived here all our lives know how the weather works around these parts," she giggled, reading the question forming on my lips. "You can trust us. If we say rain is on its way, then so it will be."

Her certainty caught me off guard, though I had no reason to doubt her. Country folk have a strange sense for these things, reading the world in ways city boys like me can't. They taste it in the air, feel it in the way the wind shifts, or the way the cows settle in the fields. They can predict everything, from a sudden downpour to the birth of a calf days before it happens.

"I'll concede to your superior knowledge," I said, bowing my head.

"Instead of heading to the glade, why don't you play for me instead?" she suggested, her gaze holding mine. A playful smile tugged at her lips.

"Here?" I glanced around, feeling the absurdity of it. We were in the middle of a field, with nothing but the whispering wheat and the quiet river to witness.

"Why not?" she teased, leaning in just enough for me to catch the faint scent of wildflowers clinging to her. "You were going to play alone in the trees, weren't you?" Her voice softened, dropping to a conspiratorial whisper as she moved closer, her breath warm against my skin. "We're alone now."

My pulse quickened. I could almost feel the words tangling around me like invisible strings, drawing me in. It felt so foolish sitting in a field, serenading a girl I barely knew, and yet...

There was something in the way she looked at me, a quiet, unspoken challenge. Like she wanted to see if I'd refuse, if I'd shy away.

"Okay," I said, swallowing hard. I swung the guitar around, settling it on my knee. She leaned back, giving me space, her eyes never leaving mine as she sat gracefully on the bank, folding her hands in her lap like she was settling in for a private concert.

"Is there anything in particular you'd like to hear?" I asked.

"Surprise me with whatever is in your heart," she answered, "something you alone own within you."

I strummed a few chords, testing the strings, feeling the familiar innate thrill. And then, without thinking too much about it, I began to play.

For the first time since I was a teenager, I played one of my oldest songs—one I'd buried deep because of the pain it always brought up. You know the one—the one I wrote right after Dad died. Why I chose that song, I couldn't tell you. But instead of the usual fear it evoked, I felt nothing but peace. Each note I plucked seemed to resonate off those same invisible walls, as if the air itself was humming in harmony with me.

I closed my eyes, trying to block out her intensity. It made me nervous, almost afraid of being judged. I didn't want to disappoint her. But then, as I played, I heard it—soft and haunting—she started to hum along. I should have been startled. After all, how could she know a melody I'd only ever played for myself? But it didn't cross my mind. I was lost, my heartbeat merging with the song's melancholy rhythm.

When I finally opened my eyes, she was swaying, moving in perfect sync with me, as if we'd rehearsed this a hundred times before.

As the final chord lingered in the air, I let out a breath and slumped beside her, exhausted but exhilarated.

"Wow," I gasped. "Just… wow."

"Did that feel good?" she asked, her smile deep and inviting.

"Better than good. It was… Christ, it was mind-blowing."

"I liked it," she said simply. "What was it about?"

"I wrote it when I was younger. It's about anguish and self-hate. I was a bit of an emo kid back then."

"Emo kid?" she repeated, her brow furrowing. "I don't know what that means."

"You don't?" I stared at her, taken aback. "Where have you been living these past few years?"

She gave a casual shrug, her eyes dancing playfully. "Oh, here and there. I don't meet many people. And the ones I do… they're not as creative as you." She nudged me with her shoulder, teasing.

"Stop it," I chuckled, nudging her back. "You're gonna make me blush. You must have met plenty of people like me."

"I've known many," she murmured wistfully. "But only a few I liked. And not everyone can dance with me."

I leaned in, feeling a sudden, inexplicable spark between us. "You know something? You're not like any girl I've ever met."

She laughed, a sound so sweet and pure it felt like aural honey. "And you're not like any boy I've ever met."

A cool drop of water landed on my hand, then another, and another. One raindrop struck the guitar string with a soft, wet twang. I looked up.

"Shit," I muttered, scrambling to get the guitar back in its case as the rain began falling harder. Thunder rumbled ominously in the distance. "Well, there goes the idea of running to the woods for cover. We don't want to be out there when the lightning starts. Come on, follow me…" I reached out my hand, expecting some resistance, but to my surprise, she took it without hesitation.

"Where are we going?" she asked as the rain turned into a downpour, soaking through our clothes in seconds.

"If we jog, we can make it back to town before it gets too bad. You can dry off at mine."

She suddenly let go of my hand, her face shifting to something guarded, almost serious.

"No," she said softly, taking a step back. "I need to get home. I'll be missed soon."

The warmth of her hand in mine had made my heart race, but the way she pulled back left me reeling.

"Can I see you again?" I asked, as the rain began to fall heavier.

"Of course," she replied, stepping closer. She kissed me lightly on the cheek and her touch lingered, a sensation so tender it almost hurt. "I *want* to see you again."

"When?" I asked, my pulse pounding, desperate for something concrete to hold on to.

"I'll find you," she replied, already turning away. Her hair, slick with rain, clung to her neck and shoulders, the soaked dress moulding itself to her skin and leaving very little to the imagination. She wasn't wearing a bra, and the sight of her like that—half bare underneath the fabric—ignited something in me. Heat surged through me; a flash of raw want so intense that it bordered on painful.

And then, just like that, she was gone—disappearing around the bridge, leaving me standing there, soaked to the bone, alone.

The walk back was hell. Rain hammered down, cold and relentless, the wind biting through my clothes. But none of that mattered. I was burning from the inside out. More turned on than I'd ever been in my life, my mind and body wound tight. No matter how hard I tried, I couldn't shut it off. Couldn't dull the ache. When I got home, I was so worked up I had to take an ice-cold shower just to try and cool down, but even that barely helped.

I have no idea when I'll see her again, and it's driving me mad. Every hour that passes when I don't see her, it just makes me want her more. It's like she's embedded herself in my head, and I can't shake her loose. I'm half-tempted to find someone, anyone, for a one-night stand, just to take the edge off. Maybe then I'll get some peace. But deep down, I know it wouldn't be enough. I don't want anyone else. I want her.

Bruv, this girl... she's something else. Just thinking about her makes my head ache. I can't stand the idea of not being near her. She's awakened something in me I thought was dead—something that feels like a soul.

I need to stop. Writing about her is doing my head in. I'm gonna try to pour this into music, see if that helps clear my mind. Got some ideas for a song, and yeah, it's about her.

Love ya, bruv.
Adam

30

Before we'd driven off, we quickly popped back into Marie's shop and take some time to stock up on gear for the trek ahead. I grabbed a second pair of hiking boots, ones sturdy enough for the dry paths but with enough grip for the slick, wet woodland, along with a heavy-duty backpack and a waterproof jacket. Jessica was more selective, settling on just a few essentials: new hiking socks and a bright pink fisherman's hat. She insisted she didn't need it, but the tiny yellow cat stitched on the front was too charming for her to resist.

Leaving the stored, we quickly ducked into a bookstore nearby to pick up some reading material and enough snacks to see us through a couple of days holed up indoors. Back in our room, we sorted everything into two neat piles—one for our stay indoors, the other for the hike.

Jessica held up the oversized bag of salt and vinegar crisps I'd tossed into the basket, shaking it lightly. "You know, none of these are going to be good for my figure," she teased, raising an eyebrow.

"Your figure will be the least of your worries if we get stuck in those woods," I shot back, stepping closer to give her waist a playful squeeze. She swatted at my hand, laughing.

"Such confidence," she smirked, slipping on her new hat. "Well, if we're trapped out there, at least I'll have a cute hat."

"Right, because nothing says, 'prepared for danger' like a pink hat with a cartoon cat on it," I joked.

"Oh be quiet, what do you think will happen? We won't get stuck up there," Jessica laughed, tossing her wet clothes onto the floor and grabbing a towel to dry her hair. "Where do you think we're going, the Canadian Rockies?"

"No, but you're going with someone who has a severe lack of coordination when it comes to directions," I admitted, taking the towel from her and rubbing it over my dripping hair before handing it back. "I could get lost on a one-way street."

"Is that why you bought enough food for more than a two-day stay in this hotel?" she teased, raising an eyebrow.

"Better to be prepared," I shrugged, trying to sound nonchalant. "This whole thing feels like a wild goose chase—based on the belief that a girl who doesn't age is out in those woods. We don't even know what we're going to find. Maybe we should've bought a tent too, just in case."

Jessica's eyes lit up as if I'd suggested something thrilling instead of a survival strategy. "Ooh! I haven't been on a camping trip since Mummy and Daddy took us to Cornwall when I was ten."

"Mummy and Daddy?" I laughed, feigning an exaggerated posh accent. "Your posh side is really starting to shine through."

"Shush!" she shot back, grinning as she pinched my side playfully. "But seriously, let's do it—let's get a tent and stay out there for a few days. It'll be fun!"

"Yeah, fun," I muttered, rolling my eyes, though I couldn't help but smile.

We started packing up everything we'd bought so far, dividing our gear between what we'd take into the woods and what would stay behind. Tomorrow, I'd call Marie to order a tent and ask what other supplies we'd need for a few nights of roughing it. As I watched Jessica neatly fold her clothes—socks, bras, underwear, toothbrush, toothpaste—I spotted her makeup bag peeking out from under a jumper.

"Hold on," I said, pointing at the small pink pouch. "What are you taking makeup for?"

"Like you said, best to be prepared," she replied, completely serious. "If we find the girl, we can bond over lipstick."

I blinked at her. "What if she doesn't wear makeup?"

Jessica gave me a knowing smile, zipping the bag shut with a flourish. "There's not a girl alive today who wouldn't want to try a little rouge on her lips."

Once we'd finished packing, we headed downstairs to let Maureen know we'd be away for a few days. She was hunched over her desk, deep in concentration as she peered at a calculator, brow furrowed like she was locked in a battle with the numbers. After settling up for our stay so far, I slipped a little extra across the counter—a small gesture of thanks.

"Did you find your friend?" Maureen asked, her fingers deftly folding up the cash and tucking it into the pocket of her navy-green cardigan.

"Not exactly," I admitted. "But we did talk to Marie. She was a big help, so thank you for the recommendation."

Maureen's stern expression softened instantly. "She's such a lovely girl, that Marie. It's a shame what she's had to endure. And now, after everything, she's caring for her mother. Where does she find the time?" She shook her head, lost in thought. "I knew Brenda well—back when I was an administrator at the hospital. She was a wonderful lady, always so caring. To hear about the state she's in now… It's heartbreaking, really. Just so sad."

We murmured our agreement and were about to back up to the room when Maureen called after us.

"I noticed you came in with bags from the shop. Off on a camping trip, are we?"

"Yes!" Jessica beamed, her eyes lighting up. "I'm really looking forward to it."

"Oh, I envy you," Maureen sighed wistfully. "I wish I could get out of here sometimes and go for a hike in the woods. Used to do it all the time when I was your age. You could spend hours out there and still not see everything. This area's full of hidden nooks and crannies that most visitors never even dream of finding. And the tales… Oh, don't get me started on the tales."

From the living room, an abrupt, dry laugh echoed, followed by the low hum of a vacuum cleaner switching on.

Maureen chuckled, as if remembering an old joke. "When we were children, we were raised on all the legends of the land. If we were being particularly naughty, our parents would warn us about the monsters that roamed the woods—beasts hungry for the blood of misbehaving schoolchildren."

Jessica's smile widened, clearly loving every word. "What sort of monsters?"

Maureen's eyes twinkled with mischief. "All sorts. Wolves, ghosts, women who bewitched men and lured them away with song, or beasts with fangs that could gobble a lost child in one bite."

Back in our room, Jessica looked at me thoughtfully. "Do you think Maureen might have a point?" she asked.

"About what?"

"The tales of the land," she said slowly.

"What are you getting at?"

"Well," she mused, her look drifting to the rain-drenched window, "historians always say that legends are often based on some grain of truth. The details might get twisted, but the core—what's at the heart of it—could be real. This place has been here since the Doomsday Book. Can you imagine what secrets it holds? What stories people used to believe?"

"You've been reading too many ghost stories," I teased. "Next, you'll tell me Maureen's right, and the villagers build a giant wicker man every solstice."

She rolled her eyes. "Well, I like her, and her stories"

"You like everyone."

"That's true," she admitted with a smile, then reached into her bedside drawer and pulled out a heavy, leather-bound book. "I like you enough to read you a few chapters from this."

"What's that?" I eyed the book suspiciously.

"A history of the village," she announced with mock seriousness, flipping through the musty pages. "I found it in the book shop. It's fascinating stuff."

"Joy," I groaned, throwing myself onto the bed dramatically. "You read, and I'll work on my prayers to the sun god."

Jessica grinned and tossed a pillow at my head. "Pig!"

"Guilty as charged," I shot back, laughing as I leaned against the headboard, watching her settle in beside me.

31

"Are you ready?" Jessica asked, holding up the book with a grin.

"Only because my sun-prayers failed," I sighed, glancing out the window where the rain lashed against the glass like thousands of tiny watery stones hurled from the skies.

"The author is a local resident," she continued, undeterred by my lack of enthusiasm. "Born in 1953, he's lived here all his life and spent most of it researching the land's history."

I couldn't imagine spending my entire life in one place. The thought of being so insular, so completely absorbed in a tiny corner of the larger world, baffled me. And listening to their stories didn't fill me with any great excitement, but then, what else was there to do? I didn't believe a history lesson would bring us any closer to finding the girl in the woods, but Jessica was determined. And since we were trapped indoors, I figured, why not?

"Carry on, then," I mumbled.

For the next couple of hours, Jessica read out loud, covering every meticulous detail—the construction of the village's oldest buildings, the lineage of the landowners, and even the evolution of the local farming practices. I tried to pay attention, really tried, but my mind wasn't built for that sort of monotony. The villages oldest tree, the towns preferred thatching materials, the religious practices of town leaders… it was all so unbelievably dull. Just as I was on the brink of completely zoning out, a phrased snapped me back.

It was the section on *ghosts.*

The book described how the villagers believed much of the land was haunted, with spirits roaming through the woods, flickering in and out of sight like mirages. There were accounts of eerie voices drifting along the quiet streets at night, whispers that seemed to beckon from the shadows. And on moonless nights, cries could be heard echoing through the hills—the sounds of those who'd wandered too far from home and were never seen again.

One story stood out—a tale about a young blacksmith who vanished centuries ago, leaving behind nothing but his tools scattered by the riverbank, as though he'd evaporated into thin air. For years, he'd spoken of a woman's voice calling to him from the dense woods or the tall reeds by the water's edge. The villagers thought he'd lost his mind. But when he disappeared, they found his home in disarray—a half-eaten meal still sitting on the table, clothes neatly folded at the foot of his bed, and a scrawled note filled with incoherent ramblings about his need to follow the mysterious voice.

"His tools were found near the river, but no body ever turned up," Jessica concluded, her eyes alight with curiosity. "Isn't it amazing? The way these stories are tied to the land, the ancient landmarks scattered around here—it all makes you wonder what else is hiding out there."

"Yeah," I lied, forcing a smile. "Much more thrilling than crop rotations and farming tools."

"Do you think any of it's real?" she asked.

"The ghost stories?"

She nodded, placing the book on her lap, her eyes searching mine.

"I believe people believe it," I said, choosing my words carefully. "But me? No, not really. Ghosts, ghouls, werewolves, vampires—they're just stories. They start as shadows in the woods, maybe a deer leaping through the trees, or bushes moving and the wind whistling through the branches. By the time the tale's been passed around, those shadows, movements and sounds turn into monsters and ghosts. They're meant to scare people—or lure in tourists. Nothing more."

"You've got no imagination," she teased, reaching over to tweak my ear.

"Oh, I've got plenty of imagination," I replied, standing up and stretching. "It just doesn't stretch far enough to believe in the undead. Come on, leave the spooky stories for the rain. Right now, I feel like we should be sociable with the living for a change."

We headed downstairs to the inn's cozy lounge, where the only other guests—a middle-aged couple—sat quietly absorbed in their own pursuits. The rotund husband was slouched in a faded armchair, his eyes glued to a dog-eared novel. A pair of green-rimmed reading glasses perched precariously on the tip of his bulbous nose, and his slick, jet-black hair looked suspiciously like a wig—too perfect to be real.

His wife, a small figure with long grey hair neatly tied back, sat by the fireplace, knitting a seemingly endless scarf in vibrant hues. Her autumn-patterned dress and worn blue slippers gave her an air of relaxed routine, her head bobbing rhythmically to some silent tune as her needles clicked away.

Both looked up as we entered. "Afternoon," the man greeted us in a thick Midlands accent, his voice warm and hearty.

"Hi," Jessica replied, taking a seat next to the woman on the sofa. I chose a chair by the window, watching the relentless rain batter against the glass, silently hoping it would take my restlessness with it.

The woman smiled, nodding in our direction, though her focus remained on her knitting.

"Atrocious weather, aint it?" the man declared, rising from his chair to join me at the window. "Me an' the missus thought we'd treat ourselves to a little anniversary getaway. Been sunny all summer, then we get here and—well, just our luck, eh? Rain nearly every bloody day!"

"Happy anniversary!" Jessica said warmly.

"Thank you," the old woman murmured, her voice soft and small, like a child's.

"The name's Gary," the man continued, offering a firm handshake. "And this here's my lovely Jeanie."

We swapped pleasantries, shaking hands and introducing ourselves.

"Are you here for long?" I asked.

"Just a week, though at this rate, it'll feel like a lifetime with all this rain." He dropped back into his chair with a huff. "Picked this place 'cause Jeanie's got some family roots here, y'know."

Jeanie nodded, her needles never pausing.

"That's right," Gary continued, clearly pleased. "Did one of those ancestry kits—turns out she's some distant cousin to the old family that used to own this place. What was the fella's name again, love?"

Jeanie paused, her fingers hovering over the wool. "Lord Ashby," she said pleasantly, her voice like the squeak of a mouse, before returning to her knitting.

"That's the one!" Gary exclaimed, puffing out his chest a little. "Turns out her great-great-whatever was a cousin to the Ashby line before it died out. Imagine that, eh? Sitting here with a bit of royalty!"

Jessica's eyes lit up with interest. "Lord Ashby? The same Ashby family that owned the woods and the old estate up the hills?"

"Exactly!" Gary grinned, clearly enjoying the attention. "The Ashbys owned most of the land around here before they all— well, you know, before they faded away. But it's funny, innit? To think she's got blood ties to all of that. We were going to head up to the visitor's centre and try to find out a bit more about him this morning, but the pissing weather is working against us."

A sudden flash of lightning illuminated the room, followed by a booming clap of thunder, as if the very sky was warning against their planned trip.

"I love a bit of history, don't you?" Gary continued, completely unfazed by the storm pounding outside. "Shame no one inherited the land when ol' Ashby kicked the bucket. I could see myself as Lord Gary of Little Ashton." He let out a hearty laugh, clearly entertained by the thought.

I mentioned that Jessica and I had planned a camping trip in the woods, though with the torrential rain, it was starting to feel more like a pipe dream than anything real.

Gary's expression shifted, and the earlier bravado faded. He shivered slightly as he leaned forward, lowering his voice. "Good luck with that. Jeanie and I took a walk out there when we first arrived. Never again. There's something off about those woods... gives me the creeps. You hear all those stories about how Lord Ashby used to deal with poachers—tying them to trees and leaving them to die from exposure. That's enough to keep me out of those woods."

Here we go again, I thought. Another round of eerie folklore. Every village seemed to have its own twisted history, designed to scare or amuse curious outsiders. I could've corrected him, maybe dampened the drama, but it was their anniversary. If they wanted to believe Jeanie had blood ties to a sadistic lord, who was I to spoil the fun?

"Well, there's nothing supernatural planned for our trip," I said with a grin, glancing at Jessica. "Unless, of course, the ghosts are looking for beauty tips."

Gary laughed, slapping me on the back before settling back into his chair and returning to his battered novel. The rest of the afternoon passed in a lazy haze. Maureen brought out tea and cakes, and we drifted through more idle conversation. Gary continued spinning stories about Jeanie's supposed family history, none as thrilling as being related to Lord Ashby, but entertaining, nonetheless. Curiously, though, he never mentioned his own past—keeping the spotlight firmly on Jeanie and her mysterious lineage.

Later that evening, as Jessica and I settled into our room, she turned to me with a smile. "I really liked Gary."

"He was definitely a character," I agreed, "a little eccentric for my taste."

We had retreated upstairs just as his stories started losing their charm, turning into random bits of trivia about places he and Jeanie had visited. Despite their apparent worldliness, the most vivid insights Gary had to offer were the dullest of facts. Luckily, Jessica had saved us from total boredom by announcing she was tired.

"Do you think we'll be like that when we're their age?" she asked, slipping under the covers.

"I certainly hope not," I scoffed. "If I ever start rattling off random facts like that, just take me out to a field and end it."

The clock had just passed 9 p.m., and the storm had finally eased, though the wind still howled outside. It shook the trees, causing their branches to scrape against the window like nails on a chalkboard.

"I can picture us older, coming back here someday," Jessica mused, her voice blending with the rhythm of the wind. "Me knitting you a winter jumper, and you with a belly hanging over a brown belt, reading some tacky crime noir novel, imagining yourself as the hero. And then a young couple asks for help with their own adventure, and you'd regale them with wildly exaggerated tales of local ghosts."

Her fingers traced a warm, teasing path around my waist before slipping into my underwear, her touch gentle yet electrifying.

"And what about you?" I asked, my fingers finding her curves, tracing lightly around her nipples. "I can't see you being as timid as Jeanie. No, you'd be the one doing all the talking. I'd just nod along while you spin tales of how deep your family tree goes, claiming you're next in line to some throne."

She kissed me softly, her lips brushing mine with a tenderness that set off a swell of goosebumps up the back of my neck. "You should be the master of our story—Lord Christopher Charles, landowner and member of high society," she teased.

"Actually, I quite like the sound of that," I replied with a grin, pulling her closer for another kiss.

That night, with the wind howling outside, we made love with a sense of urgency, as if we needed to fully connect before the world outside intruded. In the warmth of each other's arms, everything else felt distant and unimportant.

32

It was 9:20 a.m., and Jessica and I stood outside the hotel, waiting for Marie to pick us up. The morning was cool and overcast, with grey clouds stretching like a blanket across the sky. As we waited, my thoughts wandered to the local farmers already out in the fields, working hard to repair the damage from yesterday's storm. I couldn't help but wonder about the lives they led—rising before dawn, facing nature's unpredictable moods every day, and yet going mostly unnoticed by the wider world. *Better them than me*, I thought. They had my sympathies. I couldn't do it.

I also felt uncomfortably full after devouring my fourth full English breakfast of the trip. Knowing our camping supplies would be limited, I had indulged while I still could. Maureen, in her motherly way, had insisted I pile my plate high. "Double helpings; you'll thank me later," she'd said with a sly smile as if knowing exactly what we were in for.

The village was just waking up. A few shops had already opened, but there were no customers yet. In the distance, I could hear the low rumble of a tractor making its way through the narrow streets. Down the road, a couple of tourists were huddled together, their phones out as they tried to figure out directions. Nearby, two elderly men in flat caps were animatedly discussing the storm, their hands gesturing toward the sky. Overhead, a flock of geese flew by in perfect formation, heading toward the river and the open fields beyond.

Jessica looped her arm through mine, snuggling closer as a light September chill settled in. I kissed the top of her head, catching a whiff of her apple-blossom perfume, which sent me momentarily dreaming of springtime orchards.

Then, with a growl, Marie's Jeep Wrangler rounded the corner. It was clearly built for rugged adventures, its wheels caked with mud and bits of dried grass stuck in the grille, as if it had already conquered half the wilderness. Behind the streaked windshield, Marie signalled us with a bright smile, her hair tousled by the wind, looking as if she was just as much a part of the landscape as the rugged Jeep itself.

We climbed into the Jeep—me in the front seat next to Marie, Jessica in the back. The interior smelled of dirt and gasoline, the kind of earthy scent that comes from years of off-road trips. In the rear-view mirror, I saw the tent I'd ordered, bundled up and ready for us.

"Morning, you two," Marie greeted as she started the engine, pulling away from the curb. "I heard from one of the farmers this morning that the storm washed out part of the route I planned. The river's overflowed, so we'll have to take the longer way. I'll drop you off at the start of the trail near that old groundskeeper's hut I showed you on the map."

"Take us where you think is best," I said with a grin. "I'm not exactly Bear Grylls in the wild."

"It'll add another half-hour to the drive," Marie warned. "When we get there, I'll give you directions from the cabin to the glade. It's an easy route if you watch for landmarks, but just a heads-up, more rain is on the way. If it starts getting too rough, my advice is to pack it up and head back to the village."

We cruised through the modest high street, the familiar sight of Marie's store passing by. Outside, a lanky lad stood smoking a vape. Marie gave him a wave. "That's Daniel—hired help for the busy summer months. Soon it'll just be me and Gareth, my usual assistant. This time of year, not many are daft enough to go camping," she added with a teasing smile.

"Doesn't bode well for us," I replied, glancing at Jessica, who grinned back, her eyes sparkling with excitement.

"You'll be fine if you stick to the three major rules when you're out camping. One—don't light any fires in the woods. Two—don't get in the way of any randy bulls…" Marie slowed the car as we approached a sharp bend in the road.

"And three?" I asked.

"Easy—don't die," she said with a grin.

As we neared the edge of the village, the narrow roads twisted up into the hills, winding through rugged, open fields and thick patches of woodland. The landscape grew wilder with each passing mile, as if we were leaving the safety and familiarity of the village behind and heading into a world much more untamed.

"Your brother mentioned you quite a bit," Marie said, keeping her eyes on the winding road. "He was always talking about the scrapes you two got into. He told me how he'd left to travel around England and knew it would upset you that he didn't reach out. But he thought you could handle it—you were the strong one."

"He told me that a lot," I admitted, shrugging. "I never understood why. I've always seen myself as pragmatic, not particularly strong."

Marie glanced at me briefly before focusing back on the road. "I've only known you for a couple of days, but from everything he explained, I can tell he was right. When your father passed, you stepped up to take care of your brother when you both moved in with your aunt and uncle. That takes a lot of strength."

We paused at a junction, waiting for a large white truck, splattered with fresh mud and towing a horsebox, to pull out of a nearby field. Marie nodded at the driver, and I couldn't help but wonder why anyone would buy a white truck for these muddy roads.

"I did what I had to," I said. "But it doesn't compare to what you've been through. I'm not sure I'd have the strength to handle everything you've faced and still build a life for yourself here. How do you manage it?"

"My kids," Marie stated. "My husband died when my oldest was three and my youngest was just born, so they never really knew him. I did everything I could to raise them right. Then, when my father passed, I had to be strong for my mum. The kids knew their grandfather for a little while, but my mother doesn't even recognise them now. It's been hard, but I keep going for them. That, and therapy—lots of therapy," she added with a wink.

"Chris just lives on a daily dose of cynicism and a whole heap of self-deprecation to keep himself going," Jessica quipped from the back seat.

As we drove past a field full of sheep, they turned their heads to watch us, their large eyes curious. The skies had darkened, and light rain began to splatter against the windshield.

"Can I ask you something?" Marie said hesitantly. "If it's not too personal, that is."

"Go ahead," I replied. "I'll let you know if it is."

"Adam mentioned the trouble he had with his ex-girlfriend, Emily," Marie began carefully. "He said when she left, she took half of his belongings, including something that was really hard for him to talk about."

"It was a metronome," I answered, understanding where she was headed. "An antique metronome that belonged to our grandfather, passed down to Adam in our father's will."

"Oh," Marie said, her expression uncertain. Whether she didn't know what a metronome was or didn't grasp why it mattered so much, I wasn't sure.

"Our father and his father before him were musicians," I explained, feeling the weight of the story. "My grandfather was a concert pianist who toured Germany shortly before the Second World War. When he got word from the embassy that Germany was about to declare war, he rushed home and brought that metronome back with him. It was a gift from a local woman he loved, but he had to leave her behind, never seeing her again. Later, he passed it on to our dad. Adam adored our father, learned everything he could about music from him. So, it wasn't just an object—it was a piece of our family's history, something deeply personal and irreplaceable."

"Why would she steal it?" Marie asked, her voice tinged with disbelief.

"To sell it," I said, shaking my head. "For all her talk about a socialist state, she was extremely interested in her own capital gain. Thankfully, she saw sense and returned it to me, but by then, it was too late."

We continued driving in silence. Marie seemed deep in thought, probably trying to reconcile how my brother had held on to something so meaningful, while she had inherited a sketchpad with a haunting backstory and her mother's declining health.

"We've been reading up about the ghosts of these woods," Jessica chimed in, breaking the quiet.

"Which ones?" Marie replied.

"All of them," I groaned, rolling my eyes.

"Don't listen to all that rubbish," Marie laughed. "The only things you need to worry about in these woods are hidden ditches, a fox or badger den, and maybe a horny ram or two. I've lived here all my life, and not once have I seen anything out of the ordinary."

"Thank goodness someone else in this car has some sense," I said, giving Jessica a teasing glare. She stuck her tongue out at me in response.

As we left the paved roads behind and ventured onto the stony, uneven back roads at the forest's edge, the jeep began to jolt and bounce, its suspension struggling against the rough, muddy terrain. I gripped the handle above the door, bracing myself like a human jack-in-the-box as Marie fought to keep the vehicle steady.

"The storm really made a mess of these roads," Marie said, her knuckles tightening on the wheel. "It's been a long while since I've seen them this bad."

I wanted to ask Marie how she felt about driving back through this, but I was too busy trying to stop myself from sliding forward every time she braked to navigate a deep puddle.

We crossed an old stone bridge, the waters below raging from the aftermath of the storm, with the riverbanks dangerously close to overflowing.

"One more heavy rain, and the village is going to be cut off," Marie muttered, carefully steering the Jeep across the bridge. "That happened a few years ago. No one could get in or out for two weeks. While the bridges were being fixed, we had to have supplies airlifted in by helicopter."

"Thanks for the heads-up," I said sarcastically, trying to figure out if she was serious or pulling our leg.

"All part of country living," she replied with a grin.

The rain had finally stopped, and a small glimmer of sunlight pierced through the clouds. As the Jeep climbed an incline, we passed a grassy hillside dotted with grazing cattle, too engrossed in their mid-morning feast to care about us. When we reached the top, Marie slowed down, giving us a sweeping view of the forest below.

"That's where we're headed," Marie said, nodding toward the vast expanse of trees stretching out beneath us.

"What's that?" I asked, pointing to a distant building with turrets piercing through the treetops. For some reason, it made me think of one of those old manors straight out of a Gothic novel.

"We heard all about it yesterday—the story about him tying poachers up and leaving them to die," I said, recalling Gary's eerie tales.

"He probably didn't," Marie replied with a half-smile. "But I'll admit, there are a few trees that look like they still have rope marks around them. And then there's the other story—about his daughter. That one's a favourite. The Lord was said to be a paranoid man, always fretting over his family's future. When his daughter came of age, he became convinced she was too fragile to face a society that he believed was on the verge of moral collapse."

Marie shivered, as though letting the tale seep into her.

"He supposedly kept her locked away, only ever allowing her out on the grounds under strict supervision. After a few years of that, she had enough. Climbed one of those turrets you spotted and threw herself off to escape his control."

"So, which is true?" I asked, half-intrigued, half-sceptical. "The ropes or the daughter?"

Marie chuckled, her breath visible in the chilly air. "Both and neither. Take your pick."

As we drove closer, the clouds thickened, casting a grim shadow over the sprawling forest ahead. The road ended abruptly about thirty feet from the forest's edge, where a wire fence separated the farmland from the dense trees. A solitary metal gate stood between us and the wilderness. Marie brought the Jeep to a halt and rested her hands on the wheel for a moment, as if gathering her thoughts.

"This is as far as I can take you," she said finally.

We climbed out, gathering our bags and the tent from the back. Standing side by side, we observed the looming woods. The ground beneath our feet felt firm enough, despite the recent storm.

"Don't be fooled," Marie warned, watching me test the ground. "It might seem solid here, but once you're in there, it's a different story."

She led us to the front of the Jeep, opened the door, and pulled a map and a set of handwritten directions from the glove compartment. Spreading them out on the bonnet, she beckoned us closer.

"So, you're here," she said, pointing to a red dot she'd marked as our starting point. "The first part is straightforward. There's a footpath that goes all the way to the groundskeeper's hut. Some of it might be overgrown with roots and bushes, but if you follow the stone markers, you should be fine."

"Do others walk it?" Jessica asked, leaning in to study the map.

"It's probably the most walked path in the whole forest. It's the easiest hike for people, nothing too strenuous, with no chance of getting lost along the way. But all you'll find is the ruins of an old building—barely anything left standing. There used to be this coming-of-age tradition for village teenagers, where you'd spend a night alone in the keeper's hut. We believed all sorts of stupid ghost stories back then," Marie said with a laugh. "When it was my turn, all I got was a sore back and splinters in my bum. If you're interested, though, there are a few pretty spots along the way—streams and such. It's easy enough to navigate."

"I'm guessing the second part isn't so simple?" I asked, sensing a shift in her tone.

"Not as straightforward, but still doable if you know what to look for," Marie explained. "Hardly anyone walks that part— mostly locals or people who know what they're doing. I won't overload you with directions now, but I've packed everything you'll need in your tent. Use the hut as your base and read the instructions when you're there. Trust me, it'll be easier that way. One more thing—stick to the path. This forest is massive, about 17,000 hectares, and if you stray off and fail to find your way back to the trail, you'll easily get lost." She pulled out her phone and waved it slightly. "And don't expect this to work in there. No signal."

"What should we do if we run into trouble?" I asked.

"If you use your eyes and ears, you shouldn't get into bother," Marie said, raising an eyebrow. "But worst-case scenario—how many days did you pack for?"

I thought for a minute. "We've got enough for five days if we ration."

She nodded. "That should be enough." Her smile was warm but carried a hint of seriousness that lingered. "Right, I'll be back here on the sixth day. If you haven't returned by then, I'll call for help. The most important thing is not to panic. Lay markers back to the cabin if you need to, and remember, your brother managed to find the glade and return."

But perhaps not in one piece, I thought.

"And if you decide it's too much, head straight back here and up to the top of the hill," she said, pointing to the path we had driven down. "You should be able to get a signal from up there. If all else fails, just remember it's only a ninety-minute hike back to Little Ashton."

We said our farewells, slung our packs over our shoulders, and climbed over the gate, leaving behind the last bit of open sky we might see for days. As we took our first steps into the forest, we glanced back to watch Marie turn the jeep around. With a blast of the horn and a wave from the cab, she disappeared over the crest of the hill.

Jessica and I exchanged a look, the silence of the forest pressing in around us. The wind rustled the trees, their creaks and groans the only sounds for miles. We were completely alone.

33

We entered the forest cautiously, as if stepping off the edge of the known world. The grassy hillside behind us quickly disappeared, swallowed by the towering trees, and the sky above shrank to momentary glimpses through the dense canopy. The grey clouds raced between the highest leaves, giving the unsettling impression that one strong gust could send the entire forest crashing down like a house of cards. I felt a new sense of precariousness about this journey, one I had only just begun to grasp.

"Come on, let's get going," I said to Jessica, trying to shake off the strange unease. A chill breeze swept through the trees, but the weight of my pack soon had me warm enough to shed my parka, continuing in just a T-shirt. "I don't want to get drenched before we've even started."

The first few hundred yards were easy enough. The recent rains hadn't turned this part of the path to mud yet, allowing us to walk without much effort. We passed a few of the landmarks Marie had mentioned—an old stone marker, half-buried in moss, and a towering oak tree with deep, twisted roots that looked like skeletal fingers clawing at the earth. At one point, we spotted a small wooden bridge crossing a narrow ditch, its planks worn but still sturdy, its wooden handrails covered in rot and droppings. After a while, we took a brief rest by a small stream, the sound of running water soothing, momentarily distracting me from the quiet unease that lingered in the back of my mind.

But as we pressed on, the path became more challenging. The trees here had opened up just enough to let the rain soak the ground beneath, turning the trail into mud. Every step was accompanied by the unpleasant squelch of our boots sinking into the muck. I could feel my patience wearing thin. The effort of trudging through the sticky muck made me question the whole trip. I hated the sensation of my feet being swallowed by the ground with every step, and I was dangerously close to suggesting we head back.

But Jessica urged me forward. Determined, even as the trail worsened, she wouldn't let the mud, or my frustration stop us.

As we walked further into the forest, the view around us shifted dramatically. The towering trees grew denser, their trunks gnarled and twisted with age. Moss clung to their bark like faded green velvet, draping down in long strands, and thick ferns blanketed the forest floor, their fronds swaying ever so slightly in the cool breeze. Above us, the canopy was so dense that the sky was reduced to mere slivers, with only dappled patches of light filtering through, dancing across the ground whenever the wind stirred the high branches.

Occasionally, the trees parted in the distance, giving us the scenes of the land beyond the forest's edge. To the east, through gaps in the branches, we could see the rolling hills of farmland stretching back toward the village, with golden wheat fields standing out against to the dark green forest line.

"It feels like we're so far away from society, and yet close enough that we could reach out and grab it," I said to Jessica, my voice barely rising above the soft rustle of the wind.

As we walked, we passed the occasional fallen tree, its bark rough and rotting, and I couldn't shake the feeling that we were intruding on something sacred. Every time I scraped the mud from my boots against the bark or disturbed the quiet with my heavy footsteps, it felt wrong—like I was violating some unspoken rule of the forest that demanded we tread lightly, leave no trace, and simply let things be.

We soon arrived at a fork in the path. One trail led to the left, overgrown and barely visible through the thick underbrush. This had to be the path to the glade. The other trail, drier and more inviting, was lined with gravel and stones—exactly as Marie had described. I was relieved at the thought of walking on solid ground again. Ahead, the trees arched overhead, forming a natural tunnel, almost as if they were drawing us deeper into their embrace.

The path curved and narrowed, forcing us to walk single file. Everything ahead seemed to merge into a distant point, shrouded in an eerie stillness.

"Do you hear that?" I asked, suddenly stopping.

"Hear what?" Jessica replied, tilting her head and listening intently.

"Exactly—nothing," I said. "It's too quiet."

It was as if the animals and birds had abandoned this part of the forest, leaving behind an oppressive silence that made it feel like we were the only ones left in the world. The further we walked, the more isolated I felt.

After another fifteen minutes, we came across a large ditch—about six feet wide and ten feet deep—its walls lined with roots, and white moss, making it look like an ancient scar carved into the earth. At the bottom, a narrow stream trickled along, catching what little light filtered through the trees and casting faint glimmers on the water's surface. A fallen tree trunk lay parallel to the edge, its bark rough and splintered, offering a makeshift seat. I dropped my pack, sat on the trunk, and lit a cigarette, taking a long drag before slowly exhaling into the stillness.

"What are you thinking?" Jessica asked, placing her bag beside mine and sitting next to me.

"Adam," I replied, taking another drag. "For some odd reason, this walk feels like a tribute to his memory, and I'm not sure how to feel about that."

She took the cigarette from my hand and stubbed it out on the trunk. "Is your pragmatism radar going off again?"

I shrugged. "There's been so much confusion, so many peculiarities in all this, but this is the first time I've really felt close to his part in it." I gestured toward the ditch. "For all I know, he walked this same trail, came to this same ditch, sat on this same trunk, and contemplated life."

"What do you think was going through his mind if he did?"

"Music, our dad, why life had it in for him, and where he fit into his own little comedy of errors," I said, pulling her closer. I wanted to feel her warmth as I spoke about him. "But most of all, he was probably wondering how the hell he was going to get across this ditch without getting soaked."

She laughed, the sound breaking through the peace of the forest like a spark in the dark.

We kissed, then discussed our next move—cross the gap or find another way around. Marie hadn't mentioned this ditch, and we had no idea how long it would take to find an alternative route. After some deliberation, we decided the easiest option was to jump and hope for the best. Jessica went first, taking a small run-up. She leapt across gracefully, grabbing hold of a protruding tree root and carefully pulling herself the last couple of feet to the top.

Then it was my turn. I eyed the gap, estimated my chances, and backed up a few more steps than she had. With a deep breath, I charged forward and launched myself, imagining I'd land with the finesse of an Olympic long jumper—until gravity had other ideas. I came up short, slamming into the far bank halfway down. With nothing to hold on to, I slid further down until I splashed into the cold, grimy water at the bottom.

"Fuck!" I yelled.

"You're wet!" Jessica laughed, pointing and doubling over.

It took me a solid ten minutes to clamber up the embankment, grumbling the whole way, cursing nature for this little stunt. I longed for the simplicity of paved city streets, where rain only meant dodging puddles and the only jumps required were onto public transport.

As we continued, Jessica cheerfully sang about my misadventure, while I trudged along in soaked pants, each step a squelching reminder of why I preferred being indoors. Just as I was about to lose all hope and loudly questioning if I'd ever upset anyone in an earlier life, we finally arrived at the cabin.

"That can't be the place," Jessica said, frowning in confusion.

We had both expected a decrepit, old log cabin barely held together with one-hundred-year-old nails and screws. Instead, we were staring at a pristine, cottage-style, two-story cabin that looked like it had been plucked from the pages of a glossy holiday rental magazine. A freshly mowed lawn surrounded it, enclosed within a large square of wire fencing, making the whole scene feel even more surreal.

We stood there, hand-in-hand frozen in disbelief, as if what we were seeing couldn't quite register. This wasn't the run-down, abandoned gamekeeper's lodge Marie had described; it wasn't even close. Where were the crumbling walls, the overgrown weeds, the splintered beams sagging under years of neglect? There were no signs of decay, no hints of age or wear—just this picture-perfect anomaly in the middle of the wilderness.

I pulled the map from my pocket, scanning it carefully. "This has to be it," I muttered, tracing the path we'd taken. "There's no other building around here."

"It doesn't look like a gamekeeper's lodge," she said, still frowning.

"No," I agreed, shaking my head. "It really doesn't, but this is definitely the area of the lodge."

"Maybe someone bought it," Jessica suggested, "and it's been renovated, for visitors perhaps."

"Maybe," I conceded, "but it looks more like a house than a visitors centre."

The cabin was pristine. The wood façade had been freshly treated and varnished, giving it a warm glow despite the overcast sky. Gleaming windows lined the walls, and the roof, painted green, looked sturdy, with a brick chimney at one end releasing the faint scent of smoke. If this place had been remodelled, the work was flawless. But the longer I stared at it, the more unsettling it became. It exuded no sense of history, no welcoming aura—just motionlessness, as if it were a lifeless, perfect replica of something that once stood here.

Then there was another troubling question—how had this well-maintained, recently renovated cabin come to be here without leaving any signs of the necessary work? The narrow trail we'd followed bore no marks of heavy equipment or freshly felled trees, and there were no other visible paths leading to this secluded spot. With no other explanation and the need for refuge growing, I eventually pushed the thought aside.

As the first drops of rain began to patter against my cheek and the wind picked up, rustling the leaves above us, I took Jessica's hand and led her toward the cabin. I weighed the decision of whether to approach the cabin or not, but with the rain intensifying and the thought of trekking back to Little Ashton in such weather being less appealing, the choice was clear. Practicality won out—shelter was shelter, and staying dry seemed like the best option.

"C'mon," I said, taking Jessica by the hand and leading her across the lawn toward the cabin.

"What are you doing?" she asked, her voice tinged with apprehension.

"Getting dry," I replied. "Let's check this place out."

"Chris, we can't," she protested, digging her heels in.

The cabin loomed before us, offering shelter from the rain, which was now falling steadily, soaking us both through. The scent of freshly cut wood filled the air, and despite the oddness of its pristine condition, the thought of warmth and dryness overpowered my initial misgivings.

"Seriously, what's the alternative?" I said, casting a glance at the grey sky as droplets rolled down my face. "We're soaked. If no one's in there, what harm is there in waiting out the storm inside? We can camp after the rain passes."

Jessica hesitated, her eyes scanning the surrounding forest, but finally, she nodded. "Fine, but let's be quick."

We approached the door. Through its four-panel window, I could see the dim, empty interior. The place seemed as deserted as the forest around it. I knocked, the sound echoing inside, but no one answered. The rain was coming down harder now, soaking through my clothes and ratcheting up my frustration.

"Hello?" I called, knocking again, louder. Nothing. The only response was the relentless drumming of rain on the roof.

I tried the handle; the door was locked. Stepping back, I scanned the second floor for any signs of life, but all I saw were the closed blinds of the upstairs windows. The rain began to seep through my already damp clothes, heightening my frustration.

"Maybe we could sleep outside in the tent," she suggested.

Pitching our tent on the grounds of this place and shivering through the night while a warm, dry cabin sat just out of reach felt like a cruel irony.

"No," I said firmly. "I want inside this place. Maybe there's a window I could jimmy open."

"Since when have you been so eager to break into people's homes?"

"Since the day that man first started dying of pneumonia."

While I contemplated the questionable ethics of breaking and entering, Jessica had other ideas. She crouched beside a red ceramic plant pot near the door, lifting it to reveal a key hidden underneath. She grinned, holding it up triumphantly.

"Well, that was easy," she said.

"How did you know that was there?" I asked, disbelief in my voice.

"A calculated guess," she replied, unlocking the door with a satisfied click and stepping inside.

Without a second thought, I hurried in behind her, eager to escape the rain. The warm, dry air hit me, but something about the interior tugged at my instincts. It took a few seconds for my eyes to adjust to the dimly lit room. The blinds were drawn, letting in only the faintest grey light from outside. The cabin's interior was bizarre—a mash-up of clashing styles that seemed completely out of sync with each other. The air carried a strange, faint scent of aniseed mixed with the heavy, stale odour of a room long shut away from fresh air.

Paintings of various subjects lined the walls, many of them amateurish landscapes, next to the mounted heads of animals. Some of the paintings were sloppily framed, while others hung crookedly, their bright colours clashing with the dark, varnished wood panelling. A worn, mustard-yellow armchair sat awkwardly next to a sleek, modern coffee table that seemed too glossy for its surroundings, like a relic from an entirely different era. 1970s leather furniture was arranged stiffly around glass-top tables, all set on a cold granite floor that felt more suited to a showroom than a cozy cabin. It looked as if someone had gone on a frantic buying spree in a second-hand store and grabbed everything at once, without a thought for cohesion.

I closed the door behind us, sealing out the worsening weather. The sudden quiet, broken only by the steady patter of rain on the windows and the ticking of a small brass clock on a marble mantelpiece, was almost eerie.

"If we find a key and walk in, does it still count as breaking in?" Jessica asked in a hushed tone, shrugging off her jacket and draping it over the back of the sofa.

"Only if we make ourselves comfortable," I whispered back, trying to inject some humour into the uneasy situation. But the anxiety lingered. What if someone came home to find us here? I called out, "Hello? Anyone there?"

A wave of déjà vu hit me hard, as if I'd stepped into a room I'd known all my life but couldn't quite remember. The sensation was unsettling, like I'd been here before in a dream or a distant memory. Shaking it off, I told myself it was just the cabin's strange atmosphere playing tricks on me.

"What should we do?" Jessica asked, her voice quieter now.

"We're already inside, and I'm not heading back out into that rain," I said, though my words felt hollow, as if I was trying to convince myself as much as her. "If the owner shows up, we'll just say we got lost, and the door was unlocked." The excuse sounded flimsy, even to my ears.

"I'm going to look around," Jessica said, heading towards the hallway.

"Jessica, wait!" I called after her, but she was already gone.

Suddenly, the living room was bathed in light as the crystal teardrop chandelier overhead flickered on, casting a bright glow across the room.

"I found the lights," Jessica shouted from the hallway. "I wonder how they get electricity out here?"

Leaving her to investigate, I turned my attention back to the room, searching for any signs that someone had been here recently. The room was clean and devoid of the usual clutter that would indicate occupancy. I opened a drawer in a small side table beside the sofa and found an ashtray, a Bible, and a small glass container filled with blue marbles—curious but not indicative of recent activity. Within nothing more of interest, I closed the drawer and continued my search.

I then wandered over to the fireplace and noticed a brass container holding three pokers. Grabbing one, I used to stir the cold, grey ash in the hearth, it was clear the fireplace hadn't been used for months, if not longer. The room itself was so pristine, so perfectly arranged, that it felt like it was waiting for someone to arrive but had never seen any actual life. It was as if the cabin had been prepared, meticulously set up to give the appearance of habitation, yet no one had ever sat in the stiff leather chairs or placed a coffee cup on the gleaming glass tables.

The chandelier above flickered again, casting a brief shadow that made the mounted animal heads on the walls appear to shift, just for a second. I felt that familiar sensation of déjà vu strike me again, stronger, like I'd stepped into a memory that wasn't mine. What was it about this place that I found so familiar? Nothing here reminded me of anything I'd ever come across before.

From the hallway, Jessica's footsteps echoed lightly as she explored further. I turned my attention to the animal heads—one was a stag, its antlers enormous and sharp, towering over the rest of the room like some kind of silent guardian. Its glass eyes, cold and empty, seemed to follow me as I moved through the space. The sensation that we were intruding grew stronger with every second.

Jessica reappeared, settling into one of the floral armchairs. "Well, someone is — or was—living here," she said. "The larder's stocked with food, the kitchen has all the modern appliances, and there's even an unopened two-pint carton of milk in the fridge."

I set the poker back into its stand and leaned against the fireplace, my fingers absentmindedly brushing the glass of the clock's chamber. None of this made sense. The pristine condition of the place, the stocked kitchen—it didn't add up.

"This must be a holiday let," I said, trying to rationalise. "That's the only explanation."

"But no one mentioned it?" she replied, raising an eyebrow.

"Maybe Marie doesn't know it's been updated," I offered, though it felt flimsy even as I said it.

"No, that's not right. She runs the camping store. If anyone was going to know about changes around here, it's her."

She was right. "Maybe she was away when it happened, or she just forgot. The poor girl has a lot going on."

"Forgot, really, Chris?"

"Can you give me a better explanation?" I asked, frustrated at being put on the spot by her.

"She lied," Jessica countered, crossing her arms, her tone matter-of-fact.

The sudden chiming of the clock startled me. It was three o'clock. My eyes widened—had it really taken us almost four hours to complete what should've been a quick hike?

"Why would she lie?" I asked.

"Think about it," Jessica said, poking her finger into her palm, like a detective finally cracking a case. "She was pretty quick to offer to drive us out here."

"Okay, but why?"

"Maybe hearing her mother talk about her dad's death pushed her to finally confront it, to find answers."

I frowned. "So why lie about the place being an old, abandoned gamekeeper's lodge?"

Jessica's expression darkened, her brows furrowing. "What if the girl we're looking for lives here, in this cabin?"

As wild as it sounded, the logic behind it was hard to deny.

"But why the cryptic approach?" I asked, still trying to piece everything together.

"That's what I'm trying to figure out," she said, standing up with purpose. "But we're not going to learn anything if we just stand here. Let's check upstairs."

The stairs, narrow and steep, creaked under our weight as we ascended, the wooden steps echoing through the quiet house. As we reached the second floor, the atmosphere shifted. Gone was the rustic charm of the downstairs; it now felt like an ordinary countryside home. The bathroom, spotless with gleaming ceramic tiles and polished silver taps, smelled faintly of lemon and pine—as if someone had just cleaned it.

"Weirder and weirder," I said aloud as we stood in the hallway, absorbing the dissimilarity between the two bedrooms either side of us. The one on the left was plain, utilitarian even—furnished with a metal-framed bed covered in simple blue sheets, a thin pillow barely offering any comfort. A white dresser with a water-stained mirror leaned slightly against the wall, and next to it stood a narrow, flimsy cupboard that looked like it could be toppled with a gentle shove. Everything in the room felt cold and impersonal, as though it had been assembled from the cheapest of catalogues.

The room on the right, however, was a completely different story. It exuded warmth. A king-size bed dominated the space, draped in a thick, luxurious quilt with crisp white sheets that practically begged you to sink into them. The pillows were plump, and the quilt was neatly turned back, giving the impression someone had only just left. The room was tastefully decorated with elegant tapestries, a grand oak armoire, and a matching dresser table. Soft carpet cushioned our feet, giving the room an inviting, almost regal atmosphere. It was hard to believe both rooms existed in the same house.

"If she lives here, it's got to be this one she stays in," Jessica said, pointing at the plush bed.

"How do you know?" I asked.

"No girl on earth would want to be seen dead brushing her hair in that mirror," she replied, gesturing toward the moisture-stained mirror in the other room.

We entered the grand room cautiously, half-expecting someone to burst in and catch us snooping. This room felt different—more lived-in, more personal. On the dressing table, a neatly laid black cloth held an antique mother-of-pearl-handled hair set, perfectly arranged—a large brush, a comb, a hand mirror, and a small box that looked like it could be a snuff box. Jessica's theory that this might be the home of the girl we were searching for felt more plausible by the second.

"You check the cupboard; I'll check the drawers," I suggested.

I went through each drawer, finding only a few personal items: a simple blue lace nightgown in one, another Bible in another drawer, and a silver cigarette case. It all seemed strangely out of place, as though these things belonged to someone who had either left in a hurry or had never truly settled in.

"Chris," Jessica called, her voice edged with unease, "come take a look at this."

I joined her by the armoire, and my breath caught in my throat. Inside was something I hadn't expected.

"What the hell?" I muttered, leaning in closer.

The armoire was packed with men's clothes—shirts, trousers, jumpers, even shorts and ties. They were wildly varied, as if they belonged to different men. A football-inspired T-shirt that read "I Love Nottingham Forest" hung next to an old silk pyjama top, which hung beside a black dinner jacket and a garish 70s tie-dye vest. None of it matched, and the sizes were inconsistent. It was like peering into someone's strange collection, where each item represented a fragment of a different time, a different man.

I sifted through them, hoping to find in the clothing an explanation to the randomness of everything. I needed to believe that we were simply intruders in someone's strange but harmless home.

But then I saw it. "Wait a second," I said, reaching in and pulling out a red Killers band T-shirt. My heart sank when I noticed the wristband hooked around the curve of the hanger. It was a band of large black beads adorned with Scandinavian runic symbols.

I held it out to Jessica, my voice barely above a whisper. "I know this. This was my brother's."

Jessica turned the wristband over in her hand, inspecting it closely. "What is it?"

I felt a sudden ripple of dizziness and sank onto the edge of the bed. "It's Adam's," I said, my voice strained. "I got this for him at a Heavy Metal Festival in Norway, brought it back as a gift. I'm sure this was on him when we cremated him."

Jessica's eyes widened in disbelief. She sat next to me, placing a reassuring hand on my leg. "How can it be here?" she asked, her voice laced with confusion.

I didn't have an answer. My heart raced as I tried to make sense of it. I was certain—certain—that Adam had worn it when he was cremated. But now, with everything in this strange cabin making me question my own reality, had I been wrong? Had the wristband somehow been left behind here?

"I don't know," I replied, meeting Jessica's eyes, "but do you see what this means? It means my brother was here."

Jessica looked around the room as if seeing it in a new, darker light. "What about the rest of the clothes?" she asked.

I shook my head, standing and returning to the cupboard, rifling through the strange assortment. "I don't see anything else of his," I said, pulling out a faded smoking jacket. "But some of this stuff looks ancient. I mean, who even wears these anymore?"

The more I examined the clothes, the stranger it all seemed. It felt as if this house wasn't just a hiding place for someone—it was a patchwork of different lives, of different eras, all cobbled together. The assortment of furniture, the mismatched clothes... it was unsettling. The picture I was forming was no longer just of a girl hiding away in a remote cabin. It felt like we had stepped into a place that was trying to be many different things at once, as if it held onto pieces of everyone who had ever crossed its threshold.

"What should we do now?" Jessica asked, taking the jacket from me and placing it back in the armoire, closing the door with a sharp, decisive click.

"If this is her house, then we go downstairs and don't move until she returns," I replied, fastening the band around my wrist, feeling its weight, the cool beads grounding me momentarily.

Back downstairs, I sank into the sofa, my mind still spinning from our discovery. Jessica, ever the practical one, offered to make us some herbal tea she had stashed in her pack. She disappeared into the kitchen as I tried to gather my thoughts. Outside, the wind howled louder, rattling the windows, and I felt a draft through the gap beneath the blinds. The storm seemed hell-bent on reminding us just how isolated we were out here. Yet, amid all the strangeness, I found myself smiling at the sound of Jessica whistling as the kettle boiled. Her positivity was the one thing keeping me anchored in this madness. Without her, I would've abandoned this search long ago, preferring the wrath of Smith to this increasingly bizarre search.

I was about to stand and join her when a shiver ran down my spine, a cold sensation brushing the back of my neck as though someone had breathed on me. The chill seemed to settle in my bones, and instinctively, I found myself longing for her presence again. I stood to walk toward the kitchen but stopped short, something catching my eye.

Above the door leading into the hallway, barely visible against the shadowy ceiling, was a small, square hatch. A simple panel, barely noticeable unless you were looking for it. We had been so focused on searching what was in front of us that we hadn't thought to look up.

"Jessica," I called, keeping my gaze on the hatch, "come here a second. I've found a hatch," I called out, my curiosity piqued.

"A what?" Jessica replied, her voice muffled from the kitchen.

"A hatch, in the front room," I repeated loudly.

Jessica reappeared with a tray in hand, balancing two steaming mugs of tea and a small plate of biscuits. "Who has a hatch in the living room?" she asked, frowning.

"The owner, obviously," I replied, reaching up to unlatch the lock.

With a creak, the hatch swung open, and a set of stepladders automatically descended. Thick and sturdy, they were joined to the opening by casters and runners. Above us was a void of darkness so dense, it seemed almost tangible, as if I could reach in and tear away pieces of it. I switched on my phone's torch and aimed the beam into the abyss.

"I'm going up," I muttered, more to myself than to Jessica.

"Maybe you shouldn't," she said.

"There might be something up there that tells us who owns this place," I replied, already placing my foot on the first step.

I ascended carefully, the light barely cutting through the thick gloom. The higher I climbed, the louder the storm outside seemed to roar, as if the wind was trying to claw its way inside. When I reached the top, I swung the torch around, but the darkness resisted the beam, letting me see no more than a foot ahead. As I took another step, something brushed my ear—a string. I grabbed it and gave it a gentle tug.

A warm, yellow light flickered to life, banishing the shadows instantly. The attic room was full of an unexpected coziness, nothing like the floor below. A plush red shag carpet lined the floor, soft under my feet. In the centre stood an antique red leather chair facing a vintage petrol heater, the faint scent of kerosene still lingering in the air. A tall wooden bookcase stood in one corner, filled with old hardback books and manuals. Beside it, a gleaming gramophone sat, a neat stack of records ready for play. The walls were lined with dark wooden frames, all empty, as though someone had deliberately removed the pictures.

"What's up there?" Jessica called from below.

"Come see for yourself," I replied.

Jessica's head poked through the opening. "What the—?" she exclaimed, climbing up to stand beside me, her eyes wide as she took in the room that felt like a preserved sanctuary.

Nagging thoughts crept into my mind as I tried to make sense of the house's layout. The design was odd, defying what I knew about the cottage. Mapping it out in my head, this room shouldn't exist. It felt like a hidden pocket, something that extended beyond the building's boundaries, as though it had been tucked away in some other dimension. No window, no sense of where this room fit into the overall structure—it was disorienting, like the house itself was playing tricks on me. The more I tried to understand it, the more the walls twisted into something intangible.

"Make it make sense, Jess, please," I pleaded, my thoughts swirling like a ship lost in a storm.

Sensing my distress, Jess took my arm and guided me toward the armchair, gently easing me into its worn leather. She placed her hand on my forehead. "You're burning up," she whispered. "I'll get you some tea and blankets, and we'll figure this out."

"I don't understand any of this," I muttered.

"Don't try to," she whispered, wiping my eyes.

"I don't feel well."

"I think you might have caught a chill. I'm going to make you some hot soup I found in the larder. We can work through everything when you're feeling better."

I nodded weakly.

She planted a kiss on my forehead. "Just remember, I love you."

I looked up at her, managing a weak smile. It was the first time I'd heard her say those words.

Once she disappeared through the hatch, I felt too restless to stay seated despite feeling out of sorts. My mind raced at the strangeness of the room. Driven by nervous energy, I stumbled to the bookshelf. I flipped through the books, noting their bizarre mix of times and eras. There was a land registry charter from the 1860s, a 1970s crime novel, and even university geography coursework. Nestled between a faded Shakespearean folio was a battered chemistry textbook from the 1930s, while next to it, a brightly illustrated book on Victorian botany stuck out awkwardly. The collection was as random as the rest of the house. Carefully, I put them back, feeling as if I shouldn't disturb their odd order.

Then, my attention shifted to the gramophone—an exquisite relic from the past. The polished wood gleamed, and the brass horn caught my reflection in its smooth curves. The turntable and needle arm were perfectly poised, waiting. Needing something to break the unsettling silence, I sifted through the records. The mix was just as eclectic as everything else in the cabin: Johnny Cash's Live from San Quentin was piled atop a 60s bluegrass compilation, followed by Wagner's The Ring of the Nibelung beneath an Alice in Chains album. It seemed the owner's taste spanned across all genres.

I settled on Frank Sinatra's *Songs of Love*. Sinatra was one of my father's favourites, and just seeing the album brought a sense of contentment.

Gently, I slid the vinyl from its sleeve, feeling its cool, smooth veneer beneath my fingers. After placing it on the turntable, I wound the handle, the mechanical clicks a strange contrast to the room's stillness. As the LP began to spin, I lowered the needle, and Sinatra's warm voice filled the room, wrapping around me like a reassuring blanket.

I felt small sense of normalcy. The storm outside and the eerie atmosphere faded as I sank back into the armchair. Sinatra's smooth voice filled the room, pushing back the strange unease that had followed me since we arrived. I called out to Jessica, hoping she'd join me, but there was no response. The silence felt almost expectant, but exhaustion weighed heavier. Instead of searching for her, I allowed myself to drift. Frank's crooning soothed me, the melody wrapping around me like a blanket, and before I knew it, sleep began to take hold, the boundaries of the room blurring as my eyes fluttered shut.

34

"Jess, are you there?" I called down the ladder, brushing away the cobwebs of sleep. "Jessica?"

The clock had just chimed six, jolting me awake from an awkward but deep slumber in the armchair. I'd slept through the night. A blanket was draped over me, and a bowl of tomato soup—now cold—sat on the gramophone table. I stood up groggily, my arm numb from the unpleasant position I'd slept in, tingling as I shook it to get the blood flowing. The cottage was silent; the storm had passed, and the rain had stopped. I was alone.

I climbed down the ladder to find the living room cold and empty. The lights were off, the blinds still drawn, and there was no sign of Jessica. I called out again, hoping she might be asleep somewhere, but a gnawing sense of wrongness settled deep inside me. I started searching the cabin, my movements frantic. I raced upstairs, checking each room, but they were all empty. The beds were untouched, the bathroom unused. Her coat and pack were nowhere to be found.

Panic set in. I shouted her name, but my throat was dry, scratchy. My heart pounded harder with each unanswered call. Desperate for clarity, I stumbled into the kitchen, hoping a glass of water might clear my head. The water was lukewarm, far from the cold shock I needed to snap me back to reality. As I opened the fridge, searching for ice, my eyes landed on a small yellow note stuck under a magnet shaped like a delicate white flower.

I'm gone. Don't try to follow or find me.
—J.

I read the note aloud, my voice barely a whisper. As the words sank in, an instinctive certainty gripped me—I'd never see her again. She was gone. I read the note over and over, searching for some clue, some explanation, but the nine words offered nothing. Why would she leave me like this? What could have caused her to go; had something happened whilst I was sleeping? Had this house, with this weirdness she first appeared to take in her stride, affected her more than I? Why didn't she wake me? My mind was a jumble, like a washing hamper in desperate need of sorting.

I downed the water, then put the kettle on, moving as though on autopilot. What more could I do? The world outside seemed distant, muted, like I was floating through a fog that dulled my senses. Mechanically, I wandered to the front door and opened it, half-expecting to see Jessica standing there, smiling, telling me it was all just some cruel joke. But there was nothing—just the stillness of the morning. Dawn had arrived, painting the sky in soft pinks and greys. The wind had calmed to a whisper, and only the faint sound of raindrops falling from the trees and the cabin roof broke the quiet of the forest.

It was clear Jessica had decided to end her part in this search and go home. I couldn't blame her. The last 24 hours had felt like a waking nightmare. I could've chased after her, tried to convince her to stay, but something inside told me she wouldn't have returned. I was here now, and despite the desperate urge to leave, to run after her and abandon everything, I knew deep down I had to stay. I had to see this through, to whatever bitter end awaited.

My stomach rumbled, reminding me I hadn't eaten. I made my way back to the kitchen, brewed some coffee, and began rummaging through the larder. Jessica had been right about the place—it was stocked as though someone was expecting there to be visitors. The shelves were lined with tins, jars, and packets of dried goods, everything neatly organised. The fridge hummed when I opened it, revealing fresh produce, milk, and a carton of eggs. Even the bread and cheese inside were still within date. The kitchen itself was surprisingly modern for such a secluded, cabin. There was a sleek stainless-steel microwave, a fancy espresso machine, and a toaster that looked brand new. It was strange seeing all these modern conveniences in a place that felt so removed from the world.

I didn't care that I was taking someone else's food; if they came back, I'd offer to pay for it. I made myself a toasted cheese sandwich, the bread browning perfectly in the state-of-the-art toaster, the kitchen filling with the scent of melted cheese. Drink in hand, I carried my meal back to the living room and sat on the sofa, eating in silence. The house felt emptier, hollowed out now that Jessica was gone.

I wasn't shocked by her departure. I'd been left alone before—first my mum when I was a child, then Adam, and finally Alice—but this hit me harder than any of them. There was a finality to it that I'd never experienced before, and it hurt in a different way. I found myself wondering when exactly Jessica had left, whether she had slipped out during the height of the storm, trudging through the wind and rain without a word. What was it about me that made her feel she had to leave without speaking to me first? I was at a loss—the kind of loss that makes a man question everything about himself. So, I did what I do best—nothing.

After finishing my toasted cheese sandwich, I cleaned the dishes and cups, the routine bringing no comfort. With nothing else to occupy me, I headed back up to the attic. From the bookcase, I selected a novel titled Fortune Favours the Lost, an action-packed tale set during the First World War. I retrieved Enya's greatest hits from the record pile, put it on, and settled back into the armchair, letting the soothing music and the book provide some much-needed distraction until it was time to eat again. I made it through three-quarters of the novel before hunger nudged me out of my reverie. The book was nothing special, but with the calming music in the background, it was easy to let my mind break away from everything outside this cozy little room.

Briefly, thoughts of Jessica rose, but they were quickly overshadowed by the routine of preparing a simple dinner—rice, chicken from the fully stocked freezer, and some parsley sauce. Her absence hit me again as I noticed the small piece of paper stuck to the fridge door. I couldn't bring myself to throw it away. Doing so would mean erasing the last trace of her presence, the final proof that she had been here with me, and I couldn't bear that.

In an attempt to numb the ache of her leaving, I decided to get drunk. The larder held a small wine rack with several bottles, each promising a different bouquet. Not caring which wine paired best with chicken and rice, I grabbed a bottle of red from the top. Returning to the attic with my meal, I ate, finished the book, and downed several glasses of wine as the eclectic records played on in the background. By 9 p.m., tiredness began to settle in, a pressure against my wine-soaked thoughts.

Unable to face another night in the armchair, half-drunk and craving simplicity, I made my way to the smaller bedroom. I didn't need the luxury of the larger room's bed; its plush furnishings would only amplify Jessica's absence. The stark plainness of the smaller room seemed more fitting for how I felt. I opened the blinds to let the night sky in. A waning moon played hide-and-seek with the clouds, casting a soft glow that made the room feel unexpectedly homely. Stripping off my clothes, I climbed into bed. To my surprise, the bed was much more comfortable than it looked, and the simple sheets felt oddly consoling.

As I lay there, I looked up at the moon, hoping Jessica had made it back to the village safely. The image of her, from that first night I saw her, played over in my mind, offering respite—though, like the moon slipping behind the clouds, it quickly faded. In its place, visions of my brother materialised—his wristband hidden in the cupboard. Had he really been here? Did he leave it for me to find, or had someone else placed it there to twist my mind and emotions? I lay there, hoping the answers would come, even if they scared me.

With that last thought, I turned onto my side, closed my eyes, and let sleep take me—deep and long.

35

I woke the next day to a room bathed in morning sunlight—the torrential rain and unpleasantness that nature had unleashed with its full force seeming like a distant memory. The warmth and light were a welcome reprieve, and I felt like I could breathe again. The beauty of the morning felt like an invitation, and I was eager to embrace it.

After making myself scrambled eggs on toast, accompanied by a steaming cup of coffee, I sat by the window, letting the caffeine work its magic. The warmth of the drink, coupled with the sun filtering through the curtains, made everything taste better. Though I still missed Jessica deeply, and the phantom of yesterday's strange events loomed large in my mind, I clung to the joy of having been with her, even if just for those few weeks. It was something worth cherishing.

Once breakfast was over, I felt aimless. The weather made staying in the attic feel like a waste, so I decided to take full advantage of the day. I ran a bath, scrubbing away the grime, feeling the dirt and confusion of the past few days leave me with the cleansing warm water. Rejuvenated, I washed my clothes and hung them over the stair railing to dry. As I rummaged through the armoire for something to wear, I came across a light navy-blue jumper and a pair of black chinos. Oddly enough, they fit perfectly. A strange thought crossed my mind—was this cabin some sort of stage set, these clothes meant for some past or future performance? It wasn't the worst explanation, though it felt like a stretch.

Dressed and feeling more relaxed than I had in days, I grabbed a chair from the kitchen, took the directions to the glade, and settled outside in front of the cabin. The sun kissed my skin, and the autumn air was just right. The forest around me came to life with birdsong and rustling leaves. I found myself simply listening—absorbing the calm that nature offered.

I pulled out a cigarette and rolled it between my fingers, debating whether to light it. The urge was there, but the idea of inhaling the smoke's bitter taste now seemed off-putting. I'd spent the morning cleansing myself, trying to regain a semblance of control. Lighting up now felt like undoing that progress, like poisoning my lungs after a fresh start. With a sigh, I put the cigarette back in the pack and tucked it into my pocket, silently hoping this would be a small step toward leaving that habit behind.

Unfolding the directions to the glade, I began to read. The path was described in careful, meticulous detail. From the fork in the road, I would have to push through thick undergrowth, navigating several twists and turns before reaching the clearing. About halfway, Marie had circled a spot on the map and left a note: "Look for the large broken stone resembling an owl. Another ghost story."

I paused, letting her words sink in. What did she mean by "another ghost story"? Was the forest littered with spirits of creatures long gone? I wondered what a ghost owl would look like—its silent wings gliding through the trees, eyes glowing faintly in the dim light, hooting a spectral warning to travellers. The tide of it was disconcerting, though a little ridiculous.

Bored with speculating about ghostly wildlife and restless with the directions in hand, I wandered around the cottage grounds. The property was a perfect square, hemmed in by dense woods just twelve feet from each side. At the back of the cottage, a narrow, overgrown path snaked into the forest, choked by thorny vines and thick underbrush. It looked more suited for a machete-wielding adventurer than a casual hiker like me. The thought of pushing through that tangle for the glade seemed less and less appealing.

"What makes this glade so special?" I muttered to myself as I returned to the front of the cottage. I'd seen plenty of glades before—pretty enough, sure, but nothing worth braving a thorny maze. I knew I had to decide soon: venture out now or wait for another sign, for something to push me forward. But with Jessica gone, I felt more inclined to stay. Maybe the solitude had something to offer if I just let it. So, I decided to sit, to let the quiet stretch out, and wait. Wait for what, I wasn't sure—maybe for the forest to speak, or perhaps for something inside me to finally settle.

I sank into my chair, and as I stared out into the woods, my mind drifted to old memories, half-buried but persistent. My father had taken Adam and me on endless tours across Europe, dragging us from city to city as he performed. He wanted us to absorb the music, the culture, hoping we'd follow in his footsteps. Adam took to it like a prodigy. I, on the other hand, remained indifferent. Those journeys, which meant everything to him, were just trips to me—distractions.

Though he loved us both, I knew Dad had been disappointed that only Adam had shared his passion. Being here now, I couldn't shake the feeling that, in pushing Adam so hard, Dad had set this whole chain of events into motion. Was I sitting in this remote place because of him? If Dad hadn't pressured Adam to carve out his place in the musical world, would any of this be happening? And now here I was, alone, waiting in this strange cottage for a woman I didn't even know, on behalf of a man I feared.

But where was this woman? Days had passed in Little Ashton and more here in this cabin, yet no sign of her. Had I made a mistake trusting Jessica's instincts, or even my own? Waiting felt futile now. The cottage, though well-stocked, only heightened the sense that I didn't belong here, that I was intruding on a life I wasn't meant to know. I was growing tired of trying to make sense of it all.

I decided I'd give it one more day. If nothing occurred, I'd leave. Walk away and keep walking until I found something that resembled closure or safety. No more wrestling with fate or trying to find answers that refused to materialise. I needed to move on, no matter what direction that might take me.

Suddenly, I noticed I hadn't heard the clock chime in a while. I wondered if I'd missed it, too lost in my thoughts. Curious, I went inside to check. The clock had stopped, its hands frozen at 11:26 a.m. Was there meaning to that specific time, or had the clock simply wound down? A disturbing thought crept in—what if time had frozen here, trapping me while life outside continued without me?

"Enough!" I yelled, startling myself with the intensity of my voice. "Enough of these questions!"

I was fed up with the constant churn, the endless second-guessing of every decision. Why couldn't I just accept where I was and what I was doing? I felt trapped in my own head, a prisoner of my own indecision. Every action led me back to the same place—more confusion, more doubt. Why did everything have to mean something? Why couldn't I just move forward without tearing myself apart, questioning every damn choice?

In a surge of frustration, I grabbed the clock, ready to hurl it against the wall. Its weight felt unnatural in my hands, cold and heavy, as though it held all the hours, minutes, and seconds I was losing—the past, present, and future bound up in one delicate shell. If time really had stopped, maybe shattering this clock would free me from its grip.

I stood there, gripping the clock firmly, my knuckles turning white as the cold metal pressed against my skin. It felt like I was holding something more than just a timepiece—like it was a prison I had found myself trapped in. My thoughts raced, darting between memories of the past, the uncertainty of the present, and the fear of a future I couldn't predict. The more I stared at its frozen hands, the more I convinced myself that this simple object was somehow responsible for everything that had happened. The clock had become a symbol of my frustration, of the helplessness I felt over the spiralling events of the past few days. Everything seemed to hang on the edge of destruction, and breaking this clock felt like the only way to release the pressure building inside me.

But then, as I was about to throw it, something stopped me. A quiet voice in the back of my mind whispered, *What if destroying it doesn't change anything? What if it makes things worse?*

I froze, my arms trembling as the clock hovered in midair. What was I doing? Destroying a clock wouldn't change the past, and it certainly wouldn't bring me any closer to answers. I lowered the clock slowly, my heartbeat calming, the fire inside me cooling to a low ember. Smashing it would be briefly satisfying, but then what? I'd still be here, stuck in this place, no closer to understanding why I'd been drawn here in the first place.

But before I chose to do anything else, a knock sounded at the door, and everything shifted.

36

The knock startled me, pulling me sharply from my thoughts. Who could it possibly be? Jessica, coming back after a change of heart? A lost traveller, stumbling upon the cottage by chance? Or maybe the real owner of the place, returning to reclaim their home? None of it made sense. If it had been Jessica or the owner, they wouldn't have knocked. They'd have walked straight in, no hesitation.

I set the clock back on the mantel, suddenly worried that whoever was outside might have overheard me—a stranger inside, on the verge of smashing a clock and shouting about time. Running my hands through my hair, I tried to smooth my untidiness into something passable and adjusted my clothes, attempting to look less like a man who'd been living in borrowed space. My heart raced as I hesitated at the door, unsure of who—or what—was waiting on the other side.

When I opened the door, my breath caught in my throat. Standing there, smiling lightly, was the girl from the pictures. The girl with the birthmark. The one I had been searching for. She was shorter than I had imagined, maybe 5'7" or 5'8", her striking green eyes gleaming beneath the long cascade of her blonde hair. The rose-red birthmark, like a flame across her left eye, was bold and captivating. It didn't detract from her beauty—in fact, it enhanced it, drawing me in, making it difficult to look away.

"May I come in?" she asked, her voice a soothing mix of warmth and something otherworldly.

"Please," I said, stepping aside without hesitation, as if her appearance had been expected all along.

She moved with effortless grace, almost floating across the floor, her bare feet landing silently on the hardwood. I noticed they were perfectly clean—no dirt, no mud—despite the wet, wooded surroundings. She wore a pale green summer dress speckled with tiny white flowers, her slender frame exuding a calm intensity that filled the room.

"Would you like something to drink?" I offered, trying to keep my voice steady as I shut the door behind her.

"A glass of water, please," she replied, her eyes fixed on me, their glow subtly magnetic.

I escaped to the kitchen, my mind racing. I poured a tall glass of water for her, adding ice, and then filled my own glass with wine—leftover from the night before. It was early, but I had a feeling I'd need the fortification.

"Here you go," I said, handing her the water and sitting across from her.

"Thank you," she murmured, but instead of drinking it, she placed the glass carefully on the floor beside her, that serene, unreadable smile never leaving her face.

I took a long sip of wine, studying her. She was captivating, impossible to look away from. Her presence filled the room like a glowing hearth in an old mansion of gloom, casting heat and light into every dark corner.

"I hear you've been looking for me," she said, her voice calm.

How did she know? Had Jessica mentioned something before she left? Or was it Marie?

"Who told you?" I asked cautiously.

"No one in particular," she replied, still smiling. "But I've heard from some that a man and a woman have been making their way through the forest, searching for me."

Marie, I thought immediately. It had to be her. Only Marie knew that Jessica and I had ventured out here.

"I would've come sooner, but the storm kept me away," she said timidly, her voice laced with a gentle apology.

"Well, you're here now," I replied.

She glanced around the room, her eyes briefly lingering on the clock, still stuck at 11:26. Then she said, "The girl you were with... she left yesterday, didn't she?"

I stiffened. "How do you know that?"

Her expression remained serene, as if the question wasn't important. "I'm sorry she didn't have the strength to stay. But she wanted you to know she'll be fine. She's on her way home now."

"You saw her?" I asked, suspicion rising in my voice.

She nodded, her smile never faltering. "Yes."

"What else did she say?"

"She doesn't want you to look for her," the woman continued, her tone even but not unkind. "If you do, you won't find her. She'll be long gone—somewhere you can't reach."

I took a deep drink of wine, trying to process her words. Her look was penetrating, as if she could see straight through my questions, right down to my core. I felt powerless, like I was losing control of a conversation that wasn't even mine anymore.

"I'm sorry," she said again, almost tenderly. "But that's the way it is. People move at different paces. Her footsteps... they were always quicker than yours. Maybe they always will be."

"But she wanted to come with me," I protested, my voice rising with frustration, even though I sensed the futility of it.

"She did," the woman replied, her tone still infuriatingly calm, "until she didn't."

"So, I'll never see her again?" My voice cracked, thick with emotion, though deep down I already knew the answer.

She shook her head gently, and something stirred inside me—an unsettling recognition, like I had seen her before, but I couldn't place where. It felt distant, blurred.

"Have we met before?" I asked, now unsure if this woman was a stranger at all.

"Maybe," she said, tilting her head as if the answer could go either way. "Maybe not. I don't think I know you. But when you ask what you came here to ask—if you even know what that is—maybe I'll remember you."

A thousand questions surged through my mind, but I knew she wouldn't indulge them all. I could've asked about the Russian, ended the conversation quickly, and left. But instead, the first question that escaped my lips was the one I hadn't planned.

"How did you know my brother?"

Her expression softened, as a small, sad smile touched her lips. "Adam? I loved him very much. He was such a sensitive soul, much like mine. He played the most beautiful music for me. When he died, it shattered me—not just for myself, but for everyone who knew him. I don't think he ever realised how much he meant to so many people."

The way she spoke of Adam... a lump rose in my throat, the grief bubbling up too quickly to suppress.

"Do you know why he killed himself?" I asked, my voice strained, balancing on the edge of pain and anger.

She shook her head slowly, her eyes brimming with an unspoken sorrow. "If I knew, it wouldn't be my place to tell you. Some things... only the person who carries them can explain."

Frustration surged inside me, making the room feel suddenly suffocating. I stood up, pacing toward the window, and yanked the blinds open, letting the cool air rush in.

"Is this your cottage?" I asked, my impatience breaking, needing something concrete.

Her eyes drifted over the room as though she was seeing it for the first time. "It might be," she answered with a soft, uncertain shrug. "I can't really say."

"You don't know where you live?" I asked again, disbelief lacing my words.

She stood, her fingers trailing along the walls, the furniture, as if trying to conjure a memory, one that eluded her. "So much changes for me. It's hard to keep track. I can be... forgetful."

"Forgetful?" I echoed, incredulous. "Is that what you call it?"

She turned toward me, a small, almost playful smile tugging at the corners of her lips. "Don't you forget things?"

"Only the things I *want* to forget," I muttered, "and even then, not easily."

She leaned over the back of the sofa, resting her chin on her hands, her green eyes locking onto mine. "There's something else you want to ask. You've come a long way for answers—it wouldn't be wise to waste the time we have together."

Her words cut through me. There was something unnervingly familiar about her—her movements, the way she spoke, as if we'd done this dance before. I tried to place her face, erasing the birthmark in my head, reshaping her features. Then it hit me, like a flash.

"Do you know a girl named Marie?" I asked, the realisation forming even as the question left my lips.

She tilted her head slightly, her smile widening with amusement. "No, should I? Is she another girlfriend of yours?" Her voice was light, but her eyes gleamed with sharp curiosity, as though my question had revealed more than I'd intended.

"No," I said, shaking my head. "She was a friend of my brother's. You knew her father. He has a sketch of you."

Her expression softened as she seemed to drift into memory. A wistful smile played on her lips. "The artist, George. Yes, I remember him. I met him here, in the woods many moons ago… or was it less than that? I used to watch him in the glade, sketching such beautiful pictures. One day, with courage, I approached him, and he asked to draw me. I sat for him for hours, and as the night fell, he said he would complete it at home and give it to me as a gift, but… he never returned."

"He died," I said, my voice dropping. "Seems like that happens to a lot of the men you meet."

Her smile vanished, replaced by a quiet sadness. She absorbed the news in silence. "I know," she murmured, as if death was an old, familiar companion.

Without another word, she stood and wandered over to the steps leading up to the attic. Placing a hand on the railing, she turned back to me, her playful smile reappearing. But as she did, the sleeve of her dress slipped slightly, revealing a scar running around her bicep in a perfect circle. My eyes locked onto the mark, trying to place where I might've seen something like it before, but nothing came to mind. She noticed me staring and quickly adjusted her dress, her smile faltering.

"What's up there?" she asked, her voice laced with curiosity.

"Just another strange room in a strange cottage in a strange fucking forest," I muttered, irritation creeping into my tone as I sank back into the armchair. If she wanted to pretend this wasn't her house, I could play along.

She let go of the step and crossed the room, kneeling beside the chair. Her hand found mine, her touch soft but somehow settling.

"Don't be angry with me," she whispered, her voice soothing, tender. "We all carry our sins with great reluctance. I've made peace with mine; perhaps it's time you made peace with yours."

I groaned, feeling exasperation build inside me like a storm ready to break. "I didn't come here to talk about sins. There's a man—someone dangerous—who wants to speak to you. If I don't bring you to him, he's going to make sure I regret it."

Her expression shifted, softening into something almost childlike, as if what I said wounded her. "I have nothing more to say to him. His hour has passed."

She knew. She knew exactly who I was talking about. The way she spoke, the way she looked at me—there was no mistaking it. She was the same woman from the photos, the same woman who had vanished decades ago.

I shot up from the chair and walked to the corner where I'd stashed the file. Her eyes followed me, calm and resolute, as I grabbed the folder and tossed it onto the coffee table. I spread out the photos, the ones Smith had given me, hoping to finally force some clarity out of her.

"This is you, isn't it? In all three of these pictures?" I demanded.

She leaned in, studying the images with careful, almost reverent attention. I saw a flicker of something—recognition, perhaps, or maybe guilt—cross her face, but it vanished as quickly as it had appeared. Her expression remained an unreadable mask.

"It looks like me," she said, her voice timid, as if admitting to something she couldn't fully grasp. She lingered on the photo of the Russian as a boy, her fingers brushing the edge of the image. "But this one… I know who he is, but I don't know this picture," she added, handing it back to me like it was something fragile. "I don't know where this is."

"That's Russia," I said, the frustration in my voice rising. "Supposedly, you were there with him when he was just a lad."

She tilted her head, the confusion deepening in her eyes. "I don't know Russia… is that a place?"

"You recognise the family before the war in this first picture?" I pointed, and she nodded.

"That's Michael Ashby," she said, her voice barely above a whisper. "I knew him when he was a boy. He wanted to be a poet—used to write for me, pour his heart into it. But then… he disappeared. Sent to fight somewhere, someone. When he came back, he wasn't the same."

"And you recognise my brother's picture from a few years ago?" I asked, already knowing the answer but needing confirmation.

She nodded once more.

"But you don't know this one, from the '70s?"

"I can only tell you what I know," she said, her tone pleading, like she wanted to be understood but was shackled by half-forgotten recollections. "The first time I met him, he was already a man, not a boy."

"Okay, okay, calm down," I muttered. "Let's say you're right—why does he want to see you so badly? What did you say to him that's got him so desperate? What is it that he needs from you?"

She shook her head gently, her expression resolute. "I told him what he needed to hear. I can't give him more than that. He should forget we ever met and live the rest of his life in peace."

I leaned forward, gripping the edges of the photograph that featured her with my brother. "I think it's too late for that. He wants to see you again, and I need to bring you to him."

"That you cannot do," she stated, her voice steady.

Rising from my seat, I held the photo closer to her. "Who the hell are you?"

She stood slowly, smoothing her dress with calm, deliberate movements. Her eyes softened, but she offered no answer. Instead, she simply said, "I need to go now. It's late, and I need to get back."

I glanced at the clock on the mantel—it read 3 p.m. Time, which had seemed frozen earlier, had inexplicably leaped forward. I felt disoriented. Where did she need to return to? Had I been wrong all along about this being her home?

"Is this all you can give me?" I called after her, my voice raw. "I need more, please. If you can't explain what happened with Adam, I need something to bring back to the Russian—anything. If I don't, things will get worse. I've already lost enough—my brother, Jessica… haven't I suffered enough?"

She paused with her hand on the doorknob. It seemed like she was going to leave, but then she turned her head slightly. "I'll think about it. I'll return in two days. Will you wait for me?"

"I have no choice," I replied, my words bitter.

Without another word, she opened the door and stepped outside. I rushed to the window by the door, watching her barefoot figure glide across the grass, her steps light as if she floated. I stood there, frozen, as she disappeared into the thick woods, vanishing like mist caught in the wind. A shiver ran through me. Had she really been here, or had my isolation twisted my mind?

Returning to the sofa, I spotted the glass of water she had asked for—still full, untouched. I stared at it, my mind racing. I looked down at my hand, where her touch had felt so real, the warmth of her fingers still vivid in my memory. But couldn't the mind play tricks? Was I fooling myself into believing she'd been here? Yet, the cushions still bore the faint indentation of her body, her elbows having left soft marks on the back of the sofa.

Real or not, I had another 48 hours in this place, so there was no use dwelling on it. I needed to focus—losing my grip now would serve no one. With two days to fill, I knew I had to keep busy. There was food to cook, books to read, music to listen to—all distractions to stave off the growing unease.

I retreated to the kitchen, grounding myself in the routine of cooking. The simple, familiar motions—chopping, searing, boiling—helped clear the clutter in my mind. Before long, I had a plate of perfectly cooked sirloin steak, seared in butter and garlic, with boiled potatoes on the side. The scent filled my senses, a reminder of something physical, something real.

With my dinner in hand, I made my way back to the attic—what I had mentally dubbed my "entertainment loft." It was the only place in the cottage that didn't feel like I wished to escape from. Settling into the worn armchair, I balanced the plate on my lap and reopened the World War I novel I'd started earlier. The rhythmic pattern of reading and eating was a welcome distraction. Each bite of steak pulled me further away from the mystery outside and deeper into the safety of the story.

Tomorrow would likely be more of the same—cooking, reading, waiting. And after that? Only she knew what was to come.

37

The next day passed uneventfully, which turned out to be more disturbing than reassuring. With no one to talk to, I spent the morning making a large breakfast, then aimlessly wandered through the cottage's six rooms, hoping to discover hidden nooks or secret compartments like the attic space. I knocked on walls, listening for hollow sounds that might betray a secret area, and even pulled up the rugs on the ground floor, hoping to uncover a basement door. There was nothing.

Bored, I decided to reorganise the clothes in the main cupboard. First, I sorted them by the era they seemed to belong to, then by type, and finally by size. It was a pointless task, an attempt to stave off growing restlessness. Fashion, clearly, wasn't my calling. After deciding the wardrobe was no longer worth my attention, I retreated back to the loft.

I grabbed a book on fly fishing and put on an AC/DC record, letting Brian Johnson's voice fill the room. The gramophone, despite its age, played the rock album flawlessly. If You Want Blood thumped through the air as I half-heartedly flipped through the pages of the fishing book, trying to focus on knots and bait selection. The words seemed distant, like a foreign language I had no interest in learning. as though they were meant for someone else. My mind wandered, unable to engage with the content in front of me.

The music was more satisfying than anything else, and I found myself eyeing the gramophone with growing interest. Could I steal it? I wondered. I gave it a try, lifting the base, but it was far heavier than I expected—definitely not something I could smuggle under a jacket. Realistically, if the woman agreed to pass her message on to the Russian, I'd likely have enough money to buy a better one. But it wasn't about owning a gramophone. I wanted *this* one, this strange relic of an uncertain time, just like the cottage.

Lunchtime came and went, minutes ticking by at their usual, maddeningly slow pace. I ended up outside again, seated on the lawn, the midday sun warming my skin. I stared into the forest's depths, trying to piece together how many days had passed since I last saw Jessica. How long had I been here? Four, maybe five days? If it approached six, Marie would surely come searching for me soon. Oddly, I realised I didn't mind. I was content, in a strange way, with this solitude, and Marie could take her time. I wasn't in any hurry to be rescued.

With little to fill the hours beyond unremarkable novels and a collection of records, I considered whether this feeling of restlessness was a symptom of modern life—of being a man of the 21st century, dependent on distractions. I pondered this as I walked the perimeter of the property, staring into the trees. Every so often, I thought I saw something moving—a figure, perhaps, dancing among the trunks—but whenever I tried to focus, it disappeared, leaving only the sway of bushes in the wind. Was this what men lost in the desert saw before they succumbed to madness? Mirages, formed by an aching need for companionship, with vultures circling overhead, waiting for them to drop.

I glanced up, half-expecting to see a vulture circling above, but the sky was clear save for a few distant birds, too high to matter. I let out a shout, a primal yell that echoed through the empty forest, as if calling out to the nowhere people who lived in this nowhere place. I needed them to know I was still here, still alive, still waiting. Who would come? Men? Women? Deer, perhaps? Or maybe the forest's mythical creatures—the fauns, fairies, and giants from the stories of old.

I sat back down with a large sigh, the scream releasing something inside me, like a pressure valve opening. If the giants came, at least I'd hear them—feel their footsteps shaking the earth long before they arrived. What I'd offer them when they get here, I wouldn't know. For now, it was just me and the quiet forest.

Later in the afternoon, the skies darkened, and I felt the first raindrops on my face, signalling the end of the clear weather. Soon, I'd have to retreat to my little sanctuary again. I chuckled at the thought—this place had become my refuge, my shelter from the storm. Here, I could sit and wait it out, safe from the elements. I dragged myself inside just as the rain intensified, pounding the roof and windows in a relentless drumbeat, filling the silence of the cottage.

I cooked myself a simple meal, opened another bottle of wine, and settled on the sofa with my fly-fishing book while the storm raged outside. In the towns, villages, and cities beyond this forest, people would be running for cover, scrambling to escape the rain. That thought somehow made me feel more alone than ever. Jessica, Marie, and the girl were the only people in England who knew I was here, and none of them were going to walk through that door. To anyone outside that tiny social circle, I no longer existed. I felt obsolete.

The changing weather distorted how I felt about my isolation. When the sun was shining, everything seemed fine, even peaceful. But now, with the rain coming down hard, the quiet felt different—thick and oppressive, like syrup slowly pouring from a tin. I ached for another voice—any voice that wasn't my own. I rummaged through my bag for my phone, knowing it was useless but still clinging to some small hope. As Marie had warned, not a single signal bar appeared on the screen. No calls, no messages—no contact with the outside world.

I couldn't call Marie. I couldn't reach Jessica. I couldn't even hear the gravelly, drunken tones of my friend ranting about his life's disappointments—woes I would've gladly listened to for a change. Hell, I would've settled for irritating Keith with some random question about life, just to fill the silence with a voice that wasn't my own.

I tossed the phone onto the armchair, my isolation pressing on me like quicksand, threatening to swallow me whole. I craved a cigarette, but the few I had were ruined—wet and discarded when I'd tried to rid myself of the temptation. Instead, I sipped more wine, occasionally biting my nails as a poor substitute. If I drank too much more, I'd end up like my friend, drowning in self-pity, blaming Jessica and my brother for all my problems.

How was my friend, anyway? Had he taken my advice? Cut down on the booze and finally asked out his secretary, like I'd suggested? I hadn't heard from him since I left, and though I had no right to be upset, I took it personally. Maybe he was still bitter that I'd distanced myself, first—quitting the company, then disappearing without accepting his help with this bizarre ordeal. After all, we'd been through thick and thin together, and suddenly I'd cut him out, leaving while I chased ghosts in the middle of nowhere. I wondered if he thought I'd abandoned him, just like I was beginning to feel abandoned by everyone else.

I thought about the full bottles of whiskey in the larder. When I got out of here, I'd grab one on my way out. My friend and I could crack it open, toasting to this whole absurd world. A small consolation, perhaps, but better than letting this sense of abandonment take over. It felt like a snake compressing its coils around my psyche—half-starved and desperate to devour me whole.

A crack of thunder interrupted my thoughts, rattling the windows. I cursed the storm. Why did it always feel like nature was conspiring against me? Why couldn't this whole affair have taken me somewhere warm and inviting—Greece or Spain, perhaps? No, my lot was to sit here, alone, in this strange, unsettling house, while the outside took pleasure in tormenting me. Nature itself was mocking me, gleefully throwing a middle finger up to my face.

I glanced at the half-eaten dinner of sausages and mash I'd made earlier and left. Stress always did the same thing to me—killed my appetite. For someone who loved food, losing that pleasure felt like a slow death. But what did it matter? Another meal would go cold in this place where nothing seemed to move forward or make sense. "What if I just sit here and starve?" I asked the empty room. "And what happens when the girl returns to find a corpse? Will she notify the authorities, or will she leave my body to waste away into nothingness?"

Of course, there was no response. Why would I expect anything different from these walls? Another crack of thunder followed my inquiry, as if mocking me. I was getting agitated, so I decided I would pour three more large glasses of wine and end this tedious day on a blissfully drunken note. I didn't care if I could handle any more alcohol or not; sinking into inebriation was the only escape left.

"Are you sure you should get drunk?" I asked myself, my voice echoing in the empty space.

I laughed. Talking to myself—what a sight that must be. A psychologist would have a field day with me. I could picture the scene: several therapists watching this scene from behind a two-way mirror, each clutching a clipboard and pen, scribbling notes on the rapid disintegration of a man's sanity.

"Add more thunder," the psychologist in charge would say, tapping the glass with a pencil. *"It seems to be pushing him closer to the edge."*

"Do you think he'll last the night?" one colleague would ask, noting my dishevelled appearance.

"If my hypothesis is correct," the doctor would reply, *"if we increase the loneliness by a factor of four, it'll only be a few more hours before we see him self-destruct."*

The sudden burst of laughter that followed was maniacal, echoing against the walls. I threw the glass of wine at the wall, smashing it into shards. The red wine splattered across the light grey wall like blood from an open wound.

"You want crazy, doc?" I screamed, blowing an exaggerated raspberry at the imaginary two-way mirror. "I'll show you crazy!"

This house was no longer a haven. It needed renovation—a shift in energy, some feng shui to lighten the mood—and the only interior designer left on this shitty evening was me. But what tools did I have for such a task? I stormed into the kitchen, grabbed the heaviest blade from the knife block, and charged upstairs. One goal burned in my mind: the luxury bedroom was about to become luxurious no more.

First, the armoire. I would rip every piece of clothing from its depths and toss them into the mud outside. A few well-aimed kicks would shatter the antique cupboard, and I'd throw the doors from the bedroom window to join the ruined garments in the dirt, with a view to setting the pile alight when I was through. Then, the bedding—slashed to ribbons in a knife-fuelled frenzy, stripping away every trace of extravagance. And finally, the pièce de résistance: my name, carved in huge letters into the wall. Proof that I existed, right here, in this exact point in time.

My heart thudded in my ears, matching the frantic pace of my breath as I entered the bedroom. The shadows in the room seemed to stretch and distort, egging me on, whispering encouragement. I raised the blade, watching my reflection flicker in the polished wood, and imagined the satisfying sound of splintering timber, the rush of adrenaline as I gutted the furniture like a killer with a vendetta. My vision blurred, fuelled by rage and resentment, and I could already see myself tearing into the soft fabric, ripping apart this pristine mockery of calm. Each step was deliberate, controlled, but my mind was a whirlwind of chaotic thoughts—images of destruction, of fire, of finally letting loose all the madness that had been building inside me. This was going to be my masterpiece of mayhem.

But as I approached the armoire, I caught sight of myself in the dresser mirror. It froze me. The man staring back was unfamiliar to me. Dishevelled hair stuck to my damp forehead, red-rimmed eyes swollen from lack of sleep, with dark circles hanging like bruises beneath them. My clothes were wrinkled, hanging loose and twisted as if I'd thrown them on in a rage. A wild, red-eyed beast had replaced the groomed man I once knew. The knife slipped from my hand, clattering to the floor as I sat, staring at the stranger in the mirror.

Did that man within the mirrored plane of existence really look like that? I shook my head slowly, and he followed, mimicking every movement. I winked, and he winked back. I stuck my tongue out, his tongue a horrid shade of wine-red, speckled and cracked, the texture reminding me of dried blood on old leather. I tilted my head slightly, and so did he, eyes narrowing with an eerie synchronisation.

"What will become of him when I'm gone?" I questioned aloud, stepping in and out of the bedroom, and witnessing him do the same.

"I really don't want to leave here, but when you go, I follow," he whispered without sound. "Seeing how shocked you are, I believe you'd be happy with that."

"I'm sorry you feel that way," I said, my voice trembling. "But you scare me. You're nothing like me… at least, not the me I believe myself to be."

"Try being on this side of the glass, looking at you looking at me." His tone darkened. "I've lost just as much as you. I've felt everything you have, but you don't care. You just see what I am and wish to be rid of me." His face twisted with anger. "How do you think that makes me feel, knowing you hate me so much?"

"I'm sorry, I didn't mean to—" I stammered.

"You know what that is? It's selfish. A selfish desire to erase anything that makes you discomfited. Maybe Jessica left because she saw the man inside you—the one who could so easily fall apart, one blood cell at a time, and then blame me for it."

My heart sank. I placed my hand against the mirror, and the reflected Chris did the same. Our hands pressed together, separated only by the cold pane of glass.

"You're right," I admitted. "I've been terrible." I glanced around the room, the signs of my growing madness clear in the disarray. "It's this place… it's transformed who I am."

"I know, brother," he replied, a trace of kindness softening those sunken eyes. "Do me a favour, and I'll forgive you. Climb into bed and rest. Tomorrow, the girl will come. She'll give you what you need, and then you can return to your life of rationality and logic."

"I will," I murmured, wiping a smear of spittle from the glass as the restlessness slowly drained from my body. "Tomorrow is a new day."

I rose from the dresser and climbed onto the bed, feeling the creak of the mattress beneath me. The man in the mirror mimicked my every move, his eyes fixed on mine, both of us bound by the unspoken agreement that tonight, we would rest. We lay down beneath the quilt, facing each other through the reflection, as the storm outside pressed down on the house like a lead blanket.

"Sometimes all we really need is each other," he said, his voice thin, as though the energy to speak was draining away.

Despite his appearance, despite the horror of seeing myself reduced to this, I found comfort in him—a quiet understanding that we were in this together, for better or worse. Slowly, our eyes closed in unison, it was just me and him. Two halves of the same whole, finding solace in our shared plight.

38

It was 2:30 p.m., and I had been perched on a kitchen chair by the front door for two hours, waiting with growing impatience for the girl to arrive. My head still throbbed from the previous night's excesses, and the storm outside had only worsened my state. I'd forced down a slice of toast for breakfast, but my unsettled stomach refused anything more. The storm's relentless fury felt personal, like a wolf trying to tear down the last fragile house to reach the pig inside.

Despite my reflection's efforts to talk sense into me, my thoughts spiralled wildly, like a weathervane caught in the storm battering the cottage walls. I considered leaving, escaping while I still had a shred of sanity. I tried to talk myself into returning to Smith and bluffing my way through with a fake note from the girl. But I knew better. A man like Smith's boss could see through any lie with terrifying ease. The risk was too great.

As 3 p.m. approached, I had nearly given up on the girl ever arriving. My patience had worn dangerously thin; I was running out of fucks to give. Each one slipped through my grasp like sand, and soon, there'd be none left. Just a graceless man, desperate to run screaming back to the home he missed. The air felt thick with the damp smell of regret, and every creak of the house seemed to mock me, reminding me of the fragile grip I had left on myself.

Then, at 3:04 p.m., three sharp knocks echoed through the cottage, snapping me out of my anxiety. I rushed to the door, flinging it open to find her standing there, soaked to the bone. Her small frame trembled in the cold, her teeth chattering.

"I told you I'd come back," she said weakly, her voice barely audible over the howling wind.

"Come in before you catch your death," I said, concern replacing my irritation. I placed a hand on her shoulder and guided her inside. Her golden hair limp, strands clinging to the straps of her pink dress, partially concealing the familiar birthmark. She looked utterly pitiful, like a drenched puppy abandoned in the rain.

"I'm so cold," she whispered, shivering as tiny puddles formed around her feet.

"Come on," I urged, taking her icy hand and leading her upstairs. "Let's get you a towel."

She followed in silence, her small, frozen fingers sending a shiver through me. In the bathroom, I grabbed a thick towel and began drying her hair. She stood still, compliant, letting me rub her head like a father might with his daughter. The intimacy was strange—just hours ago, I had been furious, frustrated with her, but now all I felt was a deep, inexplicable sympathy. The anger that had threatened to consume me had dissolved, leaving only quiet tenderness in its wake.

"Why did you come in this weather?" I asked, though deep down, I was grateful she had. Her arrival was all I had been waiting for.

"Because I said I would," she said, her voice muffled beneath the grey wool towel. There was a vulnerability in her tone, something that tugged at a part of me I couldn't quite name.

But it's terrible out there," I replied. I resisted the urge to ask her more pressing questions—questions my reflection was practically shouting at me to ask: Where had she come from? Why now? Instead, I stepped back, assessing my hasty hair-drying attempt. "It could have waited until the storm passed."

"I don't know when it will be through. The storm is stronger than what we normally get around here," she said, her eyes glancing out the window. I stepped forward again, noticing a small patch of wet hair I'd missed and gently rubbing it dry.

"There, that's a bit better," I said, forcing a smile.

She smiled at me, a sincere, soft smile that was hidden beneath damp, tangled hair. "Thank you," she said, blowing a few stray strands out of her face.

As I lowered the towel, her small hand reached out and gently touched mine, her fingers lingering on my skin. The warmth of her touch startled me—it felt so different from the cold, lifeless sensation I had expected. My eyes drifted to the birthmark around her eye, and without thinking, I traced its outline with my fingertip, following the delicate curve. The mark seemed to pulse with a deeper hue than before, its redness more vivid, more alive.

"You're being so kind to me, and I'm not sure why I deserve it. I thought you hated me," she whispered.

"I don't hate you," I replied. "I just really need you to give me what I came for."

"I'm still not sure I can," she said, "but I can help in other ways."

She took hold of my hand and kissed it tenderly. Her green eyes locked with mine, wide and searching. I felt an unmistakable pull—a deep, irrational urge to close the distance between us, to press my lips to hers. My body leaned in slightly, the sensation of her closeness intoxicating. In my mind, I saw the scene unfold: her gown slipping to the floor, our bodies knotted together beneath the warmth of the sheets.

I shook the thought, grappling with what this girl was stirring within me. She reached behind her, unzipping her dress, ready to bare herself fully.

"Hold on," I said abruptly, pulling away. "This isn't right."

I handed her the towel, forcing myself to step back, trying to smother the sudden yearning that had flared up inside me with the cold reality of Jessica's absence. She continued undressing, her eyes still locked on mine, unblinking. I turned around, unwilling to watch the rest, not trusting myself if I did.

"There are some clean clothes in the cupboard," I said, my back to her, pointing at the armoire. "I'm sure you already know that. Just take what you want."

I retreated downstairs to the kitchen, splashing cold water on my face, trying to cleanse the lingering desire. There was no version of this where giving in would be right. How it had happened so quickly stumped me. Before her arrival, I was convinced my only goal was to retrieve her for the Russian and be done with her. Yet now, her presence seemed to grip me in a way I hadn't anticipated—a magnetic force that I imagined had ensnared men like my brother and Marie's father. It was alarming how easily I'd almost lost myself in her. I needed to remember what today was about.

I stood at the window, staring at the relentless downpour as it pooled into large puddles around the cottage. The rain became my anchor, each ripple expanding outward like a metronome, the rhythm of droplets steadying my mind. I focused on the circles forming in the puddles, counting them, using them to keep my thoughts in check, to suppress the dangerous temptation waiting upstairs.

"Hello," she said.

I turned, relieved to see her in the oversized red T-shirt with "Leeds Motorcycle Club" emblazoned across the chest. It draped loosely over her small frame, reaching her knees, still slightly damp from the rain but dry enough to make her look more refreshed. Her hair was neatly brushed and pinned back, exposing the birthmark on her face. It seemed to glow faintly in the dim light—was that even possible? The mark seemed alive, like it had a presence of its own.

I blinked, feeling disoriented, but quickly refocused. "Of all the clothes you could have chosen, you pick that?" I smiled, trying to lighten the mood.

She smoothed the fabric t-shirt down and shrugged. "I tried on some of the others, but I liked this. Don't you like it?"

I nodded. "I made you a hot drink," I said, gesturing toward the steaming mug on the table. "I wasn't sure if you'd prefer tea or coffee, so I played it safe and made you hot chocolate."

She smiled and sat down on the sofa, tucking her legs beneath her as she wrapped both hands around the warm mug. She blew into it gently before taking a sip, her lips barely touching the rim.

"I'm sorry about earlier," I began, my voice heavy with regret. "That was wrong of me."

She glanced at me, a faint smile tugging at the corners of her mouth as her tongue darted out to catch a bit of chocolate from her lip. "It's okay," she said reassuringly. "Strange situations make us do strange things. We're only human, after all."

I repeated her words in my head, *We're only human.* But was that true? Was she really like me? Because nothing about her felt entirely 'human.'

"How long does it take you to get here?" I asked. "If this isn't your house, do you live nearby?"

"I think I did live here once, long ago," she replied, taking another sip of her drink. "But that was before it looked like this."

"When it was the gamekeeper's lodge?"

She shook her head, her eyes distant as if recalling a memory buried beneath layers of time. "Before that," she said, "though I can't remember what it looked like then."

The bright, playful girl I'd met just days ago seemed a world away from the person now sitting in front of me—thoughtful, subdued, carrying a depth I hadn't noticed before. It was as if she bore the weight of something ancient, something far beyond my understanding.

"How long ago?" I asked, my curiosity piqued. If she was willing to answer, maybe I could finally begin to unravel the mystery that surrounded her.

She shook her head, her expression distant. "I can't remember. So much of my life has blurred together, only certain people and moments remain clear to me."

I paused, unsure how to respond, before saying, "I'm glad you remembered me."

"How could I forget," she said with a soft smile. "Rain or shine, I wished to return to you."

As she shifted in her seat, uncrossing her legs, I noticed something—a mark around her ankle, similar to the one on her arm. Burn marks. The sight of them stirred questions in my mind, but I pushed them aside, knowing there were more pressing matters at hand.

"Thank you," I said, trying to strike a gentler tone. "I think we got off on the wrong foot during your last visit. I didn't mean to be angry with you. It's just... I don't want to be here any longer than I have to. I need what I came for, and then I'll leave you in peace."

She nodded, her tone empathetic. "I understand. It must be hard, doing the bidding of others, especially those who threaten and bully. But you're brave to take on what most wouldn't have the courage to do."

Brave. The word felt foreign to me, almost laughable. I didn't feel brave—just worn down, my sense of self slipping away, like the rain washing into the earth outside.

"Did you decide on the note for the Russian?" I asked, steering the conversation back to the reason she was here. She nodded, her expression distant. "It wasn't easy, but I will give you a note for him, though I shouldn't. Meeting him was purely accidental. I wasn't there for him—I was saying goodbye to someone who had died. At the church, I tried to remain in the shadows, hidden, but he saw me, came over. He seemed... sincere, almost vulnerable. Maybe it was his scar," she added, absentmindedly touching her own birthmark. "Do you know how he got it?"

"No," I admitted. "I wasn't told much."

She sighed, her voice softening. "He told me his mother gave it to him. He was just six when it happened. He was busy happily playing in the street with a stray puppy one day. He wanted to keep it, begged her that he'd love and care for it, but his mother wouldn't hear of it—if they took it in, it would only be another mouth they couldn't afford to feed. She was a harsh woman, hands rough from working in a washhouse, and with a terrible anger. When he begged her, cried like only a child can, she grabbed the puppy and threw it into the river. It couldn't fight the current, and he had to watch it disappear under the water."

That poor dog, I thought, *to be thrown away like trash because of a sad little boy.*

She continued. "He was furious, lashed out and kicked her in the leg. She was furious and grabbed him by his hair and beat him across his head. He screamed at her to stop, but she told him boys shouldn't wail like little girls, then took a fish knife and cut him—straight down his face." She traced the air, from her forehead to cheek. "Told him every time he looked in the mirror, he'd remember why boys shouldn't cry."

She pointed to her thigh as she spoke, conjuring a vivid image of a small, dirt-streaked boy standing in futile rebellion, defying a cruelty he couldn't escape.

"It is," I agreed, feeling a heavy pang of sympathy. The story began to paint a clearer picture—a man shaped by harshness, driven into a life of darkness, forever haunted by the guilt of childhood tears he was told he should never have shed.

Her voice broke the silence. "I know how desperate he is to find me. He won't rest until he does. And now I realise... I can't keep refusing every person he sends after me."

"Wait... you mean I'm not the first he's sent?"

"No," she replied, her sorrow etched into every word. "You're one of many."

The realisation crashed over me like a tsunami I hadn't seen coming. I felt stupid, I was cleverer than this, I should have seen it. From the moment the Russian handed me that account full of money, when he made his threats, he already knew exactly where I was headed. He knew she was here. He had always known.

I stood slowly, staring down at her as the fragments of this twisted puzzle finally snapped into place. "Marie's father... George... he was one of those people, wasn't he?"

She gave a small nod, her eyes full of something I couldn't quite place—regret, maybe. The pieces fit too well. Marie had told us how her father came home one day with a windfall of money, no questions asked, and no strings attached—except one. He had been tasked with finding the girl and delivering her to the Russian. Smith's boss had financed his business, and Marie had paid for the sins of her father.

"But that doesn't add up," I muttered, half to myself. "Marie's father found you years after he got that money to start his shop." I paused, looking at her. "The Russian couldn't have known George would meet you then, could he?"

She looked away, a distant expression crossing her face. "I know," she answered. "But he *was* searching for me. That's why George spent so many years coming into these woods to sketch."

So, the drawings… they were a ruse, an excuse to come here. He'd been tasked from the start to look for her, failing for years, until fate—pure accident—finally brought them together.

"Is that why he drew you?" I asked, my voice growing hard with suspicion. "To show the Russian that he had seen you?"

She shrugged, her expression unreadable. "I don't know. He never told me why he was there. To me, he was just a man who interested me."

I collapsed back into my chair, the exhaustion of being played, of being a pawn in someone else's game, sinking into my bones. It felt like the ground beneath me had shifted, leaving me adrift in a world where trust was just another illusion.

"What happened?" I asked again, my voice flat, drained.

She reached out, her small hand finding mine, gripping it as if to reassure me that what I was feeling was completely natural, and acceptable.

"Just like you," she began, "George told me a man was looking for me. That the Russian wanted to see me. He asked me to go back with him, but I refused. I felt sorry for him," she admitted, her voice barely above a whisper.

"You felt sorry for him?" I snapped, anger boiling over. "All you had to do was give him a message—a single message—to take back to the man who was threatening his life! Instead, he ends up face down in a river!"

Her fury ignited in an instant. She slammed her fists into the sofa cushions, her green eyes burning with intensity. "It's not as easy as you think it is!" she shouted, her voice trembling with raw emotion. The force of it left me stunned, like I'd been slapped across the face.

I backed down, softening my tone. "I'm sorry," I muttered, struggling to contain my own rising anger. "I didn't mean to raise my voice. I just… I need to understand."

"And you will. Please, trust me."

"And what about my brother?" I asked. "Was he tangled up in all of this too?"

She exhaled deeply, her earlier anger dissipating as quickly as it had flared up. "No," she said, her voice slipping back into that calm, almost soothing tone. "With him, it was different."

I felt greatly relieved by her answer. At least my brother hadn't been caught up in this twisted web of deceit and danger. But new questions flooded in. If he wasn't involved with the Russian, then how did that man know about him? And how, for the love of God, had he gotten that picture?

A sudden crack of thunder ripped through the sky, rattling the windows and shaking the cottage as if the storm was determined to tear apart everything around us. "For fuck's sake, won't this storm ever end?" I shouted, as if the storm were another adversary conspiring against me.

"It will soon," she said, her voice turning almost ethereal again, like she knew something I didn't.

"How do you know?" I asked, my frustration clear.

"All storms must start, and they must end," she replied with quiet certainty. "They cannot go on forever. Tomorrow will be better; I'm sure of it."

Her words made no sense to me, but I was too worn out to try and decipher their meaning. I sank onto the sofa beside her, shaking my head. "You really are something else, you know that?" I muttered. "You still haven't explained how you can be the same woman in those photos taken eighty years apart. You don't look a day over twenty-five."

"Maybe I am," she teased, her lips curling into a mischievous smile, her eyes gleaming with a depth of secrets I wasn't sure I wanted to know.

I sighed, resigned to her riddles. "I bet you wouldn't tell me even if you wanted to."

She leaned in closer, her voice dropping to a near whisper, sending a shiver through me. "Let me ask you something instead: if I wanted to go, right now, would you let me leave?" Her hand rested lightly on my knee, and the simple touch sent a jolt of electricity through my body, making it impossible to ignore the gravity of her question.

Outside, hailstones pelted the windows with an angry fury, and thunder rolled so loudly overhead, it shook the very foundation of the cottage. I glanced at the raging storm, then back at her. "You can't go back out in that," I said, my protective instincts kicking in despite everything. "Stay here tonight. If tomorrow is as good as you say it will be, then… you can go."

I glanced at the clock—six p.m. already. The constant stress had dulled my appetite, but now, with the storm raging outside and the strange company inside, it returned with a sudden force.

"Do you want something to eat?" I asked, standing and nodding toward the kitchen. "There's plenty of food here."

She looked up at me, her green eyes thoughtful. After a long pause, she gave a small nod. "Yes, thank you. That would be nice."

As I stood in the kitchen, chopping vegetables for a salmon salad, my thoughts churned, mirroring the chaos of the storm outside. Why, I kept asking myself, had the Russian played such an elaborate game? If he knew where she was all along, why send people like Marie's father—or even me? A man like him, with his resources and power, could have dispatched any number of agents to track her down. Yet here I was, just another nameless pawn caught in his twisted schemes.

And that photo—the one from his youth—she said it never happened. Was she telling the truth? If so, why fabricate it? What purpose did it serve to construct such a precise, personal lie? Maybe he created it for himself, to satisfy some deep, selfish need to believe that she had always been a part of his life. It was as though he needed her to be woven into the fabric of his history, whether real or not.

But to what end? Was it just a power play? A way for him to assert control, to show me that he knew more than I ever could? Or was it something darker—a delusion? Maybe he'd rewritten his own memories, warping truths to convince himself that she had been part of his world forever. It was pathetic, really. Fabricating a history to manipulate others, or worse, to convince himself of a lie.

The more I thought about it, the angrier I became. The Russian, sitting happily in his gilded tower, had ruined my life, pulling the strings from the start. Yes, he had paid me, but what had that money truly cost me? I'd lost my job, abandoned my hometown, and, worst of all, Jessica was gone—vanished from my life because of all this. And now I was stuck in this house, which felt more like a prison with each passing minute.

I felt like a fool. I'd been played, manipulated, and the sting of that realisation hit hard. A toxic mix of anger and shame pulsed through my veins. My pride, once a shield, had been shattered, leaving me vulnerable in a way I hadn't allowed myself to feel in years. And with that vulnerability came a simmering rage. I wanted to find the Russian, find Smith, and anyone else involved in this, and tear them all down. Ruin them for what they had done to me.

But beneath that rage was a nagging self-awareness. Maybe I was to blame, at least in part. I had let myself get drawn into this, driven by a toxic mix of pride and curiosity. They had found my weakest point—my brother—and used it to string me along like a puppet. And the worst part? I hadn't even resisted. I'd been so obsessed with finding out the truth about his death that I'd blindly submitted to their demands, and now I was paying for that obedience. I hadn't fought back when I should have, hadn't questioned hard enough, and now, here I was, unravelling in the middle of a storm that was far from just the weather.

Frustrated, I grabbed a bottle of whiskey from the larder and poured a shot. The burn settled in, dulling the sharp edges of my anger. It was a momentary reprieve, but at least it was something. The Russian, the girl, Jessica, my brother—they were all caught in this web of obscurities, and the more I tried to unravel it, the tighter it seemed to get.

The only shining light was that the girl agreed to give me what I came for. Come tomorrow, I would be free.

39

When I returned to the living room with our food, she was standing by the window, staring out into the darkening forest. One arm was wrapped around her torso, as if shielding herself from the world—or perhaps from the approaching night. The storm raged outside, but her gaze seemed locked on something beyond it, something hidden in the shadows between the trees.

"Tell you what," I said, as her attention shifted toward me. "Why don't we take the food up to the entertainment room? I'm getting bored of listening to the thunder."

She nodded, and I carried the plates upstairs. Once I set them down, I went back to grab a chair from the kitchen. When I returned, she was already in the room, her fingers lightly skimming the spines of the books on the shelves, a faraway look in her eyes.

"I'll warn you now," I joked, hoping to lighten the mood. "Those books are only useful if you want to know what bait to use for trout or how many people died around here between 1744 and 1780. Otherwise, I'd skip them."

She laughed, a gentle sound that somehow filled the room with warmth despite the storm outside. "Not all deaths are recorded," she said, taking her plate and sitting in the armchair. "Some pass unnoticed, but others—they leave a deep crater in our hearts, as wide and as deep as the ocean."

"Very poetic," I replied, trying to brush off the chill that her words gave me.

"As is death," she added quietly, taking her first bite of the salmon.

"How about some music?" I suggested, eager to change the tone. "Anything in particular you'd like?"

"Whatever you wish," she replied. "This is your time, after all."

I browsed through the records, unsure what would suit the mood. Somehow, heavy metal didn't feel right, but neither did Beethoven or Lady Gaga. As I flipped through the stack, I found a few records that seemed unfamiliar, almost as if they'd appeared there without me noticing before. Finally, I landed on something that seemed to fit—an LP of ancient folk songs from Northern England.

"Here, you might like this," I said, placing the needle on the record and sitting across from her.

The room was soon filled with haunting melodies—songs from a long-forgotten England. The singer's voice told the story of a lonely wanderer who had fallen in love with a girl who died too soon. The acoustic guitar, mournful fiddle, and eerie hum of the hurdy-gurdy created a sound that felt as though it belonged to another age entirely but fit the character of this young girl completely.

"This is beautiful," she whispered, closing her eyes and swaying gently to the music.

As she began to hum along with the tune, I felt a strange familiarity in her voice—an otherworldly echo that reminded me of Jessica. It tugged at me, blurring the line between memory and reality. For a second, it was as if I was hearing Jessica's voice, blending seamlessly with the melody. I was mesmerised, watching her sway, lost in how she seemed to embody the music, her movements delicate.

Maybe I was projecting memories where they didn't belong, searching for something that wasn't there. But it didn't matter. It all felt right, even amidst the storm, even with all the questions left unanswered, everything was as it should be.

"Can I ask you one final question, and then there'll be no more?" I asked, my voice steady, though inside I felt anything but.

She opened her eyes, locking with mine—piercing, as though she could see everything I was and wasn't. "One more question," she said with a smile, still swaying gently to the fading notes of the song.

"What are you?"

"I am me," she replied simply, as if it were the most obvious answer in the world. And just like that, the mystery hovered between us, unresolved but final.

We finished our meal in silence, a strange calm settling over us like a blanket. Her cryptic response reverberated through me, forcing me to confront something deeper. Maybe, just maybe, I could let go—of the search for answers, of the endless battle with myself. Perhaps she was the key to stepping into something new, something beyond this room.

Her voice, her presence, everything about her seemed designed to make me believe that here, in this isolated space, I could be free—free from the chaos of the outside world, from the pain, from the past. She enchanted me with her singing, weaving a quiet spell that made me want to surrender to the idea that I could be my own man, that I could let go of everything else.

Outside this room, I merely existed—moving from one part of the day to another, a ghost in my own life. But here, with her, there was love. Or maybe it was just the feeling that in her presence, I could surrender, fully and completely, and let her guide me wherever I needed to go.

Later that night, as we walked upstairs, I hesitated in the hallway, just a foot apart from her. Desire carried m forward, stronger than before. I stepped closer, her breath soft and sweet, igniting a fire deep within me.

"I…" I stammered, unsure if I had the strength to stop.

She gently stroked my face, her touch soothing. "It's okay," she whispered, her voice low and reassuring.

I had always believed in free will, but it felt like it had slipped away, lost to the force of surrendering. I took her hand and nodded, leading her into the bedroom. At the foot of the bed, she removed her top, and I couldn't tear my eyes away. Her deep, steady breaths seemed to draw me in—the softness of her breasts, the flatness of her abdomen, and the small, delicate patch of hair between her legs. Instead of lust, I was overwhelmed by an unexpected tenderness.

She took my hands, guiding them over her body. My fingers traced the warmth of her skin, feeling the rise of her breasts, the softness of her curves. My heart pounded, filled with a longing that went beyond physical desire. Her eyes never left mine, a silent understanding passing between us, something that felt deeper than words. I pulled her closer, our bodies pressing together, two hearts beating in rhythm.

But as I leaned in to kiss her, something on the dresser caught my eye—a wristband. My brother's wristband.

"Adam," I whispered, suddenly pulling back, existence crashing into fantasy.

"What?" she asked, confusion etching her face.

"Adam," I repeated. "No, I'm not going to do this."

She pulled me closer again, her hands warm on my skin. "It's okay," she whispered, her voice smooth and coaxing. "You're not doing anything wrong."

I shook my head, a surge of clarity breaking through the haze. "This isn't why I came here," I said, pushing her away more firmly. I reached for Adam's wristband on the dresser, slipping it around my wrist as if it could tether me to the real world. Looking at her, standing there with her body glowing softly in the dim light, I spoke with more resolve. "I may not know why he killed himself, but I'm not going to dishonour his memory. I'll sleep downstairs, and in the morning, you can give me the message for the Russian."

I turned my back on her, leaving her standing naked and alone. I could have stayed in the spare room, but I needed space—and another drink. Sleeping downstairs would make it easier to resist whatever this pull was between us.

As I exited the room with a blanket and pillow in hand, I cast a final glance back and saw her climbing into bed, disappointment flickering across her face. Perhaps she had expected me to give in and couldn't see why I didn't. But when my eyes caught the mirror across the hallway, something was wrong. The bed reflected in the glass was fully made, untouched, as if no one had ever lain there. Confusion surged through me, gripping me like a vice. It was as if I was witnessing two different realities—one where she lay beneath the covers, and another where the bed had never been disturbed.

"You look pale," she said from behind me, her voice cutting through the fog of my thoughts.

I couldn't tear my eyes from the mirror, where the bed remained pristinely neat, and I stood alone, as if her presence had been nothing more than an illusion.

"Everything is fine," I lied, forcing myself to look away from the reflection. "I'll see you in the morning."

I stared back at the mirror, where the bed remained neatly made. In that reflection, I was as alone as I had been before she arrived.

She gave me a gentle smile, but there was something in her eyes—something dark and implicit. "If you find it hard to sleep," she whispered, "you can return to me."

I nodded quickly, then hurried downstairs, my pulse pounding in my ears. I needed to get away from her, from the mirror, from the strange distortion that I couldn't comprehend. I needed something—anything—to confirm what was real.

In the kitchen, the dinner plates still sat on the counter, exactly where I had left them. That was normal. In the living room the mug of hot chocolate I had made for her sat on the table; its contents congealed at the bottom. She hadn't drunk from it. She had eaten and spoken to me, sat beside me, yet upstairs was a ghostly echo of a girl I had almost given myself to.

Bile rose in my throat, and I fought back the urge to vomit. My hands trembled as I leaned against the doorframe, trying to steady myself. It was as if I had left my body, like I was watching someone else spiral into madness, helpless to stop it. The house felt alive, like a malevolent force watching me, toying with me, while I moved blindly through its traps. I was playing a game I didn't understand, with an opponent I couldn't see.

What could I do? Leaving now was impossible with the storm raging outside. If I tried to flee, the darkness of the forest would swallow me whole. It wouldn't take long for me to lose myself in its depths, another soul wandering aimlessly, never to return. I was a lost child, ensnared in a trap I hadn't realised I'd set. There was no escape.

I sank onto the sofa, wrapping the blanket around me, as if it could protect me from the unsettling experience pressing in from all sides. My mind replayed the events of the night—the girl upstairs, the mirror that reflected a lie, the feeling that though I was here on the couch, something continued to watch me. I knew I wouldn't sleep, not with the phantom of her presence looming upstairs, waiting for me to falter.

Yet, exhaustion, heavy and relentless, began to pull me under. Despite the terror clawing at my back, my body craved rest, my mind desperate for an escape, however brief. I downed another glass of whiskey, hoping it would numb the fear, dull the edges long enough for sleep to claim me.

And it did.

40

The clock chimed 3:33 a.m., jolting me from a nightmare I couldn't quite grasp. Its remnants clung to the edges of my consciousness like smoke, fading but never fully dissipating. I blinked into the oppressive darkness, aware that sleep had been ripped away, replaced by the crushing stillness of the night. A throbbing pain pulsed behind my eyes, as if my skull were a fragile vase on the verge of shattering. The pounding in my head amplified every thought, every shadow in the room. *No more drinking,* my inner voice screamed, intensifying the ache in my skull.

Groggy, with an uneasy reluctance to return to the dark corners of my dreams, I forced myself to sit up. My limbs felt heavy, leaden, as if I had been encased in ice. But the chill didn't come from the air—it was something absorbed, radiating from within, an unsettling coldness that had seeped into my bones. I raised my hand in front of my face, but it disappeared into the blackness. I couldn't see it. Panic flared. *Was I blind? Or was the darkness itself pressing in, suffocating me?*

I strained to listen, desperate for any sign of the girl upstairs, for something familiar. But all I could hear was the steady, rhythmic pulsing of my own heart, a drumbeat inside the hollow of my chest. A compulsion surged within me—to go upstairs, to confront her, to demand answers for what I'd seen, for everything I didn't comprehend. Yet, when I tried to move my legs, they remained numb, as if I had been drugged or paralysed by fear. *Was I still asleep, locked in some twisted nightmare?*

Then, I noticed something. The storm had stopped. No more rain hammering the windows, no more thunder shaking the house. It was as if the world had drawn in a breath and held it, waiting for something to happen. Through a gap in the curtains, I glimpsed the moon, a full, silvery orb illuminating the night. Broken clouds drifted lazily across its face, casting an otherworldly blue glow through the room. I counted, almost mechanically, waiting for the moon to reemerge from behind its veil: *3... 4... 5...* The room brightened, bathed in that spectral light, cleansing me like a balm, easing some of the dread that had knotted itself around my brain.

Then, breaking the silence, a voice whispered from the far corner of the room, where the chair sat in shadow. "Life's beautiful when it wants to be."

My heart lurched, and I froze. I knew that voice. I would know it anywhere.

Adam.

41

"Sorry, I didn't mean to scare you," my brother's voice came faintly from the corner.

In the moonlight filtering through the broken clouds, I saw him—a familiar figure dressed in black canvas trainers, blue jeans, and a black Guns N' Roses shirt. His long, slender arms, tattooed with thorns and roses, ended in calloused fingers—the hands of a guitarist. The figure was undeniably his. But his face—his face remained obscured, wrapped in an impenetrable shade that added a surreal substance to the moment.

"Who said I was scared?" I shot back, my voice shaking as I tried to shake off the feeling that I was still trapped in some twisted nightmare. "I feel great, perfectly fine. But I'll be waking up soon, so if you could leave the way you came, I'd appreciate it."

"You don't think I'm really here?" he asked, amused.

"Oh, I know you're here," I replied, glancing around the room. "But if this isn't a dream, and that chair you're sitting in is the one in a cottage I'm stuck in, and this is the same sofa I fell asleep on, it means I'm wide awake, having a conversation with someone who might just be my dead brother. Which is... a little disconcerting."

"So, you haven't forgotten me then?" he said. "I was a bit worried you wouldn't recognise me. It's been a few years."

"You sound like my brother," I admitted, feeling the tug of familiarity in his voice. "But I can't see enough of you to be sure. Maybe bend forward a little, let me see your face."

He leaned forward obediently, but the shadow stubbornly clung to his features, hiding them from me.

"Nope, still can't tell if it's you," I sighed.

"What other way can I prove who I am?"

"Maybe tell me one of your crappy jokes—one only you would think is funny."

"Fair enough," I said. "I believe it's you. But I'd still like to see your face. Like you said, it's been a while."

Though I couldn't see his expression, I could sense that sad, familiar smile of his. "I'm afraid I can't do much about that," he said with a shrug. "It's part of the package. I get to see you for a brief while, but"—he spread his arms wide— "this is all you get of me."

"So, time isn't on our side," I sang softly, a bittersweet note sneaking into my voice.

"I like what you did there," he laughed. "Maybe the Rolling Stones need to rethink their lyrics."

Hearing my brother's laugh—his real, unmistakable laugh—after five years was like being hit with overwhelming joy and sorrow all at once. I wanted to run to him, pull him into a hug, and let the tears spill out. But despite my fierce longing, I was frozen, rooted to the spot. Joy and dread twisted inside me, leaving me incapacitated, afraid that if I moved, this moment—if that's what it was—would shatter.

"Can I admit something to you?"

"Sure, bruv, anything."

"Though it was your favourite, I always fucking hated that song…"

He burst out laughing again, the sound filling the room with warmth. "Duly noted. No encore from me tonight, then."

I scratched my neck, my throat suddenly dry, but my body still wouldn't cooperate enough for me to grab the glass of water on the table. He must've noticed because, with a casual gesture, he reached beside the chair and pulled out two bottles of lager, seemingly from nowhere.

"Here," he said, handing one to me with a smile in his voice. "Let's share a final drink together."

I took the bottle, and as I cracked it open and took a sip, I tried again to get a clearer look at his face. But no matter how he shifted, the shadows clung to him, stubbornly refusing to reveal his features.

"Thanks," I said, cracking open the bottle and taking a long gulp.

Outside, the moon began to disappear behind the clouds, yet the room stayed illuminated, as if we'd captured the light within its walls. This no longer *felt* like a nightmare. The beer in my hand was real, the sofa beneath me solid, and the soft glow on my skin undeniable.

"You know," I said, setting the bottle down on the table, "I think this will be the last time I drink. Alcohol hasn't exactly been my ally these past few days."

"You've been through the wringer," he replied, his tone gentle.

"Have you been watching?"

The shadowy figure that was his head nodded. "Every second of it."

"So why show up now?"

"You were at a low point. It looked like you needed a friendly face."

"Yet I can't *see* your friendly face?" I smirked.

He nodded again. "Touché. But seriously, I was worried about you. When you first arrived here, I thought you'd manage fine. But it turns out we're all just one bad misstep away from falling apart. And if there's one person I don't want that to happen to, it's you. So, I thought I'd drop in and help you out."

"So, the ghost of my brother's here to stop me from losing my mind," I laughed, raising my beer bottle toward him in mock salute.

He shrugged. "Honestly, I didn't really think it through before I showed up."

"Then you are who you say you are," I said, shaking my head, a bittersweet smile tugging at my lips. "Acting without thinking—that's the most *Adam* thing possible." My mind flashed back to earlier in the night. "The wristband—was that you?"

He raised his arm, the band snug around his wrist. "Yep. My last-ditch effort to stop you from doing something *ridiculously* stupid. By the way—thank you for what you said about honouring my memory. If you'd gone through with what you were about to start up there, it would've made things... awkward."

"I wasn't thinking," I admitted. "I can't even explain it. It just felt so right in the moment. And after Jessica leaving me... I don't know, I didn't expect to feel anything like that again so soon."

"Don't beat yourself up," he said, his tone reassuring. "That girl—she makes men feel that way. You weren't thinking clearly."

We both took a swig of our lager, letting the peace settle between us like an unspoken truce.

"I found the wristband earlier in the week, upstairs in the cupboard. Does that mean you've been here before?"

His form seemed to shift slightly, like my question had touched something raw. "Yeah," he said, his voice quieter. "I came here once, a few days before… well, you know. Before my little trip to the other side."

"What's oblivion like?" I asked.

"Not too bad, honestly. It's peaceful—no stress, no anxiety. None of that noise that fills your head down here." He chuckled. "The music sucks, though. And no guitars anywhere... go figure."

I shivered, not from the cold, but from the chilling truth of what he was describing. The idea of oblivion, of nothingness, left me feeling emptier than before. I pulled the blanket around me, trying to shake the hollowness bleeding in.

"Why didn't you reach out?" I asked, my voice trembling with the sadness I had buried for years. "I could've helped you."

He shook his head, the movement slow and heavy. "I know it's hard to hear, but nothing you could've done would've changed things. Your practicality, your level-headedness—it would've made it worse. By the time I decided to do it, my mind was made up... several times over."

"You didn't even leave me a note," I whispered, the pain I'd kept locked away finally breaking free. "Do you know what it's like to think you didn't even care enough to say why?"

He looked down, his expression sombre, almost regretful. "Actually, I did write letters... while I stayed in the village. But when it came down to it, I didn't have the guts to send them. I wish I had. Maybe if you'd read them, it would've stopped you from following me down here."

I took another drink from the bottle. No matter how much I drank, it seemed perpetually half-full.

"So," I said, leaning forward slightly. "if you really are a ghost, and this isn't just some hallucination brought on by lack of sleep, whiskey, and the urge to get the hell away from this place; what the fuck happened?"

"Perhaps," he said slowly, "to answer that, I need to tell you what was going through my mind on my last day."

42

"The choice *not* to sit in my car and breathe in the sweet, noxious fumes of the exhaust was taken away from me when I left the village," my brother said calmly. His voice was detached, clinical. There was no emotion behind his words, no pain—just a flat statement of fact.

I struggled to understand. "What drove you to take such a drastic step?" I asked, my voice catching in my throat. How could he talk so casually about something that had torn my world apart?

He gestured vaguely toward the stairs. "I think you already know."

"Her? The girl?" I scoffed angrily. "Come on, man, that's a weak excuse if I've ever heard one. Maybe if you'd said Emily, I'd still struggle to believe it, but the girl? No. I'm not buying it. I've had my fair share of failed relationships, and none of them made me want to do what you did."

He raised his hands in surrender. "I'm not here to argue. I was weak. I know that now. The whys and what-ifs didn't matter in those final days."

He stood and wandered to the other side of the room, running his fingers along the wall, tracing the shadows. His hand stopped at a small dent in the plaster, about the size of a tennis ball.

"This," he said, pointing to the mark, "is where I lost control. Where my choices no longer mattered."

"Enough with the riddles, Adam. I've had more than I can handle these past few weeks."

He turned toward me, his face still hidden in shadow, but his voice steady and calm. "I'll make it clear; I swear. I died because my soul was stolen—by the same girl who took Marie's father, and almost took yours."

"Even if that's true, it still doesn't explain why you had to die."

"Doesn't it?" he asked, sinking back into the chair. "When Jessica left, didn't you feel something shift inside you? Like a tiny seed planted in your heart, slowly draining you?"

His words hit me, but instead of fear or clarity, I felt irritation. My mind, already worn and fragile, couldn't make sense of what he was saying.

"As soon as I met her, that seed took root," he continued, his voice tinged with quiet misery. "It was a weakness—something no one else could see or grasp. Like a weed, it grew inside me, choking me until there was nothing left. I didn't have the strength to rip it out, and that's what killed me, what claimed my soul."

"There's no such thing as a soul," I scoffed, trying to inject some logic into the conversation. "I can believe you felt a certain way—clouded by depression, disease, whatever—but a soul? That's too far."

He sighed, as though he had expected my scepticism. "Maybe you're right. I can't say for sure. But if that's true, then what am I now?"

"Whatever you are, you're still the lost little brother, running away from anything that hurt him," I snapped. "You left because you couldn't face it."

"I left home because I was depressed," he shot back, his voice sharp and pained, matching mine. "I didn't want you—or anyone—to see me like that. I was terrified I'd drag you down with me. But what happened here…" He trailed off, placing a hand on his chest as if searching for a heartbeat that had long since stopped.

"Go on," I urged, my anger ebbing as I watched him struggle to find the words.

"My weakness, my need to escape the feelings I had for Emily… that's what let her in. I couldn't fight her. Even if you had been here, looking out for me, warning me to stay away from her, it wouldn't have altered my course."

"But what did she want from you?"

"My attention, my heart, my passion—everything I was willing to give," he said bitterly, shaking his head as if trying to rid himself of the painful recollections. "Only when it was too late did I realise my mistake."

"So, she what—lied to you? Betrayed you like Emily? I don't get it."

His voice trembled. "I was so wrapped up in her promises of a brighter future, I didn't see what was happening. She wasn't lying—she was just draining me, pulling me away from the world piece by piece."

His words drifted into the realm of the metaphysical—a place I'd usually dismiss without a second thought—but something in his tone kept me hanging on, unable to pull away from the gravity of what he was saying.

"And that's what killed me in the end," he said, his voice laced with regret. "Love really *is* blind."

"What about me," I asked, "is it too late for me?"

Adam shook his head slowly. "You had the strength to stop. You saw the warning—*my* warning—and you turned away. If it had been me... I would've ignored it. I would've walked straight into her arms. But you—you resisted."

"It still doesn't explain the most important thing in all this," I told him. "If she's not human—and I'm starting to believe she isn't after seeing that she has no reflection—then what *is* she?"

"That... I don't know. I don't think *she* knows either. Maybe she's a ghost. But that doesn't explain how real she felt. You felt it too, right? She's more than a ghost or a ghoul. So, what does that leave?"

"A demon... a succubus, maybe?" I suggested, grasping at straws, throwing out any possibility that came to mind.

"No, she isn't evil," he replied. "I think you feel that too. There's no malice in her, just... this desperate need to please. She says all the right things, touches the deepest parts of our psyche, making us crave more. It's crude to say, but she's more like a parasite—feeding on our energy, draining us until there's nothing left."

"So, once that attachment forms, there's no escape?"

"I couldn't escape, Marie's father couldn't, and the Russian... he's in deeper than anyone."

"What about me?"

He leaned forward, and I caught a small glimpse of his face—the sharp outline of his chin, the lower half of his mouth visible in the soft glow of moonlight.

"No," he said slowly, his voice steady, "you're different. Your logic, your scepticism… it's a problem for her. She can't latch onto you completely because you don't crave anything more than what you already have."

Was that really my saving grace? My refusal to want more, my ability to be content with what I had? It seemed almost absurd—my cynicism, my jaded view of the world—being the very thing protecting me from her pull. Pragmatism had always been my strength, but hearing it described as a shield against something far more dangerous left me both heartened and unsettled.

"Ask yourself this," Adam said, "in all the time you've spent with her, have you ever asked for her name?"

I thought about it. He was right—I hadn't. I shook my head.

"I didn't think so," he continued. "George didn't ask either. And just before I died, I realised I never knew her name. I don't think she wants us to know. Or maybe... maybe she doesn't even have one."

"Does the Russian know?" I asked.

Adam shook his head.

"So what does he want from her?"

"He's in love with the idea of her," Adam explained, leaning back. "She listened to him—really listened—and maybe no one else ever has. He's spent his life controlling others, but with her, it's different. He can't control her, and that's driving him insane. The irony is, he'd probably be better off without her, but he can't see that. He's like a pressure valve ready to explode, and he thinks she's the only thing that can stop it."

I leaned forward, steepling my fingers under my chin. "Let's say I believe you—that you're really here, and the girl upstairs is some kind of soul-draining spirit. What is this cabin?"

Adam hesitated, then shrugged. "That, I can't tell you. Not because I don't want to, but because I don't know. Maybe it's a manifestation of a person's mind. Maybe it's limbo. Or maybe she conjures it up to offer solace to the men who fall in love with her."

It didn't feel like any of those things, but I had to accept his answer. "What happens now?"

"In the morning, you'll get up, gather your things, and go home."

"Just like that?"

"Just like that," he said, his voice soft but certain. "You might feel her pull and want to follow her call, but you're strong enough to resist it. I'm sure of it."

"And you?" I asked.

"Me? I go back to where I came from. But don't worry, it's not a bad place. I'm at peace there, though I wouldn't mind a music studio with a soundboard the size of the Titanic," he added with a wistful smile. "But you can't have everything."

"Will I see you again?"

"Maybe. One day. But after today, you won't need me anymore. You'll remember me, sure, but you won't be haunted by my absence. I guess you could call me 'spectral closure,'" he snickered, though there was a finality in the sound.

"Anything you want me to pass on?" I asked, suddenly feeling like a medium, waiting for the spirits to speak. "Not that I think anyone will believe me."

He smiled. "If you can, give Marie my regards. Tell her to forgive her father. He was lost, like I was—past the point of no return. And tell her she's a good woman. Everything will work out for her, I'm sure of it. I think you should get to know her better. She'd be good for you."

"Haven't we had enough trouble with women lately?" I joked.

"Ah, yes. Jessica."

"Did you see her leave? Did she make it home safely?"

His voice softened, as if cushioning a blow. "She made it home fine. I think she's already thinking about returning to her old life."

"I thought about going after her, despite what she said."

Adam shook his head. "Don't. If you met again, you'd see that the cord between you is already severed. You wouldn't feel the same for each other. It's a sad ending but trying to relive what's gone... it'll only hurt more. Don't put yourself through that pain."

I couldn't argue—deep down, I knew he was right. I would come out of this a different person, disconnected from the life I once knew.

"Right, I need to get going," he said, rising from his seat.

"You're leaving me with her? Is that really a good idea?" Panic flickered through me.

"She's gone," he said calmly. "She left while we were talking. She left something for you at the foot of the bed. Take it, and leave. Don't look back, not even once. Head to the village and nowhere else; do not go to the glade under any means. You know your way back home—you won't get lost. And one more thing."

"Anything," I said.

"When the Russian gives you your payment, build a life somewhere else. Use the money to move forward and do your best to forget all of this."

"Oh, I plan to," I replied, trying to sound confident.

He extended his hand. "I'm glad I had this last chance to see you."

"A handshake? Really?" I scoffed.

I stood up and pulled him into an embrace. His body felt strange—like I was hugging a resonance of myself, a fading memory—but there was still a familiar essence to him, the brother I'd always cared for. And when I hugged him, he hugged back. It felt like we were whole again, brothers in the truest sense.

"Love you, Chris," he whispered in my ear, his voice carrying the years lost.

"Love you, little bro," I whispered back, tears spilling down my cheeks, releasing emotions I hadn't allowed myself to feel for so long.

Within a few blinks, the world outside dimmed, the moon swallowed by clouds, and just like that, my brother vanished with the night. All that remained was me—standing alone in the silence of the cottage, exhausted and utterly spent.

43

I woke up refreshed, sunlight streaming through the open blinds. The unnatural events of the past twenty hours—part of an already bizarre week—seemed to dissolve in the gentle morning light. The cottage, which had once felt suffocating with fear and mystery, now seemed welcoming, almost serene. My brother had been right—without needing to verify it, I knew the girl was gone. An odd longing settled in. I was glad I didn't have to confront her again, yet her absence left an unsettling void, somehow more troubling than Jessica's departure. It was as if I had lost something unhealthy but significant, a ghost of an attachment that still clung to me.

The clock chimed 6 a.m., but there was no rush to leave. Oddly calm and detached, I felt like a prisoner awaiting release. The person I had become over the past few days seemed distant, almost unrecognisable. Stretching, I made a simple breakfast—cornflakes and orange juice—but today it tasted sweeter, as if the stress of the past days had lifted, allowing me to savour the present.

After breakfast, I washed, shaved, and dressed. Only when I felt fully composed did I venture into her bedroom. As expected, there at the foot of the bed was what the girl had left for me to take back—a small wooden box. The wood was rough, gnarled, and clearly handcrafted, with twine hinges adding a rustic simplicity. My hands hovered over the box, half-expecting some kind of trick. But when I opened it, there were just two pieces of parchment folded neatly inside.

The first was a letter addressed to me, outlining how to deliver the second note to the Russian. I was not to read his note under any circumstances; I was simply to hand it over, no questions asked. I hoped that whatever she had written would be enough to convince him to stop searching for her—to let her go—or at the very least, to leave me out of his future plans. I just wanted me life back.

There was no mention of our encounter, no lingering affection—just an indifferent request for my time and effort. It was businesslike, devoid of sentiment. A strange pang of hurt hit me at her coldness, a fissure where I had expected something more. My brother had warned me about her effect on men, and now I felt it—a curious emptiness where there should have been warmth. But it was for the best. Distance, both physical and emotional, was safer.

I smiled wryly, remembering Jessica's remark to Marie: "His is a life of cynicism, with a dash of sarcasm."

"Not a bad way to live," I muttered, folding the note and placing it back in the box.

I packed the box into my backpack and prepared for the journey home. *Home*—the word felt like a beacon of warmth. I could already imagine the small comforts: a hot bath, real food, the soft embrace of my own bed—my sanctuary, my cave.

With everything packed, I took one last look around the cottage. I had tidied up more than I ever would have in my own home, making sure everything was in its place. If the owner ever returned, they wouldn't feel violated by strangers—not that I particularly cared. This place, like the memories of the last few days, was behind me now.

With a final, satisfied sigh, I opened the door and stepped outside. The cool morning air met my face, crisp and refreshing. It was over.

44

Standing at the threshold, bathed in warm sunlight, the world felt almost surreal in its perfection. The sky, a vast expanse of serene blue, stretched endlessly, unbroken and undisturbed like a calm ocean. I was momentarily intoxicated by the beauty surrounding me—the birds singing in the trees, the vibrant greenery, the scent of fresh air. It felt too idyllic, as though I'd stepped into a scene from a Disney animation, and I half-expected woodland creatures to join me in song.

The storm that had once raged through the land had left no trace of its fury. The air was dry, the ground firm and untouched by rain. There were no puddles, no fallen branches, no remnants of the anarchy that had enveloped the last few days. When I knelt to touch the grass, it felt as though the storm had been nothing more than a fever dream—everything was dry, crisp, and impossibly still. Strangely, I wasn't surprised. In fact, it made perfect sense, as though the world had reset itself, wiping clean the extraordinary events that had unfolded.

I closed the door behind me and placed the key under the same flowerpot where Jessica had found it. Finally, I moved away from the cottage, walking slowly, deliberately, as if any quick movement might somehow rouse it from its slumber. I didn't want to give it a chance to reclaim me, as though unseen arms might reach out from the door and drag me back into its shadowy maw. I was done with this place, and I intended for it to stay that way.

At the edge of the forest, I paused, tempted to turn around and take one final look at the cottage. But something stopped me—an insistent voice in my head warning that if I did, I wouldn't see it as I remembered. Instead, I'd see the dilapidated ruin it had been all along: overgrown, decayed, and swallowed by the forest. So, in a quiet act of defiance, I walked on without looking back, trusting that leaving without a final glance was the only way to preserve this fragile equilibrium.

The path through the forest was clear, yet oddly undisturbed. There were no footprints, no signs of passage, as though Jessica and I had glided through these woods like spirits, our feet never touching the ground. A nagging unease settled in; without the reassurance of footsteps to follow, I worried that I might somehow lose my way and, worse still, find myself back at the cottage. But I continued forward, straight-backed, forcing myself to trust the path ahead, each step drawing me closer to home.

When I reached the large ditch I had fallen into earlier, I braced myself, expecting to find the murky stream swollen into a raging river, the aftermath of the storm barring my escape. But, like everything else, it was bone-dry—its bed, once filled with dark water, now reduced to dirt and scattered stones. Crossing it was effortless. I felt stronger, more confident, more alive. Yet, a small voice of disbelief lingered in the back of my mind, a quiet reminder that the end wasn't quite here.

I sat on the same fallen trunk beyond the ditch, pulling a chocolate bar and a bottle of water from my pack. I closed my eyes and let out a deep, soothing breath. My mind was clear—no questions, no anxieties—just the present. The quiet hum of the forest surrounded me, the soft rustle of leaves and the occasional bird call blending into a peaceful symphony.

I finished my snack, stood up, and stretched, feeling a lightness in my body that had been absent for too long. As I slung my pack over my shoulder, something white flickered in my peripheral vision—moving swiftly through the distant trees. Was it her? Was she watching me, ensuring I was safe? Or was she simply witnessing my departure, a silent guardian seeing me off from this chapter in my life?

I reached into my pack and pulled out the directions Marie had written for me, the route to the glade. I considered following them. If she was there, maybe I could say goodbye—no questions, no demands. It would be nice to see her one last time, to sit together without the notion of everything that had passed between us. Perhaps she was just lonely, craving companionship.

I knew that feeling well. She had offered me love when I needed it most. What harm could there be in returning the favour?

The decision felt right. It wouldn't take long, and I could still be home by evening.

Satisfied, I slung my backpack over my shoulder, ready to set off. As I moved, something tumbled from my jacket pocket—a thick bundle of folded papers, about ten pages, stapled together. I bent down to pick it up, and there, on the first page, was my brother's unmistakable handwriting:

These are letters I should have sent to you. Read them when you're ready.

A.

Adam—when had he left these for me? Had his apparition returned while I slept, slipping the letters into my jacket? Or had it been earlier, before I even knew to look for them? Regardless of the timing, the sight of his handwriting jolted me from the path I'd been so sure of seconds ago. Just as his wristband had once pulled me back from the dangers of infatuation, these letters were his way of steering me away from another mistake. He had succeeded. Whatever the girl was hoping from me, reaching home and reading my brother's words was now far more pressing.

With that decision made, I carried on, my feelings no longer drifting to the girl. The letters in my pocket making it much easier to leave her behind. Oddly, as soon as the choice was final, the sense of her presence—watching, lingering—vanished. It was as though she grasped that there was nothing more she could do to pull me from my path.

Twenty minutes later, I emerged from the edge of the forest. The sight of rolling, cow-dotted hills greeted me like old friends, filling me with a quiet sense of triumph. It felt truly over—until I saw the black SUV parked on the dirt road ahead. Standing beside it, like a spectre of grim inevitability, was Smith. His face, as lifeless as ever, doing his best impression of living death.

45

"I'd like to say it's nice to see a familiar face, but if I'm honest, it wasn't yours I was hoping to see," I said bluntly to Smith.

"Very droll," he replied, his face as blank as a sheet of paper. "Still, it's fortunate for you that we were here to meet you. Finding you elsewhere would have required too much effort."

"How did you know where to find me?"

"Do you think us foolish, Mr. Charles?"

"I never had," I shot back, sarcasm thick in my voice. If his aim was to intimidate me, he'd have to try harder. Not today. Not after everything.

Smith, as usual, was dressed impeccably—dark blue duster, pressed shirt, and perfectly ironed trousers. But his freshly shined shoes had taken a hit from the dirt of the hillside. That detail alone almost made me smile.

"I wouldn't have pegged this place as your kind of scene," I remarked, gesturing to his scuffed shoes with a smirk.

He dismissed the comment with a flick of his gloved hand, his voice stern. "We must do what we must, when we are asked to do it, and we must do it without question. That is simply how things work."

"I see," I said casually. "So, what's the reason for this personal greeting? Worried I wouldn't return? Or did you just miss me?" I flashed him the biggest smile I could muster.

"I'm not here alone," Smith replied, his accent slipping ever so slightly, as though struggling to keep his cool. He nodded toward the sleek black SUV parked behind him. "The boss wanted to greet you himself. Though I advised against it, he's a man of strong will and even stronger attachment to his agenda."

"I suppose I should be flattered," I said, glancing toward the vehicle. "But it seems a bit... excessive, doesn't it?"

Smith's expression didn't change, though his eyes narrowed just a fraction. "Excessive or not, it's his decision. When he sets his mind on something, there's little room for negotiation. Now, do you have what we asked for?"

"I don't have the girl," I said, setting my backpack down and retrieving the small wooden box. "But I have a message for him. From her."

Smith reached out to take it, but I pulled it back just as his gloved hand grazed the air.

"There are conditions," I added, my voice steady, deliberate.

A flicker of irritation crossed his face, though he masked it quickly, taking a slow, measured breath. "Speak then," he said through gritted teeth. "And we'll see what these conditions will cost you."

"First," I said, standing firm, "I want to know the connection your boss has to this land, because it goes deeper than you've let on. How did he come across the picture of my brother? And second, this is non-negotiable: I want to deliver this box to him directly."

Smith's stare didn't waver, but I could see his mind turning, weighing my demands. After a tense moment, he spoke, his voice clipped. "Wait here." He turned and strode toward the black SUV.

The rear window rolled down slowly, revealing only darkness inside. Smith leaned in, speaking in low tones to the unseen figure within. I couldn't make out the words, but after a brief exchange, Smith nodded and returned, his expression still unreadable.

"Very well," he said, his voice steady as ever. "Your request is granted. You'll hand the box over to him personally. As for your first question..." He paused, eyes narrowing slightly. "As you've clearly deduced, the boss's ties to this land run deep."

I gave a small nod. It wasn't news to me, but I could feel there was more.

"The funeral at which he first encountered the girl took place in a church not far from here," Smith continued, his words precise. "She mentioned living in the area but revealed little else. He searched for her, combing the land for weeks without success. That's when one of his men brought him a photograph from a local museum—one of Lord Ashby and his family."

I listened carefully as Smith went on, "In the photograph, the girl—unchanged from the day he met her—stood beside Ashby. From that point on, the boss knew she was more than just a woman he had met by chance."

"The one in the file?" I asked.

Smith nodded. "The very same. With nothing else to go on, the trail ran cold. Despite his resources, his power, he couldn't explain why he continually failed to find her. That's when he decided... instead of sending men to search the land, he'd simply buy the land itself."

"The land?" I asked, though I wasn't really surprised. Men like him, when denied what they want, often believe owning more is the solution.

"Yes. Much of the farmland, the manor, half the village," Smith replied, his tone matter-of-fact. "He even invested in several businesses I can't disclose to you."

"And the restaurant where my brother performed?" I asked, already knowing the answer.

Smith's lips twisted into a faint smirk. "Yes. Part of the package."

"And Marie's father?" My voice sharpened.

"Merely a transaction," Smith said coolly. "He came to London looking for money, and we provided it to him, with the proviso that he would be called upon if we ever needed him. Ultimately, he failed us... and was punished for it."

My hand stiffened at my side, fingers curling into a fist that I fought to keep steady. Every fibre of me wanted to knock the smug look off Smith's face. "But he told his wife the money was given to him 'no strings attached.'"

Smith's eyes glinted coldly. "Would you tell your family where you'd gotten money like that from?" His voice dripped with condescension, as though it were a stupid question to even ask.

I ground my teeth, suppressing the rising fury. "He didn't deserve what happened to him," I spat.

"What about his wife and daughter? The shop?"

"They do not concern us. The debt died with him."

I stared at him, incredulous. "So, with all this power at your disposal, why use the men from the village? Why not send your own people after her?"

Smith's smirk deepened, a cruel spark in his eyes. "Why waste good men—valuable resources—when the locals serve just as well? They're... disposable."

"Is that all we are to you?" My voice was low, barely masking the disgust that churned inside me.

Smith's sneer remained insufferable, but I forced myself to stay composed.

"You must have known Adam had a family," I continued. "So why threaten my friend just to get to me?"

Smith's expression stiffened. "You were an unknown variable. Pulling the right strings was the most efficient way to ensure your compliance."

"Does that include the photo of your boss at the fair? I know it isn't real, so why bother create it?"

"Would you have believed us otherwise?" Smith's tone was cool, calculated.

I couldn't answer honestly. If they'd come to me with wild claims and empty threats, I would've brushed them off without a second thought. I hated admitting it, but they'd played me well. Still, I wasn't about to linger in Smith's company any longer than necessary.

"Well," I said, forcing a smile, "I suppose I should hand this over to your boss now, if you don't mind."

Smith stepped aside, lifting his gloved hand in a silent signal for me to move forward.

I approached the SUV cautiously, peering into the darkened interior. From the shadows, a weathered, wrinkled hand emerged, its skin mottled with liver spots, gesturing me closer.

"Come, come," a voice called, thick with a Russian accent.

The man's face slowly came into view—bald, deeply lined with wrinkles and marked by moles. His nose, large and flushed like the colour of cherry brandy, stood out. A jagged scar ran from his forehead down to his cheek, cutting through one of his small, deep-set eyes. Despite his weathered appearance, that eye flickered with unsettling life.

"You have something for me?" he asked, his voice brimming with barely restrained eagerness.

I handed him the box, watching as his gnarled fingers gently caressed it with a reverence I hadn't expected. It was as if he was feeling his way around it as if it was an extension of her body. He studied it for an instant, his expression softening, before turning back to me.

"Yes, yes, this is definitely from her," he murmured, almost to himself. Then, his eyes locked onto mine, sharper now, more probing. "How did it feel, meeting her?"

"Like meeting anyone else," I lied.

A bitter smile crept across his face, the corners of his mouth jerking with a strange kind of thirst. "But you've seen her—those eyes, those beautiful green eyes, and the mark… as if she's been blessed, set apart from lesser beings. When she looks at you, doesn't it feel like she sees entire universes within you? Like gravity has shifted, and you're orbiting her instead of the sun?"

"Yes," I admitted, the truth slipping out before I could stop it.

His smile faltered for a second, replaced by something darker. "How did you manage to turn away from her?" he asked, his voice low, almost desperate.

I straightened, feeling the attraction of the landscape around me. "I suppose I had more pressing concerns," I said, forcing my tone to stay dry, unaffected.

His face changed instantly; the flicker of anticipation replaced by cold disdain. It was clear I hadn't given him the answer he craved.

"Go," he said sharply, dismissing me with a flick of his hand. "We are finished here."

The window slid up, sealing him away in the darkened SUV. I turned back to Smith, who stood waiting, expressionless as always.

"Our business is concluded," Smith said flatly. "I've been authorised to transfer the remainder of your payment, plus a bonus. You'll find it quite generous."

A soft ping sounded from my phone, and I glanced down to see a notification confirming the deposit. It was more than generous. I wouldn't have to worry for money for years."

"We can arrange transportation back to town if you need it," Smith offered, his tone formal now that the transaction was complete.

"No, it's a nice day for a long walk," I replied, ready to distance myself from them as quickly as possible.

Smith studied me, his eyes narrowing slightly. "What will you do when you return?"

I thought briefly of my brother's letters, still tucked safely in my jacket. "I've got some reading to catch up on," I said, already turning to walk away. Then I stopped, glancing back over my shoulder. "Can I ask you something? Just out of curiosity."

"Speak," Smith said, his voice sharp as always.

"What's the deal with your hand?" I asked, gesturing toward the gloved hand he always kept hidden.

Smith's eyes gleamed as he raised the gloved hand in front of him, almost as though displaying a relic. "This hand was raised by greatness," he said, with a reverent glance toward the SUV. "Since then, I would not dare waste its touch on anything lesser."

"Right," I muttered. His almost religious devotion to his boss was disturbing, to say the least. "Well, don't take this the wrong way, but I hope I never have to see any of you again."

Smith's lips curled into a thin, knowing smile. "Farewell, Mr. Charles. Know that you have done a great thing for a great man."

With that, I hoisted my bag over my shoulder and turned my back on Smith, the Russian, and everything they represented. The road stretched before me, and I welcomed the solitude of my own company, leaving behind the darkness that clung to them like a bad smell.

46

"So that's it, then?" Marie's voice was soft, almost hesitant on the other end of the line. "It's all over?"

"Yep, all finished," I replied.

"How do you feel?"

I paused, searching for the right words. "I don't know," I admitted, then added with a hint of finality, "I just feel… satisfied. Like I've finished a nice meal I'll soon forget."

"At least you've got your life back."

"Not all of it," I said, with a touch of melancholy, "but enough to get by."

A train roared past the station, the noise swallowing the pause between us. I stood from the bench and wandered into the waiting room. It was small and bleak, the faint scent of bleach lingering with something worse. The grime-covered chairs didn't exactly invite sitting, so I stood by the window, staring at the empty platform.

"I bet Maureen at the B&B was sad to see you go," Marie ventured.

"She didn't seem to mind," I sniggered. "I left her a little bonus, which she was happy to take. But she had questions. The usual nosy kind—mostly about why Jessica left before me."

"Ouch," Marie winced, her tone sympathetic.

"Yeah. Jessica told her it was some urgent family matter, thankfully leaving out the real details."

"Do you think Jessica was working with them? Maybe another way to make sure you followed through?"

It was a fair question; one I'd wrestled with after she left. "No," I said firmly, "When she told me she refused to have anything to do with the Russian, I believed her. Of course, I'll never know for sure unless I track her down, but what good would it do? Nope, whatever her reasons for leaving were, I truly wish the best for her."

A loud ding-dong echoed over the station's speakers, followed by an announcement crackling to life, explaining a delay—apparently, sheep were blocking the tracks somewhere down the line. I sighed, wondering if the girl had something to do with it, as if she were still trying to keep me from getting home.

"Well," I said, resigned, "looks like I'll be here for a while longer."

Stepping back outside to escape the stale air of the waiting room, I stood in the quiet of the station. Birds chirped, the air was fresh, and suddenly, the delay didn't feel so bad.

"How do you feel now, after everything I told you?" I asked Marie, half-expecting her to dismiss it as fantasy. "Honestly, I didn't think you'd believe any of it."

"At first, I thought you'd gone stark-raving mad, especially when you told me about the lodge," Marie admitted. "But the more I thought about it, your bat-shit story started to make sense. I'm angry at my dad for taking the money to open the store, but I can't stay mad at him for how things turned out. I just wish there was something I could do to prove it to the authorities. They've got away with murder."

"Take my advice," I said gently, "move on from it. And if you ever get a visit from anyone who looks like a snake in human form, with an accent that shifts between posh and cockney on a whim, refuse whatever offer he makes you."

The line went quiet, as though Marie was weighing the danger that still lingered, the threat hovering over her future.

"The idea of selling up and leaving this place gets more appealing with every minute I'm on this call," she finally said, her voice carrying a mix of resolve and reluctance.

"I think that would be a brilliant idea," I said, then added, "but what would you do? And what about your mum?"

"The money I'd get from selling the shop would give me enough to set up somewhere else, buy me time to figure things out. I've always been drawn to carpentry—maybe I could learn a trade, start fresh."

I smiled, picturing Marie as a carpenter. It fit her. She had that quiet strength.

"And Mum," she continued, her voice faltering. "While you were up at the lodge, she had a visit from the doctor." There was a heavy sigh on the line. "He told me to prepare for the worst. I don't think she's got much fight left in her."

"I'm so sorry," I said. Another loss for Marie, but maybe, now that her father's story had come to light, her mother was ready to go, free of the burden she'd carried.

"When she goes, it'll be a blessing," Marie admitted, her voice thick with emotion. "What she's living with now—it's not a life. And when she's gone, I won't have anything tying me to this place anymore."

As if on cue, the station's loudspeaker blared once more, repeating the delay due to sheep on the tracks.

Marie heard it too. "I should let you go," she said. "I've complained enough."

"Not at all. I've got some reading to do," I replied, patting my pocket to make sure my brother's letters were still there. But then, an idea began to take shape. "Before you go," I added, "I've been thinking... The Russian paid me well, and I've been considering leaving the country for a while. I haven't booked anything yet, but I was wondering if you'd like to join me."

Marie fell silent, processing the offer.

"I don't know..." she said eventually, uncertainty lacing her words. "The kids..."

"Bring them," I insisted. "Look, I know you've only known me for a couple of days, but when I was walking back to the village, I realised you and I are the only ones left who carry the scars of everything that's happened here. If anyone deserves a break from all the crap life keeps throwing at them, it's you."

Another pause. I could almost hear the gears turning in her mind.

"The trip will be fully paid for, and there are no strings attached. I'm offering this as a friend—nothing more. If you say no, that's okay too."

"Yes," she interrupted.

I blinked. "Yes?"

"Sod it. It'll have to wait until after Mum… you know… but yes, thank you," she said, her voice lighter, as if a load had been lifted. The relief was plain, like this offer was something she had been wishing for, for a very long time.

"That's great," I said, truthfully pleased. "We'll keep in touch, and when you're ready, we'll sort it all out."

We talked a while longer, discussing places she'd always dreamed of visiting and how much her kids would love the chance to go abroad. The excitement built between us, replacing the earlier burdens that had weighed us down like iron chains. When we finally hung up, I looked up at the bright, open sky and murmured, "Thanks, Adam."

With the train still twenty minutes away, I leaned back on the bench. The air felt lighter, and for the first time in a long while, I could breathe easily. Reaching into my pocket, I pulled out my brother's letters. A bittersweet smile tugged at my lips as memories flooded back—some I knew I'd eventually choose to forget, but not today.

Deciding to start at the end and work my way backward, I unfolded the last letter he ever wrote me and began to read.

Epilogue

The Final Letter

47

Hey Chris,

I want you tell you I'm sorry. Sorry this will be the hardest thing you'll ever read. Sorry for what it will put you through. Sorry I didn't have the strength to talk to you sooner.

I'm sorry about a lot of things, but what I'm most sorry for... is meeting her.

Things were going so very well. I met her every morning when the weather was good. I'd get up early, hike to the glade, and we'd talk. I'd tell her about who I was, about where my music took me when I wrote and performed. I'd play guitar, and she'd sing—God, her voice was incredible, like a nightingale. Afterward, we'd kiss, and sometimes, we'd make love right there in the glade. I felt complete, untouchable, like nothing could ever break me. All because of her.

But it all went wrong. So wrong.

One day, I played her a song I'd written just for her. Maybe the best thing I'd ever written. I called it *The Girl with The Mark of Fire*. She was curled up against me, eyes closed, listening to the words that were a love letter only for her. No one else would ever hear them.

Then the sky darkened, and it started pouring. We needed shelter. Instead of heading back to the village like I usually would, she told me about a place nearby where we could wait out the storm.

I didn't think twice. I followed her.

She led me to a cottage—right where I thought the old gamekeeper's lodge should've been. It felt strange, but I didn't care. Whether it was hers or not, I didn't ask. We lit a fire to dry our clothes, made love in front of the hearth, and eventually fell asleep in each other's arms.

When we woke up, the storm had passed, and sunlight streamed through the windows. All I could think about was the life I wanted with her. So, I did the one thing left for me to do.

As she got dressed, I wrapped her in my arms and said, *"Marry me."*

I was certain she'd say yes. After everything we'd shared, I couldn't imagine another answer. But instead of agreeing, she shoved me away, yelling, calling me *ridiculous*. I was stunned—she'd never reacted like that before. I was so sure she felt the same as I did. Her words knocked the breath out of me. It was as if I'd been speaking to a stranger all along, someone I'd never known.

I broke down, Chris. I wept harder than I ever have in my life. I fell to my knees, begged her to forget I'd ever asked. I told her I didn't need marriage; I didn't need anything—as long as I had her. But she wouldn't budge. She kept saying it was over, that nothing could ever be the same. Her voice was like a door slamming shut, and I knew I'd never get back in. No matter how much I pleaded, it was as if she'd already decided I didn't exist anymore.

I was wrecked. Furious—at her, at myself, at everything. I pulled my hair, cursed myself for being so stupid. In a blind rage, I punched the wall. Me, Mr. Anti-violence, smashing my fist into the wall like some idiot. I injured my hand, but I didn't care. That's what she did to me—how desperate I was not to lose her. The pain in my hand was nothing compared to the pain tearing through me, like something inside me had cracked, and I knew wouldn't be able to fix it no matter how hard I tried.

I slumped to the floor, completely broken. Then she walked over, lifted me up, and held me. For an instant, I thought maybe she'd changed her mind, that we could fix it.

But then she whispered five words in my ear.

Five words.

I don't have the guts to repeat them here, but they made everything clear. I knew then that I couldn't go on living like this. I gathered my things and walked out of that cottage, knowing I'd never see her again.

And that's how I ended up here. As I finish this letter, I'm sitting against the door of my rental car. The engine's running. I needed a lot of Dutch courage for the next part, so you'll find a half-drunk bottle of vodka and my guitar with me. The windows are taped up. I'll sit inside and wait to be free of this madness, because that's what it is—madness. I'm scared, but not because I don't want to die. The thought of death doesn't terrify me—it's the thought of leaving you behind, of never seeing your face again, never laughing with you. That's the only thing that still hurts. But this madness? I'm ready to let it go.

You'll want to know why. The truth is, she has turned me into someone I can't identify with. The anger, the violence, the recklessness—none of it is me. And I know, unless something changes, I'll never be myself again. I'll always be searching for her, draining every fibre of my being, hoping to return to what we had. Knowing full well that I never will. Every time I think about her, it's like a she is cutting away the parts of me that once felt whole. And the worst part? I know I'd chase that feeling forever, even though it's already gone.

I'm tired, Chris. Tired of chasing a dream that's killing me. So, I'm quitting early. It's for the best.

Before I go, consider the last part of this letter a warning: stay away from that village. Don't look for the reasons behind my death. And if a beautiful blonde girl with a birthmark around her eye ever approaches you—run. Don't look back. Just leave. You'll thank me.

Now comes the hardest part.

Goodbye, Chris. I'm so sorry.

Love you, brother.

Adam.

Thanks

My thanks as ever to all those who support me. Without you I would not be able to keep on creating. I am forever grateful. My eternal thanks to Darren, who always pulls out all the stops to create my book covers. Finally, I give thanks to my brain. Although it is a constant battle to keep you on an even keel, you never stop providing me with the word-splurges that somehow allow me to write.

Cover design by Darren Pilkington. www.danda-media.com

Other Titles by Arron Hickman

Sebastian

"...this shall be my confession to him who shall forever be bound to me."

Adam is a young writer beset by personal tragedy. Using his creativity to channel his struggles, he tries in earnest to make something of himself, and his writing. One day, a friend he hasn't seen in years unexpectedly turns up on his doorstep, and from that moment his life changes forever. With his volatile temperament, Sebastian will do anything to see that Adam becomes a success, even if it means taking everything that he believes in. Sebastian is a psychological melodrama about the depths that friendships can reach, and the creative spirit that can be used to endure uncertainty.

Nightmare Alley

Short Story Collection

My nightmares were once described to me as a "mind cleansing". The diagnosis wasn't the most eloquent, my mind was just a hazardous waste bin after all, but from that razor-edge description burst forth the fourteen tales contained here-in. They explore, in all its twisted glory, a dissection of a brain that cannot stop thinking; the adaptations of whatever horrendous fever-dream my mind plagues me with. Enjoy.

Sounds of a Broken Radio

Poetry Collection

I don't believe in free will. Don't be scared, everything will be okay. Our lives are determined by choices we already know the answer to. It was at the point of the big bang that our lives began. Every one of us began our journey that day, and the paths we now walk on, and the footsteps we leave behind, will continue for all eternity. Each person we meet and interact with along the way tread their own road and the sparks we create with them at those intersections we call relationships begin new moments that we'll never even see. This book that you hold in your hands was being written long before I was created. If you manage to make it through to the end or whether you merely read the first few pages, I want you to know that these words come from something more than me, an essence I have not quite come to understand. This book that you hold in your hands was being written long before I was created, and the words that I speak will last forever.

Available on Amazon

Milton Keynes UK
Ingram Content Group UK Ltd.
UKHW022109091224
452292UK00009B/70